Duke and Alice

November 2010 to September 2011

By

Dallas A. Dixon

This novel is a work of fiction. Names, characters, places, and incidents are the product of the author's imagination or used fictitiously. Any resemblance to actual events, locales, or persons, living or dead, is coincidental.

ISBN-13: 978-0615977126
ISBN-10: 061597712X

First Printing

For my lovely wife, Rita, and our daughters,
Trisia and Dawn

Chapter 1

Jason awoke abruptly when he heard the front door slam shut. He knew his father, Calvin, had arrived home after another Saturday night carousing around town. Jason had retired to his upstairs bedroom about an hour earlier, while his mother, Mary, had retired to her first-floor bedroom in the fancy, 4-bedroom, 4,000 square feet, 2-story house located in Redwood City, California. Jason rolled onto his side and wiped the sleepiness from his eyes. He saw the digital clock located on his nightstand displaying 11:00 p.m. *I suppose the fighting will soon begin,* he thought. *They have been fighting occasionally for the last few years, so it will not be anything new.* Jason rolled onto his back and again drifted off to sleep. A cold air return register, an essential component of the central heating and cooling system, occupied a space in the baseboard directly behind Jason's headboard. Jason could hear many sounds from downstairs drift upwards through the ductwork and out through the register, especially sounds from his parent's bedroom. Jason did not think his parents realized he could hear them so plainly, or if they did, they did not care. Ten minutes later, Jason awoke startled when he heard two loud slapping noises and his father hollering with slurred words, “Goddamn it, Mary! Our divorce will not be finalized until about six months from now, which means it will happen sometime in April or May of 2011. I mentioned those dates just in case you have not been able to figure them out by yourself. Until then, you will have sex with me whenever I want, especially if you want me to keep supplying you with cocaine.”

Jason heard his mother sobbing as she replied, “You do not have to tell me the dates. I have been an accountant for several years. I am certainly capable of calculating dates, and very accurately, too. Before we have sex, I want to snort another line of cocaine. From now on, I want you to refrain from slapping and pinching me during sex, and please do not expect me to do the things your secretary does for you while you are in her bed.”

“You will do anything I ask after you snort another line of that wonderful white powder. Furthermore, I will slap you and pinch you anytime I have the desire. I have never left any bruises on you that you could not hide under your clothes. Besides, when we have sex together, you always tell me that you enjoy the mild violence. Take off your robe and sit down on the edge of the bed.”

For the next twenty minutes, Jason tried to muffle out the sounds from his parent’s bedroom, but the sounds continued drifting upwards through the cold air return pipes and flowed freely out of the baseboard register. He wrapped the pillow around the back of his head and held the pillow ends against his ears. At 1:00 a.m., Jason heard his mother giggling between words as she said, “I really think we should sit down with Jason and discuss a few things with him. His school grades have been deteriorating rapidly, and I am concerned about him. Jason has recently become terribly withdrawn and acts as if he is a loner most the time."

"I will not discuss anything involving Jason's problems until later today, like at about 3:00 p.m.," replied Calvin with rapid, slurred words. "Jason will turn sixteen on December 15, which is only a month from now. He should be able to solve his own problems by this time. Damn it! Marrying you was the worst mistake I ever made in my life. The second biggest mistake in my life occurred when I impregnated you, and I blame you entirely for that, because you conveniently forgot to take your birth control pills. Good night!"

"Your biggest mistake occurred when you began using drugs and running around with other women, something you never did until right after your parents perished in the car accident a few years ago. After you inherited all their money, you began hanging around with your phony, rich friends at all those crazy drug and sex parties."

"I enjoy myself at the parties. It beats the hell out of working all the time. I have worked in the business world ever since I graduated with my master's degree from San José State College in 1991. Good night!"

"You do not have to remind me. I graduated the same year from the same college with my master's degree in accounting. I have worked ever since then, too, and I enjoy my job. Perhaps, I should have stayed home to raise Jason. I could have if we would not have been so money hungry, but we wanted to live the rich life. We have been so busy all these years. The only time I have ever returned to Waterfield, Iowa, was for my brother's funeral in March of 1991. I saw my parents then, but did not see them again until they drove out here to visit us five years ago."

Calvin sat up in bed, brushed back his brown hair with his right hand, and said, "Yes. Your parent's stay with us was definitely an experience. I could certainly tell that your parents were from the cornfields in Iowa. Your dad had little to say. Hell! It was extremely difficult for me to get a word out of him, and when he did speak, he spoke very slowly. I liked your mother a little better than your father. At least she acted friendly enough." Calvin stretched out onto his back and said, "You should take a sleeping pill, so you can wind down. Good night."

"We certainly did not treat my parents very nice while they were here. We should have taken a few days off work and took them sightseeing, or at least spent more time with them. It is no wonder we never hear from them."

Calvin opened his eyes and said, "You never bother to pick up the telephone receiver and phone them. That might be one reason you never hear from them. I think your parents became upset with me when I mocked your father's slow talking. Actually, I think they were extremely upset, because they did not stay here long after I mocked him. They shortened their visit by two days. Christ, your father talks slow, but I will admit that when he did speak, he spoke very intelligently, especially for someone who never attended college. I need some sleep, so good night."

"I feel wide awake," replied Mary. After ten seconds of silence, Mary began talking, "I wish you would not have convinced me to attend that July 4 party last summer. I should have never attended it, because you and your friends coerced me into snorting cocaine. Immediately after that, you and that other woman crawled into bed and watched while I spent time in the other bed with her husband, a man I had never met before then. I am now addicted to cocaine. I need to abstain from snorting it before it ruins my life. I certainly do not want to end up like you. Your consulting business is almost failing because you only work half the time." Mary saw that Calvin had fallen asleep, so she quit talking.

Jason spent the next hour wondering whether his

parents loved him, as well as worrying about the pending discussion. He felt positive his father did not love him, and felt unsure about his mother. He hoped that she loved him. Jason finally fell asleep at 3:00 a.m.

At 10:00 a.m. Sunday, Mary hollered up the stairwell, "It is time to get out of bed, Jason."

Jason felt very tired, but replied, "Okay, Mom." He rolled over to the edge of the bed, sat up, and began dressing. He did not like the reflection he saw in the large wall mirror located near his bed. *I am so fat and ugly*, he thought. *I need to lose some weight. It's no wonder the kids always tease me at school. Several of the jocks are big bullies, and always mock my slow talking. I hate attending school.* Jason finished dressing and went downstairs where he found Mary sitting at the kitchen table. He could not believe her unkempt appearance. She had not bothered to brush her hair, and had tucked in only half of the sleeveless, white blouse tails. The rest of the blouse tails hung down on the outside of her skirt waistband. Jason poured some Cheerios into a bowl, and then opened the refrigerator door and removed a gallon jug of milk. He carefully poured milk into the bowl of cereal, some into a glass, and returned the milk jug to the refrigerator. As he sat down across from Mary, he noticed a large bruise on her upper, left arm. "Gee, Mom. How did you get that bruise on your arm?"

"I stumbled a few days ago and bumped my arm against a door casing," said Mary while lightly rubbing the bruise. "It is okay, so do not worry about it. Your dad and I want to talk with you this afternoon about your school grades. One of your teachers phoned me at work last week and told me that you have failed some of your weekly tests. If your dad ever gets out of bed, we will all sit down together and discuss your study habits and grades."

"Why are you so nervous this morning? Several of your

muscles are twitching."

"I am fine, Jason," replied Mary as she began biting the tip of her left index fingernail. "I have no idea why I am so nervous this morning."

Calvin entered the kitchen and slumped down into a chair at the kitchen table. He glared at Mary and with a mean tone of voice, said, "Well! Are you going to get off your butt and pour some coffee for me? I am waiting."

Mary quickly stood up and walked toward the coffee pot. Jason studied his father for about ten seconds and saw that Calvin acted as nervous as Mary. Jason rose from his chair and placed his silverware, glass, and bowl into the dishwasher before saying, "I will be in my room. Let me know when you want to have our discussion." As Jason walked up the steps of the spiral staircase, he thought, *Mom and Dad should quit taking drugs before they ruin their lives. I am positive their drug use is what has caused them to file for a divorce. Mom and Dad fight more all the time. Mom still lets Dad sleep with her, even though the judge granted them legal separation.* Jason entered his bedroom, sat down at the desk, and opened his laptop computer. He began searching websites for things that interested him. A few of the adult websites especially attracted his attention.

Calvin and Mary entered Jason's bedroom at 3:00 p.m. Jason quickly closed the laptop and swiveled his desk chair so he could look directly at them. "Let's have a discussion, Jason," said Mary as she sat down on the edge of the bed.

Calvin sat down beside Mary and glared at Jason. "Your mother told me that your grades have been lousy. What seems to be your problem? You have always maintained A's and B's prior to this year. Are your sophomore classes that difficult for you, or are there other problems?"

Jason stared at the oak hardwood floor as he replied slowly and softly, "The classes aren't really that difficult, but I haven't felt like studying. I haven't been able to sleep well at night, so I'm always tired. Another problem is that I have trouble with five boys, all jocks, in my class. Whenever they see me in the hallways or outside, they shove me around and tease me about my slow talking. They sometimes say that I am fat and ugly, and tell me that I will never be able to date girls. I think they want me to start a fight with them. Three or four of the preppy girls in my class tease me while saying that I am a fat, gay boy."

"Well! You naturally inherited your slow talking from your grandpa," Calvin replied. "It would not hurt you at all to lose some of that body fat. Hell! You are 5'-10" tall, the same height as me, but you weigh about 200 pounds. That is 30 pounds more than I weigh, and I could stand to lose about 10 pounds."

"Calvin!" Mary snapped as she quickly stood up. "You are very rude." Mary approached Jason and began rubbing his shoulders. "You are certainly not ugly, Jason. You are very handsome with those blue eyes and blonde hair. Perhaps, the best thing you can do is ignore those bullies at school. Try to stay away from them. You need to study a lot more in order to improve your grades; otherwise, you will probably fail your sophomore year."

"So in other words," Jason said as he pushed Mary's hands off his shoulders, "neither one of you will talk with my school principal about the problems I have with other students. Thanks a lot! Could you at least quit fighting at night? Maybe, I could sleep a little better."

Calvin stood up and said, "I am going downstairs to phone in an order for two pizzas. I feel as if I am starving to death."

"I will be down in a few minutes," replied Mary. She put her right hand on Jason's shoulder and said, "Your dad and I will try to be quieter at night so you can sleep better. Make sure you study more from now on, because I would certainly hate to see you fail your sophomore year. I will let you know when the pizzas arrive."

As Mary exited the bedroom, Jason thought, *My parents only think about themselves. They have never cared about me. If they would have, they would have spent a lot more time with me through the years. Instead, they have always made me stay in this house after school and during the summers while they worked, or attended the fancy parties. I hope things will change when the divorce is final and Dad moves out for good. He is such an ass.*

Forty-five minutes elapsed before Jason heard his mother hollering that the pizzas had arrived. Jason went downstairs and sat at the dining room table. Calvin placed two large pizzas upon the solid oak table while Mary brought the drinks from the kitchen. She set a can of soda in front of Jason and one at her table setting. "Do you want a beer, or a soda?" she asked Calvin.

"Get me a can of beer and a glass."

Immediately after Jason finished his sixth piece of pizza, he put another piece on his plate, and took a handful of barbequed potato chips from the bag. Calvin looked sternly at Jason while saying, "It's no wonder you are so fat, Jason. Are you actually going to eat all eight pieces of that pizza?"

"Yeah," said Jason as he began slowly licking the reddish brown potato chip salt from his fingers, "I haven't eaten anything since this morning, so I'm hungry."

Jason had devoured all eight pieces of his pizza by the time they finished eating. He finished his second can of soda, stood up, walked over to the refrigerator, opened the door, and removed another can of soda. Then, he approached the pantry, opened the pantry door, removed two Twinkies, and said, "I'm going upstairs to study. I'll eat these Twinkies for desert, and wash them down with this soda."

"Study hard, Jason," Mary said as she slid back her chair and stood up. "We will see you in the morning."

Calvin slid his chair away from the table, stood up, and said, "I am going to take a shower, Mary. I expect to see you in our bedroom as soon as you finish clearing the table."

"Okay. I will be there within ten minutes. A shower sounds fantastic. I will take one as soon as you finish yours."

At 6:00 p.m., Mary stepped out of the shower stall, and after drying off, joined Calvin on their king-sized bed. She stretched out her 5'-6" tall, 125-pound, nude body, and snuggled firmly against Calvin's right side. "Do you have any more cocaine?" whispered Mary. "I would enjoy snorting a small amount of it this evening, as long as we do it early. I need enough time to recuperate, so that I can go to work in the morning." Calvin didn't reply immediately, so Mary kissed him passionately. When their lips separated, Mary said, "I will give you something special in return."

Calvin slid over to the edge of the bed and reached underneath the bed frame. He returned to Mary's side while holding two small plastic bags of cocaine. "This is all I have right now, but it is enough for this evening. I will drive to San Francisco in the morning and purchase more cocaine. Perhaps, I will purchase a large quantity this time. I want to throw a huge party here at the house next spring for all my friends. I think we will schedule it for the first weekend after our divorce is final. Just think, Mary! We will be able to go to bed with anyone we want after our divorce, and we will not have to feel guilty. I look forward to it."

"Do you not worry about getting into trouble with the

law when you purchase cocaine?" asked Mary as she brushed a few locks of blonde hair to the side her forehead.

"No. I will hide the cocaine behind the car battery in the engine compartment of my car. When I get back into town, I will take the cocaine to my office, repackage it, and lock it inside the safe. I have been doing that for a while, and I have sold a lot of cocaine to my friends. They pay me several dollars for those small packages. It is definitely worth my time to repackage it."

"Are we going to snort a little, now?" asked Mary. "I need something to perk me up."

"Yes, as long as you allow me to do what I want with you."

"That will be fine. I just need some cocaine."

Jason quit studying at 8:00 p.m. He held his laptop computer on his lap as he sat down on the bed. Then, he began searching for interesting websites. He soon heard slapping and screaming sounds drifting out through the cold air return register. *My parents must enjoy fighting all the time,* Jason thought. *They sure do enough of it. I don't understand why they have to fight. It's driving me insane. I should run away from home, but I don't know where I would go, or where I would stay, let alone support myself. The only relatives I know of are Grandpa and Grandma, but I haven't seen them since I was ten years old. Maybe, I should phone them one of these days. I doubt if they even know that Dad beats Mom all the time.* Jason spent the next few hours exploring and reading many different websites, and then tried to fall asleep. Again, he held the pillow ends over his ears in order to silence the sounds of fighting mixed with sounds of sobbing and occasional giggling.

Things returned to normal Monday morning. After

breakfast, Jason left for school and his parents left for the day, Mary to her accounting job, and Calvin to whatever he had planned for the day. As the days and weeks elapsed, Jason felt as if things at home were improving. The fighting seemed to have dissipated somewhat, but only because Calvin did not come home very often. On the nights Calvin showed up, Jason did not get much sleep because his parents went from being overly happy to angrily fighting, all which made a lot of noise. On December 15, 2010, Mary stopped after work and purchased a small birthday cake so they could celebrate Jason's sixteenth birthday. Calvin did not appear at the house that day, even though he had promised Jason that he would be there for the birthday celebration. Jason imagined his dad had gone home with his secretary that evening and had forgotten all about the birthday celebration. Jason noticed that his mother acted very nervous after they sat down at the dining room table. She stuck the bottom ends of sixteen small candles into the cake, lit the candlewicks, and then sang Happy Birthday. When Mary finished singing, Jason inhaled deeply, and then blew out all the flames with one sweeping breath. Mary removed the candles and cut the cake. Jason thought, *I really appreciate Mom doing this for me.* He noticed the dark circles surrounding her eyes, and saw that her fingernails and hair needed a lot of attention. *Mom isn't taking very good care of herself,* he thought.

At 9:00 p.m. the following Saturday, Calvin arrived at the house, and by 11:00 p.m., all hell broke loose. Jason awoke when he heard his mother screaming, "You bastard! I want you to leave this house right now. Go stay with your secretary for the night."

After hearing two loud slaps, followed immediately by Mary's sobbing, Jason heard slurred, rapid words from Calvin, "If I leave, you will have to find someone else to supply your drugs. Do you think you can do that on your own, bitch?"

"No," Mary sobbed. "I guess you can stay. I am sorry for screaming at you. Let's snort another line. Please."

"That is fine with me. I have two kilos of cocaine locked in my safe. I found a dealer in San Francisco who agreed to sell me a kilo at a time. I plan to purchase at least one more kilo from him before our spring party. Shit. I've been repackaging it and selling it like crazy. I earn a hell of a profit from all my sales."

The next few weeks faded away quickly. Jason and Mary had spent Christmas Day together. Jason had received an iPad along with a cell phone from his parents, but the fifty-dollar gift card inside the Christmas card he had received from his grandparents made him happier. The note inside the card instructed Mary to take Jason shopping and spend the fifty dollars to buy a pair of jeans and a denim shirt for him. His grandparents had sent him a Christmas card and money every year with the same instructions. Jason enjoyed it so much, because the only clothes his parents had ever furnished him were dress slacks and shorts, along with dress shirts. Calvin had shown up at the house a few nights between Christmas Day and New Year's Day. He and Mary fought most the time, especially after they snorted cocaine and engaged in sex. By the middle of March, Jason began worrying constantly about his mother. He noticed that she appeared very depressed during the breakfast times they shared together, especially on the mornings when she had not seen Calvin the previous nights. On the mornings following Calvin's nighttime appearances, Mary acted very anxious and jumpy, but by the time she returned home from work in the evenings, she acted depressed. Jason began suffering from stomachaches and anxiety problems, and the continuous bullying he endured during school hours made him feel more agitated every day.

During Saturday, April 30, Jason spent several hours with his mother, but Mary acted very depressed the entire time. Jason went into his bedroom that evening and decided to research the subject of drug abuse. Utilizing his laptop computer, he found an abundance of information on the internet, and by 10:00 p.m., admitted to himself that his mother displayed many symptoms of cocaine abuse. *I should talk with Mom about her drug problems*, thought Jason as he closed the laptop. *She won't be going to work tomorrow, so I will talk with her about it during breakfast.* Jason went to bed, but could not stop worrying about his mother. It took two hours for sleep to overtake his worries.

Jason went downstairs at 8:00 a.m. Sunday, prepared a bowl of instant oatmeal, and sat down at the kitchen table. A few minutes later, Mary walked into the kitchen, and said, "Good morning, Jason. Did you sleep well?"

"Not really, Mom."

"Why not?" asked Mary as she tightened her robe belt. She opened the refrigerator door and reached for a bottle of orange juice.

"I am worried about you, Mom. You act depressed most the time."

Mary poured orange juice into a glass, and sat down across from Jason. "I am fine, Jason. Do not worry about me."

Jason saw tears forming slowly in his mother's bloodshot blue eyes. She quickly took a table napkin and patted away the tears. "Why are you crying?" asked Jason.

Mary began sobbing loudly, but between sobs managed to say, "My boss fired me last Friday. He informed me that he had received complaints about me from three different clients." Mary wiped away some tears and continued, "He also said that he realizes I have a severe problem, and advised me to seek professional help." Mary continued dabbing away the tears as her loud sobbing subsided gradually. "It is my own fault. He warned me several different times during the last few months. To top things off, I received a letter yesterday from the California State Board of Accounting, informing me that they are in the process of investigating three complaints against me." Mary began nibbling on the tip of her right index fingernail. "I will probably have to appear before the state board members for a hearing, and they could suspend my accountant's license."

Jason held a spoon in his right hand and used it to stir his bowl of oatmeal while thinking about what Mary had just told him. After fifteen seconds, he said, "I used my laptop to do some research last night, and learned about the symptoms of cocaine abuse. You have many of those symptoms, Mom. I know you and Dad have occasionally been using illegal drugs for at least the last six months."

"How do you know that?" snapped Mary angrily as she slid her chair away from the table.

"I hear you and Dad fighting almost every night when he is here. I hear him slapping you, and I've heard both of you talking about drugs."

"Well!" Mary said as she jumped up from her chair. "Perhaps, you should mind your own business and stay the hell out of mine." She stomped out of the kitchen and headed for her bedroom. Jason heard her bawling loudly, much like a small child, after she had entered her room and slammed the door. He felt so bad for her, but didn't know what he could do to help her. He remained at the kitchen table for ten minutes, hanging his head in disgust while contemplating a solution. In the end he thought, *Maybe, I will phone Grandma and Grandpa in Iowa and ask them what I should do to help Mom. I don't know anybody else I can talk with about it.* Jason did not see his mother again until a few minutes before he left for school Monday morning. She did not tell him good-bye as she normally did.

After walking six blocks, Jason entered onto the high school property. Many students had already arrived and had assembled with groups of friends in the schoolyard while waiting for school to begin. As Jason walked along the main sidewalk toward the building, he saw two of the boys who always bullied him. He debated whether to continue walking, or to wait at his present location until time to enter the school building. *I'm tired of those guys bullying me all the time*, he thought. Jason continued walking toward the main entrance and when he approached the two boys, the bullying began. "Hey, fat boy," the largest boy said. "It appears as if you have gained ten pounds of fat during the weekend." The other boy laughed and shoved Jason very hard. Jason almost fell down, but recovered his balance and continued walking toward the main entrance. The largest boy, a boy about the same size as Jason but fat-free with solid muscles, shoved Jason backwards, and said, "Where do you think you're going, preppy boy? I'll bet that you still sleep with your mama. You're such a wimp. She probably helps you dress in those fancy dress clothes every morning."

Jason had heard enough, so he replied, "I do not sleep with my mother, you dickhead. Get out of my way and leave me alone."

The largest boy suddenly slapped Jason in the right side of his head and said, "Don't call me a dickhead again, or I'll beat the hell out of you."

Jason rubbed the right side of his head as he tried to walk toward the main entrance. The largest boy shoved him backwards, just as the other boy shoved him sideways. Ordinarily, Jason did not have a mean streak in his body, but something clicked in Jason's mind as the smaller boy shoved him. With a haymaker of a swing, Jason slugged the smaller boy in the left side of his head. The boy staggered a little, but then swung at Jason. The larger boy joined in, and Jason soon fell to the sidewalk. Both bullies slugged and kicked Jason while he tried to defend himself, but he was definitely no match for either one of the boys, let alone both of them together. A minute went by before one of the coaches ran out of the school building and broke up the fight. The coach escorted Jason and both bullies into Principal Hogan's office. Principal Hogan listened to their stories and excuses, and then gave all three of them two-day suspensions. Principal Hogan also promised to have phone conversations with their parents. Jason ended up with a black eye and several bruised ribs. Neither bully sustained severe injuries, only a few sore knuckles.

Jason took his time walking home because he worried about what his mother would say to him about receiving a suspension. As soon as he opened the front door and entered the house, Mary began hollering at him. "I have just finished a phone conversation with Principal Hogan, and he informed me that he has suspended you for two days because of fighting. You should know better than to fight. Fighting never does anybody any good. It only creates more problems."

"Well!" Jason shouted. "You should talk. You and Dad fight nonstop when he is home, and I'm sick and tired of listening to it. I'll be glad when the divorce is final. I can't wait for Dad to leave for good."

"You had better buckle down and walk the straight and narrow in school from now on. There are only about three weeks remaining in your sophomore year, so you had better study hard for your finals."

Jason stomped toward the spiral staircase while

hollering, "Who cares? You and Dad don't care a darn bit about me. If you did, you would both talk with the teachers and principal about all the bullying that I put up with every day in school."

At 6:00 a.m. Tuesday, May 3, Jason heard Mary leave the house. He wondered where she was going and why she had left so early. Jason decided to look for his grandparent's telephone number. He went into the dining room and located Mary's address book inside the secretarial desk. The phone number appeared with the address, so Jason jotted down the information on a small piece of paper and took it to his room. *I'll wait for a while before I phone Grandpa and Grandma,* he thought. *Maybe, Mom and Dad will stop fighting so much.*

Chapter 2

Mary's mother, Alice, awoke at 7:00 a.m. Saturday, May 14, 2011. She looked out through the east double-hung windows of the upstairs bedroom in their 1,400 square feet, 1½-story, Colonial-style house built in 1938. She saw the serene sky with the sun shining brightly, and heard muffled sounds of several robins along with a lone cardinal chirping and singing merrily. *It's going to be another beautiful day in Waterfield, Iowa*, she thought. Alice slid over to the side of the bed, stood up, and dressed in a pair of jeans, a long-sleeved, floral print blouse, and a lightweight, blue sweater. She went downstairs and entered the bathroom where she washed her face and brushed her collar-length gray hair. When she finished applying a small amount of rouge to her cheeks, she carefully applied bright red lipstick onto her lips. When she felt happy about her appearance, she shut off the bathroom lights and headed for the kitchen.

She looked out through the double-hung kitchen window located above the white, cast-iron kitchen sink and saw Duke, her husband of a little over 45 years, sitting on the garden bench enjoying a cup of coffee while smoking a cigarette and gazing out over the backyard. *He looks quite handsome with his graying brown hair and those blue eyes*, she thought. *He is still in wonderful shape with his 5'-10" height and those solid muscles. Duke doesn't have an ounce of fat anywhere on his body. I should be so fortunate as to not have any fat on my body. If I worked out with weights every other day like he does, I wouldn't have any fat either, but I guess I'm too lazy.* She poured a cup of coffee and carried it carefully as she walked from the kitchen through the dining room, onto the 3-season porch, and then outside to sit with Duke on the garden bench. Duke looked up at her as she approached, and said, "Good-morning, Alice. How did you sleep last night?"

"I slept quite soundly, thank you. How did you sleep? What time did you roll out of bed?"

"Oh," Duke replied, "I had one of those nights where I was half awake the entire time. I just couldn't fall completely asleep. I finally crawled out of bed at 5:00 a.m. After I dressed, I made a pot of coffee and watched the weather report. I came out here at about 6:00 a.m. It's still a little chilly, but the local meteorologist said that the temperature is supposed to reach 65 degrees, and it's supposed to stay nice and clear today with no wind. Rain is in the forecast for tomorrow, so I might spade up some more of the garden plot today."

"What would you like for breakfast?" asked Alice as she brushed a mosquito off the back of her right hand. "The darn mosquitoes are already out this spring. I can make some pancakes and fry some of the Italian sausage I bought the other day. I don't know if we will like the taste of it, but we will try it. I doubt if it will taste as delicious as our homemade sausage. If you are going to spade more of the garden, you should eat a big breakfast."

"I ate a bagel earlier, but pancakes sound pretty good to me."

Alice finished her coffee and went back inside to begin making breakfast. Duke remained on the garden bench until Alice informed him that she had breakfast waiting on the dining room table. He removed his rubber garden boots when he entered the 3-season porch and set them on a 2' x 3' gray carpet sample lying on the terra cotta stained, concrete porch floor. He slid his feet into his slippers, and entered the dining room. As he sat down at the round, solid oak table, Alice poured coffee into his cup, and said, "I'm glad you're so good about taking off your boots before you come into the house. It sure helps keep the scratches out of these oak hardwood floors. One of these days, we should buy a new braided rug for under this table. This rug is almost worn-out."

"I know," Duke replied, "but the new braided rugs are overly expensive these days, compared to when we purchased this one. Heck! A new eight-foot diameter rug similar to this one costs about 500 dollars. This one cost about 300 dollars; of course, we bought it about fifteen years ago."

"Everything is expensive now days," Alice said as she sat down in her chair. What were you thinking about earlier, while you were sitting on the garden bench? I watched you occasionally through the kitchen window while I made breakfast, and I saw you staring out over the backyard. You acted as if you were in deep concentration."

When Alice finished pouring syrup on her pancakes, she handed the syrup bottle to Duke. He set it beside his plate, and softly replied, "I was thinking back to Monday, March 4 in 1991, the day of Tony's funeral. That is the only time Mary ever came back to see us since she left to attend college in California. The only reason she came back home then was to attend her brother's funeral. I was reminiscing about the fun times we had during the years our kids grew up here. The time went so fast. I still miss Tony something terrible. I miss Mary just as much. Thank God she is alive and well, at least as far as we know."

Alice took a sip of coffee and looked into Duke's light blue eyes. He noticed tears forming in her brown eyes as she said, "I often think of Tony. I miss him so much. Memorial Day will soon be here, so we will take a bouquet of flowers to the cemetery and place it by his tombstone." Alice quickly wiped away her tears. "It's too bad Mary is such a stranger to us. It seems as if she became too good for us after she began attending college. She acted even more high and mighty after she graduated. I think Mary's college education went to her head."

"Yeah. I don't think it helped matters when she married Calvin, the rich lawyer's son. Mary and Calvin began earning tons of money after they each received their master's degree. Then, they began living the high society lifestyle." Duke took a bite of sausage, and after chewing and swallowing, enjoyed a sip of coffee. "This sausage doesn't taste too bad, but it isn't nearly as tasty as our homemade Italian sausage."

Duke and Alice remained silent while finishing their breakfast. Duke slid back his chair, stood up, and said, "I'm going outside to sit on the bench and enjoy a smoke."

"You should quit smoking those terrible cigarettes. They aren't good for you."

"I know that's what the medical professionals always preach. I've tried quitting several different times through the years, but I have never remained smoke free for longer than six months. Heck, Alice. I began smoking at the age of twelve. In the fall time, my brother Dave and I used to enter the cornfields and pick dried corn silks. We stuffed them into a little ol' corncob pipe we bought downtown at the Ben Franklin dime store. The corn silks burned almost as good as tobacco, but the smoke was a lot stronger. I turned sixty-eight years old last December, and smoking hasn't killed me, yet, but it probably will someday."

"I'm glad I gave up smoking a long time ago," said Alice

as she straightened the right sleeve of her sweater. "Mercy! It's been almost 20 years since I quit. I would still be smoking cigarettes if I hadn't developed chronic bronchitis. Luckily, I haven't had any trouble with it since I quit smoking, but I think that's why I gained weight."

"Oh, hell. You haven't gained much weight through the years. You still look mighty good to me. You are very pretty for a woman of sixty-nine years. A hundred and twenty pounds suits your 5'-5" height. I'm going outside, now."

"I'm going to clear the table and wash the dishes. After that, I will wash and set my hair."

Duke sat on the garden bench until he finished his coffee and cigarette. Then, he entered the unattached, double garage and grabbed the garden spade off the hanger. Five minutes later, he forced the spade blade eight inches into the earth at the northeast corner of the garden plot and began turning over dirt, one spade width after another, working his way west across the 20-foot wide garden plot. When he reached the northwest corner of the plot, he stopped spading so he could catch his breath and straighten his back. *My ol' back is getting sore as hell*, he thought as he stretched upright and rubbed his lower back with his left hand. *I should hire somebody with a huge tiller to till this garden plot, but I don't really feel like removing one of these fence panels, just so the guy could maneuver his tiller onto our backyard. I should have left a wider gate opening when I put up this six-foot tall, wooden privacy fence.*

After a few minutes of rest, Duke began spading to the east, working his way across the garden plot. When he reached the east side of the garden plot, he looked at his wristwatch and saw it displaying 10:00 a.m. The temperature had warmed to 65 degrees, so Duke had worked up a good sweat. He removed his long-sleeved denim shirt and headed for the kitchen to get a fresh cup of coffee. When he entered the dining room and neared the stairwell leading upstairs, he heard Alice talking on the upstairs telephone. She sounded upset, but he did not pay much attention as he walked into the kitchen. By the time he poured a cup of coffee, Alice had entered the dining room and stood by the kitchen doorway opening. "Who were you talking with?" asked Duke. "You sounded a little bit upset."

"You won't believe this, but I was talking with Jason."

"Do you mean Jason, our grandson?"

"Yes. I talked with him for about thirty minutes, and now I'm extremely worried about what's happening to Mary."

"What are you talking about?" asked Duke as he entered the dining room and set his cup on the tabletop.

"You'd better sit down before I tell you, because I know you will blow a fuse. Promise me you will remain calm."

Duke glared at Alice, but did not offer a reply. Duke and Alice sat down before Alice said, "When I picked up the phone receiver, I heard Jason, and I couldn't believe it was him. Jason was sobbing, so I knew he felt very upset. He told me between sobs that when Calvin came home last evening, Mary surprised him with a birthday cake for his 44th birthday. Everything was fine until they finished eating some of the cake. Then, Calvin informed Mary that their divorce had been finalized earlier in the day."

"Divorce?" Duke said gruffly as he rubbed his forehead. "We didn't know they were getting a divorce."

"That's not the worst part of what Jason told me. He said that at about 9:00 p.m. last night, Calvin and Mary went into their bedroom, and it wasn't long afterwards when Jason heard slapping and screaming noises. Jason said that his parents have been snorting cocaine occasionally for the last several months, and immediately after they snort drugs, they begin having some kind of wild sex. Afterwards, they usually fight for a while. Jason said that Calvin slaps and punches Mary during those times."

"That bastard hits her?" asked Duke as he hit the tabletop once with the heel of his right fist.

"Yes, that's what Jason told me. He said that during the last few months, he has seen bruises on Mary, and when he saw her at breakfast this morning, she had a black eye. It sounds as if Calvin is beating her worse all the time. Jason said that Mary is not taking very good care of herself. I guess her hair is a mess all the time, and she is depressed a lot. He told me that Mary has lost her accounting job and that the California State Board of Accounting is investigating complaints against her. Jason told me that Calvin and some of his friends coerced Mary into snorting cocaine. Jason has researched drug abuse and is quite sure that his mother and father are both addicted to cocaine."

"What in the hell is wrong with those two?" asked Duke as his fist slammed onto the tabletop. "They should be smart enough to know that illegal drugs ruin lives." Duke jumped up from his chair and began pacing back and forth between the dining room and living room. His voice became louder as he said, "I didn't especially care for Calvin the first time I met him. Then to top it off, when we were out there visiting them five years ago, he mocked my slow talking. That really made me mad, almost to the point that I wanted to slug him. I think Calvin acted very arrogant toward us. I also felt as if he looked down on us because neither you nor I attended college."

"You don't need to holler," Alice said. "Calm down a little before you have a stroke, or a heart attack. I felt the same way about Calvin; of course, Mary didn't act much differently."

"Maybe that's because she married that arrogant bastard."

"Jason asked me what he should do to help his mother." Alice began to remove her sweater as she said, "It's getting hot in here." After she removed her sweater and hung it on the chair back, she said, "I told Jason that maybe we could travel to California and visit them for a while. We could try to calm things between Calvin and Mary."

"Good God, Alice," Duke said as he stopped pacing and stood next to her. "That is two thousand miles away from here. It would take us at least four days of driving time."

"We could buy airline tickets and fly out there. I think we would only be onboard the plane for about four hours."

"I am not flying onboard a doggone airplane. I've been scared shitless more than enough times during my life. I sure as hell don't want to board an airplane and end up being scared some more. I'll phone Mary and try to find out some additional information about what's going on out there. Do you have her phone number?"

Alice opened one of the solid oak hutch drawers, took out an address book, and handed it to Duke. "Mary's phone number is listed underneath her name and address."

Duke searched for his reading glasses for five minutes before he found them in the living room. He grabbed the mobile phone off the coffee table and returned to the dining room. Duke sat down at the dining room table and fumbled through several pages in the address book until he found Mary's phone number. He punched the numbers into the mobile phone keyboard, and after hearing several rings, heard, "Hello. Jason speaking."

"Hello, Jason. This is your Grandpa Duke. How have you been, anyway? I haven't talked with you for ages."

"Yeah, it's been quite a while, Grandpa."

"I want to talk with your mother. Is she home?"

"Yeah, Grandpa. She's in her bedroom. Hang on while I go tell her that you want to talk with her."

Two minutes later, Duke heard, "Hi, Dad. What a surprise to hear from you."

"Hello, Mary. I don't know if you're aware of it or not, but Jason phoned here earlier this morning and talked with your mother. He told her that Calvin has been hitting you and that you and Calvin are both taking drugs. Jason is very worried about you. He didn't know what to do, so he asked your mother. We are very concerned about you. Jason said that you have a black eye. Did Calvin hit you in the eye?"

Mary began crying, and between sobs, said "Calvin has been hitting me occasionally, but only on the parts of my body where he knows I can hide the bruises with my clothing. He became excessively violent last night and after he slapped me several times, he punched me in the eye. I almost blacked out from the pain. Now that our divorce is final, I want to enter a drug treatment program, so that I can become drug free. I cannot enter a program, though, because I need to be available here at home for Jason. I do not want Jason to spend time with Calvin, because Calvin is high on drugs and alcohol about half the time. He cannot be trusted any longer."

"Would you enroll in a drug rehabilitation program if you could send Jason out here to spend the summer with us? Maybe your mom and I could drive out to your place for a visit. We could spend a day or two with you and Jason, and then bring Jason back here with us. Do you have enough money to support yourself and to enter one of those programs? Jason said that you lost your accounting job."

In between sniffles and sobs, Mary replied, "Money is not a problem. We have always used Calvin's earnings to live on, so I have saved all my earnings. My investments have performed well through the years. I have sole ownership of this house now that the divorce is final, so I could sell it if I needed additional money to support Jason and myself."

"Okay. How about if you find a drug rehabilitation program and arrange an entrance time? Discuss things with Jason, too, as far as if he would want to come out here for the summer. I would like you to arrange things as soon as possible, and then let us know right away, like maybe tomorrow. When is Jason's last day of school this spring?"

"His last day of school is Friday, May 27. I will make some phone calls today and find out if I can enroll in a drug treatment program. I will also discuss things with Jason. Will it be okay if I call you at 8:00 a.m. your time tomorrow?"

"That will be just fine, Mary. Please enroll in one of those drug treatment programs and get yourself straightened out. Stay away from Calvin, too."

"Okay, Dad. I will talk with you tomorrow. Thanks for phoning me. Good-bye."

Duke shut off the mobile phone and placed it upon the dining room tabletop. "Mary said that she will call us at 8:00 a.m. tomorrow, so we will know a little more then. I'm going outside for a smoke. After that, I will spade more of the garden plot. I'm sure glad I planted three rows of seed potatoes Good Friday. I need to finish spading the plot, so I can plant more vegetable seeds and seedlings."

As Duke walked out of the dining room and onto the 3-season porch, Alice said, "It's 11:00 a.m. What time do you want to eat lunch?"

Duke stopped walking, turned to look at Alice, and replied, "How does high noon sound to you? I just want a couple of bologna sandwiches and some potato chips."

"I'll have lunch ready at noon. I'll eat some leftover

vegetable soup. I can't stand that fatty bologna."

Duke snickered and replied, "You should be able to eat all the fat you want since you take those pills for your cholesterol problem."

Duke and Alice began eating lunch at noon. They remained silent during lunch while thinking about Mary and Jason. Duke went outside to the garden plot as soon as he finished eating. Alice cleared the dishes and silverware from the tabletop, washed dishes, and then began cleaning house. At 2:45 p.m., Duke pulled a putty knife out of his back pocket and scraped the dirt from his spade. He entered the garage and hung the spade onto the hook. Duke made his way along the sidewalk located between the garage and house. He opened the side door, entered the house, and walked slowly down the stair steps until he reached the basement. He opened the refrigerator door and grabbed a can of beer. At 3:00 p.m., he popped open the beer can lid tab and took a large gulp. *This cold beer really hits the spot,* he thought as he swallowed and headed upstairs to find Alice.

Duke awoke at 5:00 a.m. Sunday. He lay still for about five minutes while listening to the raindrops splattering against the roof. His entire body felt very stiff and sore, but he stood up and dressed in jeans and a short-sleeved denim shirt. By the time he walked down the stair steps and into the dining room, his soreness had disappeared. *I'm getting too old to be spading the garden plot,* he thought as he poured a pot of water into the coffee maker. *I think I'll hire somebody to till the garden plot next spring.* Just as he dumped the third spoonful of new coffee grounds into the coffee maker basket, Alice walked into the kitchen. She finished tying the belt of her floral-print, silk kimono, and said, "Good morning, sweetheart. You're up early."

Duke grinned and said, "You're up pretty darn early, too, Peach. I thought you were going to sleep late, since it's

Sunday."

"My goodness, Duke. You haven't called me Peach for quite some time. I was going to sleep late, but I am so worried about Mary and Jason. I didn't sleep very well last night."

"I hope Mary has arranged to enter a drug rehabilitation center. I guess we'll find out before much longer, that is if she calls as she said she would. I'm going to sit on the 3-season porch while I drink my coffee and enjoy a cigarette. I'll take the mobile phone with me."

The phone rang at 8:00 a.m., just as Alice entered onto the porch. Duke picked up the mobile phone as he snuffed out a cigarette. "Duke speaking."

"Hi, Dad," Mary replied. "I phoned several different rehab centers yesterday and finally found one that will accept me into their program."

"That's good. When will you enter the center to begin treatment?"

"The program director said that I could check into the center at 8:00 a.m. Monday, June 6. I will have to live there for at least a month."

"Did you ask Jason if he would be okay with coming out here to live with us for the summer?"

"Jason likes the idea. I phoned Calvin and talked with him about it. He said that he could care less about what Jason does. Actually, it does not matter what Calvin thinks, because he gave up all his rights to Jason, so I have sole custody of him."

"Do you know if your mother and I will need some kind of legal guardianship over Jason while he lives with us?" Duke mumbled as he lit up a cigarette. He inhaled a large amount of smoke, held it in for a few seconds, and then blew a huge smoke ring into the air as Alice rolled her eyes at him.

"I thought about that yesterday," replied Mary, "so I

called a lawyer friend of mine and asked him. He said that Jason could voluntarily sign an affidavit to give Mother and you temporary guardianship, but we would all have to attend a judge's hearing on the matter. Jason agreed to it. My lawyer friend said that if a California judge approves it, the State of Iowa should approve it, but you will still have to submit the documents to an Iowa court for their approval."

Duke took a sip of coffee, and said, "Doggone! That's sure a lot of red tape to go through, but I guess we need guardianship; otherwise, we probably wouldn't be able to get any kind of medical treatment for Jason if he needed some."

"I want to finish the rehabilitation program, and then sell the house and move to Iowa. I should be able to find a good enough job there to support Jason and myself. I am tired of all this high society living we have been doing for so long. I think it is time to get back down to earth. I could spend more time with Jason, and with you and Mom."

"So you might not be able to move here before school begins in the fall, huh? In that case, we will definitely need guardianship over Jason; otherwise, we won't be able to register him in school."

"My lawyer friend said to let him know when we want the hearing. He has a very good friend who is a judge. My friend said that he could easily arrange a date and time for the hearing."

"Okay," Duke said. "My ear is getting tired, so I'll let you talk with Alice for a while. Alice and I will discuss your situation later. I'll phone you tonight and let you know our plans." Duke handed the mobile phone to Alice as he stood up and said, "I'm going upstairs to get ready for church. Tell Mary that I will call her tonight at 8:00 p.m., California time."

Alice nodded her head and whispered to Duke, "I'll be

ready for church by 9:45 a.m., so let's attend the 10:00 a.m. service.

The heavy rain along with the 20 mph south wind at 9:50 a.m. hindered Duke and Alice a little bit as they walked the thirty feet along the sidewalk leading from their house to the unattached, double garage. As they slid onto the front seat of the navy blue, 2002 LeSabre, Alice mumbled something about how nice it would be to have an attached garage. Duke ignored her mumbling and waited for her to buckle her seatbelt. During the eight-block drive to church, Alice said, "I look forward to Reverend Smith's sermon this morning. It will be his first one at our church. Perhaps, we will be able to introduce ourselves to him. I guess he moved his family here from Topeka, Kansas, just last week. The rumors from the churchwomen are that the minister and his wife are parents of two teenagers, a boy and a girl."

"I imagine all those gossipy churchwomen know everything about the new preacher and his family by this time."

"Oh, Duke. They don't gossip very much."

Duke steered the LeSabre off Kane Avenue and onto the church parking lot. He parked in a parking space located about two hundred feet from the church. As Alice and Duke opened the car doors and stepped onto the parking lot, the rain and wind ceased abruptly. "My goodness," said Alice as she looked up at the sky. "The good Lord must have stopped the rain and wind for us, just so we can walk into the church without getting wet."

Duke grinned and said, "He's taking extra good care of us, Alice."

When they entered the Methodist Church, Alice said, "Let's sit as close to the front as possible."

Duke reluctantly replied, "I guess we can, but you know doggone well that I prefer to sit in the back row."

"It won't kill you to sit close to the pulpit. I want to make sure I can hear and see the new minister."

At one point during the church service, Reverend Smith asked everybody to sing along as the organist played The Old Rugged Cross. During the song, Duke reached up and wiped some tears from his cheeks. *That song always brings tears to my eyes for some reason*, he thought, *kind of like when I sing along to God Bless America, or hear a bugler playing Taps.*

An hour and ten minutes after they had entered the church, Duke and Alice slid out of the pew. Reverend Smith and his family stood beside the front exit as everybody began filing out of the church. Reverend Smith and each member of his family shook hands and introduced themselves to each church attendee. When Alice shook hands with Reverend Smith, she introduced herself first, and then said, "You definitely preached a wonderful sermon this morning, Reverend Smith. I look forward to your future sermons."

Duke shook hands with the reverend and said, "It's nice to meet you, Reverend Smith."

Alice did not say much to Duke on the way home, other than remarking that it appeared as if the sun would soon shine. When they entered the kitchen, Alice said, "You sure didn't say very much to the reverend. You could have at least welcomed him and his family to the community."

"Oh, Alice. Reverend Smith had shaken hands with so many people by the time we were leaving the church. I figured he just wanted everybody to leave as soon as possible, so he and his family could go home and relax for a while. Of course, if we wouldn't have been sitting in the front pew, we could have been home a half hour sooner. Reverend Smith sure doesn't preach anything like the ol' fire-and-brimstone preacher he replaced. Heck! It is already 11:45 a.m."

Duke went upstairs and changed into his jeans and short-sleeved denim shirt. Then, he went downstairs and walked directly into the living room. He opened the coat closet door, and began shuffling through some books stacked on the top shelf. He removed a State Farm Road Atlas, and sat down on the sofa to plan a trip to California. Alice entered the living room a few minutes later and saw Duke concentrating on a page in the atlas. "Planning a trip?" she asked as she sat down beside him and began lightly rubbing his right thigh.

"I'm just trying to figure out a route and timeline for the trip to California. If we take Interstate 80 all the way, it will take us about four days. I think that if we were to leave here at sunrise Tuesday morning, we would arrive at Mary's house late Friday night. How do you feel about it?"

"That's fine with me. Let's lounge around here for the rest of today. We can pack our suitcases tomorrow."

"Our ol' 2002 LeSabre should be ready to go. I had the Firestone employees change her oil and filter last week. The tires aren't in very good condition, but they might last long enough for a round trip to California. That doggone car already has fifty-five thousand miles on it, and those are the original tires."

"We should leave a house key with Janice. She is always good about checking the house for us when we are away. We are fortunate to have good next-door neighbors."

"That's for sure. I've been on many different land surveys through the years, and many times, it was because the people were in disputes with their neighbors. People sometimes fight over the craziest things."

"I'll give our extra house key to Janice tomorrow." Alice again began lightly rubbing Duke's right thigh. Then, she slid her hand slowly along his thigh, following a path from his knee to his hip and back to his knee. After a few trips back and forth along the path, she rested her hand by the waistband of his jeans. Duke scooted around a little as Alice slid two fingers in between the waistband of his jeans and his belly. "I think we should spend a little quality time together in bed this afternoon," whispered Alice. "What do you think of that idea?"

Duke leaned over and planted a kiss on Alice's lips. "That sounds like an excellent idea. I've been waiting for at least two weeks for you to suggest something like that. Let's eat lunch so we can get an early start this afternoon."

At 10:00 p.m. Sunday, Duke entered the dining room, picked up the mobile phone, and walked onto the 3-season porch where he sat down in his favorite wicker chair. The rain had stopped earlier in the afternoon, and he could see the full moon shining brightly through some white, wispy clouds. He punched Mary's phone number into the mobile phone keyboard and listened for the rings. After five rings, he heard Mary answer, "Hello."

"Hi, Mary. Your mother and I have decided to leave here at daybreak Tuesday morning. We should arrive at your house sometime late Friday night, if everything goes okay."

"Excellent! Jason and I will be so happy to see you both. It has been five years since we have seen you."

"We plan to stay with you until Tuesday, May 31. Will that be okay with you? We'll leave your house early that morning and begin driving toward home."

"That will be just fine, Dad. I will have one of the bedrooms ready for you."

"I suppose you should try to arrange a hearing date for the guardianship business we discussed. Do you think the hearing could be scheduled sometime during the week of the 22nd?"

"I will call my lawyer friend and tell him to arrange it. He did not seem to think it would be a problem, since his friend is a judge. Actually, my friend and the judge are both gay and have been living together for several years."

"They're gay? Doggone! That must be a different kind of lifestyle, but I guess if they are happy, nobody else should complain. We will see you late Friday night. Talk to you then. Good-bye, Mary."

"Good-bye, Dad. Drive carefully."

Duke and Mary slept until 8:00 a.m. Monday. They both woke at the same time. Duke looked directly into Alice's dark brown eyes, smiled, and said, "I believe you almost wore me out yesterday afternoon. I still feel pretty tired, but I'll have to admit that I feel very relaxed, more relaxed than I have been for a few weeks."

"I feel wonderful this morning," Alice replied as she slid over to the side of the bed and began dressing. "You still have a lot of firepower in that old, muscular body."

Duke laughed a little and said, "Yeah. I still have a little power left, but it isn't easy for me to keep up with a spicy-hot half Italian."

Alice headed for the stairway as she laughed and replied, "You sure love trying to keep up with me."

Duke and Alice enjoyed eating scrambled eggs and bacon for breakfast. As Alice began clearing the tabletop, she said, "We should buy some kind of artificial flower bouquet today and put it next to Tony's tombstone. We won't be here for Memorial Day like normal, so we won't be able to put real flowers by his gravesite."

"We'll go to Walmart and see if they have any fake bouquets for gravesites. If they don't, we will look at Kmart. Let's do that as soon as you finish washing the dishes."

Duke and Alice spent an hour browsing through the Walmart store before they went to the Kmart store. There, they purchased a bouquet of artificial red roses mixed with white baby's breath. They left Kmart and went directly to the cemetery where they placed the bouquet next to Tony's tombstone. They held hands as they recited The Lord's Prayer, after which they each wiped tears from their cheeks. Fifteen minutes later, they arrived at their house and began discussing the trip to California. Duke reminded Alice to pack conservatively, because they would need enough room in the car for Jason and his luggage during the return trip. When Duke reminded Alice the third time, her Italian temper flared up instantly. Her cheeks glowed bright red as she waved her hands into the air, and with a high-pitched voice, loudly said, "I realize we need room on the return trip, so you don't need to keep reminding me." She stomped toward the staircase and stomped all the way up the stair steps. After entering the master bedroom, she stomped toward the walk-in closet.

Duke grinned when he heard Alice yanking the suitcases out of the bedroom closet. Duke hollered up the staircase, "Doggone, Alice! Try to leave some of the woodwork paint in place. You're banging things around pretty good up there."

Duke did not hear a reply, nor hear any additional banging noises coming from the upstairs bedroom. He waited about thirty minutes before going upstairs to begin packing his suitcase. By then, Alice had cooled down and acted normal. As soon as Alice finished packing, she said, "I'm going next-door to Janice's house. I'll visit with her for a while and give her our spare house key. I know she won't mind watering our house plants and keeping an eye on the house while we're gone."

"Okay. I'll see you when you get back. I'll carry your luggage downstairs. Tell Janice hello for me."

Chapter 3

Duke had carried all his and Alice's luggage out of the house and loaded it into the car trunk by 5:00 a.m. Tuesday, May 17. He and Alice slid onto the front seat of the LeSabre and left for Des Moines at 5:30 a.m. At 7:15 a.m., Duke steered the LeSabre onto westbound Interstate 80 and set the cruise control at 75 mph. He reached over and put his hand on Alice's thigh. "It has been a while since we've made a long road trip," Duke said. "I hope this doggone ol' car will make it all the way to California and back without too much trouble."

Alice patted Duke's hand and replied, "I hope so, too. It should. It's been a good car so far." Alice shifted body positions a few times before saying, "I need to use a bathroom before much longer."

"I saw a sign for a rest stop a little while ago, so the exit should be coming up before long. There should be a coffee machine inside the rest stop building, so we'll grab a couple cups of coffee to take with us when we leave."

Duke parked the LeSabre in front of the rest stop building ten minutes later. They did not waste any time at the rest stop, and were soon driving at 75 mph on westbound Interstate 80, heading toward Omaha,

Nebraska. Alice eventually reached into a canvas shopping bag located next to her feet, removed a romance novel, and placed the paperback book upon her lap. "I guess I'll begin reading this novel," she stated as she opened the book to the first page.

"You may as well read. There isn't much else to do, other than view the scenery. What's the name of that book, anyway?"

"The title is *Miss Nancy: June 5, 1964, to September 13, 1964*. A guy from Iowa authored it, and it's supposed to be very spicy. He wrote a sequel to it, too."

"I might read it when you're done with it, especially if you think it is spicy enough for me."

"Yes, Duke. I know you enjoy everything hot and spicy. The spicier the better. Right?"

Duke shifted positions slightly and replied, "That's right, Alice."

Everything went fine for the next two hours. As they neared the halfway point along the decline leading into the Missouri River Valley, Duke glanced at the dashboard clock and saw it displaying 9:30 a.m. They suddenly heard a very loud bang. Duke immediately struggled with the steering wheel and applied the brakes, trying to maintain control of the car. He eventually slowed enough, steered onto the asphalt shoulder of Interstate 80, and parked the car. He let out a deep breath of relief, wiped his forehead with the back of his right hand, and reached into his shirt pocket for a cigarette. He looked at Alice as he lit the cigarette and said, "I was afraid this would happen. One of the doggone tires must have blown out." Duke opened the door and stepped onto the asphalt shoulder. He looked forward and aft before saying, "The left rear tire blew out. I'll have to unload the luggage from the trunk, so I can get out the spare tire. It's underneath the trunk floor."

As Duke began emptying the trunk, an Iowa State

Trooper parked his cruiser about fifty feet behind the LeSabre. He switched on the flashing red top lights, opened the door, and stepped onto the highway shoulder. Duke saw him when he was about twenty-five feet away. The trooper approached Duke and said, “Hello, sir. Is there anything I can do to help?”

“Hello,” replied Duke. “I’m in the process of changing a flat tire. I think I can manage it okay.”

The trooper extended his hand for a handshake and said, “My name is Dan. I noticed by your bumper sticker that you support the military troops, and I see that you have a magnetic freedom ribbon stuck to your car.”

Duke shook hands with Dan and said, “I’m Duke. Yeah. We support the troops as much as we can. We lost our son over in Iraq during Desert Storm in 1991. He was a US Marine corporal.”

“I am very sorry for your loss, Duke. I was over there during Desert Storm, but I was in the US Air Force, so I spent most of my time in airplanes. Are you a veteran?”

“I spent four years in the US Navy, three of them aboard a submarine.”

“Darn! I always thought you would have to be crazy to serve aboard a submarine. I would not have been courageous enough for submarine duty.”

Duke grinned as he replied, “I always thought that about airborne military people.”

Dan pointed toward Alice and asked, “Is that your wife in the car?”

“Yeah,” Duke replied as he wiped some sweat from his forehead. “She’s my wife of a little over forty-five years.”

“I need to see your driver’s license, Duke. It is one of my job requirements.”

Duke removed his wallet from his left rear jean pocket, took out his driver’s license, and handed it to Dan. “I understand, Dan.”

After carefully inspecting the driver's license, Dan handed it back to Duke. "Thank you," said Dan. "I'll help you unload the luggage and change the tire. It is dangerous out here with all this speeding traffic whizzing past us. The red flashing lights on my cruiser will help slow the traffic considerably." Dan wiped the beads of sweat from his eyebrows, and said, "Whew! It is very hot today, unusually hot for this time of year."

"Yeah. It must be about 80 degrees. Humid as heck, too. I sure appreciate your help, Dan."

Forty minutes later, Duke and Dan finished changing the tire and returned the luggage into the trunk. They loaded the ruined tire into the rear passenger area where they wedged it in between the front of the backseat and the rear of the front seat. Dan and Duke said their good-byes as Duke slid in behind the steering wheel. Alice thanked Dan for helping just before he began walking toward his cruiser. As soon as Dan crawled into his cruiser, Alice said, "Good gracious, Duke! You sure used God's name in vain a lot while you changed that tire. Perhaps, you should take a moment and pray for his forgiveness."

Duke lit a cigarette and turned the ignition key. As the car engine started, he said, "If God had been doing all that work, he might have sworn quite a lot, too, so I'm not going to worry about it."

Alice gave Duke a nasty look as Duke stepped on the accelerator and increased the speed. He soon steered the car onto the westbound, outside lane of Interstate 80, where he maintained the speed at 55 mph. *Cars used to come from the factory with a full-size spare tire*, thought Duke, *but now they all come with the doggone little space-saving spare tires. You can't even drive very fast with one of those on a car.* Dan followed them with his cruiser for a while, and then suddenly passed them as his top red lights began flashing. Duke said, "Dan must be on his way to an emergency call."

Duke eventually saw a sign advertising an Omaha Firestone Store located close to Interstate 80. He took the exit and soon located the store, so he steered the LeSabre onto the asphalt parking lot and parked in front of the tire store. Duke and Alice went inside and talked with the store manager. They spent 400 dollars for five new tires, and while waiting to get them installed, walked across the street to eat lunch at a family owned restaurant. When they returned to the tire store, they learned that the LeSabre needed new front brake pads and calipers, so they spent another 250 dollars. Of course, tax increased the total amount considerably. Duke grimaced a little when he handed the store manager a credit card and said, "Put it all on this credit card."

At 3:00 p.m., Duke and Alice rode away from the store in their LeSabre. Ten minutes later, they entered upon westbound Interstate 80, heading toward Grand Island, Nebraska. Two hours later, Duke steered the car off Interstate 80 and onto an exit ramp. He steered onto a Grand Island city street, and soon parked the car in front of a motel. At 5:30 p.m., Duke opened the cooler lid and removed a cold can of beer. He popped open the lid tab, took a huge swallow, and sat down on the edge of the queen-sized bed in their rented motel room located on the second floor. Alice sat down next to him, leaned over until her body snuggled against his, and said, "I should have brought a bottle of wine. I could sure use a drink right now."

"I'm going outside for a smoke, so when I walk through the lobby, I'll ask the desk clerk where we can buy a bottle of wine. There should be a liquor store around here somewhere."

After spending two additional long days of driving along

Interstate 80, Duke and Alice crawled onto the queen-sized bed in a motel room located near Elko, Nevada. The bedside clock displayed 10:00 p.m. as they snuggled together and Alice said, "This motel room is a lot nicer than the one we rented last night in Rawlins."

"Yeah. This room cost less, too. Good night, Peach. I'm exhausted."

"It's nice of you to call me Peach. You used to call me that a lot, but not too often, lately. Good night, Duke. I love you."

"I love you, too, Peach."

At the same time as Alice said good night to Duke, Jason entered the living room and sat down on the sofa. A few seconds later, at 8:00 p.m. (California time), Jason heard Mary talking on her bedroom phone. Mary had not bothered to close the bedroom door, so Jason could hear her very clearly, as she said, "I know it is late, but I need some cocaine. Can you bring some over to me?" Jason did not like the next thing he heard when she said with a sarcastic tone of voice, "Okay, then! I will see you at your secretary's house in about thirty minutes."

Mary walked into the living room a few minutes later, and said, "Oh, there you are, Jason. I have been looking for you."

"I was upstairs in my bedroom studying until about ten minutes ago. I have two final tests tomorrow, one for math and one for history. I came downstairs to see what you're doing."

"I will be leaving in a few minutes. I do not know when I will return home. Will you be okay here by yourself?"

Jason's face turned bright red as he jumped up from the sofa. He stomped the floor with his right foot as he raised his hands and waved them around far above his head. "You must have been talking with Dad," hollered Jason. "I heard you ask for cocaine. I thought you were going to quit taking illegal drugs."

"Oh, honey! I am trying to quit, but it is very difficult. I will quit in a few weeks, as soon as I enter the rehabilitation program. I promise."

Tears came to Jason's eyes as he lowered his hands and headed for the spiral staircase. He stopped walking, turned and looked at Mary, and hollered, "You must be crazy. You keep taking drugs with Dad, and then he slaps you and treats you mean. One of these days, he might hurt you severely, or else kill you."

"Please do not get so upset, Jason. I promise I will change my ways."

"Yeah, right!" replied Jason loudly as he began bounding up the stair steps. He entered his bedroom and slammed the door so hard that some of the white paint on the fir doorstops flaked off. Jason fell onto his bed and began weeping. He heard Mary leave the house a while later, and thought, *Well, I guess she doesn't care about herself. I wonder if she will bother to come home tonight.* Jason eventually went to sleep, but awoke several times during the night, wondering if his mother had come home.

Jason awoke at 6:00 a.m. Friday and immediately went downstairs to see if his mother had returned home. He could not find her anywhere in the house, so he went upstairs and dressed for school. When he left for school an hour later, Mary still had not shown up. Jason worried constantly about her during his six-block walk to the schoolhouse. He quit worrying about Mary when he began taking his first final test, because he knew it was important for him to concentrate entirely on the test, so that he would not flunk his sophomore year. When the morning classes ended, Jason ate lunch in the cafeteria before going outside to enjoy the beautiful spring weather and breathe a little fresh air. He strolled along the main sidewalk, back and forth between the street and the main entrance to the school building. A few of the bullies grouped together and watched as Jason passed beside them. They gave him some dirty looks, but said nothing. When everybody began returning to the classrooms, Jason followed a group of students through the main entrance and into the hallway. One of the bullies bumped forcefully against Jason's left side and said, "We're going to get you on your way home this afternoon, fat boy."

Jason ignored the bully and continued walking toward the classroom so he could take another final test. *I wish those bullies would leave me alone*, he thought. *Now, I'm worried about walking home this afternoon.* The second final test of the day seemed very difficult for Jason, but after he finished the last question and handed in the test, he believed he had answered all the questions correctly. When the final bell of the day rang, Jason headed for home. He kept a close watch for the bullies while walking the six blocks, but never saw any of them. He unlocked the front door and entered the house. "Are you home, Mom?" he yelled.

"Yes, I am in my bedroom. I will be right out."

Jason helped himself to a Twinkie and a glass of chocolate milk. He sat down at the kitchen table to wait for Mary. As Jason finished washing down the Twinkie with some milk, Mary sauntered into the kitchen, sat down at the kitchen table, and asked, "How was your day?"

"It was okay. I took two final tests. They were quite difficult, but I believe I answered all the questions correctly."

"I am certainly glad to hear that," replied Mary as she lightly stroked her right temple with her right index finger.

"Why didn't you come home last night?" asked Jason as he stood up. "I worried about you all night."

"Oh, dear. You should not worry about me. I guess time passed so quickly that I lost tract. Your father introduced me to Betty, his new secretary. I had never met her before, but she has only worked as his secretary for a few weeks." Mary began nibbling on the tips of her right fingernails, alternating between them. "I believe your dad began dating Betty a few months ago. He moved in with her a week ago. She became quite rich when she divorced her husband last year. The house she obtained through the divorce settlement is gorgeous. It contains four bedrooms and three bathrooms. Three of the bedrooms each have two queen-sized beds, and the fourth bedroom has a king-sized bed. It is a very impressive home."

Jason walked across the dark sand-colored, ceramic-tile floor, and set his empty glass upon the beautiful light sand-colored granite countertop next to the polished stainless-steel sink. He turned around, looked at Mary, and said, "You haven't answered my question, Mom." Jason paused a few seconds before asking, "Why do you bite your fingernails so much?"

"I am sorry, Jason," Mary said as she quit biting her fingernails. She nervously rubbed her right cheek with her right hand. With her left hand, she brushed aside a few locks of blonde hair from her forehead. "I decided to stay there last night. It was very late when we finished talking, so Betty said that I could sleep in one of the spare bedrooms. Actually, I am going over there tonight, too. Betty insisted that I attend her birthday party tonight, and I certainly could not refuse her invitation. I guess several of her and your father's friends plan to attend."

"You do remember that Grandpa and Grandma are supposed to arrive here sometime late tonight."

"Yes, I remember. I will be home by the time they arrive. We need to leave for the lawyer's office, now, so we can sign the guardianship papers. I talked with the lawyer last Wednesday, and he said that the papers would be ready for our signatures at 4:30 p.m. today, so we should leave for his office right now."

Mary and Jason left the lawyer's office at 5:30 p.m., and on their way home, stopped at McDonalds so Jason could purchase something for his supper. He ordered two Big Macs and two orders of fries at the drive-thru. Minutes later, they were on their way home, and when they arrived, Mary went straight to the bathroom so she could shower and get ready for the party. Jason set his sack of food upon the kitchen table. He walked over to the refrigerator, opened the door, and removed a bottle of ketchup and can of soda before shutting the door. He walked over to the table where he sat down and unwrapped one of the Big Macs. He took a large bite, and after swallowing, ate a French fry. After a sip of soda, Jason thought, *This food is much tastier than the frozen junk food Mom always makes nightly for supper.*

When Jason finished eating, he cleared off the table, and went upstairs to take a shower. After showering and drying off, he dressed in the new jeans and denim shirt his mother had purchased for him with the money his grandparents had sent him for Christmas. He returned downstairs and entered the living room at 7:00 p.m., just as Mary came out of her bedroom. Mary said, "You are very handsome in those jeans and that denim shirt. You remind me of the Iowa farmers. Many Iowa people wear denim clothes; at least they did when I lived there."

As Jason thanked Mary for the comment, he noticed she had dressed very sexy for the party. He thought the skin-tight, white slacks, along with her black satin, long-sleeved, low-cut blouse appeared as unusual attire for her, especially since she wore no bra. Her black, high-heeled shoes made her appear taller. Jason wondered how she could possibly walk without tripping. "I am leaving, now," stated Mary. "If I am not home by the time your grandparents arrive, welcome them to our home. Make sure you help them with their luggage. They can use the bedroom directly across the hall from yours. I have it ready for them."

As Mary left her house for Betty's birthday party, Duke and Alice exited a GM dealership building located near West Sacramento. They had left Elko, Nevada, at 8:00 a.m. that morning, and everything had gone smoothly until they stopped to eat lunch at 2:30 p.m. in West Sacramento. They walked out of the restaurant at 3:30 p.m., and as they approached their car, Duke noticed a large spot of oil upon the asphalt parking lot underneath the front right side of their car. He cussed silently before saying, "Look at that, Alice. It appears as if our car has an oil leak." Duke kneeled down and looked underneath the car, trying to see the oil leak. After a minute, he stood up and said, "It's leaking quite badly from the right front axle seal. We'd better find a GM garage and see if we can get it repaired before we continue driving toward Redwood City."

"My goodness," said Alice, "It's the middle of the afternoon. Do you think we can get it fixed today?"

"I don't know, but it needs to be repaired. I will go back into the restaurant and ask somebody where we can find a GM garage. You may as well wait in the car."

Alice sat in the car and waited ten minutes before she saw Duke walking toward her. Duke opened the car door and slid in behind the steering wheel. "I managed to find a local man inside who knew this area. He said that there is a GM dealer located about five miles from here, quite close to Interstate 80. We'll stop there and ask them if they can repair the leak."

Duke and Alice entered the service department at the dealership ten minutes later. After Duke told the service manager, Carlos, about the oil leak, Carlos replied, "You are fortunate, because we have an empty stall, and a mechanic who has been looking for something to work on.

We'll check out that leak and give you an estimate right away." Carlos pointed toward a doorway and said, "If you want, you can wait in our lounge. There's a television, coffee, and snacks in there. It's right through that doorway. "

"That sounds good to me," Duke said as he handed the car keys to Carlos. Duke faced Alice and said, "We may as well sit in the lounge while we wait for the estimate."

Fifteen minutes passed before Carlos entered the lounge. He approached Duke and said, "You were right. The axle seal is leaking badly. We have the parts in stock. I totaled the prices for parts and labor. The repair will cost you 300 dollars plus tax. It will take the mechanic about three hours to replace the axle seal."

"Can he begin working on it right away?"

"Yes, as soon as I give him the okay."

Duke looked at the wall clock located above the TV and said, "It's 4:00 p.m. right now, so it will be 7:00 p.m. by the time our car is repaired. Is that correct?"

"That's right, Duke. We stay open late on Friday nights, so you lucked out in that respect, too."

"Go ahead and fix it," Duke said. "Our car is about due for an oil and filter change. Can you take care of that for us?"

"Sure thing. That will add 35 dollars plus tax to your bill."

That's fine," Duke said. "Is there anything exciting to do within walking distance of here?"

"Not much", replied Carlos as he pointed toward the west windows. "If you like to shop, there is a strip mall located about two blocks west of here."

"Are there any restaurants in the mall?" asked Alice.

"There's a family style restaurant there," replied Carlos as he slid his right fingers through his long, coal-black hair. "The restaurant employees make everything from scratch, all American style food. The food there is excellent. Well, I'll go tell the mechanic to begin repairing your car."

"Okay," Duke said as he rose from the chair. "We'll be back here at 6:45 p.m., just in case your mechanic finishes the repairs a little early. Will you still be here?"

"I'll be here until closing time at 9:00 p.m."

Duke and Alice spent some time browsing through the stores in the strip mall. Actually, Alice did most of the browsing while Duke spent most of his time pacing back and forth along the sidewalk located in front of the mall. Of course, he smoked a few cigarettes while pacing along the sidewalk. Duke and Alice entered the restaurant at 5:30 p.m. and selected a booth near the front windows. As they slid onto the booth seats, Duke said, "A great big cheeseburger along with some burnt hash browns sounds good to me. I could sure drink the hell out of a cold beer, but I'd better not, since I still have a long ways to drive today."

Alice smiled at Duke and said, "I have a taste for some fried chicken and some fried potatoes, but I want to look at one of the menus before I decide for sure."

"You should be able to eat anything you want, since you take that doggone cholesterol medicine all the time."

"Well! You don't even know what your cholesterol count is since you have never had a doctor test you for it."

The waitress approached the booth as Duke began to reply, so he stopped talking and began looking at the menu, even though he knew what he would order. Duke and Alice eventually finished eating and left the restaurant at 6:30 p.m. They returned to the GM garage, charged 358 dollars to their credit card account, and drove away in their car. As Duke steered the car from an entrance ramp onto westbound Interstate 80, he said, "Just think, Alice. We should arrive at Mary's house in about three more hours, that is, if we don't get lost in San Francisco."

"We can't get there soon enough as far as I am concerned. I'm so tired of riding in this car."

"I know what you mean," replied Duke.

When Duke and Alice reached San Pablo, Duke stopped at a rest stop so they could use the bathroom. He spent some time looking at his California road map before continuing their drive. As they entered onto Interstate 80, Duke reached over and put his right hand on Alice's left forearm. "I think we will bypass San Francisco," he offered. "Maybe, we can stay away from some of the heavy traffic. I'm not used to driving with all these cars and trucks passing us as if we're standing still." Duke continued driving on Interstate 80 until they reached Oakland where he maneuvered the car onto southbound Interstate 880. He continued driving until they saw a sign for the junction of westbound Highway 84. Duke almost caused an accident when he quickly changed lanes at the last minute so he could turn onto Highway 84. They soon reached the Dumbarton Bridge tollbooths, and after paying a toll of 4 dollars, Duke continued driving across the bridge. When they reached the junction of Highway 101, Duke headed north and soon saw a sign for Redwood City. Duke said, "I don't know if I remember how to get to Mary's house. We haven't been there for five years."

"When we arrive in Redwood City, we will probably remember where to turn off to get to Mary's house."

Twenty minutes later, Duke steered the LeSabre onto Mary's driveway and parked in front of the attached, double garage. He looked at the dashboard clock and said, "I hope somebody is still awake. It's already 10:00 p.m."

"The living room is all lit up, so somebody must be awake."

Duke opened the car door and slowly slid out from behind the steering wheel. He stood up and stretched his body for about thirty seconds before walking around the rear of the car to open the door for Alice. "Well, thank you, Duke. It might take me a while to get out. I'm very stiff from sitting in this car for so long."

As soon as Alice stood up and stretched a little, they approached the front door and rang the doorbell. When the door opened, they saw Jason dressed in his new jeans and denim shirt. "Hi, Grandma and Grandpa. I've been waiting for you."

"My goodness," Alice said as she hugged the gentle giant. "You have grown so much since we saw you five years ago."

"Doggone!" Duke said as he took his turn hugging Jason. "You are way bigger than your ol' Grandpa."

When Jason finished hugging Duke, he asked, "Do you want to go inside and rest for a while? I can unload your luggage and bring it inside."

Duke looked at Alice and said, "You may as well go inside, Alice. Jason and I will bring in the luggage."

"Okay," Alice said. "Is Mary home, Jason?"

As Jason headed for the car, he replied, "No. She went to a birthday party that Dad arranged for one of his friends. Mom told me that she would be home by the time you arrived, but she's evidently running late."

Alice went into the kitchen and helped herself to a hot cup of tea as Duke and Jason unloaded the luggage and brought it all into the upstairs bedroom located directly across the hallway from Jason's bedroom. When Duke saw the room, he said, "This is a nice big bedroom, Jason, and fancy, too."

"Mom did a little decorating in here after she found out you and Grandma planned to visit us."

"That was nice of her. I'm going out to the car and grab a can of beer out of my cooler. I think I'll sit on the front stoop and have a smoke."

As they walked toward the spiral staircase, Jason said, "I'm going to talk with Grandma for a while. You could put all your beer in the refrigerator."

"I might do that, because I think the ice in my cooler is nearly melted. Thanks for helping me with the luggage, Jason."

"You're welcome, Grandpa."

Duke went outside and opened the car trunk lid. After opening the cooler lid, he removed a can of beer from the cooler, and sat down on the front stoop. He popped open the lid tab, lit a cigarette, and took a large swallow of beer. *Boy!* thought Duke. *This beer really hits the spot, even though it isn't very cold.* He finished drinking the beer within ten minutes, and then removed another can of beer from inside the cooler. Duke admired the full moon for about fifteen seconds before popping open the beer can lid tab. He lit a cigarette and began pacing back and forth slowly along the driveway, from one end to the other. When he finished the last swallow of beer, he looked at his wristwatch and saw it displaying 11:30 p.m., so he decided to go inside and take a shower. Duke saw Jason sitting at the kitchen table, "Did Alice already go to bed?"

"I don't know, Grandpa. I know she went upstairs a little while ago to take a shower."

"I'm going to take a nice warm shower pretty soon," replied Duke. "Doggone! I thought Mary would be home by this time."

"I thought so, too, Grandpa. I phoned her a little while ago, but she didn't answer her cell phone. I also phoned Dad, but he didn't answer his phone. They must be busy doing something."

"Well, I'm going to bed right after I take a shower. I'm not waiting up for her any longer. My ol' body is sore and stiff, and I feel tired."

Chapter 4

The clock on the nightstand displayed 11:55 p.m. Friday by the time Duke and Alice had crawled into bed and pulled the top sheet up to their chins. Alice told Duke about her earlier conversation with Jason, the conversation about how Mary had been suffering from Calvin's abuse. Most the birthday party guests had left Betty's house just before midnight Friday, so the only people left were Calvin, Mary, Betty, and Ike, a very handsome, muscular 45-year old Guatemalan who had arrived in town earlier Friday to attend a business meeting with Calvin. Mary and Ike had danced several dances together earlier Friday night, and Mary sensed that he had more in his mind for her than just dancing. Ike began flirting excessively with her when they finished dancing, but remained very courteous and professional. Calvin and Ike had gone outside for some fresh air at 11:15 p.m., and as they stood on the front porch, Ike said, "Your ex-wife is very attractive. She has captured my total attention."

"She is extremely attractive and has an exquisite body, but I am glad we are divorced. She is a witch to get along with most the time. If you want some of her tonight, I will give a few packets of cocaine to you. Then, if she asks me for cocaine, I will tell her that you have it all."

"You would do that for me?" asked Ike as he reached

up with his right index finger and rubbed his speckled gray, right sideburn.

"I enjoy treating my business clients as well as possible, so yes, I will do that for you. Mary will agree to anything you ask of her, as long as she knows that you will give her some cocaine." Calvin brushed a fly off his forearm and continued, "I snorted a little cocaine with her a little while ago, but I know she will want to snort more tonight, sometime before she goes home. Hell! You can take her upstairs to one of the bedrooms and spend the night with her for all I care."

"That sounds exciting to me," said Ike as he swirled around his glass while listening to the ice cubes clanking together in the bottom of the glass. "I would love to undress Mary and spend some time with her. I am ready for another rum and coke, Calvin. I have finished this one."

Calvin reached into his right front pants pocket and pulled out two packets of cocaine. He handed them to Ike and said, "Mary is definitely built like a brick shithouse. I am certain you will love her firm, size 38C breasts. Let's go back inside and I will mix another drink for you. Then, I will inform Mary that you have all the cocaine. If she wants some more of the good white powder, she will have to ask you. I know she will go upstairs with you as soon as you promise to give her some cocaine. I certainly hope you will entice Mary into going upstairs with you, because Betty and I would enjoy joining both of you. Perhaps, we can all have a little fun together."

"Okay. If Mary asks me for some cocaine, I will tell her that if she wants some, she will have to spend some time in bed with me." Ike opened the front door and said, "Shall we go inside, so I can get another drink?"

"Sure, Ike. Let's go inside and I'll mix one for you." Calvin followed Ike into the house and mixed a rum and coke. After Calvin handed the drink to Ike, he approached Mary and informed her he had given all the cocaine to Ike. Within ten minutes, Mary began flirting with Ike, and soon asked him for some of the white powder. Ike and Mary went upstairs a few minutes later, so Calvin approached Betty and said, "Let's go upstairs in about five minutes. We will snort some cocaine with Ike and Mary."

Duke awoke at 6:00 a.m. Saturday, and dressed quietly so he would not disturb Alice. He went downstairs and eventually found the coffee filters and a can of Folgers coffee. As soon as he readied the coffee maker, he opened the door leading to the attached, double garage and checked to see if Mary had parked her car inside. It was not there, so he went outside to see if Mary had parked her car in the driveway. When he did not see her car, he thought, *I wonder if Mary is okay. I can't believe she didn't come home last night. She knew we would be here*. Duke lit a cigarette and sat down on the front stoop while waiting for the coffee to finish brewing. He went inside ten minutes later, poured a cup of coffee, and returned to the front stoop. Alice opened the front door fifteen minutes later, and stepped onto the front stoop. "Good morning, sweetheart," she said while buttoning the top button on her pink cotton robe. "Do you know if Mary came home?"

"Good morning, Alice. Mary's car isn't here. I hope nothing has happened to her."

"Goodness gracious. She knew we would arrive last night. I'm surprised she wasn't here to greet us. I guess she will eventually come home."

Duke felt very irritated about Mary being so disrespectful, "This is not like her at all. It really upsets me that she wasn't here to greet us last night. Hell! She could have at least phoned Jason and told him that she wouldn't be coming home. He probably worried about her all night."

"Jason told me that Mary has been doing some strange things since she began using cocaine." Alice placed her hand on Duke's right shoulder and said, "Well, my dear. I'll get dressed, and after I drink a cup of coffee, I'll start making breakfast. What would you like to eat?"

"I could go for some good ol' homemade pancakes, and some bacon."

"Okay. I'll see if Mary has enough ingredients in the kitchen for pancakes. I don't know if she does or not."

Duke stood up and said, "Eggs will be okay if there isn't anything to make pancakes. I'm going inside to get another cup of coffee." Duke held open the door for Alice and followed her inside. Alice went directly upstairs as Duke went into the kitchen. As soon as he poured a cup of coffee, he returned to the front stoop. He stood there for a minute, and then walked onto the driveway and began pacing slowly back and forth, along a route from one end of the driveway to the other end. After pacing for 5 minutes, he sat down on the front stoop and lit a cigarette. He checked the time and saw his wristwatch displaying 7:00 a.m. Jason opened the front door and joined Duke on the front stoop. "Good morning, Grandpa. Did you sleep okay last night?"

"Good morning, Jason. Yeah. I slept like a baby until 6:00 a.m."

"I wonder why Mom didn't come home last night," Jason said as he used his right hand to rub his belly lightly with circular motions. "She knew darn well you and Grandma would be here."

Duke saw Jason rubbing his belly, so he asked, "Is your stomach bothering you, Jason?"

"It does when I worry about Mom. I sometimes feel pain, right in the middle of my belly area, especially when I'm hungry."

"I hope you don't have an ulcer. You can get one from

constantly worrying." Duke snuffed out his cigarette, and then continued, "I developed a stomach ulcer several years ago, not too long after Mary's birth. The doctor put me on a strict diet. Heck! I couldn't even drink a beer, or smoke a cigarette. After I followed that crummy diet for a month, I decided to give it up." Duke took a sip of coffee before continuing, "I began a normal diet again, and yes, I went back to my daily ration of beer and cigarettes. I simply made up my mind to quit worrying about everything. That wasn't easy, but every time I caught myself worrying, I just said to hell with it, and put it out of my mind. The ulcer healed within a few months, and I've felt great ever since." Duke stood up and said, "We should go inside and see if your grandma has breakfast ready. Maybe, you just need a little food in your stomach."

Jason stood up, opened the front door, and held it open for Duke. As they entered the dining room, Duke said, "Just smell that aroma, Jason. Your grandma must be cooking pancakes and bacon."

Duke and Jason sat down at the kitchen table as Alice set a large platter of pancakes upon the tabletop. A minute later, she set a large platter of fried bacon next to the pancakes. She sat down across the table from Duke and said, "I hope you both enjoy the pancakes."

"I know I will," replied Duke as he put two pancakes on his plate. He grabbed the syrup bottle, poured syrup onto his pancakes, and handed the bottle to Jason.

"I will for sure, Grandma," said Jason as he stabbed his fork into two pancakes and put them on his plate. This is a treat for me. I usually eat cold cereal for breakfast. Mom never takes time to cook a big breakfast, except sometimes on weekends."

"No kidding?" remarked Alice. "I suppose she is always rushing around getting ready for her work day."

Just then, they heard the front door open, and saw

Mary enter the dining room. Mary acted as if she were in pain as she walked slowly through the dining room and entered the kitchen. Alice and Duke arose from their chairs as Mary said, "Good morning, Mom and Dad. I'm sorry I wasn't here when you arrived, but the party didn't get over until 2:00 a.m., so I decided to sleep at Betty's house."

Alice and Mary briefly hugged each other, and when they separated, Alice backed away two steps, put her hands on her hips, and looked closely at Mary. "My goodness, Mary! Have you lost weight? You look so thin, compared to the last time I saw you."

As Duke hugged Mary, she looked at Alice and replied, "I have probably lost a little weight, Mother, but not very much." When Duke let go of Mary, she walked over to the coffee maker and poured a cup of coffee. She sat down next to Jason, looked into his blue eyes, and asked, "How are you this morning, Jason?"

Jason finished chewing and swallowing a piece of bacon. "I worried all night about you, wondering if you were okay."

Mary acted very skittish and nervous as she replied, "You should not worry so much about me."

Duke finished the last bite of his pancakes, slid back his chair, and headed for the coffee maker. After he poured a cup of coffee, he said, "I'm going outside for a while."

Alice observed Mary lifting her cup for a sip of coffee, but Mary's hand shook so badly that she spilled some of the coffee. She quickly set the cup on the table, and slid back her chair. "I need to take a bath and change into clean clothes," said Mary as she arose from the chair. "I will see you in a little while."

A few minutes after Mary left the kitchen, Alice said, "My goodness, Jason. Is your mother always so nervous? Did you see how much her hand trembled when she tried to take a sip of coffee?"

"Yes," replied Jason. "She goes in streaks. Sometimes, she is very nervous, but at other times, she acts very depressed. I think that is because of the drugs. She's been acting more depressed since she lost her job." Jason took another pancake from the platter and put it on his plate. "These pancakes are very tasty, Grandma. Thanks for making such a good breakfast."

"You're welcome, Jason. When we get back to Iowa, you can eat a home-cooked breakfast with your grandpa and me every morning."

"I'll like that a lot," said Jason as he poured some syrup onto his pancake.

Alice stood up and said, "Could you clear off the table when you finish eating? I want to talk with your mother for a while."

"Go ahead, Grandma. I'll take care of the cleanup. When I finish, I'll go outside and talk with Grandpa."

Alice walked into the dining room and entered the hallway leading to Mary's bedroom. When she reached the bedroom door, she saw it closed, so she tried the doorknob. She discovered it unlocked, so she quietly opened the door and entered Mary's bedroom where she heard the sound of running water coming from inside the bedroom bathroom. The opened bathroom door allowed Alice to see Mary sitting in the bathtub. "May I come in and talk with you, Mary?" she asked while standing beside the open doorway.

"I guess so, since you are standing there. You could have at least knocked before entering my bedroom."

"Well, excuse me!" Alice said as she walked into the bathroom. She closed the toilet lid, sat down on it, and looked closely at Mary's back. She felt half-sick when she saw that Mary had several bruises and red marks on her back. "How did you get all those bruises on your back?"

she asked with a concerned sound of voice.

Mary laughed and said, "Oh, Mom. You know how men are always so rough."

With a stern, loud voice, Alice said, "That isn't true, Mary! All men aren't rough. Did you receive all those bruises from Calvin?"

Mary did not reply as she rinsed soap from her breasts and legs. A few minutes later, Alice again asked, "Did you get all those bruises from Calvin?"

Mary giggled a little as she stood up in the bathtub. She slowly turned to face Alice, and said, "Calvin gave me most of these bruises. Look at all these bruises on the front of my body."

Alice could not believe the number of bruises and red marks on Mary's breasts and inner thighs. "What do you mean most of them? Did someone else hit you, too?" Alice almost barfed, but choked back her partially digested food as she managed to say, "How long has Calvin been abusing you?"

"Calvin has been abusing me for quite a while, but I do not care. Actually, I rather enjoy it, especially after I snort a little cocaine. I know it is crazy to think that way, and I realize the drugs have a weird effect on me. I need to enter the rehabilitation program, so I can stop taking drugs. Perhaps then, I will think differently."

Alice quickly rose to the standing positing, removed a bath towel from the towel bar, and handed it to Mary. "Cover up your body. I feel half-sick from looking at all those bruises. It's completely ridiculous how you continue to allow Calvin to abuse you. There is definitely something wrong with your thinking."

Mary quickly grabbed the towel and wrapped it around her body. She thought, *Mom would more than likely have a stroke or heart attack if I told her that Calvin had handcuffed me to the bed earlier this morning, and let Ike have his way with me while Calvin and Betty took turns slapping, and pinching me. At least Ike did not hit me. He was an excellent lover. I will go to bed with him anytime, and enjoy every minute of it.*

Alice stormed out of the bedroom bathroom, through the bedroom, and into the hallway. She went directly outside and saw that Duke had opened the hood on the LeSabre. Duke and Jason stood side by side, peering into the engine compartment, while Duke slowly explained the many different engine components to Jason. *My goodness,* thought Alice. *Duke and Jason are sure bonding well.* Alice approached them and said, "It looks as if you two are enjoying yourselves, looking at all those mechanical things."

Jason turned and looked at Alice, "Grandpa is explaining the purpose of each engine component. Dad never explained anything to me, so I am really interested in learning all about cars."

"Your grandpa knows a lot about cars. It's too bad your father never took an interest in helping you learn. Do you have your driver's license yet?"

"No. I don't even have a learner's permit. I asked Dad and Mom to teach me how to drive, but they never took the time."

"We'll fix that when we get back to Iowa," Duke offered. "I'll teach you how to drive. How does that sound to you?"

"That will be so exciting for me, Grandpa."

Mary opened the front door and stepped onto the front stoop. "Would you all like to take a ride to the Fisherman's Wharf in San Francisco? We could look around for a while before eating lunch there."

Jason quickly replied, "That's a good idea, Mom." He looked at Duke and asked, "Do you want to go, Grandpa?"

"Yeah. That sounds okay to me."

"It sounds good to me," replied Alice.

"Great!" Mary said, "Let's all get into my car, and we will ride up there. The drive takes about forty-five minutes."

"I need to use the bathroom before we leave," said Duke as he turned and gently closed the car hood. As he walked toward the front door, he noticed Mary had elected to wear a long-sleeved, white satin blouse and a pair of navy-blue slacks. *I wonder why Mary is wearing a long-sleeved blouse*, he thought. *It's already hot as hell outside, and the temperature will climb higher during the day.*

"I'd better go to the bathroom, too," said Alice.

Ten minutes elapsed before Mary slid in behind the steering wheel of her car as Alice slid onto the front passenger seat. Duke and Jason occupied the backseat. During the drive along Highway 101, Duke and Jason discussed many different kinds of car engines. Mary pointed out several points of interest along the way, but Alice remained silent during the ride en route to Fisherman's Wharf. Duke observed Alice's quietness during the trip, and thought, *I wonder if Alice and Mary had some kind of argument this morning. Alice has sure been quiet.*

Mary eventually found a vacant parking space near Fisherman's Wharf, and as she carefully parked the car, Duke said, "I didn't think we would ever find an empty parking space, Mary. I'm sure glad your mother and I live in Iowa. At least we don't have to fight the doggone traffic all the time, not like here."

"I know, Dad," replied Mary as she opened the car door and slid out from behind the steering wheel. "The only problem about living in Iowa, is that there is nothing much to look at except vast cornfields."

"I'll take the cornfields over all this traffic," replied Duke as he opened the left rear door, slid off the backseat, and stood up on the asphalt parking lot.

"Do you all want to eat right away," asked Mary as she looked at Duke, "or should we look around for a while before we eat?"

"It doesn't matter a bit to me," said Duke. "Whatever you all want to do is fine with me."

"I'm hungry," Jason said as he opened the right rear door and exited the car.

Duke opened the car door for Alice and when she exited the car, they began walking toward the buildings at Fisherman's Wharf. After walking a few blocks, they located a restaurant and went inside. When they were almost finished with lunch, Mary said, "Would you enjoy touring the *USS Pampanito*, Dad? It is moored at Pier 45, which is within walking distance of here."

Before Duke had a chance to reply, Jason said, "I want to go on the tour." Jason quickly finished his soda, and asked, "Do you want to go, Grandpa?"

Duke set his coffee cup on the tabletop and said, "If you all want to take the tour, I'll walk to Pier 45 with you, but I'm not going aboard the submarine. I'll wait on the pier while you all tour the sub."

"I would enjoy going aboard the sub," said Alice merrily as she set her empty water glass beside her plate. "I've never been aboard a submarine."

Duke offered to pay for the lunches, so Mary said, "If you insist on paying for the lunches, Dad, I will not argue with you. I will pay for our tour tickets."

"That's fine with me," replied Duke as he picked up the lunch tickets. He looked at the total price, and almost fainted. *Damn!* he thought. *It's expensive as hell out here in California.*

They left the restaurant, and walked onto Pier 45 thirty minutes later. As they approached the *USS Pampanito (SS383)*, Duke thought back to a day in the spring of 1962, the day he reported for his first day of duty aboard the *USS Banger*, a submarine almost identical to the *Pampanito*. Several flashbacks quickly passed through Duke's mind. He suddenly felt chills traveling up and down his spine, so he quickly put the thought of his time on the *USS Banger* out of his mind. Mary purchased three tour tickets, and after waiting for two hours while many other tourists finished their tours, Mary, Alice, and Jason boarded the *Pampanito*. Duke eventually saw them go below deck, so he sat on the edge of the pier and dangled his lower legs and feet over the side. Fifteen minutes later, he suddenly stood up, lit a cigarette, and began pacing back and forth along the pier. An hour elapsed before Duke saw Mary, Jason, and Alice appear on the deck of the *Pampanito*. Duke watched as they walked across the brow and onto the pier. When he approached them, Jason said, "Wow, Grandpa. That was an interesting tour. It's hard for me to understand why anyone would want to live on a submarine. It's so crowded inside. I kept bumping against things, and even hit my head on the top of a watertight hatch opening."

Alice and Mary both agreed with Jason. With a pitiful appearance on her face, Alice looked at Duke and went so far as to say, "I believe a person would have to be very patriotic, and absolutely crazy to serve in the Silent Service."

Mary acted a little irrational as she waved her hand in the air and loudly said, "Dad has always been half crazy."

Mary's words struck Duke the wrong way, and he quickly replied, "What do you mean by that remark, Mary? I always worked hard to make sure you and Tony had everything you needed, at least the necessities, while you two were growing up."

"I am only kidding, Dad," replied Mary as she giggled and smiled.

Alice whispered into Mary's ear, "Your father always

takes things so seriously." Then, Alice looked toward Duke and said loudly, "Your father is a good man."

Duke smiled and decided to change the subject, so he offered, "I'm glad you all enjoyed the tour. What are we going to do, now?"

Mary glanced at her wristwatch and said, "We could visit the Presidio of San Francisco. It is not far from here and it is open 24 hours a day. It is already 4:00 p.m., but we will have plenty of time to look around there before we leave for home."

"What's the Presidio?" asked Duke.

Mary rolled her eyes as she smiled at Duke and said, "It is currently a huge national park, but it was a huge military base, one of the oldest in the USA. It dates back to the Civil War days. We will be able to view the beautiful Golden Gate Bridge, as well as the Bay Bridge from the park."

"I love Mother Nature, as well as architecture," Alice said, "so the park sounds good to me. I would certainly enjoy looking at those bridges."

"Okay, then," Mary said as she began walking. "Let's walk back to the car and we'll ride over to the park."

After a short drive, they arrived in the park. They spent an hour viewing the bridges, and spent two hours walking through the park while viewing the scenery. At 7:30 p.m., Mary said, "Let's leave for home. There is a very fancy steak house in Redwood City. It is one of my favorite restaurants. I want to take you there for supper, and do not fret about it Dad, because I will pay for our suppers."

"I'm not going to fret over anything," replied Duke gruffly. "Why would you think that, anyway?"

"I saw the look on your face when you paid for our lunches."

No one spoke much during the ride from the Presidio of San Francisco to the steak house in Redwood City. Duke remained a little bit upset over what Mary had said about him fretting, and Alice still felt upset about Mary allowing Calvin to abuse her. Jason slept during the entire trip, but woke very quickly when Mary parked in the steakhouse parking lot. Duke snickered and said, "You must have smelled the smoke from the barbeque grills, huh, Jason? You sure came to life in a hurry."

"Yeah, Grandpa. I smelled the smoke as soon as Mom parked the car. Are you going to eat a big steak, Grandpa?"

"Darn straight, Jason. Since you mother is buying supper, I am going to order the most expensive steak listed on the menu."

Two hours later, Mary parked the car inside her double garage. Alice and Mary went directly into the house. Jason said, "Are you going to stay outside for a little while, Grandpa?"

"Yeah. I want to sit on the front stoop for a while. It is such a beautiful night. Would you go inside and get me a cold beer?"

"Sure, Grandpa. I'll be right back with your beer. Do you care if I sit on the stoop with you?"

"I will enjoy your company, Jason."

Jason and Duke sat on the front stoop, neither saying much, until 11:30 p.m. when Duke said, "My ol' body is stiff and sore, so I'd better take a shower before I go to bed. How about you, Jason?"

"Yeah, I'm tired, too," Jason said as he stood up and opened the front door. He held open the door for Duke, and then followed Duke into the house and up the spiral staircase. When Jason opened the door to his bedroom, he said, "I'll see you in the morning, Grandpa."

"Okay. Sleep tight."

Just as Duke finished his shower and began drying off, Alice entered the upstairs bathroom. "I already took my shower," she said. "I just need to brush my teeth. I like this bathroom. It's nice to have two sinks. We can both get ready for bed at the same time."

"Yeah. It's very nice. I don't have to wait for you to finish brushing your teeth every night, so that I can brush mine."

"Oh, Duke. You never have to wait very long."

As soon as Duke and Alice crawled into bed, they pulled the top sheet up to their chins. Alice immediately began telling Duke about all the bruises and red marks she had seen on Mary's body. Duke became very upset, so upset that he swung his right arm up into the air and hollered, "Why, that son of a bitch! I never did like Calvin very much, but after what you have just told me, I hate the arrogant bastard."

"Shush!" Alice whispered as she grabbed Duke's right forearm and pulled it down to her side. "Please quiet down a little. I don't want Jason to hear us talking about his parents."

Duke spoke softly while saying, "I'll give Calvin something to think about the next time I see him. That arrogant bastard deserves a good lesson."

"Oh, Duke. Please don't do anything crazy."

"You never know, Alice. My craziness might just appear the next time I see Calvin. If you are with me, you might find out how crazy I can really become."

Alice and Duke talked about Mary's situation for an additional fifteen minutes before saying good night to each other. Actually, Alice had talked the most while trying to calm Duke.

Duke awoke at 5:00 a.m. Sunday, but before he could ready the coffee maker, Jason appeared in the kitchen. Duke looked at Jason and saw that his blue eyes were squinty and very sleepy appearing. "Well, good morning, Jason. You're sure awake bright and early this morning."

"I know, Grandpa. I had planned to be awake and out of bed before you, but I didn't make it in time. I wanted to have the coffee ready and waiting for you this morning."

"That is thoughtful of you, Jason."

Duke poured a pot of water into the coffee maker, closed the lid, and said, "Are the clothes you have on the ones your mom bought for you with the money we sent you for Christmas? I like the looks of those jeans and that denim shirt."

"Yeah, these are the ones. Thanks a lot for sending me the money. These are my favorite clothes."

"I'm glad you like them, Jason. Now that the coffee maker is percolating, I'm going outside to have a smoke."

"I'm going to eat a bowl of cereal. When the coffee is ready, I'll bring a cup of it to you."

"That will be mighty nice of you, Jason. I'll be on the front stoop, or maybe on the driveway."

Jason poured Cheerios into a large bowl and set the bowl upon the kitchen table. Just as he opened the refrigerator door and reached for the gallon milk jug, Alice walked into the kitchen. "My goodness, Jason. You're up early this morning. It's only 5:30 a.m."

"I thought I could wake up earlier than Grandpa, but he was already in the kitchen when I came downstairs. He went outside a little while ago to have a smoke."

"It's very hard to wake up earlier than your grandpa. He is usually awake early every morning. He occasionally has trouble sleeping, but he still gets out of bed early."

Jason sat down to eat his cereal. Alice sat down across the table from him and said, "I could have fried some eggs and bacon for your breakfast."

"That's okay, Grandma. This cereal will fill me up."

Mary did not come out of her bedroom until 9:00 a.m. Sunday. She heard Alice and Jason talking in the living room, so she closed the front of her white terrycloth robe, tied the cloth belt, and sauntered wearily into the living room where she sat down next to Alice on the burgundy-colored leather sofa. Alice looked closely at Mary and said, "Do you feel okay, Mary? You slept so late. You appear to be dragging, as if you don't have any energy."

Mary glanced at Jason as she replied, "I sometimes feel slightly depressed, Mother, and this is one of those times."

"Sometimes, Mom?" said Jason. "You're depressed more than you're normal, and you have been for the last several months. You should stay away from Dad. It seems like you're always happy when you're with him, but within a few hours after he leaves, you become very nervous, or else depressed."

"I know, Jason. I am sorry. I promise to stay away from him after I finish the rehab program."

The front door opened and Duke walked through the dining room and into the living room. He sat down in the brown leather recliner as Alice asked, "Do you and Jason ever attend church, Mary?"

"No. We have not been to church for at least five years. We used to attend church, until Calvin and I began having marriage problems."

"Really?" remarked Alice as she stood up. She smoothed down her floral-print, cotton dress and said, "We should all go to church this morning. Is there a Methodist Church near here?"

Jason rose to his feet and said, "There's a Methodist Church located five blocks from here. They have an 11:00 a.m. service, so I'll go change my clothes right now. We can walk to church."

With a scowl on his face, Duke arose from the recliner and said, "I guess if we're going to church, I'd better change into something more appropriate."

After a huge yawn, Mary said, "I am surprised you do

not wear your jeans to church, Dad."

"Be nice, Mary," replied Duke.

"You can all go to church without me," Mary said as she brushed a few strands of blonde hair to the side of her forehead. "I am not in the mood."

On her way out of the living room, Alice offered, "A little religion would probably do you tons of good, Mary. The Good Lord will help you in many ways, if you allow him the opportunity. Are you sure you don't want to attend church with us?"

"No thank you, Mother," said Mary with an agitated tone of voice. "I do not want to go, period."

Duke, Alice, and Jason entered the church at 10:55 a.m., and after listening to a very lengthy, but enlightening sermon, they began walking back to Mary's house. At one point during the walk, Duke took Alice's right hand with his left hand and stated, "That doggone preacher was really long winded. I didn't think he would ever finish his sermon."

Alice squeezed Duke's left hand and said, "That lengthy sermon probably did you a world of good, Duke."

Duke mumbled a reply, but neither Alice nor Jason could understand it. When they approached the house, Alice and Jason entered through the front doorway opening. "I'll come inside before too long," said Duke. "I'm going to stay out here and smoke a cigarette."

"I'll see if I can come up with something for dinner," Alice said just before she closed the front door. Jason went directly upstairs to change clothes while Alice looked for Mary. She found Mary, still dressed in a robe, lying on her bed. Alice sat down on the edge of the bed and asked, "Aren't you going to put on some makeup and get dressed today?"

"I have a migraine headache, Mother. I am staying right here until I get over it."

"You should have come to church with us. The minister preached an uplifting and interesting sermon. It might have made you feel better about yourself."

"Will you please leave me alone, Mother?" snapped Mary as she covered her ears with her hands. "I do not feel like talking, or listening."

Alice became very upset, but did not reply. She walked briskly out of the bedroom and went upstairs to change out of her church clothes. After she changed her dress, she went back downstairs and explored the kitchen, looking for something to cook for dinner. Jason entered the kitchen as Alice opened the freezer door. "Are you finding everything you need, Grandma?"

Alice checked to see what she could find inside the freezer, and said, "My goodness, Jason. Does your mother ever buy regular food? Everything inside this freezer is pre-made crap."

"That's all Mom ever buys. It doesn't take very long to cook any of that pre-made stuff in the microwave."

"I'll ask your grandpa to take us to the grocery store later this afternoon. We need to buy some decent food, so I can do lots of good old-fashioned cooking this week. I have no choice right now, except to heat up some of these TV dinners. Mercy sakes! I know your grandpa isn't going to like the taste of this pre-made crap. He'll probably have a fit when he sees me set the TV dinners on the table."

Chapter 5

Mary appeared in a much better mood as she entered the kitchen at 9:00 a.m. Monday. “Good morning, Mom and Dad,” she said cheerfully. “Did you sleep well last night?”

Duke and Alice each replied, “Good morning, Mary. Yes, I slept very well.”

Alice took a sip of coffee, and after swallowing, said, “My goodness, Mary. You act very happy this morning. Your migraine must have disappeared.”

“Yes, Mother,” replied Mary while removing a clean coffee cup from inside a cabinet. She set the cup beside the coffee maker upon the granite countertop and poured a cup of coffee. “I took two pain pills late last night,” she said while walking toward the table. Mary sat down and said, “The pills certainly made me feel better. Actually, they made me feel like a new person within five minutes after I swallowed them.”

“Did you bother to eat anything before you swallowed those pain pills?” asked Duke while glaring at Mary. “I’ve heard the medical professionals say that you are supposed to eat something before you take pain pills; otherwise, they will damage your stomach and make you feel as high as a kite.”

With a scowl on her face, Mary glanced at Duke and

replied, "Don't worry about it, Dad. I always follow the directions on the pill bottle. Did Jason leave for school on time this morning?"

"Yes," Alice quickly replied. "I made him two scrambled eggs and some toast for breakfast. Your father walked with him to school, so he arrived on time. Do you ever make breakfast for him, or does he make his own?"

"Mother! Jason is sixteen years old. He is certainly old enough to make his own breakfast. I should not have to make it for him."

Duke sneered and asked, "Do you spend much time with Jason, or does he spend most the time alone when he's home? He told me that he spends most of the time in his bedroom."

"Well! For your information, Dad, Jason spends most the time in his room using his laptop computer to search the internet. I do not see much of him when he is home."

Duke did not like Mary's snippy attitude, so he slid back his chair, stood up, and said, "Excuse me for asking, Mary." He looked at Alice and said, "I'll be outside if you need me for anything."

As soon as Duke went outside and closed the front door, Mary said, "Dad is in his usual mood this morning. He definitely has a dry sense of humor."

"Your father is concerned about Jason and you; and besides, you know how he always takes everything so seriously."

"Whatever," Mary replied sarcastically as she stood up. "Would you enjoy looking at five acres of roses today? I thought we could ride up to San Jose and look through the rose gardens. Dad should enjoy it, since he dabbles around with the roses in your yard."

"That sounds like something we would enjoy."

"Okay," Mary replied as she headed for the bedroom. "I will put on a little makeup and get dressed. Then, we will leave for San Jose. Do you want to inform Dad of our plans?"

"I'll tell him," said Alice as she rose to the standing position.

At 10:30 a.m., Duke, Alice, and Mary entered the San Jose Heritage Rose Garden. They felt amazed as they viewed all the roses while strolling slowly through the rose garden. Alice read about the rose garden in a pamphlet she picked up at the rose garden shop, and learned that the rose garden contained about 4,000 plants made up of 3,000 varieties. Seven-hundred and fifty volunteers had initially planted the garden in 1995. When Duke, Alice, and Mary returned to the car two hours later, Mary suggested eating lunch at her favorite restaurant in San Jose, a restaurant specializing in barbecued meats. At one point during lunch, Mary said, "We have an appointment with my lawyer friend, Larry, in his office at 4:00 p.m. Wednesday, so as soon as Jason gets home from school Wednesday, we will leave for Larry's office. He received the guardianship papers from Iowa, so we all have to sign them. Jason and I have already signed the California guardianship papers, but you will also need to sign those."

Duke finished swallowing a mouthful of barbecue pork, and then quickly gulped some ice water. "Wow!" Duke said while trying not to choke. "I put way to much hot sauce on that pork. Damn! It's really super-hot sauce." After another huge gulp of ice water, Duke cleared his throat, and asked Mary, "Is Larry your gay lawyer friend?"

"Yes, Dad, and please try to be nice during our appointment with him. In other words, do not say anything about his feminine actions, or his diamond earring."

"He actually wears an earring?" asked Duke as he reached up and tugged lightly on his right earlobe.

"Now, Duke." Alice said. "I've seen a lot of men wearing

earrings."

"I have too," replied Duke, "but I can't believe a lawyer would wear one while he's meeting with clients."

Mary finished drinking the last of her soda, and set the empty glass on the tabletop. "You need to catch up with the modern times, Dad."

"I know, Mary, but it's difficult for me to understand the modern way of thinking. I guess I'm just not liberal enough."

"We have to appear in front of a judge Friday afternoon," Mary said. "The judge is Larry's significant other, but he is much different than Larry. The judge appears as if he is pure man, very macho, and extremely muscular. I saw him and Larry together at Pebble Beach one time, so I talked with them for a little while. They are definitely opposites."

Alice straightened her blouse collar and said, "They always say that opposites are good for each other in relationships."

Duke slid back his chair and stood up. "Are you ready to head for home? All this talk about gay people is making me ill."

Mary stood up, picked up the cashier tickets, and said, "Perhaps, the reason you feel ill is because of all the hot sauce you ate with the pork. That would definitely make me ill."

"I'll take some Tums when I get back to your house," Duke mumbled as he used his right hand to massage his belly area.

The remainder of Monday, all of Tuesday, and the first part of Wednesday passed by, and then at 2:45 p.m. Wednesday, Duke began walking from Mary's house to the school building, so he would be there when Jason exited the school building. Jason felt very happy when he saw Duke waiting for him. They walked six blocks to Mary's house, and when they entered her driveway, they saw Mary and Alice standing beside Mary's car. As Duke and Jason approached, Mary said, "Hi, Jason. Are you ready to leave for Larry's office?"

"I'm ready to go," replied Jason.

"I need to use the bathroom before we leave," said Duke as he headed for the front door. "I'll be back in a minute."

Twenty minutes later, they arrived at Larry's office and checked in with the receptionist. She lifted the telephone receiver and informed Larry his clients had arrived. A few minutes later, Larry opened his office door and invited them into his office. "Hello, sweetie," he said to Mary as he patted her on the shoulder. Larry turned toward Alice, offered his hand for a handshake, and said, "And you must be Mary's mother, Alice. Oh, dear. You appear so young and beautiful."

Alice blushed as she shook Larry's hand and replied, "Yes. I'm Alice. It's so nice to meet you, Larry."

"Oh, Alice," Larry said as he let go of her hand and backed away from her a few steps. He placed the tip of his right index finger against the tip of his chin, and with incredible concentration, looked up and down as he closely inspected the front of Alice's dress. "I love the awesome colors in your floral-print dress. Did you purchase your dress in a store near here?"

Alice continued blushing while replying, "No. I bought the dress at the Walmart store in Waterfield, our hometown.

"Well, it is certainly a gorgeous dress." Larry turned toward Duke and offered his hand for a handshake. With a very feminine voice, Larry said, "My, my! This handsome young man must be Duke."

"It's nice to meet you, Larry," said Duke dryly as he hesitated briefly before shaking Larry's hand.

"Wow, Duke!" Larry said as he smiled and let go of Duke's hand. "You have a very firm grip." Larry eyed Duke's biceps and said, "You have awesome biceps, Duke. You evidently work out with weights a lot."

Larry quickly turned toward Jason, looked up at him, placed his right palm lightly against Jason's left cheek, and asked, "How are you, sweetie?"

Jason's face immediately turned crimson red as he replied, "I'm fine."

"Okay, everybody," Larry said as he clasped his hands together. "Let's all sit down and get comfortable. I will quickly explain all the legal gibberish about guardianship, and when I finish, you may sign all these documents. That will take care of everything until the hearing with Judge Socko at 2:00 p.m. Friday."

"Do we have to go to the county courthouse for the hearing?" asked Mary as she stared into Larry's eyes.

"The hearings are normally held at the courthouse," replied Larry as he nervously shifted positions in his plush, black leather upholstered, swivel desk chair, "but I have made special arrangements with Judge Socko. He is a very dear friend of mine. When I first asked him to hold the hearing in my office, Judge Socko told me that my request was very unusual. I promised him something he will enjoy, so he finally agreed to hear the case here. His court recorder will accompany him. She will use her stenotype machine to record the entire hearing. Everything will be perfectly legal, so do not worry your sweet little hearts over it."

Duke glared at the large diamond earring dangling from Larry's pierced left earlobe while thinking, *I wonder what Larry had to do, or is going to do for Judge Socko. It's probably better that I don't know. I'd love to grab that doggone earring and rip it out of Larry's ear."*

Larry explained the guardianship documents, after

which each person took turns signing the documents. Duke signed the documents after everybody else had finished. Larry actually grasped Duke's hand lightly and tried to guide it toward the last line that needed Duke's signature, but Duke jerked away his hand, and scowled at Larry while saying, "I don't need your help, Larry. I can see the doggone X on the line that needs my signature."

"I am only trying to be helpful, Duke," replied Larry while stepping away from Duke.

Ten minutes later, as Duke, Alice, Mary, and Jason exited Larry's office, Larry said, "Don't forget. The hearing is at 2:00 p.m. Friday, here in my office."

Mary glanced at Larry and replied, "We will see you then, Larry. Have a nice evening."

"You, too, sweetheart. Bye bye, all."

After the short drive home, Mary parked the car in her driveway. Alice opened the right front car door and said, "I think we should fry some chicken and sliced potatoes for supper tonight. How does that sound to everybody?"

"Do you actually want to go through all that work, Mother?" asked Mary as she opened the car door. "We should eat supper at a restaurant. It will be much easier and more relaxing."

"I thought you would enjoy helping me prepare supper," Alice replied as she maneuvered off the front seat and stepped onto the driveway.

"I would rather go to a restaurant and pay for all our meals," offered Mary as she slid out from behind the steering wheel and stood upon the driveway. She looked across the car roof at Alice and said, "I have other things I need to accomplish tonight. Besides that, I feel as if I am getting a migraine headache."

From his sitting position in the backseat, Duke looked at Jason and grinned from ear to ear while whispering, "We may as well sit here while the women make a decision about supper."

Jason smiled at Duke while showing him a thumbs-up gesture. Alice suddenly poked her head through the right rear side-window opening, looked at Duke and Jason, and asked, "What do you guys want to do about supper?"

Duke opened the left rear door, stepped onto the driveway, and said, "I'm going to sit on the front stoop and smoke a cigarette while you two women decide. Anything you decide is okay with me."

Jason quickly slid across the backseat, exited the car, and stood beside Duke. He looked at Alice and said, "I'll sit with Grandpa until you guys decide."

Alice and Mary bickered back and forth for an additional five minutes. Then, with a crimson red face, Alice raised her hands above her head, waved them around in the air, and said loudly, "Okay, Mary! You win! Let's eat supper at a restaurant."

Two hours later, at 7:00 p.m., Alice and Mary sat down on the plush cushions of the leather sofa in the living room. Jason removed a can of beer from the refrigerator, brought it outside, and handed it to Duke. Jason sat down beside Duke on the front stoop and said, "That hamburger I ate for supper tasted delicious, Grandpa. How was your chicken sandwich?"

Duke popped open the beer can lid tab and said, "The sandwich tasted very good, Jason. The hash browns were extra delicious." Duke took a large swallow of cold beer, and said, "This beer really hits the spot."

Duke eventually asked Jason about his school time. Jason told Duke about the bullies, and how his parents had refused to talk with the teachers about Jason's problems in school. Jason also told Duke about how some of the kids in school teased him about being fat and ugly. Duke patted Jason on the right shoulder. "Stand up, Jason. I want to take a good look at you."

Jason stood up and faced Duke. After about thirty seconds, Duke said, "Turn sideways."

Jason turned sideways and stood still. Duke stood up, walked over to Jason, and put the palm of his left hand against Jason's belly. With a circular motion, Duke moved his hand around on Jason's belly area. He felt no muscle, only mushy fat, so he removed his hand and took a large swallow of beer. Then, with his right hand, Duke reached up and squeezed Jason's flabby left biceps muscle a couple times. He released Jason's biceps and grabbed Jason's right hand. "Grip my hand as hard as you can," said Duke. Jason gripped Duke's hand, but Duke could not feel much pressure, so he pulled his hand away from Jason and reached into the pocket of his T-shirt for a cigarette. He lit the cigarette, took a drag, and then blew a huge smoke ring into the calm evening air. Duke began walking toward the street end of the driveway, so Jason sat down on the front stoop and watched him.

Duke returned to the front stoop five minutes later and dropped his cigarette butt into an empty beer can he had substituted for an ashtray. Jason said, "You sure have big hands, Grandpa. I had trouble getting a good grip on your hand. Why are the knuckles on your hands so big and knurled?"

Duke sat down beside Jason and replied, "I suppose there are many reasons for my knuckles being so large and knurled. Old age plays a big part of it. All the hard work I have done during my life also plays a role. Another cause is probably from when I boxed in the smokers during my navy years."

"Mom never told me that you boxed. What are smokers, anyway?"

"Oh, that's just a navy term for boxing matches. Your mom never told you, because I've never told her about my boxing days."

"Gee, Grandpa. Maybe, the boxing you did years ago contributed to keeping you in such good shape all through the years." Jason leaned back against the front door and said, "You remind me of Popeye, Grandpa. Your build is very slender with no fat, and your muscles bulge out so distinctly. Do you know who Popeye was, Grandpa?"

"Of course I know. I used to watch him in the cartoons."

"What did you think of my grip? Do you think it is firm enough?"

"I hate to burst your bubble, but I could barely feel your grip. Heck! As big as you are, you should be able to break my hand with your grip. If you want to hear some more of my opinions, I will gladly tell you what I think about your body."

Jason's face turned red as he replied, "I would like to hear more of your opinions, Grandpa."

"Okay, Jason. I can see that you need to lose about thirty pounds of weight, but most of your extra weight is from all the baby fat that's still on your body. When we get back to Iowa, I will help you with that problem. I have a nice weight bench and some cast iron weights in our basement. I work out with weights about every other day during the winter months, but not as often during the summer months. I get plenty of exercise working around the yard and riding my bicycle during the summers." Duke took a huge swallow of beer, and continued, "You can work in the yard and garden with me and go bicycling with me. You can work out with the weights if you so desire. I will develop a special weight-lifting program for you, and help you get started on it."

"That sounds like a good idea, Grandpa." After a short silence, Jason asked, "How much do you weigh, Grandpa?"

"My weight varies during the year. Right now, I weigh

about one hundred forty-five pounds. During the winters, I usually weigh somewhere between one hundred and fifty to one hundred and fifty-five pounds."

"Gee, I guess I need to lose a lot of weight. We're about the same height."

Duke tipped up the beer can and swallowed some more beer. He pulled a cigarette from the pack in his pocket T-shirt, lit it, and said, "If you will follow the program I develop for you, you'll eventually lose all your baby fat and turn the rest of your flab into solid muscle. Of course, you will have to quit eating all the junk food and quit drinking so much soda. So what do you think, Jason? Do you want to work that hard?"

"I look forward to it, Grandpa. I think it will be fun working with you in the yard and garden, and working out with weights. I definitely need to shed this fat from my body. I promise you I will work hard to lose weight."

"Okay!" said Duke as he grinned. "Now that we have that settled, let's go inside and visit with your mother and grandmother for a little while."

A few minutes later, Duke removed a can of beer from the refrigerator and popped open the lid tab. Then, he and Jason walked into the living room. Alice looked at Duke and said, "Mary wants to take us to San Francisco tomorrow and show us the Painted Ladies. Duke slid his right fingers through his grayish brown hair as he sat down in the leather recliner. "What are the Painted Ladies?" Duke asked with a confused appearance on his face. "I've never heard of them."

"Oh, Duke," Alice replied with a smile. "They are beautiful Victorian houses that were constructed during the late 1800s. There are seven of them, all in a row. I've seen pictures and read about the Painted Ladies, but I would really enjoy seeing the actual houses."

"I wouldn't mind seeing some of the tourist attractions

in San Francisco," said Duke as he leaned back in the recliner. Maybe, we could find a good place to eat lunch, too. I want to walk with Jason to school in the morning, before we leave."

"Jason knows how to get to school, Dad," Mary said. "He's a big boy."

"I am aware of that, Mary, but I want to walk with him in the morning."

"Fine, Dad!" Mary replied as her face reddened. "We will wait until you get back from the schoolhouse."

Jason sat down in a chair and said, "Grandpa is going to teach me how to work out with weights. Maybe, I will lose some of my body fat."

"Well!" Mary said. "That is certainly nice of your grandpa."

Duke cleared his throat, and said, "So, Mary. Is Calvin coming over here one of these days to see us? I wouldn't mind seeing him again, just so I could tell him good-bye for the last time. We'll probably never see him again."

"I phoned him late last night," Mary said as she smiled. "I invited him to come over here Friday evening. I told him that you and Mom were visiting us. Calvin sounded reluctant, but finally said that he would arrive here at about 6:00 p.m. Friday. He invited me to a party he is throwing this coming Saturday. He planned to have it here, but when he heard that you and Mom are here, he decided to have it at his secretary's house. I hope you do not mind, but I plan to attend his party."

"I thought you were going to stay away from Dad," Jason said with an upset tone of voice.

"Not until I enter the rehabilitation program," replied Mary as she stood up. "I have a migraine, so I am going to bed. I will see you in the morning."

Alice stood up and said, "I'm going to bed, too. I'm rather tired tonight."

"I'm going to stay up for a while," said Duke.

Jason and Duke talked with each other until 10:00 p.m. Then, Jason went upstairs to his bedroom, and Duke went outside to smoke his last cigarette of the day.

Duke and Alice entered the kitchen together at 6:00 a.m. Thursday. While Alice prepared the coffee maker, Duke sat down at the kitchen table and stared out through one of the kitchen windows. "It appears as if it's going to be another beautiful day," he said while using his right hand to smooth the grayish brown hair on the right side of his head. "My hair is sure wild. Gray hair seems hard to control, much harder than my brown hair."

Alice turned toward Duke and smiled. "Tell me about it, Duke. My hair is all gray, and very wild. That's why I keep it short all the time. It's easier to manage short hair. Sometimes, I feel like shaving my head, so I could wear a wig. There are some pretty wigs on the market, but a well-made one is very expensive."

Duke laughed a little before offering, "You'd look pretty funny baldheaded, Alice. Hell! I'll probably be completely bald before much longer. I don't have much hair left on the top of my head."

Jason and Mary entered the kitchen and sat down at the kitchen table. "What do you all want for breakfast?" asked Alice. "I thought about making some omelets. Is that okay with everybody?"

"That sounds okay to me," Jason replied.

"All I want for breakfast is a bagel," said Mary.

"I'll eat an omelet," replied Duke as he continued smoothing down his hair. "Can you put some chopped onions in my omelet?"

"Yes, Duke," Alice replied as she opened a cabinet door and reached inside for a frying pan. "I bought a huge white onion when we were grocery shopping the other day. I knew you would want some while we're here."

Duke grinned as he looked at Jason and said, "You appear very spiffy in that white shirt and those navy blue dress slacks this morning, Jason. Do you plan to preach somewhere today?"

Jason grinned and chuckled a little before replying, "No, Grandpa. I'm not preaching anywhere. I always wear dress clothes to school, but only because Mom insists on it."

Alice turned from the stove and glanced at Jason. "Well, Jason. You know that when you wear nice clothes, it gives other people a nice impression of you."

"I've heard that before, Grandma. I'm not sure my nice clothes help very much, as far as impressing anybody."

"Well, Jason," Mary said loudly. "It is extremely important to dress nicely anytime you are in public view."

That statement ended the discussion about clothing. Duke stood up and said, "I'm going outside for a smoke. Please let me know when breakfast is ready."

"I'll come outside and tell you when breakfast is ready, Grandpa," replied Jason.

At 8:00 a.m. Thursday, Duke and Jason left the house for the six-block walk to the schoolhouse. As soon as Duke returned to Mary's house, she asked, "Are you ready to leave for San Francisco, Dad?"

"Is it okay if I drink a cup of coffee and smoke a cigarette before we leave?"

"I guess so, but we should leave here by 9:00 a.m. It will take us about an hour to get there, probably a little over an hour by the time we arrive near the Painted Ladies."

Duke slid onto the backseat of Mary's light-gray, 2011 Mercedes C300 sports sedan at 9:00 a.m. Mary and Alice occupied the front seat. Mary turned the ignition key and as soon as the car engine started, she quickly backed out of the driveway and turned onto the street. She pulled the gearshift lever to the drive position, and floored the accelerator. The rear wheels squealed mercifully. As Duke felt his upper body being forced against the rear of the backseat, he remarked, "Good God, Mary! You drive as if you hate your car."

"We California drivers do not drive the same as Iowa drivers, Dad," Mary said as she let up on the accelerator.

After an hour of riding, Mary found a parking spot on Steiner Street, only two blocks from the Painted Ladies. Duke, Alice, and Mary exited the car and strolled along the sidewalk until they arrived on the corner of Steiner and Grove Streets. They continued walking slowly along Steiner while inspecting all seven Painted Ladies. When they reached Hayes Street, Mary said, "Let's go across the street to Alamo Square Park. We can sit on a park bench and view the Painted Ladies for a while."

As they sat on a park bench viewing the Painted Ladies, Duke asked, "How much do you suppose one of those houses would sell for these days, Mary?"

"The house at the corner of Steiner and Grove sold last summer. I saw it advertised, and the asking price was almost four million dollars. I do not know what it actually sold for, but I imagine it was close to that amount. Can you believe that back in the 1970s those houses were selling for about seventy thousand dollars?"

"Good God!" replied Duke while waving around his right hand over his head. "I can't believe anyone in their right mind would pay four million dollars for one of those old houses. That's just plain ridiculous."

"Property is very expensive in California, Dad. My house is worth about seven hundred thousand dollars. The best part is that we paid off the loan about a year ago. My house was worth a million dollars five or six years ago, but then the housing and real estate market crashed."

"Well, at least your house is fairly new," Duke said.

"You should sell your doggone house and move to Iowa. You could retire if you had enough money to invest, although now days, the interest doesn't amount to squat on any of the federally insured investments. You have to invest in the stock market if you want to earn much return, but it's very easy to lose your butt in the market."

As Alice continued gazing across the street at the beautiful Painted Ladies, she said, "Those houses are so beautifully decorated. I just love all the ornate trim, and all the different paint colors the owners have selected."

Mary glanced at her wristwatch and said, "It is 11:30 a.m., so let's go to China Town and eat lunch. When we finish eating, we will browse through the gift shops in that area."

"Lunch sounds good to me," replied Duke as he stood up. "I'm hungry. It's been a long time since I've eaten any Chink food."

"Duke!" Alice said as she stood up. "You shouldn't call it Chink food. That's not very nice."

Duke began walking toward the car and replied, "I don't always say things politically correct, Alice. You should know me by this time."

Alice quickly caught up with Duke and with her left hand grabbed Duke's right hand. While walking hand in hand, Alice said, "I do love you, Duke."

"I know, Alice. I love you, too."

Mary walked closely behind Duke and Alice, and while observing them, thought, *Mom and Dad should purchase some different clothes for their summer wear. Mom always wears a floral-print, cotton dress, and Dad usually wears jeans and a pocket T-shirt, or else cut-off jeans and a short-sleeved denim shirt.*

After spending an hour at the Chung Lai Restaurant, fifteen minutes of which went for decisions on what to order from the large menu offerings, Mary, Duke, and Alice finished eating. When they left the restaurant, Mary and Alice browsed through several gift shops while Duke spent most of his time waiting for them while standing upon the city sidewalks located in front of the shops. He did not mind waiting outside for Mary and Alice, because he enjoyed smoking a cigarette occasionally while enjoying the California weather. They eventually returned to Mary's car and headed for Redwood City. When they arrived at Mary's house, Duke walked directly to the refrigerator and removed a can of cold beer. Mary went to her bedroom, and Alice went upstairs to freshen up a little. Duke popped open the lid tab and took a huge swallow of beer. He didn't see Jason anywhere downstairs, so he went upstairs to see if Jason was in his bedroom. Duke approached the closed bedroom door, and knocked while saying, "Are you in there, Jason?"

"Yeah, Grandpa. Come in."

Duke entered the bedroom and found Jason sitting on the bed, looking at the screen on his laptop computer. "Hi, Jason. Are you doing some homework, or studying?"

"Sit beside me, Grandpa. I'll show you what I'm looking at on my laptop screen."

Duke sat down beside Jason and peered at the laptop screen. He saw a beautiful picture of the seven Painted Ladies. "How did you find that picture of the Painted Ladies?" asked Duke.

"You can find almost every kind of information you want on the internet. I just did a search on Google and found all this information within seconds. This particular website describes the history of the Painted Ladies. Do you want to read some of it?"

"Go ahead and read it to me, Jason. I don't have my reading glasses with me."

"Okay. Well, it reads that a developer by the name of Kavanaugh built all seven of the Queen Anne Era homes.

He began building the first one in 1892 and finished the last one in 1896. It reads here that they are Victorian style homes, very beautifully decorated. Do you want to hear any more?"

"No," Duke replied as he stood up, "but that's some interesting history."

Jason closed the laptop and asked, "Don't you have a computer, Grandpa?"

"No. I used a computer when I still worked for a living. When I retired, I decided not to mess around with any more computers, so I never bought one. Sometimes, I think it would be nice to own one. I probably should buy a computer, but I don't know if I would use it very often."

"I could help you learn all about the internet and computers, Grandpa."

"Thanks, Jason. Maybe we will go shopping for a computer when we get back to Iowa. I'm going outside for a smoke. Do you want to come along?"

"I'll come outside in about ten minutes. I still need to read a few more articles."

Chapter 6

The remainder of Thursday, May 26, expired quickly, and the first part of Friday went even faster. When Jason arrived home at 1:30 p.m. Friday, after the last day of his school year, Mary, Alice, Duke, and Jason left for the guardianship hearing at Larry's office. When they arrived inside the office, Larry fluttered around as if he were an exuberant butterfly. With his unmistakable feminine voice, Larry introduced Mary, Duke, Alice, and Jason to Judge Socko. As Duke observed Judge Socko's actions as well as his muscular build, he wondered how such a one hundred percent macho man could possibly be interested in such a pencil thin, feminine acting man such as Larry. After the introductions, Judge Socko sat down in Larry's plush, black leather swivel chair, looked at the stenographer seated near the end of Larry's desk, and asked if she were ready. She nodded her head, so Judge Socko immediately brought the hearing to order.

Judge Socko began inspecting the signed guardianship documents. He asked several questions as he reviewed each one. Larry answered some of the questions, but Alice, Mary, and Duke answered most of them. After the judge gave final instructions to Duke and Alice, pertaining to what they needed to do when they arrived in Iowa to make the guardianship documents legal in Iowa, Judge Socko ended the hearing. Duke looked at his wristwatch and saw it displaying 3:30 p.m., a half hour past his normal beer time. Larry thanked the judge several times for holding the hearing. Then, Larry fluttered flamboyantly around the room while saying his good-byes to everybody as they left his law office.

When Mary steered the Mercedes sedan off the street and onto her driveway, she said, "Now remember, Dad, Calvin is supposed to arrive at 6:00 p.m., so we will not eat supper until after he leaves. I hope you will not become too irritated. I know how you prefer eating supper at precisely 5:00 p.m. Perhaps when Calvin arrives, you could invite him to sit on the front stoop with you and Jason. I am sure he would enjoy visiting with you while drinking a few beers."

"I can hardly wait to see him again," replied Duke dryly. Then, he thought, *I wouldn't care if I never saw that wife beating, arrogant son of a bitch. I hope he doesn't mock my slow talking, because I will really get mad at him.*

When they all went inside, Duke and Jason headed straight for the kitchen. Jason opened the refrigerator door and grabbed a cold can of soda. "Do you want a beer, Grandpa?"

"You bet I do, Jason. I'm really parched right now, like I've been in a desert for a while."

Jason handed a cold can of beer to Duke. "Do you want to sit on the front stoop for a while?"

"Yeah, let's do," replied Duke as he headed for the front door. He heard Alice and Mary conversing in the living room as he walked through the dining room, and thought, *They seem to be getting along pretty good.*

Duke and Jason sat on the front stoop while talking about many different subjects. At one point, Jason said,

"My dad thinks I talk too slow. He told me a while back that I inherited my slow talking from you. Do you believe that's true?"

"I don't know, Jason, but your father shouldn't be so rude. Just because a person talks slowly doesn't mean they're ignorant, although, many people judge others by how they talk. I know for a fact that when some people meet me for the first time, they think I'm as dumb as a rock, just because I talk so slow." Duke checked the time and saw his watch displaying 5:55 p.m. "Let's go inside and refresh our drinks. Your dad should be arriving soon."

Duke and Jason went into the kitchen and replenished their drinks. "It sounds as if your mom and grandma are talking almost nonstop in the living room," Duke said as he popped open the beer can lid tab. "We may as well go outside and wait for your dad to show up."

Jason popped open the soda can lid tab and said, "Okay, I'll follow you."

As Duke and Jason entered the dining room, the front door swung open. Calvin, dressed in a tailor-made, light-brown suit, a brilliant white shirt, and a pale-yellow necktie, entered the dining room. He sneered and laughed a little as he looked at Duke and Jason, and said, "Well, well. You two are like two peas in a pod." As Calvin approached Duke and extended his hand for a handshake, he lowered the tone of his voice an octave to match Duke's voice, and talked very slowly, slower than Duke talked, as he drawled, "How is the ol' slow talker from the Iowa cornfields?"

Duke quickly transferred the beer can from his right hand to his left hand, but instead of shaking hands with Calvin, Duke's right fist suddenly shot out and struck squarely on the middle of Calvin's forehead. Calvin's head snapped back as he raised his right fist to strike Duke. Suddenly, Calvin's eyes rolled back, so that only the whites were visible. He moaned and slowly collapsed until he lay on his back upon the hardwood floor. Duke poured half his beer on Calvin's face and chest. Then, he dropped the half-empty beer can onto Calvin's chest and watched as the remaining beer gurgled from the can. As Calvin moaned, Duke said, "My fist is much faster than my talking, you arrogant bastard."

Duke heard Alice holler, "What are you doing, Duke? Are you crazy or something?"

Duke kicked Calvin in the right rib cage several times as Mary screamed, "Leave him alone, Dad. Please do not hurt him worse."

Duke suddenly sat straddle of Calvin's waist and quickly punched him several times in his chest and ribs. Calvin cried out, "Please quit punching me, Duke. I'm sorry I made fun of you."

Duke raised his right fist into the air, preparing to deliver a hard blow to Calvin's face. Suddenly, Alice grabbed Duke's right arm, so he quickly stood up. He pulled his arm away from Alice's grip, stared into Calvin's glazed eyes, and hollered, "If you ever again slap or punch my daughter, I will find you and beat on you until you're half dead. You stay away from Mary. Now, drag your arrogant, sorry ass out of here and go crawl into a hole somewhere."

Calvin turned over and managed to get on his hands and knees. He crawled as fast as he could toward the front door. When he reached the door, he stood up, opened the door, and ran toward his car. Duke slammed the door and mumbled, "Good riddance." Then, Duke listened to Alice as she waved her hands in the air and scolded him. *I'll just listen to her,* Duke thought while using his left hand to massage the pain away from the top of his right hand. *I'm not going to say anything, because that would only aggravate her hot Italian temper.*

Five minutes later, when Alice finished venting her Italian temper, Mary became hysterical and began crying as she yelled, "You are mean, Dad! You should not have hurt Calvin. He did not deserve that beating. I'm going to my bedroom."

Mary stormed out of the dining room and stomped through the hallway and into her bedroom. When she slammed the bedroom door, Alice scowled at Duke and said, "Now, look at what you've done. Mary is very upset." Alice followed Mary's footsteps as she headed for Mary's bedroom.

Continuing to massage the top of his right hand, Duke turned and saw Jason standing motionless, leaning against the side of the archway located between the kitchen and dining room. Duke grinned and asked, "Do you have anything to say, Jason?"

"No, Grandpa," said Jason as he smiled. Then, Jason quickly looked at the floor. "I think Mom and Grandma scolded you more than enough."

Duke walked toward the kitchen and when he approached Jason, said, "I need to get another beer, and I'd better put some ice on my hand. It hurts like hell."

"I'll put some ice cubes in a plastic bag for you, Grandpa. Boy! You have a powerful punch. Dad sank to the floor like a lead anchor. I'll bet his head hurts a lot."

"He evidently has a hard head," replied Duke as he grinned from ear to ear and sat down at the kitchen table. "I thought that blow would knock him cold, but it just dazed him. I imagine his ribs hurt quite a lot. I could sure drink some cold beer. It might make my hand feel better."

Jason handed a can of beer to Duke before filling a plastic bag with some ice cubes. He handed a kitchen towel and the bag of ice cubes to Duke while saying, "The top of your hand is really swelling up, Grandpa."

"It'll be okay. Let's go outside for a while so I can

smoke a cigarette. Maybe, that will calm my nerves. We'll talk for a while."

Calvin arrived at Betty's house in San Carlos at 6:45 p.m. Friday. He immediately went into the kitchen and filled a small plastic bag with ice cubes. He held it gently against his forehead as he began looking for Betty. He soon found her enjoying a bath in her bedroom bathroom. When he entered the bathroom, she looked at him and asked, "What's with the ice?"

"I had a disagreement with someone. He punched me so hard that I almost blacked out. He hit me in the ribs several times, too. Actually, I feel as if a truck ran over me."

"Who punched you?"

"It does not matter who punched me," Calvin snapped back sarcastically, "so do not worry about it. I have a drug deal lined up, so I am soon leaving for San Francisco. We need some cocaine for the party tomorrow. I want you to meet me in my office at 11:00 p.m. tonight."

"What are we going to do at the office?" asked Betty as she teasingly slid a bar of soap slowly from her right breast to her left breast.

"I am going to purchase a kilo of cocaine from the dealer. Then, when I arrive in my office, we will repackage some of it to use during the party tomorrow. I could have saved myself a trip tonight, if I would not have sold all my other cocaine."

"Well, you made a lot of profit selling it," said Betty as she slowly rinsed soapsuds from breasts."

Calvin lowered the ice bag from his forehead, glanced into the mirror, and said, "I suppose this large bump on my forehead will turn black-and-blue. Well, I guess I will leave for San Francisco. Remember to meet me at the office."

"I'll be there at 11:00 p.m.," replied Betty as she stood

up and gently massaged both her breasts. "You could give me a little loving before you leave."

Calvin leaned over and planted a kiss on Betty's right breast. He straightened up and said, "It would be impossible for me to perform well tonight. My ribs hurt like hell and I have a pounding headache. You will have to settle for the kiss."

"You should take two pain pills before you leave. There are some oxycodone pills in the drawer of my nightstand."

"Okay, I will."

Duke awoke startled and found himself lying upon a sweat soaked sheet Saturday morning. He glanced at the clock located on the nightstand and saw the bright red numbers displaying 4:00 a.m. He reached over and lightly touched Alice's upper arm, but she did not stir. He lay completely still for about five minutes as he thought, *I wish I would quit having the doggone nightmares. It has been 46 years since I left the submarine. By this time, I shouldn't be having any more nightmares. Now, I'll have to change the sheets*. Duke rolled to the side of the bed and sat up. He debated whether to get up and dress for the day, or to go downstairs for a glass of ice water, and then return to bed for a while. He decided to dress before going downstairs, so he put on his jeans and pocket T-shirt, and headed for the spiral staircase. As his right foot touched the top step, he heard extremely loud knocks on the front door. Then, he heard someone hollering, "Police! Open the door."

Duke went downstairs and opened the front door. Two plainclothes police officers, one who appeared to be in his early thirties and one who appeared to be about fifty, forced their way past Duke and entered the dining room. The oldest officer held up a piece of paper and said, "We have a search warrant to search this residence. Are you the owner?"

"No," Duke replied as he gently rubbed the top of his

swollen, bruised right hand. "My daughter owns this house. Why do you want to search it?"

"Where is your daughter?"

Just then, Mary arrived in the dining room. She tied her robe belt while asking, "What is going on, anyway?"

"Do you own this house?" asked the oldest officer.

"Yes. This is my house."

The officer handed the search warrant to Mary as he asked, "Do you have any illegal drugs in this house?"

"No. There is nothing illegal in this house."

Just as Jason and Alice arrived at the top of the spiral staircase, a uniformed officer holding a leash attached to a drug sniffing German shepherd walked through the front doorway opening and entered the dining room. The oldest officer looked toward Jason and Alice, and ordered, "You two people at the top of the stairs come down here and have a seat." He looked at Mary and asked, "Are there any other people in this house?"

"No," Mary quickly replied. "There are only four of us."

"Okay," replied the oldest officer. "I want all four of you to sit down at the dining room table, and remain seated while we conduct the search." He looked at the other two officers and said, "I'll stay with these people while you guys search upstairs. When you finish searching up there, search this level. There is no basement, so you can search the garage and cars after you finish searching this level. Make sure you search that Iowa car, too."

Duke reached into his front pocket, pulled out his car keys, and said, "Here are the keys to the Iowa car." He tossed the keys to the younger plainclothes officer.

After searching upstairs for an hour, the officers and dog came downstairs and began searching rooms on the first floor. They finished searching the first floor rooms and entered the attached garage at 6:00 a.m. The front door suddenly swung open, and Larry appeared wearing a pin-striped, navy blue suit, a light-pink dress shirt, and a floral-print necktie. He fluttered flamboyantly through the front doorway opening and into the dining room. "Hello, everybody," he said very femininely. "I thought you sweet little dears might need my assistance."

The oldest officer stood up, stared at Larry, and gruffly asked, "And who are you?"

Larry walked over to Mary and placed his hands on her shoulders. "Oh, officer. My name is Larry, this little sweetheart's attorney."

The officer sat down and said, "Well, Larry. You may as well sit down. We are almost finished searching this residence. The officers are searching the garage and cars as we speak. When they finish, they will let us know what they have found."

Fifteen minutes passed before the younger plainclothes officer returned to the dining room. The oldest officer asked, "Did you find any illegal items?"

"No, sir," replied the younger officer. "The dog signaled only once during the entire search. He kept sitting next to the bed in the master bedroom, so we tore apart the entire bed, removed all the dresser drawers, and looked behind and underneath the dressers. We couldn't find any illegal drugs. The dog must have smelled some drug residue on the mattress, or else something other than drugs. We found a bottle of pain pills in one of the dresser drawers, but they are prescription drugs."

The oldest officer glared at Mary and asked, "Did you ever use any cocaine while you were in that bedroom?"

Larry quickly responded, "My client does not have to answer your question. You didn't find anything illegal, so there should be no further questioning."

The oldest officer stood up, scowled at Larry, and said, "We will leave, now. You people can go back to bed, or whatever."

As all the cops headed for the front door, the youngest plainclothes officer looked at Duke and said, "Your car keys are on the front seat of your car."

Duke followed the officers outside and watched them leave in their cars. He lit up a cigarette and thought, *It's a doggone good thing they didn't find any drugs. They would have arrested all of us.* He walked to the LeSabre and opened the left front door so he could check to see if everything was still in one piece. He noticed a few maps and his car record book lying on the front floor. Other than that, everything seemed to be okay. Duke picked up the car keys and dropped them into his left front jean pocket. He closed the car door, and then walked to the street end of the driveway where he stopped to look up and down the street. He did not see anything other than a few parked cars, so he walked toward the house. As Duke approached the front stoop, he saw Jason carefully opening the front door while holding a cup of coffee with his right hand and a can of soda with his left hand. "I brought you a cup of coffee, Grandpa."

"That's great, Jason. I need a good cup of coffee after all the crap that has happened during the last few hours." Duke lit a cigarette and asked, "Are you going to sit out here with me?"

"Yeah. I'll sit with you, Grandpa. Boy! I am sleepy. I don't think I have ever been up so early in the morning. Larry is telling Mom all about how the police arrested Dad and his secretary late last night for drug related crimes. Larry said that the cops stormed Dad's office a little before midnight. They entered the office just as Dad and his secretary finished filling a whole bunch of small plastic bags with cocaine."

"No kidding? I'd better finish smoking this cigarette and go inside so I can hear more about what happened."

Duke and Jason went into the living room and listened

while Larry told Mary all about the events during his early morning hours. Mary asked Larry, "How did you find out the cops arrested Calvin?"

"Calvin phoned me at 1:00 a.m. this morning. He informed me that the police had arrested him and taken him to the police station. He asked if I would come to the station and represent him. I informed him that I am not a trial lawyer, but until he could hire one, I would represent him. I quickly crawled out of bed, dressed, and told my sweetheart good-by. I felt overwhelmed with shock, so I drove to the police station as fast as possible. I just could not believe Calvin had participated in illegal drug activities."

Alice rose from the leather sofa and asked, "Does anyone want more coffee?"

Larry loosened his colorful, floral-print necktie, and replied, "Oh, Alice. You are such a dear. I would love some more coffee."

Mary nervously shifted her body position upon the sofa and asked, "How did Calvin appear when you saw him at the police station? Did he appear to be high, or drunk?"

"Oh, my dear Mary," Larry said, "Calvin did not act drunk or high, but he had a huge, black-and-blue bump in the middle of his forehead. I asked the arresting officer if Calvin had fought with the officers. The officer replied that Calvin had offered no resistance. Calvin would not tell me what happened to his forehead."

"How long will Calvin be in jail?" mumbled Mary as she began nibbling on the fingernail tip of her right little finger.

"I am not sure at this point, Mary," replied Larry as he reached over and grasped Mary's left hand with his right hand. "The judge might allow Calvin to post a bond, so that he can remain free while awaiting trial. I am quite certain Calvin will end up spending many years in prison. If he is found guilty of all charges, he could receive a sentence of at least twenty-five years. Officers working with a federal, state, and county drug task force have followed Calvin for the last several months. They know he purchased large quantities of drugs in San Francisco, and that he repackaged and sold those drugs."

Larry let go of Mary's hand and moved away from her a little. Then, he continued, "Several undercover cops will testify against Calvin. One of the undercover cops observed Calvin purchasing a kilo of cocaine last night. The same cop had also observed Calvin purchasing cocaine several other times. Some of the officers followed Calvin all the way from San Francisco to his office here in town. They had a search warrant to search his office and car. They found several thousand dollars of cash inside Calvin's office safe, not to mention all the drugs. They even found a few packets of drugs inside his car. The drug task force cops arrested several people early this morning, all of them tied to Calvin in one way or another."

Alice handed a fresh cup of coffee to Larry, and then approached Duke. She still felt upset with Duke for beating up Calvin, but asked, "Do you want some fresh coffee, Duke?"

With his swollen right index finger, he reached up and lightly rubbed his temple. "Yeah. I'll drink some more coffee."

Alice saw the black-and-blue, large swollen area on the top of Duke's right hand. "My goodness, Duke. Do you need to see a doctor about your hand? It looks terrible."

Duke lowered his right hand and rested it on the chair arm. "No I don't need to see a doctor. I think some of the small bones located in the top of my hand are broken, but they will heal eventually. It isn't the first time this has ever happened to me."

Larry quickly stood up, fluttered across the room, and approached Duke. "My, my, Duke," Larry said as he gently put his hand on Duke's right forearm. Larry lightly massaged Duke's forearm, but for only five seconds, because Duke jerked his right forearm away from Larry's hand. Larry stepped away from Duke and said, "Oh, my dear Duke. I cannot imagine how painful that must be. You should let me take you to the hospital emergency room, and let the health professionals inspect your hand."

Carefully holding a cup of coffee with her right hand, Alice returned to the living room and approached Duke, so Larry fluttered across the room and sat down next to Mary upon the leather sofa. As Alice handed the coffee cup to Duke, he grinned while looking at Larry and said, "My hand will heal okay, Larry. I appreciate your concern, but you shouldn't worry about me."

With a huge smile on his face, Larry replied, "Oh, Duke. You are so welcome. I just wanted you to know that I am concerned about you. I love helping people."

Alice sat down next to Larry on the leather sofa, just as Jason stood up. "I've heard enough about Dad," stated Jason with a very upset tone of voice. "I'm going to my room."

Duke took a sip of coffee, swallowed, and with a serious, almost scolding tone of voice, said, "It's a good thing you didn't have any drugs in this house, Mary. If the cops would have found any, we would all be in jail right now."

Mary scowled at Duke and replied, "I am not stupid, Dad." Then, Mary asked Larry, "Do you think I should delay my entry date into the rehabilitation program? Calvin might need my testimony, or something to help him."

"You should enter the rehabilitation program as soon as possible," Larry replied, "and forget about Calvin. Stay completely away from him, or anybody else involved with drugs. I think the world of you and want you to get your life back together. I would be extremely happy if you will allow me to take you to the rehab center. You are supposed to check in Monday, June 6, so I will plan to take you there. Will that be okay?"

Mary slowly slid the fingers of her right hand through her blonde hair as she replied, "I will appreciate it very much. Thank you, Larry."

Duke coughed a little, and with a very serious tone of voice, said, "I'll tell you one thing, Mary! If I ever find out you get involved in drugs after your rehabilitation, I'll call the cops and file a report."

Mary quickly stood up and stomped from the living room into the dining room as she replied, "Thanks a lot, Dad." Mary went directly to her bedroom and slammed the door so hard that everybody thought the ceiling plaster would fall to the floor.

Larry finished drinking his coffee, stood up, and said, "I need to go home and get some much needed sleep. I am very tired."

"I'll walk with you to your car," Duke said. "I need a smoke, anyway."

"Oh, thank you, Duke." Then, Larry extended his right hand and lifted Alice's right hand. He kissed the back of her hand before saying, "I hope to see you again before you leave for Iowa, Alice. You are such a sweetheart."

As Larry let go of Alice's hand, she blushed and replied, "We had planned to leave for Iowa early Tuesday morning, May 31, but we have changed our minds. We will leave early Wednesday morning, June 1, so we might see you again before then. If we don't see you, I want you to know that it has been nice meeting you. Take good care of yourself, Larry."

"Thank you, my sweet Alice," Larry replied while

waltzing flamboyantly across the room toward Duke. "You take good care of yourself, Alice, and take good care of Duke." Larry stood next to Duke and said, "I'll follow you outside, Duke."

Duke stood on the front stoop and watched Larry carefully back his silver, 2011 BMW convertible out of Mary's driveway. Duke glanced at his wristwatch and thought, *Shit, it's already 10:00 a.m. I haven't even eaten breakfast.* Duke entered the house and searched for Alice. He couldn't locate her on the first floor, so he went upstairs. He heard her in the bathroom, so he opened the door and asked, "Are you going to make breakfast for us?"

"There are some frozen pancakes in the freezer," Alice snapped back with an irritated tone of voice. "You can heat some of those in the microwave and eat them for breakfast? I'm going back to bed for a while. Jason went back to bed a while ago. Mary must have gone back to bed, too."

"Oh!" Duke said as he raised his left hand into the air and waved it around. "You're sure cranky this morning."

"I'm just upset. I'll feel better after I get a little more sleep."

Duke stormed out of the bathroom, through the hallway, and trotted down the steps of the spiral staircase. He went outside to smoke a cigarette, and when he finished, went back inside. He entered the kitchen, and found the frozen pancakes without a problem, but he could not find a bottle of syrup inside the refrigerator. As the pancakes heated in the microwave, he searched through several cabinets before finally finding a new bottle of maple syrup. Duke sat down at the kitchen table ten minutes later and took a bite of a pancake. Jason walked into the kitchen and asked, "Are those pancakes good, Grandpa?"

Duke finished chewing, swallowed, and said, "They

taste pretty good, but freshly cooked pancakes, or eggs would taste much better. I couldn't get your grandmother to make a doggone thing for breakfast."

Jason warmed some pancakes, poured a glass of milk, and sat down across the table from Duke. With sadness in his eyes, Jason offered, "I'm worried about Dad."

Duke looked seriously at Jason and said, "I know you are, Jason, but there isn't much you can do about his problems. Usually, when people become involved with drugs, their lives end up in ruins. Let's just pray that your mother will be cured of drug use by the time she gets out of rehab."

"I guess Dad wasn't as smart as he thought. He is stupid for getting involved with drugs. Mom is just about as bad, but if it wouldn't have been for Dad, she probably wouldn't have become addicted to drugs."

"Yeah. Well, now they will have to pay the price, especially your dad."

When Duke and Jason finished eating breakfast, Duke stood up and grinned at Jason. "I suppose we should put our dishes and silverware into the dishwasher; otherwise, we'll be on Alice's shit list."

Jason giggled a little bit before saying, "I will do the cleanup, Grandpa. Are you going outside for a smoke?"

"Yeah, but first I'll help you load the dishwasher."

As soon as the dishwasher began its wash cycle, Duke poured a cup of coffee and headed for the front door. Jason followed behind Duke, and as they walked through the front doorway opening, Jason asked, "Do you want to shoot a few basketball hoops with me, Grandpa?"

"Sure. I'll shoot some hoops with you."

Jason went into the garage and brought out his basketball. Duke looked up at the basketball hoop attached to the garage peak. "There's not much left of that doggone net, Jason."

"I know, Grandpa. Dad told me a month ago that he would replace it, but he never did. There is a new one in the garage."

"Do you have a ladder?"

"There's a ladder inside the garage."

"Well then, Jason. Get the new net and the ladder, and climb up there and replace the net. You should be able to do it with no problems."

"I wanted to replace it a while back, but Mom wouldn't let me, because she worried that I would fall off the ladder."

"She worries too doggone much. I'll hold the ladder for you."

When Jason finished replacing the net, he and Duke took turns shooting hoops, but Jason held an advantage over Duke, because Duke could only use his left hand. Duke discovered that Jason played basketball very well. Jason rarely missed sinking the ball through the basketball hoop. "You can really make those shots count, Jason. Are you on the school basketball team?"

"No. Dad said that I am too fat to play basketball, so he wouldn't let me try out for the basketball team."

"Are you on the school football team?"

"No," Jason said as he made another perfect shot. "Mom and Dad said that they didn't want me to get injured, so they wouldn't let me play football. They said that if I played ball, I wouldn't have enough time to study. They always expect me to get straight A's."

Duke sat on the front stoop and watched Jason shoot a few more hoops. Then, Jason sat down next to Duke and said, "If I could ever get in good enough shape, I would enjoy playing football."

"We'll get you in shape this summer. Maybe, you can play football next fall when school begins."

"I hope so, Grandpa." They sat silently for about five

minutes, and then Jason asked, "How come your right eye droops so much, Grandpa? Can you see out of it okay?"

Duke snickered a little and said, "I guess there are several reasons why my eye droops so much. I think the first reason is that way back when I was about ten years old, my brother Dave and I were across the street from our house throwing rocks at an ol' tomcat that had climbed way up high in the neighbor's apple tree. I remember that the black cat was a stray in the neighborhood. Dave threw a big rock and it glanced off a tree branch. The doggone rock fell and hit me just below my right eye. Blood splattered everywhere, so we ran home. Mom phoned the family doctor, a nice woman doctor, and she drove to our house and ended up installing three staples into my face." Duke pointed toward his right eye and said, "You can still see the scar if you look closely."

Jason looked closely at the small scar and said, "Wow! I'll bet that hurt."

"It didn't hurt very much when she installed the staples, but it really hurt when she removed them ten days later. I almost threw up from the pain as she cut those staples and pulled them out of my face."

"What else happened to your eye?"

"Well, one night way back in 1961, when I was stationed at the Great Lakes Naval Station, one of the sailors lipped off to me, so I punched him in the face. My punch didn't even faze that guy, so he immediately punched me back, right on my right eyebrow. Man! That ended the fight. My eye swelled up and turned black-and-blue in no time at all."

"Did you guys get in trouble for fighting?"

"No. Nobody reported us for fighting. Heck. My next fight happened while I attended submarine school in New London, Connecticut. I won that fight, but the guy reported me. I thought for sure the commanding officer would court-martial me that time. I knew the master-at-arms in our barracks, so I convinced him the fight wasn't my fault. He discussed my situation with one of his officer friends. That officer destroyed the report, so the commanding officer didn't find out about the fight."

"What would have happened if they would have court-martialed you?"

"Oh, they probably would have busted me one rank, but I didn't have much rank anyway, so it wouldn't have mattered much. Later on, while I served on the submarine, I boxed in some of the smokers, so I received several more blows to my eyes. That probably didn't do my eyes much good, but I can still see okay." Duke lit a cigarette, inhaled, and blew a smoke ring into the air. "Oh! I almost forgot to tell you about when I worked construction. I was using a grinder to bevel the end of an eight-inch diameter, fifteen feet long joint of ductile water main pipe. I was in a hurry, so I neglected to wear my safety glasses. A piece of steel flew into the iris of my right eye. I didn't even feel it until about 2:00 a.m. the next morning when I woke up with severe pain in my eye. Your grandma took me to an eye specialist later that morning. He removed a substantial piece of steel from my iris, and said that I was fortunate the steel hadn't penetrated my pupil. If it had, I would have been blind in my right eye."

Just as Duke finished talking, the front door opened. Alice leaned through the opening and said, "My goodness. You two have been out here a long time. You must be having quite the discussion. What have I missed?"

Jason looked at Alice, and with major excitement in his voice, said, "Grandpa has been telling me all the different reasons why his right eye is so droopy."

"Your grandpa must really like you, Jason. He has never told me any of the reasons. I know he once had a piece of steel removed from his right eye. Are you two hungry for a nice lunch? Mary just woke up, so I thought I would make some ham-and-cheese sandwiches."

Duke glanced at his watch and saw it displaying 3:00 p.m. "Sandwiches are fine with me. Are you hungry Jason?"

"I could eat two ham-and-cheese sandwiches," Jason replied, "along with some potato chips."

"I'll make some sandwiches," said Alice, "so come inside at 3:30 p.m. and we'll eat. I'll heat some tomato soup to go with the sandwiches."

As Alice closed the door, Duke stood up and said, "It's my beer time, Jason. Are you going to drink some soda?"

"Yeah, I will." Jason stood up and opened the front door. "After you, Grandpa."

"Well, thank you, Jason."

During Sunday breakfast, Alice insisted that Duke and Jason attend church with her. She also tried to convince Mary to attend church, but did not have any luck. Just before they entered the church, Alice said, "You should take communion this morning, Duke. While you're at it, you should ask for the Good Lord's forgiveness. He might forgive you for beating up poor Calvin."

Very dryly, Duke replied, "That arrogant bastard had it coming. I'm not a bit sorry for beating on him. I should have beat on him a lot more, but you stopped me."

The minister finished his long-winded sermon at 11:30 a.m., so Duke, Alice, and Jason returned to Mary's house. After lunch, all four of them sat down in the living room and spent much of the afternoon discussing plans for Jason's upcoming stay in Iowa. They talked about many different things, including Jason's medical insurance cards, his financial needs, Duke and Alice's rules, and anything else they could think of to eliminate potential problems during Jason's stay with Duke and Alice. They also discussed Mary's planned stay at the rehabilitation center.

During Memorial Day, May 30, Alice, Duke, and Mary spent much of the day thinking about the tragic loss of Tony during Operation Desert Storm in 1991. Jason also felt the sorrow, even though he had never met his Uncle Tony. Jason felt as if he had known Tony, because Mary had told him many stories about her and Tony's childhood days.

Since Duke, Alice, and Jason planned to leave for Iowa on June 1, the day of Mary's 44th birthday, Alice decided they should all celebrate Mary's birthday on Tuesday, May 31. Alice wanted to make a German chocolate cake for the occasion, so right after breakfast Tuesday, she searched through the kitchen cabinets for the recipe ingredients. A few ingredients were missing, so Alice sent Duke and Jason to the grocery store. Alice thought it took them a long time to purchase the items, but they eventually returned, so she began making the cake. Jason took an interest and helped Alice whip together the ingredients. When the cake finished baking, and had cooled enough, Jason helped Alice spread a thick layer of homemade chocolate frosting onto the cake. Later that evening, Alice and Jason carefully inserted 22 candles into the cake, one candle for every two years of Mary's life. They informed Duke and Mary to join them at the dining room table, and after everybody sat down, Jason lit the candlewicks. Duke, Alice, and Jason sang Happy Birthday to Mary as she sat silently with a huge smile on her face. When the singing stopped, Mary made a wish while inhaling as much air as possible. After Mary blew out all the candles, Alice reached down to her lap and picked up a beautifully wrapped, small box. She handed it to Mary and said, "That is something special, Mary. Your father and I want you to take it with you when you check into the rehabilitation center. It might help you cope a little easier with everything while you're there."

Mary opened the package and saw a beautiful gold bracelet containing several small diamonds. "Thank you, Mom and Dad. This is certainly a beautiful bracelet."

With a tear forming in her eye, Alice said, "My mother wore that bracelet for many years. Her mother purchased the bracelet in Italy and brought it to the USA when she immigrated here in 1900. She gave it to my mother in 1931 for her 16th birthday."

"Do you think those are real diamonds?" asked Mary while inspecting the bracelet.

"I'm not sure," Alice replied, "but they sparkle just as much."

Duke looked at Jason and asked, "Do you have your luggage all packed, Jason?"

"Yeah, Grandpa. I have two suitcases packed. I set them next to my bedroom doorway. I'll have to remember to bring my laptop. What time are we leaving tomorrow?"

"I'll wake you at 5:00 a.m. You can help me load the luggage into the car. I want to be on the road by 6:00 a.m. It's a long drive from here to Elko, Nevada, and that's where we have motel reservations for tomorrow night."

"I wish I could travel with you all," Mary said as she stood up. She approached Jason and put her hands on his shoulders. "I will miss you so much, Jason."

"I'll miss you, too, Mom, but you need to become drug free."

Duke stood up and said, "It's very important for you to enter that rehab program, Mary. As soon as you're drug free, you'll be able to move on with your life. Your mother and I sure hope you and Jason move to Waterfield. We would love having you both near us.

"That is my plan, Dad. I should be able to make the move, so that I am there by the time Jason begins school next fall, but it all depends on how long it takes to sell this house. I know it will take quite a while for me to adjust to living in Iowa."

As Duke turned to head for the front door, he said, "I'm happy to hear about your plans to return to Iowa, Mary. I'm going outside for a smoke."

"You should quit smoking," Alice said sarcastically as she slid her chair away from the table and stood up. "My goodness, Duke. I've noticed recently that your right thumb and index finger have yellowish-brown stains on them from all that cigarette smoke. Besides, smoking is not good for you. It's actually quite disgusting."

Duke simply ignored Alice's advice while continuing to walk toward the front door. Jason joined Duke on the front stoop a few minutes later.

Chapter 7

Duke awoke at 4:30 a.m. Wednesday, June 1. He gently nudged Alice until she opened her eyes. "Wake up, Peach. We need to start our day."

"I hate the thought of riding in the car all day, but I am eager to get home," replied Alice as she scooted to the side of the bed and sat up.

Duke sat up, began dressing, and said, "You might want to dress warmer today. I heard the meteorologist last night say that the warmer than normal temperatures we've had in California would end during the night. The temperature this morning is supposed to be forty-five degrees."

"I'm sure glad it was unusually warm during our entire visit," Alice said as she pulled her jeans on."

Just as Duke entered the hallway, Jason opened his bedroom door and peered into the hallway. "Good morning, Grandpa. Are you almost ready to load the luggage into the car?"

"Hi, Jason. You must have woken early. I see you're already dressed. Let's eat some breakfast before we load our luggage."

"Okay. I'll see you in the kitchen." Jason carried two of his suitcases downstairs and set them near the front doorway. Then, he returned upstairs to get the rest of his luggage, and as he entered the upstairs hallway, saw Alice entering the bathroom. "Good morning, Grandma. When I finish taking my luggage downstairs, I'll carry your luggage downstairs."

"Good morning, Jason. That's very nice of you. I'm going to freshen up a little before I make breakfast."

Jason went into his bedroom to get his laptop and overnight bag. He returned downstairs a few minutes later and set them beside his suitcases. Jason went into the kitchen and removed a can of soda from inside the refrigerator. He noticed the full pot of freshly brewed coffee, so he put the unopened can of soda into the front pocket of his shirt. He poured a cup of coffee, and carefully carried it to the front stoop where Duke sat smoking a cigarette while staring into space. "I brought a cup of coffee for you, Grandpa."

"Thank you, Jason. Doggone! I'm sure glad I brought a jacket with me. It's pretty cold out here this morning."

"Yeah. It does feel cold. I'm going inside to get my jacket. I'll be right back."

As soon as Jason returned to the front stoop, Duke asked, "Is your grandma making breakfast?"

"Yeah. She's making some omelets, and Mom is setting the table."

"That's good. You'd better eat a big breakfast, because we might not stop to eat until late this afternoon. We'll have to stop somewhere to fill the gas tank, so I guess you could get a snack then, if you're hungry at the time."

"Don't worry about me, Grandpa. I'll eat a big breakfast."

Ten minutes later, Duke and Jason went into the kitchen and sat down at the kitchen table. Alice set a platter of omelets on the table a few minutes later, and said, "I hope you all like these omelets. I put some bacon bits and cheese in them."

Twenty minutes later, Duke slid back his chair, stood up, and said, "Are you ready to help me with the luggage, Jason."

Jason quickly finished his soda, and stood up. "Yeah, Grandpa. I'm ready."

Jason and Duke made a couple of round trips between the front door and the upstairs bedroom to get the rest of Duke and Alice's luggage, and then began loading the luggage into the LeSabre. They managed to get most of it into the car trunk, all except for one of Jason's suitcases. They set it on the rear floor, directly behind the front passenger seat. Duke closed the trunk lid while Jason closed the car doors. Duke lit a cigarette, placed his hands on his hips, and said, "Well, Jason. I think we're ready to hit the road. What do you think?"

"I'm ready when you are, Grandpa. Do you want me to tell Grandma that we're ready?"

Duke looked at his wristwatch and said, "It's 5:45 a.m., so let's go inside and tell your mother good-bye. We'll leave at 6:00 a.m."

When Duke and Jason entered the kitchen, Mary handed a stack of cash along with a check to Duke as she said, "I want you to use the thousand dollars cash to pay for Jason's expenses. I wrote that check in your name for thirty thousand dollars. When you arrive in Waterfield, you should deposit it in a separate bank account with your and Mother's name on it. When Jason needs or wants something, you and Mom decide whether he really needs it or not. That money should certainly be more than enough to take care of Jason until I move to Waterfield."

"Can you afford to give us all this money?" asked Duke as he sat down at the kitchen table.

"Absolutely, Dad. Calvin inherited tons of money after his parents perished. He gave me half of it, so money is not a problem."

"Okay, we'll use it wisely for Jason's needs. It'll sure help, because your mother and I live on our social security money along with our savings." Duke looked across the table at Alice and asked, "Are you about ready to leave for home?"

Alice stood up and said, "Yes. I'll go to the bathroom, and then I'll be ready."

As soon as Alice came out of the bathroom, everybody congregated outside near the LeSabre. After all the hugs and good-byes, Duke opened the car door and slid in behind the steering wheel. Alice chose to sit on the front seat while Jason sat on the backseat. Duke fired up the car engine and slowly backed out of the driveway. Tears flowed down Mary's cheeks as she stood near the front stoop waving good-bye to her son and parents.

After completing a 530-mile trip eleven hours later, Duke steered the LeSabre onto the asphalt parking lot of a motel in Elko, Nevada. He parked in front of the motel office, opened the car door, and slowly planted his feet upon the parking lot. "I'll go inside and check in. I hope they still have two rooms available. They should, since we reserved them earlier."

"Do you want me to come inside with you, Grandpa?"

"You can if you want to, Jason."

"I'll wait here," offered Alice.

Duke grabbed the doorpost and pulled as he exited the car. Jason quickly exited the car and watched Duke spend thirty seconds stretching in order to remove the kinks and stiffness from his back. "Are you okay, Grandpa?" asked Jason.

"Yeah, Jason. My ol' body is just sore and stiff. Like they always say, 'It's hell to get old.' "

Fifteen minutes later, Duke and Jason began hauling the luggage from the car to their rented, second-floor adjoining rooms. As soon as they finished, Duke went outside and removed a cold can of beer from inside his cooler. He popped open the lid tab and took a huge swallow of beer. Just then, Jason and Alice appeared. Jason asked, “Does that beer hit the spot, Grandpa?”

“It sure does,” replied Duke as he tipped the can for another gulp of beer.

After another huge swallow of beer, Duke reached for a cigarette. As he lit it, Alice said, “Jason and I are going to the motel office, so we can see if they have any brochures describing tourist attractions in this area.”

“We aren’t going to be here long enough to look at any tourist attractions,” replied Duke. “I want to leave early in the morning.”

As Alice and Jason began walking toward the office, Alice snapped a reply, “If we think there are some interesting attractions to look at, we might have to stay here an extra day.”

“Whatever!” replied Duke as his right hand shot up into the air. “As soon as you guys come back, we’ll walk over to the next-door restaurant and eat some supper.”

Alice and Jason returned fifteen minutes later, each holding a handful of brochures. Duke dropped a cigarette butt into his empty beer can, scowled at them, and asked, “Are you two ready for supper, or are you going to study all those doggone brochures? I’m almost starving to death.”

Alice smiled as she looked at Duke and said, “My goodness. I wouldn’t want you to starve to death, so I guess we’d better eat supper.”

Three hours elapsed, and then at 9:00 p.m., Jason entered Duke and Alice’s room, and sat beside Alice on the edge of the bed. Ten minutes earlier, Duke had switched on the TV and chosen to sit in a chair near the corner of the room. He intended to watch the weather report before going to bed. Just as the meteorologist began to report the weather news, Jason saw Duke's head slump forward. After thirty seconds, Jason saw Duke's head go backwards, and then sideways as Duke dozed. Jason said, "Gee whiz, Grandma. Grandpa must really be tired tonight."

"He was going to watch the weather news, but it appears as if he'll miss it. He's nodding off pretty good. I'll have to wake him soon, so he can get ready for bed. Since you and I didn't find any tourist attractions that would interest us, he wants to leave at 6:00 a.m. tomorrow. Maybe, when we arrive in Rawlins, Wyoming, we'll discover some interesting tourist attractions."

"I guess I'll go to bed, Grandma. Tell Grandpa good night for me."

"Okay, Jason. Sleep tight. Your grandpa will wake you in the morning. You don't have to worry about over sleeping."

Duke, Alice, and Jason left the motel parking lot in Elko at 6:00 a.m. Thursday, June 2. A short while later, Duke steered the LeSabre along an entrance ramp leading to eastbound Interstate 80 and soon merged onto the outside lane. He set the cruise control at 75 mph and said, "Well, we might as well settle in for another long day of driving."

From her location upon the backseat, Alice replied, "At least the weather is supposed to be nice today."

"I didn't get a chance to hear the weather report last night," replied Duke as he grinned. "I had a little difficulty staying awake."

Jason snickered and said, "Yeah, Grandpa. I saw your head bobbing around while I was in your room last night."

Duke lit a cigarette and rolled down his side window a little. Jason asked, "How is your hand, Grandpa? The swelling has disappeared, but it's still very black-and-blue."

"It still hurts a little, but not very much. It'll be okay."

"I'm glad it feels better," replied Jason. "I did a little research before I went to bed last night. There is supposed to be an old prison in Rawlins, and it's open for tourism. Do you think we could stay in Rawlins long enough to take a tour through the prison? The hours are from 9:00 a.m. to 5:00 p.m."

Duke rubbed his forehead lightly and replied, "How did you do research? I thought you had to have your computer connected to the internet."

Jason laughed a little and said, "It was easy, Grandpa. I just used my laptop to sign into the free Wi-Fi system at the motel."

"Oh," replied Duke while glancing into the rearview mirror. "What does Wi-Fi stand for, anyway?"

"Wireless Fidelity," replied Jason. "It's a system that allows computers to correspond with each other by using radio waves."

"I didn't know there was such a thing, let alone knowing that the internet was available to motel guests." Duke shifted his body position a little, trying to get comfortable. "Well, let's see how our day goes. We probably won't arrive in Rawlins early enough to tour the prison today. We're going to lose an hour of time today, because we'll be crossing into a different time zone."

Alice leaned against the back of the front seat and said, "We could tour the prison tomorrow morning. A few hours delay shouldn't affect our travel schedule very much."

"We'll decide when we arrive there, Alice. I really want to get home so I can finish spading and planting the garden."

"Oh, Duke!" Alice said as she began rubbing Duke's right shoulder. "Relax for once in your life. Forget about the garden for a while. I'm sure Jason will help you with the garden."

"I look forward to helping you, Grandpa," Jason offered.

At 6:00 p.m., Duke parked the LeSabre in front of a motel office located near the city limits of Rawlins, Wyoming. "Thank God," said Alice as she opened the rear car door and stepped onto the parking lot. I'm glad we have finally arrived. My butt is completely numb."

Duke opened the car door and turned his body enough so he could place his feet upon the parking lot. As Jason opened the front door and exited the car, Duke looked at Alice and said, "I have a thought, Alice."

"What's that?" asked Alice.

"You and Jason should go into the office and register. While you're doing that, I'll sit here and wait for you. I'm as stiff as a board."

"We can do that, Duke. Come with me, Jason."

When Duke saw Alice and Jason carrying several brochures while exiting the motel office, he swung his legs and feet back into the car. As they approached, he asked, "Were you able to rent a couple rooms?"

"Yes," Alice replied as she looked at the receipt. "We have rooms 301 and 303." Then, Alice pointed toward the far end of the building and said, "The rooms are located way down at the other end of the building, so you may as well drive the car there and park it. We'll walk."

By the time Duke and Jason had carried the luggage to the third-floor rooms, Duke had decided that after this trip, he would never again go on any long trips. He sat on the edge of the bed, trying to recuperate from walking up and down all the stair steps. Duke watched Alice and Jason as they sat down at a small table in the corner of the room to begin reading the brochures. *I suppose they will find all kinds of interesting tourist attractions they'll want to visit tomorrow*, Duke thought. He stood up and stated, "I'm going out to the car and get a cold beer out of the cooler. I'll drink a beer and smoke a cigarette while you're looking at those brochures. Let's eat supper pretty soon. I'm hungry."

Alice grinned at Duke and said, "We'll come outside when we finish looking through these brochures. There is a restaurant within walking distance. I saw it when we pulled into the motel parking lot. Let's eat supper there."

"That's fine with me," replied Duke as he opened the room door and stepped into the hallway.

Duke, Alice, and Jason slept until 8:00 a.m. Friday. They went downstairs at 8:30 a.m. and ate free continental breakfasts offered by the motel owners. When they finished eating, Duke and Jason loaded the luggage into the LeSabre. After dropping off the room keys at the motel office, they drove to the Wyoming Frontier Prison, formerly known as the Wyoming State Prison. They spent a total of one hour and thirty minutes touring through the prison and the Wyoming Peace Officers' Museum. They finished touring the prison at 11:30 a.m. and reluctantly crawled into the LeSabre. Alice told Jason to sit in front, because she wanted to stretch out on the backseat and take a nap. Ten minutes later, Duke drove the LeSabre onto eastbound Interstate 80 and began driving the first mile of a 360-mile trip to North Platte, Nebraska. Jason looked at Duke and said, "I enjoyed the prison tour. That place has quite the history. I'm sure the new prisons are much nicer than that one."

Duke snickered and said, "Heck, Jason. I've watched some of those prison shows on TV. It appears to me that the prisons are pretty fancy these days. It's too bad they aren't like the one we toured this morning. There probably wouldn't be so many repeat offenders."

"Yeah. Did you hear the tour guide say that the cornerstone for the Wyoming State Prison was laid in 1888, but it remained vacant until December of 1901? The state didn't have enough money to operate it until then."

"I didn't hear that, but I heard the guide say that there wasn't much heat in the prison during the early years." Duke quit talking as a tractor-trailer semi began moving from the passing lane into the outside lane, right in front of them. Duke tapped the brake pedal a little to shut off the cruise control. "That doggone fool nearly hit us," Duke said loudly. As soon as the semi sped up and spread the gap between them, Duke set his cruise control and said, "Yeah, Jason, it sounds as if the prisoners nearly froze to death during the Wyoming winters."

"That prison was open for a long time, up until the state closed it in 1981. It remained vacant until 1988 when they began using it as a tourist attraction. I know one thing for sure; I never want to be locked away in prison."

"Well, Jason. Just make sure you never break any laws. Then, you won't have to worry about prison time. I'd better quit talking so much and concentrate on my driving. The traffic is kind of heavy right now."

"Okay, Grandpa. I'll be quiet so you can concentrate better."

Several hours later, Duke steered the LeSabre off Interstate 80 and onto an exit road leading into North Platte. Just as Duke turned onto a city street, he heard the song Jingle Bells blaring away from somewhere near Jason. The sudden sound of the song startled Duke, and his shoulders jerked back a little as he looked at Jason and asked, "What in the hell is that?"

As Jason reached into his front pocket for his cell phone, he replied, "It's just my cell phone, Grandpa." Jason answered the phone and heard his mother's voice, "Hello, Jason. How is the trip going? Where are you now?"

"We have just arrived in North Platte, Nebraska. We're going to stay here tonight."

"Are you getting along okay with your grandparents?"

"Yes, Mom. We have been getting along great. We went on a tour of an old prison in Rawlins, Wyoming, this morning. It was interesting."

"Well, it sounds as if everything is going okay, so I'll let you go on with your day. Tell my parents hello for me."

"Okay. Good-bye, Mom."

Jason put the cell phone back into his front pocket and said, "That was Mom. She said to tell you each hello."

"That damned cell phone song scared me for a second. I didn't realize you had your phone with you. For a second, I thought I was imagining things."

Jason laughed a little and said, "Yeah, Grandpa. I've had my phone with me. You and Grandma should each have a cell phone, especially for when you're traveling."

At 9:00 p.m., Duke maneuvered the LeSabre off a city street and onto a motel parking lot while replying, "I thought about buying a cell phone, but decided not to spend the money."

As soon as Mary hung up after talking with Jason, she punched some phone numbers into the keypad of her home phone, the numbers for a motel in Santa Rosa. When the motel desk clerk answered, Mary asked for Ike, the Guatemalan she had spent time with at Calvin's party. Mary remembered that during the party, Ike had told her that he would be staying at the motel until Sunday, June 5. The desk clerk rang Ike's room and after three rings, Mary heard Ike answer, "Hello."

"Well, hello there, good looking. Do you remember my voice?"

"I most certainly do, Mary," said Ike with his sexy Guatemalan accent. "I could never forget your voice, or anything else about you."

Mary giggled for a few seconds, much like a teenager, and then said, "I feel lonesome tonight. Would you like to come over to my house and visit for a while? Perhaps, you could bring something to make me feel better. I will make it worth your time."

"I'd love to come over to your house. I know something that will make you feel better. I still have something left from Betty's birthday party we attended May 20th."

Mary glanced at her wristwatch and said, "So what time will you arrive at my house? I want to be ready for you."

"I should arrive there about 9:00 p.m., depending on traffic."

With a very sexy tone of voice, Mary purred, "I'll be waiting for you, good looking."

As soon as Mary ended the phone call, she went into the bathroom and took a warm shower. After she dried off, she entered her bedroom and stood in front of the full-length wall mirror. As she looked into the mirror, she thought, *I still have a great body for my age*. She massaged her breasts for about ten seconds, and then slowly slid her hands downward across her belly area and onto her inner thighs. She turned so that she could see her side view in the mirror, and after viewing the reflection for about ten seconds, thought, *Ike should enjoy my body*. Mary walked over to the dresser and picked up a bottle of her favorite perfume. She put a dab of it on the side of each breast and a dab on each inner thigh. Then, she went to her closet, selected a beautiful silk kimono, and slipped it on. She tied the silk waist belt as she left her bedroom and entered the hallway. The doorbell rang just as she entered the dining room, so she walked to the front door and opened it. She saw Ike holding a bouquet of red roses with his left hand and a bottle of champagne with his right hand. Ike felt quite surprised when he saw Mary's choice of clothing. He handed the roses to Mary and said, "Hello, Mary. Gosh! You are absolutely gorgeous."

"Thank you, Ike. You look very handsome." Mary smelled the roses and said, "Thanks for the roses. It is nice of you to bring the champagne. Let's go into the kitchen. I will put these roses in a vase of water. We can set that bottle of champagne into a bucket of ice."

Mary allowed Ike to walk in front of her as they headed for the kitchen. She noticed a faint scent of aftershave lotion as she closely followed him. She did not know what kind it was, but it smelled very sexy, sexy enough to cause a tingle in her body. Mary selected a beautiful emerald green vase for the roses and filled it half full of water. She carefully inserted the rose stems into the water and set the vase upon the granite countertop. As Ike stood near her, Mary removed an ice bucket from a cabinet and set it on the granite countertop next to the refrigerator. Ike smelled the slight aroma of Mary's perfume drifting through the air. The scent along with Mary's sexy appearance caused Ike to feel turned on sexually. Just as Mary reached for the refrigerator handle, Ike pressed his body tightly against hers. She quickly turned around and put her right hand on the back of his neck and her left hand on his right shoulder. She pulled his head toward her and their lips quickly locked together.

Mary felt the pressure of Ike's tongue tip as he tried forcing it into her mouth, so she parted her lips slightly and began sucking on the tip of his tongue. When he thrust it deeper into her mouth, she sucked very hard, trying to keep it there, but Ike's tongue kept thrusting in and out. Ike reached down and fumbled with the silk waist belt on Mary's kimono. He finally untied it and pulled open the front of her kimono. Their lips separated, and as Mary panted heavily, she began frantically unbuttoning Ike's white sport shirt. When she finished, she spread open the front of his shirt, so Ike quickly removed it, baring his upper body.

Mary moved toward Ike until her breasts pressed tightly against the smooth, dark skin of his muscular chest. They began kissing passionately, while using their hands to explore each other's body. After a few minutes of tongue thrusting and heavy panting, Mary kneeled onto the ceramic-tile floor and quickly unbuckled Ike's belt. She unbuttoned his slacks and zipped down the zipper. Then, she grabbed the waistbands of his slacks and underwear, and tugged on them as she lowered them toward his feet. She continued lowering both waistbands together until they surrounded his ankles. As Ike stepped out of his slacks and underwear, Mary removed her kimono, exposing her completely nude body. Ike slowly backed away from Mary until he felt the cool, stainless steel refrigerator door pressing against his buttocks and back. He grabbed the refrigerator door handle with his right hand, stood straight and tall, and said, "I'm waiting for you, Mary."

Twenty minutes later, Ike asked, "Do you care if I take a shower?"

Mary slipped into her kimono and said, "I am going to take a shower. Do you want to join me, or do you want to take one separately?"

Ike put on his undershorts, and picked up his slacks and white sport shirt. He smiled and said, "I'll take a shower with you, but you have to promise not to bother me."

"Okay. Follow me. I'll lead you into my bedroom bathroom."

They spent fifteen minutes showering together, and then dried off and entered the bedroom. Mary sat on the edge of her bed, and with a begging sound of voice, asked, "Did you bring anything else to cheer me up?"

"Ike picked up his slacks and reached into the front right pocket. He pulled out four small plastic sacks, each containing white powder, and said, “I saved these for a special occasion. Calvin gave them to me at the birthday party.”

Mary stood up and approached Ike. She pressed her breasts against his bare muscular chest while hugging him tightly. “Can we snort some of that tonight?”

“That’s why I brought it with me. If you let me stay with you tonight and tomorrow night, we can snort some tomorrow, too.”

“Since I am entering a rehab program Monday, I’ll let you stay. I may as well enjoy my last weekend of drug highs. I will never again use illegal drugs after this weekend.” Mary released Ike and stepped away from him. She smiled as she gazed into his eyes. “We should put that bottle of champagne on ice before we snort any cocaine, because later on, I want to drip champagne onto your sexy body and lick it off as I savor the taste.”

“May I do that to you, too?”

“You certainly may, but I want you to bind my wrists and ankles to the bedposts before you drip champagne onto my body. That is much more exciting for me. Wait here while I go into the kitchen and ready the champagne. I will bring it back with me.”

Ike flopped onto the bed and said, “I’ll be waiting for you. I’ll get the cocaine ready so we can snort some when you return.”

Duke awoke at 4:30 a.m. Saturday, June 4. Alice woke a few minutes later, just as Duke sat on the edge of the bed and began dressing. “Good morning, Duke,” said Alice as she sat up and yawned. “Are we going all the way to Waterfield today, or just part way?”

“We’ll see how it goes, but we’ll probably stay overnight in Des Moines.” Duke buttoned his short-sleeved denim shirt before saying, “We’re still about five hundred and thirty miles from home. It’s a little over four hundred miles from here to Des Moines."

Alice moved to the side of the bed and stood up. As she removed her cotton nightgown, Duke stood up and looked at her. "You sure are well built, Alice." Duke walked toward Jason's room door. "I'll wake Jason so he can help me load the luggage right away, and then we'll eat breakfast."

Duke knocked on Jason's room door several times before Jason opened the door and appeared. With very sleepy, squinty eyes, Jason looked at Duke and mumbled, "Good morning, Grandpa. Gee whiz. The night sure went fast."

"It's like they always say, 'Time flies when you're having fun.' " Duke headed for the hallway. "I'm going outside to smoke a cigarette. I'll be back when I finish."

As Duke stepped into the hallway, Alice cheerfully said, "Good morning, Jason. You'd better get dressed so you can help your grandpa carry the luggage to the car. You know him; he's always in a big rush."

"Okay, Grandma. I'll be ready shortly."

At 7:00 a.m., Duke steered the LeSabre onto an entrance ramp to eastbound Interstate 80. After he merged onto the outside lane of Interstate 80, he set the cruise control at 75 mph, looked at Jason, and said, "We will cross a time zone line today, so we'll lose another hour."

"At least we're out of the mountains, so driving should be easier. I can't believe how flat the land is in Nebraska."

"Flatland is great for farming. Iowa is quite flat, too."

"Yes," Alice chimed in, "and the farmland near the Waterfield area is some of the best in the entire world."

Just as the dashboard clock displayed 3:00 p.m., Duke said, "I'm tired of driving, not to mention I'm thirsty as heck, so let's find a motel here in West Des Moines."

"I'm definitely ready to get out of this car," Alice said as she leaned against the back of the front seat. "I could go for a nice warm shower."

Jason pointed at a billboard and said, "There's a sign for an AmericInn motel. The exit ramp should be about a mile ahead of us."

Ten minutes later, Duke parked the car in front of the AmericInn office. "Are you coming inside with me, Jason?"

"Sure, Grandpa."

At 11:00 p.m. (Iowa time) Saturday, Duke, Alice, and Jason said their good nights to each other and went to bed. At the same time (9:00 p.m. California time), Ike and Mary decided to party big time, because they knew it would be their last weekend together. They still had two packages of cocaine. They had used the full bottle of champagne for the dripping and licking games they had played very early Saturday morning. At 10:00 p.m. Saturday, Ike and Mary decided to shower together. When they finished drying off, Mary slipped into her initialed, white terrycloth robe, and asked, "Do you want to wear Calvin's robe? I'll get it for you."

"Either that, or I will remain nude," Ike replied as he flexed his right biceps.

Between giggles, Mary said, "I will get the robe for you." Mary went into the walk-in bedroom closet, removed Calvin's initialed, white terrycloth robe, and handed it to Ike. "I have some pain pills in my dresser drawer," Mary said as she watched Ike put on the robe. "We should each take one before we snort the rest of the cocaine. Do you think that would make us feel higher?"

Ike grinned a little and said, "I don't know, Mary. That combination could make us very ill. I'm going to mix a rum and coke. Do you want a drink?"

"Yes, a rum and coke will taste very good. I believe I will try a pain pill with my drink and see what happens. Mary removed a pill bottle from her dresser drawer, opened the bottle, and shook it enough for a pain pill to land in the palm of her hand. She popped the pill into her mouth, swallowed, and walked toward her bedroom door. "Let's go into the kitchen and mix a couple drinks," she said as she entered the hallway.

Ike and Mary mixed two rum and cokes, and then brought their drinks into the bedroom. Ike set his glass on the nightstand, and reached down beside the bed. He picked up a serving tray, and asked, "Should I ready the cocaine?"

Mary teasingly removed her terrycloth robe as she walked toward the closet. "Yes, please," said Mary with a very seductive tone of voice. "When you have it ready, take off your robe, and we will sit on the bed. When we finish snorting the cocaine, we will finish our drinks. After that, I will tie your wrists and ankles to the bedposts." Mary opened the closet door and removed four, cloth robe belts from the closet.

Ike and Mary partied all through the late night hours of Saturday and the early morning hours of Sunday. After Mary had tied Ike to the bed, she had convinced him to take several pain pills, along with several rum and cokes. He had passed out at 4:30 a.m., after enduring several hours of Mary's aggressiveness. At 5:00 a.m. Sunday, Mary felt as if she were coming off her high, so she left her bed and took the pill bottle out of her dresser drawer. She swallowed two pain pills on her way into the kitchen where she mixed a rum and coke. She carried the drink to her bedroom and sat on the edge of the bed. Mary swallowed some rum and coke, and with glazed eyes, looked at Ike. *I should untie him, but he is sleeping so soundly*, she thought as she swallowed some more rum and coke. *I do not want to wake him, so I will lie down beside him and enjoy my high.* Mary set the empty glass upon the nightstand, and snuggled against Ike. She felt high for about thirty minutes before slipping into total blackness.

Chapter 8

Duke, Alice, and Jason had become somewhat comfortable in the LeSabre by 10:00 a.m. Sunday while traveling north of Des Moines on northbound Interstate 35. Alice reached over the back of the front seat at 10:15 a.m. and put her right hand upon Jason's left shoulder. "You should phone your mother and surprise her, Jason. I know she would love to hear from you."

Duke glanced into his side mirror and said, "Mary should be out of bed by now. It's 8:15 a.m. in California."

Jason squirmed around as he reached into the right front pocket of his jeans and pulled out his cell phone. He flipped open the keypad and entered several numbers. After hearing five rings, he heard Mary's answering machine, so he left a message for Mary to phone him. Jason flipped shut the keypad and said, "Mom didn't answer, so I left her a message. She will probably phone me right back."

"For some reason," Alice said while settling back against the backseat, "I have a bad feeling this morning. I'm worried about Mary. If she doesn't phone you back within a half hour, you should phone her again."

Duke looked into the rearview mirror and asked Alice, "Do you think we should stop at the Reiman Gardens in Ames? It's such a beautiful morning."

With her right hand, Alice patted the right side of her

short gray hair a little. "I guess we could stop there. It's not too far out of our way."

"We can enter onto US Hwy 30 at the next exit," replied Duke.

Jason looked at Alice and asked, "What's at the Reiman Gardens, Grandma?"

"It's actually part of Iowa State University, and it has many different flower gardens. My favorites are the rose gardens, especially the one planted with several different varieties of rose bushes that Professor Buck developed. There is also a beautiful glass-enclosed building that they call the butterfly wing. It houses about eight hundred butterflies and many varieties of plants. There is also a large conservatory filled with plants. Reiman Gardens is one of the largest public gardens in Iowa. We haven't been there for about three years, so it is probably developed much more by now."

"It sounds like a nice place," replied Jason. "I would love to see all the butterflies."

Thirty minutes later, Duke steered the LeSabre onto the Reiman Garden parking lot. He parked the car, opened his door, and said, "Do you want to phone your mother again before we tour the gardens?"

"Yeah. I'll phone her right now," replied Jason as he opened the front car door.

Duke exited the car and opened the car door for Alice as Jason phoned Mary. Jason heard the answering machine, so he ended the call and said, "Mom isn't answering the phone, Grandma."

Still sitting on the backseat with her feet upon the parking lot, Alice said, "I think we should phone Larry. I have his cell phone number. He would probably check on Mary for us."

"How did you get his cell phone number, Alice?" asked Duke as he lit a cigarette.

"Larry gave me his business card," replied Alice as she stood up. "He wrote his cell phone number on it, just for me."

"Wow," Duke replied as he waved his hand into the air. "Lucky you, Alice. I guess you should be the one to phone him, since he admires you so much."

"May I use your phone, Jason?" asked Alice.

Jason exited the car and handed Alice his cell phone. Alice reached into her purse and removed Larry's business card. She did not know how to use the cell phone for sure, so she asked Jason to phone Larry. After three rings, Larry answered, so Jason immediately handed the phone to Alice.

"Hello, Larry. This is Alice. How are you this morning?"

"Oh, my. It is so nice to hear your voice, Alice. What is up, anyway?"

"We've been phoning Mary, but she isn't answering the phone, so I wonder if you would be so kind as to check on her for us. I'm worried about her."

"Oh, my dear Alice. Sure, anything for you. I will drive over to her house and see if everything is okay. She asked me to list her house with a realtor, so she gave me her spare house key a few days ago. Now, do not worry your little heart, Alice. I am sure Mary is okay."

"Thank you, Larry. We really appreciate your time."

"I will reluctantly tell my sweetheart good-bye, and then drive to Mary's house. Tell me your cell phone number, and I will phone you after I check on her."

"I'm using Jason's phone, so I'll hand it back to Jason and he can tell you the phone number. I'll talk with you later. Good-bye."

Alice handed Jason the phone and said, "Tell Larry your phone number. He's going to call us after he checks on Mary."

Jason told Larry the phone numbers before he

terminated the call. Then, Jason handed the phone to Alice and said, "You may as well carry the phone, Grandma. When Larry calls, just flip it open and answer it."

Duke, Jason, and Alice admired the beautiful June day as they strolled to the entrance of the Reiman Gardens. Duke's wristwatch displayed 11:00 a.m. as he purchased three admission tickets.

At 9:30 a.m. (California time), Larry parked his silver BMW 335is convertible beside a white car in front of Mary's garage. As Larry exited his car, he thought, *Hmm. I wonder who owns that car.* He rang the front doorbell several times, but received no reply, so he knocked loudly several times on the front door. When he received no answer, he pulled his cell phone from its holder and punched in Mary's home phone number. He heard the answering machine, so ended the call and punched in her cell phone number. He heard another message about voice mail, so he ended the call. Frustration began setting in, but he finally unlocked the front door, opened it, and hollered, "Hello, Mary. Are you home?" No one answered, so he hollered two more times. He heard no reply, so he cautiously entered the dining room.

Then, he heard a man's voice, "Hello. We're in Mary's bedroom. Please come into the bedroom."

Larry did not feel comfortable about going into Mary's bedroom, so he stood in the hallway and said, "Are you sure it is okay for me to come into the bedroom? Is Mary in there?"

"Yes, Mary's in here. I think she might be unconscious. She needs our help, so please come in. The door is unlocked."

Larry turned the cut-glass doorknob and slowly opened the door. He could not believe what he saw"

He rushed into the room as Ike's face turned beet red.

"You have caught me in an awkward position," said Ike with great embarrassment. "Would you please untie me?"

"Let me first check on Mary," replied Larry as he shook Mary a few times. She moved a little, so Larry quickly freed Ike's wrists.

While Ike untied the cloth robe belts binding his ankles, Larry shook Mary several times. She finally opened her eyes, and with a garbled whisper said, "What time is it? Why are you here, Larry?"

Ike quickly began dressing and said, "I believe Mary took too many pain pills and drank too many rum and cokes." While Larry lifted and pulled Mary into a standing position, Ike finished dressing and said, "I'm getting the hell out of here. Good luck with her."

By this time, Larry acted completely hysterical, but managed to keep Mary in the standing position while grabbing her robe off a chair. He eventually convinced Mary to put her arms through the sleeves, so he could slip the robe onto her. "Let's walk into the kitchen, my dear Mary. I will pour a nice glass of ice water for you. You need to keep walking with me, so you can wear off the drugs. You need to drink a lot of water, too."

"Okay," Mary mumbled.

With Mary's right arm around Larry's shoulders, and Larry's left arm around Mary's waist, they continued walking throughout the house except for the times they stopped in the kitchen, so Mary could drink some water. When she finished drinking her fifth glass of water, she suddenly heaved. Some of the vomit splattered onto Larry's light-gray slacks and brown, patent-leather shoes. Larry jumped away as far as he could without letting go of Mary's arm, and said, "Oh my God, Mary. Let's sit you down so I can clean up the floor. I need to clean off my shoes and slacks, too."

Larry helped Mary walk to a chair located at the

kitchen table and steadied her as she sat down. Then, he began cleaning the vomit from the ceramic-tile floor. After the floor appeared spotlessly clean, he began removing the vomit spots from his shoes and slacks. By the time Larry finished, the kitchen wall clock displayed 1:00 p.m. Mary felt much better, so Larry said, "I need to call your mother and let her know you are okay."

"Please do not tell her that I took too many pain pills," Mary replied.

"Oh, Mary," said Larry sympathetically as he removed his cell phone from its holder and sat down at the kitchen table. "I really hate to lie to your mother. Well, I guess I could tell her that you have the flu."

"That will work," replied Mary as she placed her elbows upon the tabletop and supported her head with her hands.

At 3:15 p.m. (Iowa time), Duke, Jason, and Alice exited the glass-enclosed butterfly wing at Reiman Gardens and began walking toward the LeSabre. Just as they arrived at the LeSabre, Alice heard Jason's phone ringing, so she quickly reached into her purse and removed the phone. When she answered, she heard Larry's feminine voice, "Hello, my dear Alice. I am with Mary at her house, and everything is super fine. I found Mary sleeping when I arrived. She has a bad case of flu. That is why she didn't answer her phone."

"That's a relief," Alice said as she opened the left rear car door.

"My sweet Mary said that she will phone you when she feels better. I have decided to stay here with Mary until tomorrow morning. Then, I will take her to the rehab center at 9:00 a.m."

"Oh, Larry! That's so nice of you. I will quit worrying about Mary, now that I know you will take good care of her."

Larry giggled a little and cheerfully replied, "That's what friends are for, Alice. I love helping people. Well, my dear Alice, I must say good-bye so I can go home to get some clean clothes and tell my sweetheart that I plan to stay here overnight."

"Okay, Larry. Thanks a lot for letting me know everything is okay. Good-bye."

"Good-bye, Alice. Oh! Make sure you take good care of that handsome husband of yours."

"I will, Larry." Alice smiled as she ended the call and handed the cell phone to Jason.

Duke fired up the LeSabre engine while glancing into the rearview mirror at Alice. "So, Alice. Is everything okay?"

"Everything is fine. Mary just has the flu. Larry told me that he'll stay with Mary until he takes her to the rehab center tomorrow morning. I'm so glad. He's really a super nice guy."

Duke placed the gearshift lever into the drive position, and as he began driving the LeSabre out of the parking lot, replied, "Yeah. Larry is a very nice young man. I don't know if his priorities are right or not, but I guess that's up to him."

"Oh, Grandpa," Jason offered. "There are a lot of gay people in the world, and there always has been. They just don't hide it as much these days."

Duke looked at the dashboard clock and saw it displaying 3:30 p.m. "We should be home by 5:30 p.m., unless you both want to stop somewhere to eat."

"Let's find a restaurant in the next town," Alice said as she reached over the back of the front seat and began rubbing Duke's shoulders. "I'm hungry and I'm sure Jason is too."

"I'm very hungry," Jason replied as he smiled and looked at Alice.

Duke steered the LeSabre from a Waterfield street onto a gravel-surfaced alley at 6:30 p.m. He pressed the button on the remote control garage door opener, and watched the overhead, double garage door slowly opening. "Well," Duke said, "we've finally arrived."

Jason saw Duke's shiny, black S-10 ZR-2 pickup parked inside the garage. "Gee whiz, Grandpa. I didn't know you had a pickup. What year is it?"

"It's a 2003. I bought it about six months ago."

"Wow! That's a sharp looking truck. Those extra-large tires are really neat."

Duke decided to back the LeSabre through the garage doorway opening and park inside the garage. As he began slowly backing the LeSabre through the doorway opening while alternately glancing into both side mirrors, Alice and Jason heard him mumbling something about how it is so doggone difficult to judge where the car fenders are on the newer cars. Duke finally parked the car and shut off the engine. "It's good to be home," Duke said as he opened the car door and placed his feet upon the garage floor. He exited the car, placed his left hand against his lower back, and while trying to stand straight, remarked "Boy! I'm really stiff and sore this evening."

As soon as Alice and Jason exited the car, Duke opened the trunk lid and said, "Let's carry some of this luggage into the house."

Duke pushed the open/close button for the overhead garage door opener and watched as the overhead door closed. Alice opened the small garage door and said, "I'll let you men carry the luggage into the house. I'll hold open the storm door for you."

"Well, you could carry a light weight piece of luggage, Alice," Duke replied as his right hand shot up into the air.

Alice grinned as she ignored Duke and strolled along the sidewalk leading to the side door of the house. She opened the storm door, unlocked and opened the interior door, and waited for Duke and Jason to arrive with the luggage. As Jason approached, Alice held open the storm door and said, "Just set your luggage on the kitchen floor, Jason. We have to figure out which bedroom you can use."

Duke heard Alice, and said, "It'll probably take you three hours to remove all your knickknacks from whichever bedroom you let Jason use. Both downstairs bedrooms are terribly cluttered."

"Oh, Duke," Alice replied as Duke walked through the doorway opening and into the kitchen. "I don't have very many knickknacks."

Duke set the luggage on the kitchen floor, turned around, and walked toward the side door. As he exited the house, he looked at Alice and said, "You could give away half your knickknacks, and you'd still have more than enough. You ought to give away some of your doilies, too. I hate cleaning all that stuff."

Alice scowled and replied, "Well, you could give away half your junk, too. You don't clean the house near as often as I do, so don't complain."

Jason exited through the doorway opening and headed for the garage, so Alice released the storm door and went inside. As she walked through the kitchen and into the dining room, she thought, *They can open their own darn doors. I have better things to do.*

Duke lifted the last two suitcases out of the car trunk. He handed one to Jason and said, "You can carry this one, Jason."

As Jason took the suitcase, he said, "Grandma acts like she is upset with you."

Duke walked through the small doorway opening of the garage and replied, "She'll get over it."

When Duke and Jason entered the house, they found Alice standing in the front bedroom looking at numerous knickknacks occupying several shelves and the full-size bed. Duke asked, "What are you doing, Alice?"

"I guess I'll pack these knickknacks into boxes and take them upstairs to the storage closets. Jason can use this bedroom. It's a little larger than the rear bedroom."

"I'll go upstairs and get some empty boxes," Duke replied as he shook his head and thought, *Those damned knickknacks are nothing more than extra work for me.*

"Do you want me to help you, Grandpa?"

"Yeah. You can go into the basement and get some newspapers out of the recycle bin. Then, you can help your grandma wrap the knickknacks so she can pack them into boxes."

As Jason headed for the basement, Duke went upstairs. They returned to the front bedroom five minutes later. Duke set the empty cardboard boxes on the floor and said, "I'll let you two wrap and box all those knickknacks. I'm going to drink a cold beer and smoke a cigarette. I'll be outside checking out our yard, or else sitting on the 3-season porch. Have fun."

Alice and Jason spent two hours wrapping and packing the knickknacks. Then, Alice looked at Jason and said, "Will you please find your grandpa and tell him to come in here and carry these boxes upstairs? He's probably sitting in his favorite wicker chair on the 3-season porch."

Jason quickly left the bedroom and as he entered the dining room, said, "I'll find him, Grandma."

Sure enough, when Jason entered the 3-season porch, he saw Duke sitting in his favorite wicker chair and staring out through the Jalousie windows while smoking a cigarette. Jason said, "Grandma wants you to carry the boxes upstairs. I'll help you."

Duke snuffed out his cigarette and dropped it into a large glass ashtray located upon an 18-inch diameter, glass-topped wicker table. "Okay," replied Duke as he looked at his wristwatch and saw it displaying 9:00 p.m. As they walked through the French doorway opening and into the dining room, Duke said, "Gee, Jason. You might have a bed to sleep in by 10:00 p.m."

Jason laughed a little and said, "I hope so, because I'm tired."

Alice walked out of the bedroom and stopped in the hallway. As Duke and Jason walked through the hallway and into the front bedroom, she said, "While you guys carry the boxes upstairs, I'll make something for supper. I think we have a frozen pizza in the freezer. I can put that in the oven and it'll be ready to eat in about thirty minutes. Will that be okay, or do you want something else?"

"I like pizza," replied Duke as he picked up a box. "My stomach never likes it very much, but I sure do. I'll just take a few Tums before I go to bed."

Jason picked up a box and said, "Pizza sounds good to me."

Duke awoke at 5:00 a.m. Monday, June 6. He remained lying on his back for a few minutes while listening to the cardinals and robins chirping their early morning songs. He looked through the open, east double-hung windows and thought, *The sky is sure clear this morning. It'll be a good day to finish spading the garden plot.* He looked at Alice, and saw her sleeping soundly with a slight smile on her face. *Alice must be having a pleasant dream*, he thought as he scooted over and sat on the edge of the bed. Duke dressed in jeans and a light-blue pocket T-shirt. He went downstairs, and when he finished in the bathroom, went into the kitchen and readied the coffee maker. Then, he knocked on Jason's bedroom door and said, "It's time to wake up, Jason."

With a sleepy tone of voice, Jason replied, "Okay,

Grandpa."

"Put on your work clothes, because we're going to spade the garden plot today." Duke turned around and headed for the 3-season porch. Just as he opened the French doors between the porch and dining room, he saw a Cooper's hawk fly away from the large, lower bowl of the garden fountain. I hope that doggone hawk doesn't nest around here. If it does, we won't have many songbirds left in our neighborhood. Duke cranked open several Jalousie windows, and then sat down in his wicker chair. Jason arrived on the porch ten minutes later and sat in the other wicker chair. Duke looked at Jason and said, "Your grandma will wake up pretty soon. We'll eat a big breakfast before we begin spading the garden plot." Duke pointed toward a group of potted small seedlings located on the porch floor. "I want to finish spading the garden plot today, so we can get some of those seedlings planted."

Jason looked at the seedlings and asked, "What kind of plants are those, Grandpa?"

"There are eight tomato plants and twelve bell pepper plants in those pots. I planted the seeds in small pots about the middle of March, and kept them under a grow light in the basement. I transplanted them and moved them out here shortly before we left for California."

Just then, Alice appeared in the French doorway opening and said, "Good morning. I imagine you guys want a big breakfast this morning."

"That's for sure," replied Duke. "I'm going to teach Jason how to spade a garden plot."

Alice smiled and replied, "There's not much to learn about it, other than working very hard. I'll get a cup of coffee for you, Duke. Then, I'll begin making breakfast."

"You're sure a sweetheart, Alice," Duke replied as he reached into his shirt pocket and removed a cigarette. He looked at Jason and asked, "Do you want something to drink?"

"No thanks. I'll wait and drink something during breakfast."

Alice returned to the porch and handed a cup of coffee to Duke. She looked at Jason and said, "We don't have any milk, Jason. Can you get by with a glass of water with your breakfast? I'll go grocery shopping later this morning."

"Water will be fine, Grandma."

Duke, Alice, and Jason finished eating breakfast at 8:00 a.m., so Duke scooted his chair away from the dining room table and stood up. "Are you ready to begin working, Jason?"

Jason quickly stood up and said, "Yeah, I'm ready."

Alice said, "As soon as I finish washing these dishes, I'm going to the grocery store. If you see Janice outside, will you thank her for taking care of everything while we were gone?"

"Sure thing, Alice," Duke replied. "I'll thank her. She'll probably be outside sometime this morning."

Duke and Jason headed for the garage, and as they neared the small door, Duke reached into his pocket for the keys. "I'll have to unlock that door, Jason."

As Duke unlocked the door, Jason viewed the garden fountain located three feet from the sidewalk and three feet from the garage. He moved closer to the fountain, and rubbed his hand lightly across the river stone and cement composition of the large, lower basin. "Did you make this fountain, Grandpa?"

"Yeah, Jason. I'll turn on the pump switch so you can see how the water flows." Duke entered the garage, turned on the pump switch, and returned to the doorway. Ten seconds later, Jason saw water bubbling out of a half-inch diameter vertical pipe opening at the top of the six-foot tall fountain. He watched as the water slowly flowed into the small, upper fountain bowl. When the upper bowl filled with water, the water flowed over the sides of the bowl and free fell into the lower fountain bowl. After a few minutes, the lower bowl filled, and the water flowed through an overflow pipe and free fell thirty inches into the westerly end of a kidney-shaped, twenty-five gallon, PVC sunken pond located directly below the east edge of the large, lower fountain bowl.

"Gee, Grandpa. That's really cool. Does that water just keep recirculating?"

Duke pointed at the kidney-shaped pond and said, "Yeah. See that submerged pump near the west end of the pond. That pumps the water from the pond back up through a pipe vertically located through the center of the fountain, the same pipe you see at the top of the fountain. I usually have to add water to the pond every day, especially during hot, windy weather. That's because some of the water evaporates, and some of it splashes onto the ground. Well, my boy, we'd better get busy and do some spading." Duke went into the garage, grabbed the spade off the wall hook, and headed for the garden plot. Jason followed Duke and when they reached the plot, Duke said, "I'll spade the first row across the plot while you watch me. Then, you can spade the next row across. It's already seventy-five degrees and humid, so we'll be sweating something terrible before the day is over."

"Good. Maybe I'll lose some of my baby fat."

Alice came out of the house and walked toward the garage. As she stood on the sidewalk near the garage, she hollered, "Okay, men. I'm going to the grocery store. Don't work too hard."

Duke rammed the spade into the earth at the west side of the garden plot, and replied, "Okay, Alice. We'll see you when you get back." When Duke turned over the first spadeful of dirt, he felt pain in his right hand. "Oh, yeah," he half screamed. "I'll have to work very slowly, because my hand still hurts quite a lot."

Jason did not reply as he watched Duke continue spading across the garden plot. When Duke reached the east side of the plot, he slowly straightened up before saying, "Okay, Jason. It's your turn. You can start right here and work your way across to the west side."

Jason took the spade from Duke and stepped on it, forcing the blade into the ground. He struggled as he turned over the spadeful of dirt, but slowly continued spading his way across the garden. By the time he reached the west side, his dungaree shirt appeared completely sweat soaked. "Boy, Grandpa. It's really hot today," said Jason while tugging lightly on the front of his wet shirt to allow a little fresh air to enter between his shirt and belly area.

As Duke took the spade from Jason, he said, "It's going to get a lot hotter before the day is over. I'm going to put on my straw hat. I have a couple of baseball caps. Do you want to wear one of those?"

"No, I don't need a hat."

At 11:00 a.m., Alice returned home with several bags of groceries inside the car trunk. She walked out of the garage and along the sidewalk until she could see Duke and Jason. "I need a good man to carry the groceries into the house for me."

Duke ignored Alice and continued spading, so Jason said, "I'll carry the groceries for you, Grandma."

When Jason approached Alice, she said, "My goodness, Jason. Your clothes are completely soaked. Is your grandpa working you too hard?"

"It's definitely hard work, but it's good for me," Jason replied as reached up with his right hand and wiped beads of sweat from his forehead. "I need to lose some of this fat."

"You should be wearing a hat, Jason. I don't want you to have a heatstroke." Alice hollered at Duke, "You should give Jason one of your hats to wear, Duke."

"He didn't want one when I asked him earlier," grumbled Duke.

"Well, he wants one now," Alice snapped.

Duke straightened up and said, "I'll go inside and get a hat for him. I need a break anyway." Duke checked the time and saw his wristwatch displaying 11:10 a.m. As he walked toward the porch door, he thought, *I wonder if Mary has checked into the rehab center.* Duke entered the 3-season porch and slipped off his rubber garden boots. Then, he went into the rear bedroom and found a baseball cap. Duke jammed the cap into his rear left pocket as he walked into the kitchen. He poured a cup of hot coffee and carefully carried it onto the porch where he sat down in his wicker chair. He lit a cigarette and watched as Jason made several trips carrying the groceries from the garage into the kitchen. When Jason carried the last bag of groceries into the house, he set them upon the kitchen floor, and immediately returned outside. As Jason walked past the 3-season porch on his way to the garden, Duke said, "I have a baseball cap for you, Jason."

Jason entered the porch and took the baseball cap from Duke. He put it on and said, "I'll start spading again, Grandpa."

"Did you drink some water while you were in the kitchen?"

"I drank three glasses of water."

"That's good," replied Duke as he watched Jason exit the porch. "You need to drink plenty of liquid on these hot summer days. I don't want you to suffer a heatstroke."

Duke finished his coffee ten minutes later and headed for the garden to help Jason. Duke watched as Jason nearly fell to his knees when he turned over a spadeful of dirt. "Doggone, Jason. Is your back hurting, or something? You were practically on your knees a second ago. You'd better take a break and let me spade for a while."

Jason wiped the sweat from his forehead as he tried to stand up straight. "My back hurts a lot, and so do my hands. I have at least two blisters on each hand."

"Do you want me to get you a pair of gloves? I never wear gloves, because I get more blisters with gloves than without them."

"I guess I won't wear any, either," replied Jason as he stood straight and handed the spade to Duke.

Chapter 9

As Duke reluctantly rammed the garden spade into the ground at 11:30 a.m. Monday, June 6, Larry and Mary walked through the front doorway opening of the rehab center in Redwood City. The receptionist logged Mary's name into the registration book at 9:31 a.m., and then informed a rehab supervisor that Mary had arrived. Greta, a very attractive forty-year-old with shoulder length, straight brown hair, arrived at the front desk and introduced herself to Mary and Larry. Then, Greta said, "I have a few pages of rules and regulations for you to read and sign, Mary." Greta turned to Larry and whispered, "You can go ahead and leave, Larry. We'll take good care of Mary."

"Okay," replied Larry as he straightened his pink necktie. He put his hand on Mary's shoulder and said, "Take care, my dear. I will talk with you later."

As Larry walked toward the front exit door, Greta said, "Okay, Mary. Let's sit down at my desk and you can read and sign the paperwork. Then, you must pay the required amount for a one-month stay at this rehab center."

Thirty minutes later, Greta led Mary along a hallway until they stopped at a door labeled 105. Greta took hold of the brass-plated doorknob and said, "This is the door to your bedroom for the next month, Mary, unless you decide to leave before your month is finished. Let's go in and I'll introduce you to your roommate."

"Well! I certainly did not realize I would have to share a room," snapped Mary as she scowled at Greta.

Greta opened the door and walked into the room. Mary followed Greta into the room, and saw a beautiful African American woman sitting on the edge of a twin-size bed. She appeared to be in her early forties with short, tightly-curled, black hair, and dark brown eyes. Greta approached the woman and said, "Hello, Keisha. This is Mary, your new roommate."

Keisha stood up as she looked at Mary and said, "Hello, Mary."

"Hello, Keisha," replied Mary nervously while whisking several strands of blonde hair to the side of her forehead.

Greta walked across the room to a vacant twin-size bed. "Put your suitcase upon this bed, Mary. I need to search through your suitcase and personal items to make sure you didn't bring anything you're not supposed to have with you."

Mary put the suitcase on the bed, opened it, and said, "It's all yours, Greta."

Greta carefully inspected each item of clothing, and then inspected the suitcase pockets. She removed a pill bottle from one of them, read the prescription label, and then removed the bottle cap. "Hmm!" Greta said while looking suspiciously at Mary. Greta carefully inspected one of the capsules. "This bottle label reads that these are penicillin pills, but they are definitely pain pills. I'll have to confiscate these."

With much disappointment in her voice, Mary said, "I must have put those pills in the wrong bottle."

Greta put the pill bottle into her pocket and asked, "Do you have any other drugs with you?"

"No," Mary replied while clutching her purse tightly.

Greta stared into Mary's eyes. "Okay, Mary. Please give me your purse."

Mary reluctantly handed the purse to Greta. As Greta opened the purse, she asked, "Do you have a cell phone with you?"

"It is inside the purse."

Greta emptied the purse contents upon the bed and inspected each item. Then, she carefully inspected each purse pocket. Greta put Mary's cell phone into her pocket.

"Why are you taking my cell phone?" asked Mary.

"If you want to phone anybody, you will have to use the phone located on the wall near the front desk. We monitor and record all phone conversations."

Greta pointed toward the bathroom and said, "Okay, Mary. Let's go into the bathroom. I want you to undress, so I can make sure you do not have anything else that you should not have with you."

"I did not realize I would be treated this way," Mary whined. "This is worse than what I have heard about prisons."

"I don't know what to tell you, Mary. After all, you signed the papers to enter this rehab center, and those papers listed all the rules and regulations accurately. I am only doing what is needed to help you overcome your drug problem."

Keisha suddenly offered, "You might enjoy receiving a body search, Mary. It isn't so bad."

Mary glanced nastily toward Keisha, and then walked toward the bathroom. Greta followed Mary, and after they entered the bathroom, Greta closed the door. She reached into her pocket and pulled out a pair of rubber gloves and a tube of KY. Greta put on the rubber gloves and said, "Okay, Mary. Remove all you clothes."

Alice went outside at 11:55 a.m. and informed Duke and

Jason she had lunch ready. It took Duke about five minutes before he could stand up straight. Jason had almost as much trouble straightening up. Duke said, "Well, Jason. I think we'll finish spading this plot by about 3:00 p.m. We'd better listen to the weather report during lunch. It wouldn't surprise me if it rains tonight. It's so doggone humid today."

"Will we be able to work in the garden tomorrow if it rains tonight?" asked Jason as he walked toward the porch door.

"Nope," Duke replied. "It'll be too muddy."

As they entered the porch, Duke said, "Make sure you remove your shoes; otherwise, you will receive holy heck from your grandma. She becomes very upset if her ol' oak floors get any scratches in them. I should get more upset than I do, because I'm the one who would have to refinish the floors."

After Duke and Jason washed up, Jason sat down at the dining room table. Duke went into the living room and turned on the TV. After selecting the weather channel, he returned to the dining room and sat down at the table. Alice walked out of the kitchen and into the dining room. "I made two fried egg sandwiches for each of you," Alice said as she sat down at the table. "I hope that's enough to fill your stomachs until supper. We should grill something for supper, Duke."

"We?" Duke said. "I'm usually the one who does all the outside grilling."

Alice grinned as she picked up a glass pitcher three-fourths full of freshly squeezed lemonade and poured some into all three glasses. Then, she said, "It's good for you to cook once in a while. I do most of it, so you shouldn't complain too much."

Jason smiled as he looked downward so that Alice and Duke would not see his face. He thought, *I get a kick out of listening to Grandpa and Grandma quibbling back and forth. They're funny.* As Jason took a bite of his sandwich, Duke grinned as he looked at Alice and asked, "What do you want me to grill for supper tonight?"

"I bought some ground round when I went shopping this morning. I'll make some hamburger patties. You can grill those."

"Okay, my dear."

Duke and Jason returned to the garden plot at 1:00 p.m. "Let's work extra hard this afternoon, Jason. When we finish spading this plot, I want to rake it smooth and spread some fertilizer on it. It's supposed to rain tonight. Do you want to spade a row first, or should I?"

"I'll spade a row," Jason replied as he grabbed the spade.

Just as Jason began spading, Duke heard Janice, the next-door neighbor, say, "Hello, Duke."

Duke looked easterly and above the six-foot tall, wooden privacy fence. He saw Janice looking over the privacy fence while standing on her treated-wood deck. "Well, hello there, Janice." How are you this fine day?"

"I'm great. Thank you for asking."

"Thanks a lot for checking our house and watering the plants while we were gone," offered Duke as he removed his straw hat and wiped the sweat from his head.

"You're welcome, Duke," replied Janice as she quickly reached up with her right hand and shooed away a bumblebee hovering near her shoulder-length, wavy, gray hair. "It appears as if you have a good helper today."

Duke said, "Jason. Let's walk over to the fence and I'll introduce you to the neighbor lady."

Jason followed Duke to a two-foot tall cement bench centered below an eight-foot tall rose arbor and against the privacy fence. Duke stepped onto the bench and looked over the fence. Jason stepped onto the bench and stood next to Duke. Then, Duke said, "Janice, this is Jason, our grandson. He is spending the summer with us."

"Hello, Jason," replied Janice while smiling. "It's nice to meet you. How old are you?"

"It's nice meeting you," replied Jason. "I'm sixteen."

"Well, that's a nice age. I wish I were still sixteen." Janice swatted a mosquito that landed on her arm. "It seems as if there are a lot of mosquitoes this summer. Well, Jason. I'm sure your grandpa will keep you busy all summer."

"Yeah. Grandpa is going to teach me how to drive."

"That should be fun for you, Jason," replied Janice. "Well, I should let you two get back to work, so I'll talk with you later."

Jason jumped off the bench and returned to the garden plot. Duke said, "We'll talk with you later, Janice. Have a nice day." Duke grasped one of the 2"x4" vertical arbor supports as he carefully stepped down from the bench. He thought, *It would sure be nice to be young again. Well, maybe as far as the fitness part of it.*

Duke and Jason finished spading at 2:45 p.m., so Duke said, "Let's get the fertilizer and the garden rake from the garage, so we can finish this garden plot. I'm getting very thirsty. I could drink the heck out of cold beer."

"Do you want me to get a can of beer for you, Grandpa?"

"No. We'll finish raking and fertilizing before I drink a beer."

Just as Duke and Jason were entering the garage, Alice exited through the side door opening of the house and said, "I'm going over to Janice's house for a little while."

"Okay," replied Duke. "Don't forget to get our spare house key from her."

As Duke looked for the garden fertilizer, Jason looked at Duke's S-10. "This is really a nice truck, Grandpa. Are you going to let me drive it someday?"

Duke snickered as he removed a bag of fertilizer from inside a five-gallon pail. "I might let you drive it." Duke headed for the small door while saying, "Grab that garden rake off the wall hook. We'll finish our garden project."

"I see three rakes hanging here, Grandpa. Is it this heavy steel one?"

Duke grinned and said, "Yeah. Those plastic-tined rakes are for raking leaves. Bring the steel rake."

After an hour of raking, Duke scattered the correct amount of 10-10-10 fertilizer upon most the garden plot. Jason asked, "Why didn't you fertilize the south end of the garden?"

"That's where we'll plant the pepper plants. We'll fertilize them after they form peppers. If you fertilize them before that, they won't produce many peppers."

Duke and Jason returned the garden tools and fertilizer into the garage, exited the garage, and then walked along the sidewalk toward the 3-season porch. When Duke opened the porch door, he removed his straw hat and said, "I could sure drink a cold beer."

Duke removed his rubber garden boots as Jason said, "I'll get a can of beer for you as soon as I remove my shoes. You should sit down and rest for a little while, Grandpa. You look very tired."

Duke looked at Jason and said, "You look pretty tired, too. You'd better get yourself a soda and sit out here with me for a while."

"Okay, Grandpa," said Jason as he walked through the French doorway opening located between the porch and dining room. "I'll be right back."

Alice walked past the corner of the house and opened the porch door just as Jason returned to the porch. Alice looked at Duke and asked, "Did you decide to quit working for the day?"

Jason handed Duke a cold can of beer, so Duke quickly popped open the lid tab and replied, "Yes, dear. The garden plot is ready for planting."

"You look as if you are worn-out, Duke," remarked Alice as she walked past him on her way into the dining room.

Duke gulped down some beer before replying, "I feel like I've been ridden hard and put away wet." Duke removed a cigarette from the pack inside his T-shirt pocket.

Jason sat down and said, "I feel worn-out, too, Grandpa. Every part of my body aches."

Alice leaned against the side of the French doorway opening, looked at Duke, and asked, "When are you going to fire up the grill, Duke?"

Duke lit the cigarette and inhaled a huge amount of smoke. He glanced at his wristwatch and saw it displaying 4:15 p.m. Duke blew a huge smoke ring into the air, and then said, "I'll fire up the grill in about fifteen minutes. I don't even know if there is enough propane left in the grill tank, but we'll give it a shot."

"I'll make the hamburger patties," replied Alice. "Do you both want lettuce salads to go with your hamburgers?"

"I want some pork and beans, and some barbequed potato chips," Duke said. "A pure American meal is what I want."

"How about you, Jason?" asked Alice.

"I'll have the same as Grandpa."

"Okay," replied Alice as she turned and walked toward the kitchen.

Duke, Alice, and Jason finished eating an all-American supper at 6:30 p.m. Duke scooted his chair away from the table, stood up, and said, "You should take your shower, now, Jason. When you finish yours, I'll take one."

Alice cleared her throat a little and looked at Jason. "Are you homesick, Jason? You have been very quiet this evening."

"Yeah. I'm a little homesick," replied Jason as he slid his chair away from the table. He stood up and said, "I'm worried about Mom and Dad, especially Mom."

"Your mother will be okay," replied Alice as she snapped shut the ketchup bottle lid. "She will probably phone you one of these days."

Duke walked out of the dining room and onto the porch where he looked through the Jalousie windows at the sky. "The doggone sky is really getting cloudy. We'll probably get a nasty storm tonight."

Alice looked through the French doorway opening at Duke and said, "I thought we could go for a short walk before you shower."

"Not tonight. I have already had enough exercise for one day. I'm sure Jason feels the same way."

"Yeah, Grandma. I'm really tired. I just want to take a shower and go to bed."

Alice stood up and began gathering plates from the table while replying, "Well, I guess I'll let you two skip out on a walk with me, since you both worked so hard today."

By 9:00 p.m. Monday, Duke, Alice, and Jason had taken showers and dressed in their comfortable evening clothes. They congregated on the 3-season porch to relax for a while before bedtime. Duke looked through the westerly Jalousie windows and said, "Some of those doggone clouds are really getting black. I'm sure we'll receive some rain tonight."

"I'm going to take Jason shopping for some clothes tomorrow," Alice offered. "He needs some work clothes."

"That's for sure, Grandma. Most of my clothes are

dress clothes."

Duke took a sip of coffee, swallowed, and said, "If you are both going shopping tomorrow, I'll deliver those guardianship papers to our attorney. Maybe, he will be able to convince a judge to approve them, so we don't have to attend any hearings."

"That would be nice," replied Alice. "It might save us some money, too. Those courts charge for every little thing they do."

"That's for sure," replied Duke as he saw a bright flash of lightning streaking downward from the distant southwestern sky. Seconds later, they heard crackling thunder. "We'd better go inside," said Duke as he jumped out of his chair. "This porch isn't very safe during a lightning storm."

Jason stood up and said, "I'm going to bed. I'll see you both in the morning."

"I'll wake you if I hear any sirens blaring tonight," Duke said. "I listened to the weather news a little while ago, and heard that we are under a tornado watch."

"Okay," replied Jason.

Alice and Duke undressed and crawled into bed at 10:00 p.m. Duke said, "I should have turned on the window air conditioner earlier. It's really hot up here."

"Do you want to make it a little hotter?" asked Alice as she reached over and put her left hand upon Duke's right knee. She slid her left hand slowly toward his groin. "You could switch on the ceiling fan."

Duke squirmed around a little and said, "I felt very tired earlier, but I suddenly feel an abundance of energy returning to my ol' body."

Alice whispered, "We'll have to be quiet, so Jason doesn't hear us."

Twenty minutes later, Duke whispered, "That was super good, Alice. I guess we can still make love pretty darn good."

"Yes. It was tremendously satisfying," whispered Alice.

Alice snuggled against Duke and kissed him on the lips. As their lips separated, they saw flashes of light and heard crackling thunder from several nearby lighting strikes. Duke rolled out of bed and quickly closed all four double-hung bedroom windows. The high winds and heavy rain began a minute later. Then, they heard the weather-radio siren activate, followed by a tornado warning alert. Seconds later, they heard the local warning sirens blaring, so Duke said, "Shit. It sounds like the wind is gusting to at least 50 mph. Let's wake Jason and head for the basement."

Duke, Alice, and Jason spent an hour in the basement while waiting for the tornado warning to end. Duke paced back and forth along a route between the west end of the basement and the east end of the basement during most the hour, while Jason and Alice hovered directly under the basement stairway. Duke heard the all clear broadcast on his basement radio at 11:30 p.m., so they returned to their beds. Jason fell asleep within minutes. Duke and Alice snuggled against each other while talking for a while. They did not fall asleep until a few minutes before midnight.

Dressed with only a pink, silk nightgown, Mary crawled onto her assigned twin-sized bed at 10:00 p.m. Monday while Keisha sat down on the edge of her bed and began undressing. After undressing, Keisha looked across the dimly lit room at Mary, "Sleep tight, Mary. Sweet dreams."

"Good night, Keisha," Mary replied as she rolled onto her left side to face away from Keisha.

Mary felt uncomfortable sleeping in a room with a complete stranger, so she lay silently while thinking about Jason. She also thought about Calvin being in jail, and wondered what kind of prison sentence he would receive. Mary finally drifted into a deep sleep at 11:30 p.m. An hour later, she felt the mattress move a little. When she opened her eyes and rolled over, she saw the dark image of a woman sitting on the edge of the bed. Then, she heard Keisha whisper, “Do you care if I lie next to you and hug you? I feel so lonely.”

Still half asleep, Mary whispered, “I suppose that will be okay, as long as that is all you do.”

Keisha flopped down onto her side so that she faced Mary. Then, she wrapped her arms around Mary and snuggled against her. “You smell so nice, Mary. What kind of perfume did you put on?”

“I did not put on perfume. It must be the scent from my liquid bath soap.”

“Are you married, Keisha?” whispered Mary as she began lightly rubbing Keisha’s shoulders.

“No, I’ve never married. I dated several men during my early twenties, and even had sex with several of them. I never enjoyed the sex; actually, I found it repulsive. Eventually, I began attending some drug parties, and during one of the parties, I took some kind of pill that made me feel high as a kite. I had sex with another woman during my drug high. That woman gave me the greatest sexual experience I had ever had with anyone. From that time on, I had sex with many different women; of course, I continued taking drugs, too. I guess that’s why I’m here. Did you ever try making out with another woman?”

“I spent some time in bed with a woman and a man a while back, but I did not do anything with the woman. I was married for several years, up until my divorce became final several days ago. I have a 16-year-old son, but he is now living with my parents in Iowa. I plan to move there as soon as possible.”

Keisha’s hands eventually found their way inside Mary’s silk nightgown and to her breasts. Keisha whispered, “You should try making love with a woman.

You might find that a woman can make you feel much more loved."

Mary replied, "I want you to leave me alone, now. I need to get some sleep."

"Okay," replied Keisha as she crawled off Mary's bed, "but let me know if you ever want a sexual experience with me. I promise to give you the best sexual satisfaction you have ever experienced."

"I'll think about it," replied Mary. "Good night."

As Keisha sat down on her bed, she said, "Thanks for letting me hug you. I don't feel so lonely, now. Good night."

When Duke awoke Tuesday morning, he found Alice's side of the bed vacant. He looked at the clock and saw it displaying 7:05 a.m. *This is the latest I've slept for ages*, he thought as he scooted to the side of the bed and sat up. When he reached down to get his jeans from the gray-painted wooden floor, he felt several pains traveling through his nerves and muscles. *My ol' body aches all over this morning*, he thought as he pulled his jeans on. Duke looked toward the east windows and saw raindrops splattering against them. After applying underarm deodorant, Duke put on a maroon pocket T-shirt and went downstairs. As he walked through the dining room on his way to the bathroom, he heard Alice in the kitchen, and said, "Good morning, Alice."

"Good morning, my dear," she replied as she poured a cup of coffee for Duke.

Duke entered the living room and glanced through a couple of the front double-hung windows. He saw many small, broken tree branches scattered upon the front lawn. Then, he went into the hallway and knocked several times on Jason's bedroom door. He heard no reply, so he loudly said, "It's time to rise and shine, Jason."

"I'm awake, Grandpa. I'll be out in a minute."

Duke removed a can of shave cream and a new safety

razor from inside the hallway cabinet before entering the bathroom. He finished shaving fifteen minutes later and exited the bathroom, just when Jason exited his bedroom. As they nearly collided in the hallway, Duke smiled and said, "Geez, Jason. It sure took you a while to get out of bed."

Jason rubbed the sleepiness from his eyes and replied, "I know, Grandpa. My body is so painful and stiff this morning."

As Jason entered the bathroom, Duke said, "You'll feel better after you eat a good breakfast." Duke put away the razor and shave cream before heading for the kitchen.

Alice handed a cup of reheated coffee to Duke and said, "I'm making pancakes for breakfast. You may as well sit on the porch until breakfast is ready."

Duke carefully carried the cup of coffee to the 3-season porch and sat down in his wicker chair. He looked through the west Jalousie windows at the rain gauge attached to the west privacy fence and squinted as he tried to read it. He finally stood up, walked over to the door, and opened it a crack. He peered through the opening at the rain gauge and saw it registering one inch of rain. *That should be enough to settle the garden dirt*, he thought. *We should be able to plant the seedlings in a few days, if it quits raining.* Jason entered the porch as Duke returned to his wicker chair and sat down.

"Is it supposed to rain all day?" asked Jason as he sat down in a wicker chair.

Duke lit a cigarette and said, "I don't know for sure, Jason. The sky is becoming partly cloudy, so it'll probably stop raining pretty soon. We should be able to plant the seedlings in a few days."

"Grandma said that she will take me shopping for some work clothes at Crossroads Mall this morning. I hope I can get some pocket T-shirts like you wear."

"Yeah. I like my pocket T-shirts," Duke replied just after he blew a smoke ring into the air.

Alice walked through the French doorway opening and onto the porch. She put her hand upon Duke's right shoulder and said, "So, Duke. What are you going to do while Jason and I are shopping?"

"Well, I will call our attorney, and after that, I will go to our bank and open a new account so I can deposit the money Mary sent home with us. If you get home early enough, I'll take Jason out to the Department of Motor Vehicles so he can get a driver's manual to study for his driver's permit."

Alice rubbed Duke's shoulder lightly as she replied, "The DMV is located in Crossroads Mall. We can pick up a manual while we're there. We'll be home by noon."

"Great," replied Duke. "Jason and I will go outside this afternoon and pick up all the tree branches and twigs. That strong wind last night really did a number on all the trees, especially our white birch clump. There are many small tree branches and twigs scattered all over our and Janice's front yard. Is breakfast almost ready?"

"Yes," Alice replied as she turned and headed for the kitchen. "You two may as well sit down at the table. All the pancakes should be ready by this time."

By eleven o'clock, the sky had cleared and the temperature had reached eighty degrees. Duke had opened a new bank account, and delivered the guardianship papers to the attorney. After checking for aphids on all twenty-five rose bushes located along the backyard privacy fence, and next to the 3-season porch, Duke sat on the wooden garden bench located against the west privacy fence. *I should spray the rose bushes one of these days*, thought Duke while staring at the nearest rose bush. *I didn't see any aphids, but some of the bushes have black spot disease.* Duke saw Janice standing on her deck, so he hollered, "Hi,

Janice. Jason and I will pick up all those sticks lying on your front yard."

Janice looked over the fence at Duke and replied, "Well, thank you, Duke. I wanted to pick them up, but my back is bothering me something terrible."

"Jason will need something to keep him busy this afternoon. Teenagers always have abundant energy."

Janice laughed and said, "Yes, Duke. My husband and I raised seven kids, so I know all about teenagers. I have a doctor's appointment at 11:30 a.m., so I'd better get going. I'll see you later."

"Take care, Janice." Duke remained seated on the garden bench and thought about several things while staring at all the different plants in the backyard. Then at 11:45 a.m., he heard the overhead garage door slowly opening.

When Alice and Jason exited the garage through the small doorway opening, Jason saw Duke and said, "Grandma bought some T-shirts for me. They're just like the ones you wear."

"That's nice," replied Duke. "Did you get a driver's manual, so you can study for your driver's permit?"

"Yeah. We did that when we first arrived at the mall. I can't believe how friendly everybody is around here. They're much friendlier than the people in Redwood City."

"Most people in Waterfield are friendly."

Alice approached Duke and said, "I'll make some ham-and-cheese sandwiches for lunch. Did you get everything taken care of this morning?"

"Yeah. I sure did," replied Duke as he stood up and followed Alice and Jason into the 3-season porch.

Duke, Alice, and Jason finished eating lunch at 1:00 p.m., so Duke said, "Let's go outside and pick up all those sticks, Jason."

Alice butted in and said, "I'll be leaving for the church

before much longer. My bible study class begins at 2:00 p.m. I imagine when that's over, we churchwomen will sit around and visit for a while. I probably won't be home until about 5:00 p.m., so supper might be a little late."

"That's fine, Alice," replied Duke as he looked into Alice's brown eyes and grinned from ear to ear. "Don't gossip too much. Enjoy yourself."

"Oh, Duke. You know I don't gossip."

"Right," replied Duke as he headed for the porch door.

Jason quickly followed Duke and said, "I can pick up all the sticks, Grandpa, if you'll show me where to put them. You can sit on the front stoop and relax."

"Well, you need to get that blue yard-waste cart out of the garage and roll it to the front yard. You can put all the branches and twigs from our yard into the cart. I told Janice that we will clean up her front yard, too, but we'll put those branches and twigs into her blue yard-waste cart. You'll find her cart located behind her garage."

Duke and Jason went into the garage where Duke took a plastic-tine rake from the wall hook. Jason rolled the large blue cart through the open doorway and pulled the cart behind him while walking toward the front yard. Duke grabbed a pair of pruning shears before following Jason. When they reached the front yard, Duke handed the rake and pruning shears to Jason as he said, "You'll have to cut up some of those large branches. It might be easier if you pick up all the large branches first, and then rake all the small twigs into piles."

Duke sat on the front stoop while Jason raked and picked up sticks. When Jason finished cleaning up Duke's front yard, he said, "I'll get Janice's cart, now."

"I'll sit right here and watch you," Duke replied as he swatted a mosquito that had begun sucking blood out of his left forearm. *Goddamned mosquitoes*, he thought as he lit a cigarette. *Maybe the smoke will drive them away.*

Jason rolled Janice's cart onto her front yard and began raking twigs into piles. A little while later, two teenage girls, both with long, blonde hair, and both wearing swimming suits, stopped on the city sidewalk near Jason and watched him drop some twigs into the yard cart. Duke saw the girls and grinned as the oldest girl looked at Jason and said, "Hello. What's your name?"

Jason blushed slightly while replying, "Jason. What's your name?"

"My name is Jo Ann and this is Monica, my sister. We're on our way to the swimming pool." Jo Ann pointed east and said, "We live about a block east of here, in that light-green, two-story house."

Duke thought, *Jo Ann appears to have a bit of a weight problem, kind of like Jason. She is sure a pretty gal.*

As Jason reached down to pick up some more sticks, JoAnn asked, "Are you new to the neighborhood? I haven't seen you around here before."

Jason dropped some sticks into the cart and replied, "Yes. I'm staying with my grandparents this summer. I moved here from California."

Jo Ann and Monica began walking west as Jo Ann said, "We'll see you later, Jason. Don't work too hard."

"Okay," Jason replied. "I'm glad I met you and Monica."

As Jo Ann and Monica passed in front of Duke, they each said, "Hello."

"Hi there, girls," replied Duke. "Going swimming, huh?"

The girls did not hear Duke, so they kept walking without replying. Jason finished picking up the sticks, and rolled Janice's cart back to its previous location behind the garage. When he returned to the front yard, he approached Duke and asked, "Do you know those girls?"

"I've seen them a few times with their parents at

church. Their stepfather is a Waterfield police officer and their mother is a social worker." Duke stood up and said, "Let's put our tools and cart in the garage, and then we'll jump into the S-10 and take a ride downtown to the bait shop. I'll buy a fishing license for you. When we get back home, we'll fertilize the lawn. The first thing tomorrow morning, we'll go to the lake and fish for a few hours. How does that sound to you?"

"I've never tried fishing, but I think I will enjoy it. Do you have an extra fishing pole I can use?"

"Yeah. I have three fishing poles, three reels, and plenty of fishing tackle."

Chapter 10

When Duke and Jason finished fertilizing the lawn Tuesday, June 7, Duke glanced at his wristwatch and saw it displaying 3:30 p.m. "Gee whiz, Jason. It's thirty minutes past my normal beer time. Let's sit on the porch and talk for a while before supper."

"That sounds good to me," Jason replied. "I need to sit down and rest for a while. I'm about worn-out."

Duke headed for the porch while thinking, *It's hard for me to believe a sixteen-year-old kid can be so worn-out after such an easy day.*

Duke and Jason entered the 3-season porch and removed their shoes. "Do you want a cold beer, Grandpa?" asked Jason as he wiped some sweat from his forehead.

"Darn straight, Jason."

"I'll go into the basement and get one for you."

Jason returned a few minutes later and handed a cold can of beer to Duke. Jason sat down in the wicker chair and popped open the soda can lid tab. Duke popped open the beer can lid tab, swallowed a huge amount of beer, and said, "Boy. That really hits the spot. I am thirstier than somebody burning in Hell."

Jason laughed as he tried to swallow a mouthful of soda without gagging. He looked at Duke and asked, "How long have you had those tattoos on your arms?"

Duke pointed to his left forearm. "I did this small tattoo myself when I was about fifteen years old, so I've had it for a long time. Duke turned just enough so that Jason could see the tattoo on his right biceps. I went to a tattoo shop located downtown a few years ago and hired an artist to tattoo this set of dolphins on me. He charged me fifty bucks, but he touched up the small one on my left arm after he finished the dolphins."

"I saw a large set of dolphins attached to a wooden plaque aboard the *USS Pampanito* when we toured it in San Francisco."

Duke pointed to the middle of the dolphins tattoo and said, "If you look carefully, you can see what looks like a submarine in the middle of this tattoo, and then on each side of the submarine, you can see a dolphin. When submariners become qualified, they receive a set of sterling silver dolphins to wear on their uniforms."

"Does it hurt very much when you get a tattoo?"

"Not much. It burns a little, kind of like getting cut with a red hot knife."

"Is it difficult to get accepted for submarine school?" asked Jason as he continued inspecting the dolphins tattoo on Duke's biceps.

"Well first of all, I had to volunteer for submarine duty. Then, I had to go through another physical exam given by two physicians. After that, I had to talk with a psychiatrist, but he asked me only two questions. The following day, an instructor and a doctor took a group of us into a pressure chamber. As I recall, there were about eight students in the group. The instructor sealed the chamber and began bleeding air pressure into it, with the intent of pressurizing it until the pressure equaled the pressure at 400 feet of water depth. Since the pressure at 100 feet of depth is 44.5 pounds per square inch, the pressure at 400 feet of depth is 178 pounds per square inch. It felt very eerie as the pressure began building. The chamber became somewhat foggy, and I could feel intense pain building in my eardrums. I raised my hand when the pressure reached about 90 psi, because I couldn't stand the excruciating pain any longer. They stopped the test and let me leave the pressure chamber. A doctor immediately checked my eardrums and said that both had nearly ruptured. The reason my eardrums wouldn't equalize was because I had a cold at the time. Another student had the same problem with his eardrums, so he came out of the chamber a short time after I left the chamber. I went back to re-test a week later, and passed it with no problems. It's kind of weird in that pressure chamber, because when you're under so much pressure and somebody talks, their voice sounds just like Donald Duck's voice."

"That pressure chamber test sounds scary to me," Jason said as he leaned back in the chair. He swallowed some more soda before saying, "Tell me some more, Grandpa. It's interesting to hear about your experiences."

Duke swallowed some more beer before continuing, "After we passed the pressure test, we had to make buoyant ascents inside a water tower. That scared me half to death."

"How do you make a buoyant ascent?"

Duke tipped up his beer can and swallowed the rest of the beer before saying, "I'd better get another beer. This one's gone."

Jason quickly stood up and said, "I'll get one for you. Will you tell me about the buoyant ascents when I get back?"

"Sure, Jason," replied Duke as he snuffed out a cigarette and began nervously tapping the glass top of the wicker table with the tips of his left fingers.

Jason returned two minutes later and handed Duke a

cold can of beer. As Jason sat down in the wicker chair, Duke popped open the lid tab and said, "Thanks, Jason."

"So, Grandpa. Tell me more about the buoyant ascents."

"Well, we entered a room located at the top of a cylindrical-shaped water tower where we stood on a deck surrounding the water surface. If I remember correctly, the water surface diameter is about eighteen feet, and the water depth in that tower is 100 feet. First of all, the instructors explained the buoyant ascent process. What it amounts to, is that you have to inhale as much air as you can, and then blow out as much as you can. Then, you repeat it three or four times, kind of like hyperventilating. After you inhale deeply the last time, you hold your breath and enter the water. Then, you stand at attention, keep your hands to your sides, tilt your head back, and ascend slowly toward the surface while blowing out air. It is very important to blow out air as you ascend, because if you don't, your lungs will explode. You have to remember that when you do a buoyant ascent, the air you inhale is compressed air, so as you ascend toward the surface, the air in your lungs expands as the water pressure gets less and less. The whole idea of the buoyant ascent test is so that we knew how to make an ascent from a disabled, submerged submarine. Does that make sense to you, Jason?"

"Yeah, Grandpa. I understand what you've told me so far."

Duke lit a cigarette and continued, "I'm glad it makes sense to you. Okay, we are still in the room at the top of the tower, so we had to jump into the water and practice a few ascents. We had to hold our breath, pull ourselves down a ladder until we were about 8 feet underwater, and then assumed the buoyant ascent position. Then, we ascended slowly to the surface while continuously blowing out air. The divers watched each one of us to see if we did it correctly. Mostly, they watched for air bubbles to make sure we blew out air continuously while ascending to the surface. I didn't blow continuously the first time, so the diver told me that I'd better blow out air better than that when I did the actual test, otherwise he would hold me underwater for a while. He said he could stay underwater longer than I could, because he would have on his oxygen tanks and scuba gear. That kind of scared me."

Duke stopped talking long enough to inhale some smoke. After he blew a smoke ring into the air, he swallowed a little beer. "What do you think so far, Jason?"

"I want to hear more of the story."

"Well, after we passed our practice sessions, we walked down several flights of steps that lead to a chamber attached to the outside of the water tower. The instructors assigned us into several groups of eight students each. I ended up in the first group of eight, so we put on inflatable life jackets and entered the chamber where we quickly lined up along the curved interior walls. The instructor closed and sealed the watertight entrance hatch. He began flooding the chamber with water while bleeding compressed air into the chamber. A watertight hatch separated the chamber from the tower.

When the water level inside the chamber reached the same level as the top of the hatch door, he stopped flooding the chamber. By then, the water level in the chamber reached up to my chin. A small watertight light attached to the ceiling provided light, but it was very dim and foggy in the chamber, very eerie feeling. When the pressure inside the chamber equaled the pressure inside the water tower, the instructor opened the watertight hatch door. The top of the hatch opening is 50 feet below the water surface inside the tower. The student closest to the hatch had to make the first ascent, and the rest of us were to follow him, one by one.

I was fourth in line, so I watched the first two students exit the chamber, one by one. The student right ahead of me chickened out and told the instructor that he wouldn't go into the tower. The diving instructor grabbed the student by the shoulders and shook him several times while repeatedly asking the student if he was going to make the ascent. The student repeatedly said that he wouldn't go through the open hatch, so the instructor literally shoved him through the hatch opening and into the tower. It seemed like a couple minutes elapsed before all of a sudden, the student returned through the open hatch and popped up through the water surface in the chamber. A diver had held him inside the tower, and then eventually pushed him back through the open hatch. The student's eyes appeared as big as saucers and he acted very panicky. I thought the poor guy would die, because he kept gagging and gulping for air.

The diving instructor again shook the student several times and asked him if he was going to make an ascent. Still suffering a panic attack, the student repeatedly said that he wouldn't go into the tower, so the instructor finally told him that he was no longer eligible for submarine school, and told him to stand beside the entrance hatch. After observing all that, I felt very scared, but I stepped up to the hatch opening for my turn. The instructor put a small amount of compressed air into my inflatable lifejacket and slapped me on the shoulder. I inhaled and exhaled three times, then took a deep breath and held it. I grabbed the top of the hatch as I ducked through the hatch opening and entered the tower where I stood on a little platform while continuing my hold on the top of the hatch. I tilted my head back, released my hold, put my hands down to my sides as if I were standing at attention, and began blowing out air while slowly ascending toward the water surface 50 feet above me."

"Did you guys have flippers and masks?" Jason asked.

"Heck no, Jason. We just wore our navy-issued, skimpy, blue swimming trunks," replied Duke as he snuffed out his cigarette.

Just then, they heard Janice say, "Hello, over there on the porch."

Duke turned and looked through the Jalousie windows toward Janice's deck. He saw her looking over the privacy fence, so he said, "Hello, Janice."

"I have some freshly baked brownies for you," she said while holding a small plastic food container high enough so that Duke could see it.

"Well, thank you, Janice. Jason will be right there."

Jason quickly left the porch, and jogged to the concrete bench. He jumped onto the bench and took the container from Janice. "Thank you, Janice," he said as he jumped off the bench. "These will really taste good. I love brownies."

"Thank you for cleaning up my yard," offered Janice. "Enjoy the brownies."

Jason took the container into the kitchen and set it upon the butcher-block design, laminated countertop next to the white, cast iron sink. He quickly returned to the porch and sat down. "Continue with your story, Grandpa."

"Let's see, now, where was I?" Duke sat silently for about ten seconds before continuing, "Oh, yeah. After I ascended upwards for about 10 feet, I ran out of air. My first instinct was to swim to the surface as fast as I could, but I knew I couldn't do that because of the danger. I immediately began gagging and thought for sure I would drown. It's damned hard to breathe water. One of the diving instructors quickly wrapped his legs around my chest and squeezed hard while we slowly ascended together toward the surface. It seemed as if we would never reach the surface, but we eventually broke through. I had swallowed a lot of water, so I spit out water and gagged for air as I sat on the deck while trying to recover. Needless to say, I didn't pass the test, so I tried it again.

I did a little better on the second try, but I quit blowing out air for a second or two, at about the 25 feet level, but that was enough to fail me. Then, as several of us stood on the deck surrounding the water surface, the student who ascended a short time later, together with a diving instructor, popped through the water surface. The student appeared unconscious and blood oozed from his ears, nose, and mouth. The instructors pulled him out of the water, and a doctor quickly examined him. A couple of instructors and a doctor took the student to a pressure chamber. I guess he had the bends, or something similar to the bends. We heard later that he had survived, but I don't know if he ever again tried the test. Anyway, I couldn't try the ascent again that day because of the bloody water." Duke looked at his wristwatch and saw it displaying 4:45 p.m. "Well, I guess I have time to finish telling you a short version of the remaining story before Alice gets home."

"What happened next, Grandpa?"

"Several of us went back to the water tower a week later so we could re-test. When my turn for the ascent arrived, the instructor slapped me on the shoulder and said, 'You'll make it this time, buddy. Open your eyes and look for the mermaid on your way to the surface.' I thought he was shitting me, but as I ascended toward the water surface, I opened my eyes. Sure enough, I saw a huge picture of a beautiful mermaid on the tower wall. I passed the test that time, which made me eligible to begin eight weeks of submarine school classes. I felt extremely happy." Duke sat silently for about a minute before saying, "I'll have to admit; I thought about dropping out more than once, but I'm glad I stuck it out."

"I don't think I'm brave enough to go through all that kind of stuff, Grandpa."

"I don't know if I consider it bravery," Duke replied as he nervously shifted around in his chair, trying to find a comfortable position. "I think it's more like you have to be at least half crazy."

Jason swallowed some soda, and said, "So you finished sub school and went aboard the sub. Are you going to tell me about the qualification process, now?"

Duke glanced at his wristwatch and said, "Alice should be coming home before much longer. I guess there is time to tell you a short story version."

"We had to learn all the systems on the boat, like the fuel oil system, the compressed air system, the hydraulic system, the electrical system, and the fresh water system. We had to learn the systems good enough to draw a schematic of each one, showing all the piping, valves, switches, circuit breakers, etc. We also had to stand every watch on the boat, so that in an emergency, we knew how. Of course when we stood those watches, a qualified submariner supervised us."

"That sounds like a lot to learn."

"Yeah." Duke took a swallow of beer before continuing, "We were supposed to qualify within six months after we boarded the submarine, but it took me seven. Heck! It took me longer because I had to work so many hours in the engine room. I didn't have much time to work on my qualifications. The engineering officer restricted me to the boat for the entire seventh month, just so I would finish learning all that stuff."

"I don't think I could ever learn that much, at least not enough to be able to draw schematics of the systems."

"We were in the middle of the Atlantic Ocean on our way to Scotland when the engineering officer let me take the final exam. I passed it without any problems. A day or two after we arrived in Scotland, some of us rode on a train to Glasgow one night. That's where I drank down my dolphins. Afterwards, one of the senior crewmembers pinned a set of sterling silver dolphins onto my uniform. The next morning, the captain officially pinned a set of dolphins onto my uniform and congratulated me as a duly qualified submariner. I felt very proud when I received those dolphins. I still have a set of sterling silver ones upstairs in my dresser drawer."

"Wow, Grandpa. That's a neat story. What did you mean when you said that you drank down your dolphins?"

"Oh, I'll tell you that story sometime in the near future. Just remind me to tell you. We don't really have time right now."

Where did you guys go when you left Scotland?"

"Well, my boy. I can't tell you where we went, because it is still considered classified."

Just then, they heard Alice park the LeSabre inside the garage, so Duke said, "I'm glad Alice is back home. Maybe she'll make some supper for us. Will you please get another beer for me, Jason?"

"Sure, Grandpa," replied Jason as he stood up and headed for the basement.

Duke watched as Alice exited through the small doorway opening of the garage and strolled along the sidewalk while carrying her Holy Bible. "How did bible study go for you?" asked Duke.

"It went quite well." Alice replied while looking through the Jalousie windows and smiling at Duke. "You and Jason should have attended bible study with me. It would have done you both a lot of good."

"You think so, huh?" asked Duke just as Alice opened the porch door.

"Well, it sure wouldn't have hurt either one of you,"

replied Alice as she approached Duke. She leaned down and kissed him on the forehead just as Jason returned to the porch.

"Hi, Grandma," Jason said as he handed the cold can of beer to Duke. "I met two neighbor girls earlier this afternoon."

"Where do they live?" asked Alice.

"About a block east of here," replied Jason as he pointed toward the east. "Grandpa said that their dad is a cop and their mother is a social worker."

"Oh! I've seen those girls before. Their father died in a construction accident when the girls were very young. The mother eventually remarried, and her new husband, an African American, adopted both girls. I've talked with their mother and stepfather at church. They are a very nice couple. As I recall, his name is Otis and her name is Missy."

Duke looked at Alice and said, "Boy, Alice! You sure know a lot about our neighbors. I suppose you hear all kinds of information when you gossip with the churchwomen, huh?"

Alice smiled and replied, "Duke! You know we never gossip." Then, Alice said, "So, Jason. What else has been going on while I attended bible study?"

"Grandpa has been telling me all about his submarine qualifications."

"Really? He has never told me anything about it."

"That's because you've never asked," replied Duke as he popped open the can lid tab. "Oh! Janice baked some brownies for us. Jason put them in the kitchen."

"How nice of her," Alice replied as she walked through the French doorway opening and into the dining room. She laid her Holy Bible upon one of the steps in the stairway leading to the upstairs bedroom. "I'm going to make some spaghetti for supper. Does that sound okay to you two men?"

"I like spaghetti," replied Jason.

"That's fine with me," Duke said. "How long will it take? Are you going to put some meatballs in it? I feel like I'm starving to death."

"Supper should be ready in about a half hour," replied Alice as she looked at Duke through the open French doorway. "I don't have any meatballs. I'm going to use the spaghetti sauce I bought at the store. Can you survive for another thirty minutes without eating?"

Duke grinned from ear to ear. "I'm sure I can survive that long, Alice."

Duke took the last bite of his spaghetti at 6:30 p.m., and after chewing and swallowing, looked at Alice and said, "This spaghetti sauce you bought at the store isn't as tasty as your homemade spaghetti sauce."

"I didn't think so, either, but it's much easier and quicker," replied Alice as she half scowled at Duke and stood up.

Duke saw Jason grinning a little, so he said, "I'm quite sure your grandma could use some help with the dishes, Jason. While you help her, I'll take a shower. When you finish washing dishes, you can take your shower."

"That's fine, Grandpa. I'll help her. I want to study for my driver's permit after I take my shower."

"That's a good idea," replied Duke as he headed for the bathroom.

As Alice and Jason began washing the supper dishes, Greta searched for Mary in the rehab center. She found Mary sitting upon her bed reading some information about drug abuse. "Hello, Mary," said Greta. "You have a phone call. Larry wants to talk with you."

As Mary stood up, she glanced at her wristwatch and saw it displaying 4:45 p.m. She thought, *I wonder why Larry is calling me.* "Am I supposed to use the phone near the front desk?" asked Mary.

"Yes," replied Greta as she walked out of the room.

A minute later, Mary picked up the phone receiver and said, "Hello, this is Mary."

"Oh my god, Mary. I talked with Calvin at the jail a little while ago, and he is very mad at you. He thinks your parents persuaded you to report him to the police and that is why they arrested him. I told him that you and your parents had nothing to do with it, but he flat-out called me a liar."

"I did not report him to the police," Mary said with an agitated tone of voice. "I hope he is not too mad at me. My parents certainly did not have anything to do with Calvin's arrest."

"Calvin acted like a crazy man the entire time I talked with him. He told me that he would get even with you and your parents, even if it took him the rest of his life. Actually, he hollered throughout most of our conversation. I could not believe how nasty he behaved." Larry cleared his throat, and continued, "Two deputies finally entered the room we were in, and Calvin struggled with them while they escorted him back into his cell. His actions scared me half to death. At least Calvin hired a criminal defense attorney, so I will not have to deal with him any longer."

"I did nothing wrong," said Mary. "I cannot figure out why Calvin is so upset with me."

"All I know is he is extremely angry toward you and your parents. I hope the judge will not allow him bail at the hearing tomorrow morning, because I am afraid he might harm you. Calvin knows you are in the rehab center."

"Do you think I will be safe here if he gets out on bail?"

"I hope so, my dear Mary. If he gets out on bail, I will notify you and the rehab center manager. Perhaps, the manager will request more police presence around the rehab center."

"Okay, Larry. Were you able to list my house with a realtor?"

"No, not yet. I met with a realtor at your house earlier this afternoon, so now it is just a matter of listing it. Actually, I have been thinking about purchasing your house along with all your furniture. That is why I did not list it. Your house is so much nicer than my house. I am sure my sweetheart will like your house as much as I do."

"I would love for you to purchase my house and furnishings, Larry. That would certainly make it much simpler for me to move."

"Okay, Mary. I will discuss it with my significant other, and then phone you sometime tomorrow to let you know what we decide. I will phone you if the judge releases Calvin. Have a nice evening, Mary. Good-bye, my dear."

"Good-bye, Larry."

Mary walked along the hallway toward her room. Just as she reached for the doorknob, the door opened, and Keisha exited their room. "Are you ready to eat supper, Mary? I'm on my way to the dining room."

A tear rolled down Mary's cheek as she replied, "If you will wait a few minutes, I will go with you."

"Is something wrong, Mary?" asked Keisha sympathetically. "Why are you crying?"

"I will tell you later," replied Mary as she opened the door and walked into her room.

By 10:00 p.m., Mary and Keisha had finished taking their showers and dressed in nightgowns. They sat down on the edge of Mary's bed. Then, Keisha placed her left hand upon Mary's right shoulder and asked, "Why were you crying earlier?"

"That phone call I received this afternoon was from Larry, my lawyer friend. He informed me my ex-husband, Calvin, who is in jail for selling illegal drugs, thinks I informed the police about his involvement in the illegal drug business. Larry said that my ex has threatened to get even with me. I am very worried Calvin will come after me when he gets out of jail."

Tears formed in Mary's eyes as Keisha put her arms around Mary and said, "Do you think he would actually hurt you?"

"Yes. He enjoys physical violence as long as he is the one dishing it out."

Keisha began lightly rubbing Mary's shoulders. "I'm sure everything will be okay, Mary. Did you divorce him because of his violence toward you?"

"Not really," replied Mary as she wiped tears from her cheeks. "He stepped out on me several times, so I concluded he wanted the other women more than he wanted me. That is the main reason I divorced him."

Keisha quit rubbing Mary's shoulders and stood up. "I guess it's time for me to get some sleep, unless you want me to comfort you some more."

"I will be okay," Mary replied as she flopped onto her back upon the bed. "Thanks for listening to my problems. Good night, Keisha."

"Good night. I'll see you in the morning."

Duke, Alice, and Jason finished eating breakfast at 7:00 a.m. Wednesday. While remaining at the dining room table, Duke said, "How did your studying go last night, Jason? Do you think you'll be ready to take the driver's permit test pretty soon?"

"I'll be ready for the test in about a week," replied Jason as he slid his chair away from the table and stood up. "It won't take me very long to memorize the information in the driver's manual."

Alice stood up and said, "My goodness, Jason. You must have a photographic memory."

"Yeah, Grandma. I can usually read something once

and remember it for a long time."

Duke reached up with his right hand and scratched the top of his balding head for a few seconds before smoothing down the thick, grayish brown hair on the right side of his head. "I wish my memory was that good, Jason," said Duke as he slid back his chair and stood. "I usually have to read something at least ten times before I can remember it, and even then, I have trouble retaining it for long. Are you ready to go outside with me? We'll mix up some rose spray and spray the rose bushes. We'll go fishing afterwards."

Jason headed toward the bathroom and said, "I'll be ready as soon as I wash my hands and face."

Duke helped Alice clear the dishes and silverware off the table. When Jason exited the bathroom, Duke and Jason went outside and entered the garage. Jason quickly flipped on the fountain pump switch, and then went outside and watched as the upper fountain bowl filled with water. As Duke stood in the doorway opening watching Jason, he said, "That fountain must fascinate you, huh Jason?"

"Yeah, I think it's awesome. Do you think I should add water to the pond?"

Duke glanced at the pond and said, "It should have enough water until we return from fishing. You just have to make sure the pump is always completely submerged; otherwise, it will become completely ruined because of overheating. A pump like that costs about fifty dollars."

Thirty minutes later, Duke and Jason finished spraying all twenty-five rose bushes. They put away the sprayer, and then loaded three fishing poles and the tackle box into the S-10 pickup bed. Duke said, "Maybe you should tell your grandma that we are leaving for our little fishing excursion."

Jason bolted toward the small garage door opening

and said, "I'll tell her, Grandpa."

A few minutes later, Duke and Jason crawled into the S-10 and left for the lake. Just as Duke steered the S-10 from the alley and onto the street, Jason asked, "Will you show me where Jo Ann and Monica went swimming yesterday? Is that swimming pool near here?"

Duke grinned a little and said, "It's just a couple blocks from here, at Byron Park. I'll drive by there so you can see it. Do you like to swim, Jason?"

"Yeah. I wouldn't mind going one of these days. Maybe, I would see Jo Ann and Monica at the pool. Jo Ann is sure pretty, and she is so nice."

"Do you have a swimming suit?"

"No. I'll have to buy one."

"Well, you should ask your grandma if she will take you shopping when we return home."

Duke pointed out the swimming pool to Jason as they rode slowly through Byron Park. Ten minutes later, Duke parked the S-10 upon a gravel-surfaced parking lot located at the south end of Britt Lake. As Jason opened the door, he asked, "Is this a natural lake, Grandpa?"

"Nope. When the State of Iowa built new Hwy. 63 back in the 1960s, they used this site for a borrow area to obtain enough dirt for the highway. Somebody told me that this lake is spring fed, but I don't really know if that is true. There's a walking trail surrounding this lake, so let's grab our fishing gear and we'll walk to the other end of the lake. There is a gentle south breeze today, so the waves will be lapping softly against the north shoreline."

It took Duke and Jason about ten minutes of walking along the easterly trail until they reached the north end of the lake. After thirty minutes of Duke schooling Jason on the fine art of fishing, Jason formed a ball of stink bait on his hook and made a flawless cast with the spinning-reeled fishing pole. Duke couldn't believe Jason had made such a fine cast, but didn't say anything. As Duke readied for a cast with his ancient, open-reeled fishing pole, he thought, *Jason is going to be good at fishing. He sure didn't have any trouble making that cast.* Duke swung his arm and fishing pole as he made a cast toward the lake. The reel quickly backlashed, so the hook, line, and sinker splashed into the water about five feet from shore. "Goddamn it!" Duke growled loudly as he began unknotting and untangling the fishing line nest surrounding his open-faced reel.

Jason wanted to laugh at Duke, but knew better, so he just grinned and turned away so that Duke could not see his face. Duke looked at Jason and said, "I guess I should break down and buy another spinning reel. They are so much easier to use." After five minutes of grumbling while untangling his fishing line, Duke made another cast and watched as the hook, line, and sinker sailed smoothly through the air before splashing into the water about fifty feet from shore. "I'll find a couple forked sticks so we can stick them into the sand and use them to prop up our fishing poles."

"Do you want me to help you, Grandpa?"

"No. You keep your fingers on your fishing line so you can feel it if a fish bites." Duke pointed west and said, "There should be some forked sticks in that brush pile. I'll be right back. Keep an eye on my pole. If you see it sliding toward the water, grab it, and give it a good jerk to set the hook."

Duke walked about fifty feet to the brush pile and found two forked sticks that were suitable. Just as he returned to his fishing pole, he saw Jason give a mighty jerk on his fishing rod. As the rod nearly bent in half, Jason hollered, "I think I hooked a fish, Grandpa."

"Oh, good!" Duke replied as he dropped the forked sticks onto the sandy beach. "Make sure you keep tension on your line, so the fish doesn't get away."

Jason began reeling in the line. He did not feel much resistance at first, but suddenly heard the reel clicking like crazy as the automatic clutch released and the line began spinning off his reel. A few seconds later, he felt the tension subside so he reeled in some more line. "It must be a huge fish, Grandpa," said Jason with great excitement in his voice.

"It must be, Jason. Just make sure you keep tension on your line."

"I am, Grandpa." After a few minutes of struggling with the pole, Jason reeled in some more line. He soon pulled a huge fish ashore, and said, "Wow, Grandpa! How much do you think this fish weighs?"

"That's a channel catfish, Jason. It probably weighs about eight pounds. We'll weigh it when we get home. I have a nice meat scales inside the garage. Boy! You are definitely lucky. I've fished this lake for years, and I've never caught a fish that huge."

"Are catfish good to eat?" asked Jason as he reached into the tackle box for a pair of needle-nose pliers.

"They usually have a strong fishy taste, but they're not too bad. I don't like them as much as I like sunfish or walleye. Actually, walleye is my favorite, but we don't have many of them around this area. Your grandma knows how to prepare and fry catfish in a special way, so it will taste pretty darn good."

Jason removed the hook, and watched Duke attach the stringer to the fish. Duke anchored one end of the stringer to a stick and slid the catfish into the water. Then, Jason and Duke re-baited their hooks and continued fishing. Duke checked the time on his wristwatch and saw it displaying 10:00 a.m. "Let's fish until about 11:00 a.m., Jason. Then, we'll go home and clean that catfish. We'll fillet it and give the fillets to your grandmother. Maybe, she'll fry some of them for supper tonight."

"I hope she does. I want to eat some of that catfish."

"If we treat your grandma real nice, maybe we can convince her to fry some sliced potatoes to eat with the fish. I love fried potatoes."

By 10:30 a.m., dark clouds covered the entire sky and the breeze had subsided completely. The mosquitoes began viciously attacking Duke and Jason. Duke swatted at several mosquitoes while muttering and cussing to himself. He soon reeled in his fishing line, and said, "Let's get the hell out of here and head for home. It's 10:45 a.m. and the only bites we're getting are from the doggone mosquitoes."

"That's for sure, Grandpa," replied Jason as he shooed away several mosquitoes. "I'm ready to go home. These mosquitoes are driving me crazy."

Chapter 11

Duke and Jason returned home from Britt Lake at 11:00 a.m. Wednesday, June 8. At 9:00 a.m. in California, Calvin and his attorney entered a courtroom in the San Mateo County Courthouse for Calvin's bail hearing. The federal prosecutors had agreed to allow the San Mateo District Attorney to handle Calvin's trial. The feds requested the state to handle Calvin's trial, because they suspected there could be some entrapment circumstances arise in Calvin's case. Judge Waakono, a very liberal man in his early fifties, brought the court to order. He first listened to Calvin's attorney, Mr. Arnold, present his argument for Calvin's eligibility for bail. When Mr. Arnold finished, the assistant district attorney presented his argument against Calvin's bail. After listening intently to both arguments, Judge Waakono ruled that he would allow bail, mainly because the jails were very overcrowded. The judge set bail at 200,000 dollars and ruled that he would release Calvin as soon as the court received the bail money. Calvin would not have to wear a monitoring device. Judge Waakono ordered Calvin to appear for his trial at 9:00 a.m. Monday, October 3.

After Calvin and Mr. Arnold left the courtroom and returned to the jail, Mr. Arnold presented a legal document to Calvin. He read and signed the document, which legally transferred Calvin's office building ownership over to Mr. Arnold as collateral. The county records listed the 2010 appraised value of Calvin's office building at 1,000,000 dollars, so Mr. Arnold felt very comfortable with the transfer. Calvin, on the other hand, felt as if he had received the short end of the deal, but he did not have many choices. Mr. Arnold said that he would pay Calvin's bail, so that Calvin's release would happen at 8:00 a.m. Thursday, the following day. As Mr. Arnold left the jail, Calvin thought, *I will be free after spending one more night in this hellhole, at least for a while.*

By noon Wednesday, Duke had finished cleaning and fileting the catfish. He had grumbled during the entire fish-cleaning process about how he had never learned how to sharpen a knife razor sharp, even though he had tried many times through the years. Duke and Jason entered the kitchen at 12:05 p.m., and when Duke handed the pan of fish filets to Alice, she said, "I suppose you want me to fry some of these for supper, huh?"

"Jason wants to eat catfish for supper, so I suppose you should," replied Duke as he reached for an empty coffee cup. "Some fried potatoes would taste good with the fish," said Duke as he poured a cup of coffee.

"Okay," replied Alice as she set the pan of filets into the kitchen sink. "I'll wash these thoroughly before I soak them in milk."

"Why are you going to soak them in milk, Grandma?" asked Jason while peering over Alice's shoulder so he could see the filets.

"The milk helps take some of the strong fishy taste out of them. What do you fishermen want for lunch?"

"How about some of your homemade vegetable soup?" replied Duke as he headed for the 3-season porch.

"Do you want some soup, too, Jason?" asked Alice as

she opened the refrigerator door.

"That sounds good, Grandma."

Alice removed a large stainless steel kettle of soup from the refrigerator and placed it on the stove burner. She turned to look at Jason and asked, "What are you two going to do this afternoon?"

"I don't know for sure. Grandpa said that I should ask you to take me shopping this afternoon, so I can buy a pair of swimming trunks."

"I guess we could go over to Kmart and buy a swimming suit for you. I need a few other things anyway. Let's go as soon as we finish eating lunch."

"Oh, good!" replied Jason as he headed for the porch.

Duke, Alice, and Jason finished eating lunch at 1:00 p.m., and as soon as Alice cleared the dishes from the table, she and Jason left for Kmart. Duke put on his wide-brimmed straw hat and went outside to see if the garden plot had dried enough, so that he and Jason could plant the seedlings. After using his garden boot heel to scuff the dirt in several different locations, he decided it was dry enough. *I may as well get the posts and wire cages ready*, he thought. *When Jason returns, we'll plant the seedlings*. Duke looked at the magnificent blue southern sky and noticed a few white, wispy clouds drifting slowly from west to east. He looked at the outdoor thermometer attached to the garage and saw it displaying eighty degrees. *What a beautiful, calm summer day, a perfect day for bike riding*, he thought while walking toward the garage. I need to take Jason shopping for a new bicycle, so we can go bike riding.

Duke made several trips back and forth between the garage and the garden as he carried some 42-inch tall, cylindrical-shaped wire cages, several 6 feet long steel fence posts, and several plastic coffee cans missing their tops and bottoms. After he had everything lying by the garden plot, he returned to the garden bench to sit for a spell. He glanced at his wristwatch and saw it displaying 2:00 p.m. A few minutes later, he heard the overhead garage door slowly opening, and after a few minutes, saw Jason and Alice exit the garage. Jason held a pair of navy blue swimming trunks in front of him as he said, "What do you think of my new swimming trunks, Grandpa?"

Duke squinted as he looked toward Jason and replied, "I like those, Jason. Are you ready to help me plant the seedlings?"

"Yeah, Grandpa," Jason said as he hurried along the sidewalk and passed in front of Duke. "I'll take these swimming trunks into the house. I'll be right back."

As Alice strolled leisurely past Duke, she shook her head a little and said, "Jason sure has a lot of energy."

Duke grinned and replied, "That's the teenager in him. I used to have that much energy, and so did you."

As Alice went into the house, Duke looked toward the front sidewalk and saw Jo Ann and Monica dressed in their swimming suits standing by the front gate located near the northwest corner of the house. Jo Ann looked at Duke and asked, "Do you care if we come into your backyard?"

"Come right ahead," replied Duke as he reached for a cigarette.

As Jo Ann lifted the gate latch and swung open the chain-link gate, she asked, "Is Jason here?"

"Yeah. He should be coming out of the house at any minute." As the girls approached Duke, Jason exited through the side-door opening.

Jo Ann looked at Jason and smiled. "Hi, Jason. Would you like to go swimming with us?"

Jason rubbed the back of his neck and asked, "May I, Grandpa?"

Duke lit the cigarette and replied, "I want you to help me in the garden this afternoon. You could go swimming later, maybe after supper."

Jason moved closer to Jo Ann and said, "I'd better help Grandpa this afternoon. Are you going to be at the swimming pool after supper?"

"No," replied Jo Ann as she flipped some of her long blonde hair over her right front shoulder. "I have to work every night this week."

"Where do you work?" asked Jason.

"I work part-time at Wanda's Restaurant," said Jo Ann as she rolled her blue eyes.

"I might be able to go swimming with you tomorrow afternoon," said Jason with much disappointment in his voice.

"Okay, Jason," said Jo Ann as she and Monica began walking toward the front sidewalk. "We'll stop here tomorrow afternoon on our way to the pool."

After the girls walked through the gate opening and closed the gate, Duke looked at Jason and said, "Well, my boy. Let's transplant those seedlings into the garden."

Jason acted as if he were down in the dumps while replying, "Okay, Grandpa. What do you want me to do?"

Duke saw Jason's red face and disappointment, so he gruffly said, "You'll have plenty of time to go swimming this summer, so don't feel too bad about having to help me."

"Do you want me to get the seedlings from the porch and take them to the garden?" asked Jason while grinning.

"Yeah. I'll help you."

After spending nearly two hours in the garden, Duke and Jason had completed their work. After returning all the garden tools into the garage, Duke reached up with his left hand and removed his straw hat. Using his right hand, he wiped the sweat from the top of his balding head. He glanced at his wristwatch and saw it displaying 3:55 p.m., so he said, "It's way past my beer time, Jason. Let's go inside, so I can drink some cold beer. We'll sit on the porch until supper time."

At 2:00 p.m. (California time), Greta handed the phone receiver to Mary while whispering, "It's Larry."

Mary took the receiver and answered, "Hello. This is Mary."

"Hello, my dear, sweet Mary," said Larry cheerfully. "How are things going for you today?"

"It has been a great day so far. I spent most the morning in group therapy. I thought I had severe problems, but I now realize that my problems are minor compared to the other peoples' problems in this place. Their lives have been much worse than my life. I actually feel very fortunate to have had it so well."

"I am so glad you feel that way, Mary. A positive attitude will definitely help you stay away from drugs. I have some good news and some bad news for you. Which do you want to hear first?"

"Tell me the bad news, first."

"Okay." The judge allowed bail for Calvin this morning, so he will walk out of jail tomorrow morning. He will be free until his trial begins October 3. I hope Calvin has cooled off by now, so that he does not bother you."

"I do not think he will bother me, at least not very much. I cannot believe he would harm me, or my parents." Mary cleared her throat a little before continuing, "So, Larry. What is the good news you have for me?"

"Oh, dear. My sweetheart and I spent two hours looking through your house last night. We have decided to offer you 700,000 dollars cash for the house and 75,000 dollars for the furnishings. The house amount is about 5,000 dollars less than the appraised value, but you will save roughly 49,000 dollars by not listing it with a realtor, so you will actually come out better. How does that sound to you?"

"That sounds absolutely wonderful, Larry. I am certainly very happy with your offer. When do you want to close the deal?"

"When will you leave the rehab center? My sweetheart and I will pay you that same day, and then we can all sign the transfer documents."

"I am not sure of the exact day. As you know, I am supposed to stay here until about July 4, but I have been thinking about leaving sooner. I miss Jason very much, so the sooner I move to Iowa, the better."

"Well, phone me the day before you leave rehab, Mary. That will give my sweetie and me enough time to transfer the money into our checking account. I have a client waiting, so I must end this phone call. I will drive over there and visit you one of these first days."

"Okay, Larry. Thanks for calling. Good-bye."

Calvin walked out of jail at 8:00 a.m. Thursday. He took a taxi-ride to the two-story office building he had owned up until Wednesday, when he had signed over the title to Mr. Arnold as collateral to pay for bail and trial expenses. Calvin went into his office on the second floor and quickly checked inside the wall safe. As he viewed the emptiness, he thought, *The goddamn cops must have taken all my cash.* He looked inside his desk drawers and found every one of them empty. Calvin saw that his computer had disappeared. *Damn!* he thought. *The cops took everything. I hope they did not find the money I stashed away in the utility room.* After sitting silently for ten minutes while thinking about his future, Calvin headed for the stairway leading to the first floor. He switched on the utility room lights a few minutes later, and walked over to a small workbench where he picked up a screwdriver. Then, he walked across the room to a large workbench situated in the northwest corner of the room. He struggled as he slowly slid the south end of the workbench away from the west wall.

Calvin kneeled upon the wooden floor and inserted the tip of the screwdriver into a crack between the ends of two wooden floorboards. He carefully pried up the end of one board, a board measuring four inches wide by thirty-two inches long. He put his left index fingertip under the end of the board, lifted and removed the board, and laid it upon the floor next to the opening. Using his right hand, he reached down through the opening and into the space between the floor joists. He explored the area for nearly ten seconds, and then pulled out a large stack of cash. *I am glad the cops did not find this hiding place*, he thought, *or I would be missing an additional 200,000 dollars*. Calvin peeled five hundred, 100-dollar bills from the stack and placed them inside his briefcase. He placed the remaining stack of cash next to another stack hidden in the space between the floor joists, and carefully replaced the floorboard. *Fifty thousand dollars should be enough for a little while*, Calvin thought as he stood up. As he slid the workbench back to its original location, he thought, *The goddamn cops seized my car, but I should be able to replace it with a cheap car, and still have enough money to live on for a while.*

Calvin switched off the lights and exited the utility room while thinking, *Mr. Arnold said that I could keep my office building key, and sleep in my office if I wanted, at least until my trial. I am surprised the feds did not seize this entire building. Perhaps, they thought their case against me is too uncertain.* Calvin returned to his office and phoned Elaine, a thirty-five-year-old he had spent several nights with before dating Betty. When Elaine answered, Calvin said, "Hello, Elaine. Would you enjoy a little company tonight? My ex-wife will not let me stay at her house any longer."

After an entire minute of silence, Elaine replied, "I

suppose you can stay at my house until you find a place of your own, but you'll have to pay me."

"I'll give you whatever you want," Calvin replied quickly. "Will cash along with my exquisite body be enough payment for you?"

Elaine giggled for nearly ten seconds before replying, "That will be fine, Calvin. I've missed your presence during the last several months."

"Okay, Elaine. I will arrive there at about 6:00 p.m. this evening, so I will see you then. Good-bye."

Calvin ended the call with Elaine and phoned the taxicab company. While Calvin waited in front of the office building for the taxicab to arrive, he thought, *I will purchase a car today, and then tomorrow, drive to San Francisco and visit Jes'us. I am glad my cellmate, Jacob, told me about the Mexican man. For a price, Jes'us will manufacture flawless fake identification cards for me. Jacob also said that Jes'us knew all about disguises, so for additional fees, he will teach me how to temporarily change my physical appearance.* Just as the taxicab stopped in front of the office building, Calvin thought, *I will treat Mary very nice until she leaves the rehab center. After that, I will get even with that bitch and her parents for reporting me to the police. I will phone her this afternoon.*

At 11:00 a.m. Thursday, Calvin handed 20,000 dollars cash to a car salesman in exchange for a 2008 white Cadillac. At 9:00 a.m. (Iowa time), Duke handed 150 dollars to a clerk at the local Target store. "Do you want to purchase an extended warrantee for the bicycle?" the clerk said. "It's a good deal for only 20 dollars a year."

"No, thank you," replied Duke. After the clerk gave Duke some change and the cash register receipt, Duke turned and observed Jason holding onto the new 26-inch, ten-speed mountain bike, and a bicycle helmet. "Are you ready to roll that bike out to the pickup?" asked Duke as he grinned slightly.

"Yeah, Grandpa. Thanks for buying this bike and helmet for me. I really appreciate it."

"You're welcome, Jason," replied Duke as he headed toward the exit doors.

Standing in the garage an hour later, Duke put on his wide-brimmed straw hat, and said, "Put on your helmet, Jason. Let's go for a bike ride. Duke rolled his fire engine red, ten-speed mountain bike through the small doorway opening of the garage, and said, "I'll show you around the downtown area."

Jason quickly strapped on the helmet and rolled his bicycle out of the garage. Just as he cleared the small doorway opening, he heard a very low-toned voice from the other side of the wooden privacy fence, "Hello, there. You must be going for a bike ride, huh?"

Duke quickly parked his bike, and stepped up onto the wooden garden bench. He looked over the west fence and said, "Hello, Elmer. I haven't seen you for a while. How have you been?"

"I have been perfectly fine," replied Elmer as he used his right hand to shade his squinty eyes while looking at Duke. "It is very bright out here today. I should get my bicycle out of the garage one of these days and check it out mechanically. Perhaps, I will go bike riding with you sometime. Who is the young man?"

Duke motioned for Jason to join him upon the bench, so Jason stepped onto the bench, looked over the fence, and said, "Hello."

"This is Jason, our grandson," said Duke as he rested his forearms upon the fence top. "He is spending the summer with us."

"Hi, Jason. I'm Elmer," replied Elmer dryly while tugging lightly on the tips of his long, gray beard. "It is very nice to meet you, Jason. Well, I guess I should go back inside and get busy."

"What are you working on these days?" asked Duke.

"I'm writing another novel," replied Elmer as he walked toward his back door.

"Have a nice day, Elmer," said Duke as he stepped down onto the sidewalk.

Jason jumped off the bench and said, "Gee, Grandpa. Elmer looks like a mountain man with that chest-length beard and shoulder-length hair."

Duke mounted his bicycle and replied, "Elmer has never been married. He lives like a hermit most the time. Elmer is a well-known novelist, though."

"Is he about your age?"

"Yeah. Elmer told me one day last summer that he had just turned sixty-seven, so he must be sixty-eight by now. He moved into that house a few years after we moved here. He spends most of his time writing novels, so I don't see him very often. Elmer went bike riding with me twice last summer, but he didn't talk much. He did manage to tell me that he had served five years in the US Army. Elmer served in the Special Forces as an Airborne Ranger. He completed two, eighteen-month tours of duty in Vietnam during the early seventies." Duke lowered the bike kickstand and dismounted his bike. He removed his wide-brimmed straw hat and wiped some sweat from his brow. "Yeah. Ol' Elmer is one tough bastard. You definitely want him on your side. He told me once that he still spends a lot of time working out and practicing self-defense."

"Did you have to go to Vietnam, Grandpa?"

"No, but I received a letter from the navy personnel office in 1964. They asked me to volunteer for duty in Vietnam as an advisor to the South Vietnamese Navy. I replied with a letter informing them that I would volunteer. A few weeks later, I received another letter from them." Duke paused long enough to light a cigarette. "They informed me that I would have to add another year to my enlistment time, so I would have two years of active duty remaining, instead of just one. I didn't want to extend for another year, so I didn't end up going over there. It's good that I didn't, because I probably would have returned to the USA inside a body bag. They wanted me to serve on the doggone river boats to teach the South Vietnamese Navy men about engines and other mechanical things." Duke glanced at his wristwatch. "Well, we'd better go on our bicycle rides."

Jason mounted his bicycle, and followed Duke as they rode their bicycles through the open chain-link gate. They turned east onto the city sidewalk located along and parallel with Klinger Boulevard. Just then, Alice opened the front door, leaned out through the door opening, and hollered, "Make sure you return home by noon. I'm going to fry some bratwursts for lunch."

"We'll be back by noon," hollered Duke while pedaling his bike east. "You should come with us."

"No thanks," Alice shouted. "I'll ride along with you some other day."

A few minutes later, Duke and Jason pedaled past a light-green two-story house. "Is that the house Jo Ann lives in?" asked Jason while pointing toward the house.

"That's the one, Jason."

"I hope she asks me to go swimming this afternoon," Jason replied as he nearly fell when his bike wobbled off the sidewalk and onto the grass.

Duke glanced toward Jason and said, "You'd better pay attention to where you're riding. You almost fell over."

Jason caught up with Duke and asked, "How far are we going to ride, Grandpa?"

"My bike odometer will probably register an additional six miles by the time we get home."

When Duke and Jason reached the intersection of

Fourth Street and Klinger Blvd., Duke turned north onto the sidewalk along the west side of Fourth Street. They stopped long enough for Duke to light a cigarette. Then, Duke began pedaling and said, "We'll ride along this city sidewalk all the way to the downtown area."

"Do you care if I ride ahead of you?" asked Jason. "I'd like to go a little faster."

"Go ahead, but don't get more than two blocks ahead of me. Make sure you stay on the sidewalk and watch carefully for traffic before you cross the alleys and streets. People drive like crazy now days."

"Okay," Jason said as he sped past Duke.

By 11:00 a.m., Duke had shown Jason much of the downtown area located on the northerly side of the Cedar River. Duke said, "Follow me and we'll ride along the sidewalk on the Fifth Street Bridge. When we reach the southerly side of the river, I'll show you some engraved bricks at the Veteran's Memorial Hall."

Just after they reached the southerly end of the Fifth Street Bridge, Duke turned his bicycle onto a narrow sidewalk leading to a large paved area. "Let's park our bikes right here," said Duke as he stopped and dismounted his bike. Jason parked his bike, dismounted, and followed Duke as they walked to an area paved with red bricks. Jason saw that almost every brick displayed someone's name, branch of military service, and his or her service dates.

"Wow, Grandpa. This is really neat. Is your name on one of these bricks?"

As Duke's eyes scanned over several bricks, he stopped walking, pointed, and said, "My brick is right there. Cost me sixty bucks. Your Uncle Tony's brick is right beside mine. That cost me another sixty bucks."

Jason inspected the bricks closely for several minutes. "I'm glad there is a place like this to honor veterans."

Duke walked slowly toward some other bricks. "I bought a brick for my best buddy, too. It's right over here." Duke stopped and pointed down as he said, "It's right there. I wanted the bricklayers to install it beside my brick, but it ended up over here. My brother has a brick here, too." Duke took a few steps to the north, pointed downward, and said, "It's that one right there."

"Oh, I see that Dave was in the Army, huh?"

"Yeah. The draft board was about ready to draft him in 1961, so he enlisted in the US Army for two years. Heck! He served as a military policeman in the Fifth Division out in Colorado." Duke stared at Dave's brick for about thirty seconds before saying, "Well, I suppose we should head for home. Your grandma will have the bratwursts ready at noon sharp."

Jason wiped some sweat from his forehead. "It's sure hot and humid today."

"All that sweating is good for you," Duke replied as he mounted his bicycle.

Jo Ann swung open Duke's chain-link gate at 1:30 p.m., walked along the sidewalk, and approached Jason who remained sitting on the wooden garden bench. "Are you going swimming with me this afternoon, Jason?"

"Yeah. I've been waiting for you since 1:00 p.m." Jason stood up and walked toward the side door. "I'll go inside and change into my swimming suit. I'll be right back."

"Okay. Ask your grandparents if you can stay at the pool until about 3:30 p.m. I need to leave the pool by then, because my shift at Wanda's begins at 5:00 p.m."

Ten minutes later, Jason and JoAnn left for the swimming pool. Duke watched through the front window while they walked along the city sidewalk toward the pool. When they disappeared from Duke's sight, he walked into the kitchen and found Alice standing at the kitchen sink washing dishes. He snuggled against her back, wrapped both arms around her, and kissed her neck. Duke managed to slip his right hand into the top opening of Alice's low- cut cotton dress. He gently massaged her brazier-covered breasts while asking, "Do you want to go upstairs for a quickie this afternoon? Jason won't be back for a few hours."

Alice giggled as she pulled Duke's right hand away from her breasts. "I'm sorry, Duke. I have to leave for the church as soon as I finish these dishes. We churchwomen are going to begin making quilts, so we can eventually sell them. We'll donate the proceeds to the cancer society."

"Oh, shoot!" Duke said as he released her and stepped away. "Well, I guess that's nice of you all."

Alice wiped her hands, turned to face Duke, and said, "We can play around a little tonight when we go to bed. How does that sound to you?"

"I suppose, if I'm not too tired by then. Remind me at supper time to turn on the upstairs window air conditioner."

Alice grinned and said, "Okay, my dear."

Calvin phoned the rehab center at 4:00 p.m. and asked for Mary. When Mary finally answered, he said, "Hello, Mary. Is it okay if I come over there to visit you?"

"Are you going to be nice to me?"

"Yes. Why would I not be nice to you?"

"Hold on for a minute. I will ask the supervisor if it is okay for you to visit me." Mary saw Greta standing at the end of the hallway, so she approached her and said, "Is it okay if my ex-husband visits me for a little while?"

"That will be fine, as long as you stay in plain view. You can sit in the lobby, or you can sit on one of the park benches located in front of the building. You can't take him into your room."

Mary returned to the phone and informed Calvin that it was okay for him to visit her. "Okay," replied Calvin, "I'll be there in about ten minutes."

"I will wait for you outside near the park benches located in front of the building."

Calvin approached Mary fifteen minutes later. "Hello, Mary. How are things going for you?"

Mary sat down on a park bench and patted the bench seat beside her. "Sit beside me, Calvin. I have been struggling, but I am getting by okay."

"I am glad for you, Mary," said Calvin as he sat down. I want you to know that I am very sorry for introducing you to drugs."

"Are you still mad at me?" asked Mary. "Larry said that when he visited you at the jail, you blamed me for everything."

Calvin patted Mary's left knee and replied, "No. I blamed you at first, but now I know you didn't report me to the cops." *I wonder if this bitch actually believes me,* thought Calvin as he waited for Mary's reply.

"I am relieved you are not mad at me. I certainly hope you are not mad at my parents. They had nothing to do with your arrest."

Before replying, Calvin thought, *Lie, lie, lie, Mary. I want to kill that bastard, Duke.* "I am certainly not mad at your parents, Mary." After a few minutes of silence, Calvin said, "This will probably be the last time you see me, Mary. It will be better if we stay away from each other."

"I agree with you, Calvin. Larry is purchasing my house and furnishings, so as soon as I leave rehab, I will begin packing so I can move to Iowa. I miss Jason very much."

"Really? I have not missed Jason at all. I guess I am not much of a father?"

"I guess not!" replied Mary angrily as she quickly stood up, and stormed toward the front entrance. "You have turned into a first class asshole, Calvin. Good-bye!"

Calvin stood up and watched Mary until she entered the rehab center and closed the front door. As he walked toward the parking lot, he thought, *Perhaps, I should kill that bitch before I kill her father. No, I think I will follow her to Iowa and kill them both. I guess I should have Jes'us make a fake Iowa driver's license for me.*

When Duke, Alice, and Jason sat down at the dining room table for supper Thursday night, Alice bowed her head and said, "Let's recite The Lord's Prayer before we eat." When they finished praying, Alice glanced at Jason and asked, "Did you and Jo Ann have a nice time at the swimming pool?"

Sporting a big smile, Jason replied, "Yeah. Jo Ann is so cool. She introduced me to a few of her friends."

Duke poured some gravy onto his mashed potatoes before asking, "Did you guys swim while you were at the pool, or just lollygag around?"

Jason laughed a little and said, "We swam part of the time, but we spent a lot of time standing chest deep in the water near the edge of the pool, talking about all kinds of things. JoAnn said that I should apply for a job at Wanda's, and then we could work together."

"I think you should get a part-time job," Duke replied seriously. "You will eventually need some money for a car. Does Jo Ann have a car?"

"No. She doesn't have her driver's license, yet. She has signed up for a driver's training class that begins July 5. The class lasts for three weeks and costs 330 dollars. When she completes the class, she will be eligible to take her driver's license test."

"Good God," Duke replied as he waved his left hand into the air. "That's a ridiculous amount of money, just to learn how to drive. That's another law the politicians created to make everything more costly. I guess it created some new jobs, though. Heck! My brother and my dad taught me how to drive, and it didn't cost me anything but my time."

"I could wait until I turn eighteen," Jason said. "Then, I wouldn't need the driving classes."

"How does Jo Ann get to work?" asked Duke.

"Her mom or dad gives her a ride. Sometimes, they get her when her shift ends, but sometimes her co-workers give her a ride home."

Alice offered, "You should sign up for a driver's training class as soon as you get your learner's permit."

"When are you going to take the test for your learner's permit?" asked Duke.

"I'll be ready tomorrow," replied Jason. "Will one of you take me out to the DMV office tomorrow morning?"

"I'll take you to the DMV," replied Alice. "Your grandpa probably has some things he wants to do in the yard."

"Do you want me to take you over to Wanda's, so you can apply for a job?" asked Duke. "We can go over there as soon as we finish eating."

"Yeah, Grandpa. Gee! Maybe we'll see Jo Ann while we're there."

Calvin parked his white Cadillac in front of Elaine's garage at 6:00 p.m. Thursday. He saw Elaine standing on the front stoop when he exited the car. "Hello, Calvin," she said cheerfully. "It's so nice to see you again."

"It is nice to be here. You look lovely this evening."

"Thank you, Calvin. I hope you haven't eaten supper. I made a large, homemade pizza this afternoon, and it's baking in the oven. It should be ready in about fifteen minutes."

"That sounds delicious," Calvin said as he walked toward the front stoop. When he approached Elaine, they hugged and immediately kissed passionately.

When their lips separated, Elaine brushed back her shoulder-length red hair with her left hand. "Wow, Calvin.

Your kisses make me feel so hot. I already feel a burning desire for you. Let's go inside. Would you enjoy a cold beer?"

"There is nothing better than a cold beer and a hot woman," Calvin replied while following Elaine toward the kitchen. "Is that not every man's dream?"

Elaine reached for the refrigerator handle as she looked toward Calvin. "That may be every man's dream, but I have never been very successful at getting a good man. Actually, I have never been sexually active with anyone but you." She rolled her large green eyes flirtatiously while saying, "I will eagerly fulfill your desires for as long as you live with me."

Calvin thought, *Elaine certainly does not have a very pretty face, but her perfectly built body makes up for it. Her personality is exceptional, and she is a super-hot lover.*

At 9:00 p.m. Thursday, Mary pulled aside the shower curtain and stepped under the warm, spraying water from the showerhead. She poured some lavender-scented liquid bath soap onto a mesh bath sponge and began washing the lower parts of her body. While enjoying the lavender scent and the feeling of the sponge sliding across her buttocks, she thought, *I still cannot believe Calvin's attitude toward Jason. Most men love their sons, but not Calvin. I should have never married that creep. I am glad we are divorced.* Mary finished washing the lower parts of her body, and then poured a little more body wash soap onto the mesh bath sponge. All of a sudden, she felt something touch her right buttock. Startled, she turned around and saw Keisha peering into the shower stall. "What are you doing?" asked Mary loudly.

"I thought you might enjoy my company. I'll gladly wash your back. Will you let me join you?"

"No, thank you."

"Are you sure? I think you would enjoy it."

"I want you to leave right now. I have already told you that I would let you know if I wanted anything more than friendship from you."

Mary saw Keisha's hand grab the shower curtain, and then saw the curtain close with one quick jerk. "Be that way," hollered Keisha just before she slammed the bathroom door.

Chapter 12

At 10:00 a.m. Friday, June 10, Alice and Jason walked out of the Iowa Department of Motor Vehicle site located inside the Crossroads Mall. As they slid onto the front seat of the LeSabre, Jason said, "I aced that test, Grandma."

"You should be very proud of yourself. Now that you have your permit, your grandpa can teach you how to drive."

"Yeah. Do you care if I sign up for the driver's training program, the same one Jo Ann enrolled in?"

"That's okay with me, but you'd better ask your grandpa about it."

"That's the only way I'll be able to get my driver's license before I'm eighteen. If I complete the course and pass the test, I'll be able to get my intermediate license. Then, I can get my regular driver's license when I turn seventeen, if I don't have any violations or accidents."

"How long do you have to attend classes?" asked Alice as she turned the ignition key and fired up the LeSabre engine.

"I think the classes last for three weeks. I need thirty hours of class time with at least six hours of that being what they consider lab time. I believe most of the lab time is spent driving with an instructor."

"Well, it will be nice if you get your driver's license, especially if you get that job at Wanda's Restaurant."

"I'll ask Grandpa when we get home," said Jason as he tugged nervously on his right earlobe.

Fifteen minutes later, Alice parked the LeSabre inside the garage. As Alice and Jason exited the garage, Duke looked at them from his seated position on the garden bench and said, "Did you get your driver's permit, Jason?"

"Yeah. I sure did, Grandpa. I aced the test." As a huge smile appeared on Jason's face, he reached into his shirt pocket, pulled out his driver's permit, and handed it to Duke.

After carefully inspecting the permit, Duke said, "By golly, I can finally teach you how to drive. We'll start working on that tomorrow."

When Alice walked past Duke and Jason on her way into the house, she smiled at Duke and said, "So, Duke! Did you accomplish any work while we were gone?"

"No. I've just been sitting on this bench watching all the different birds enjoying their baths in the fountain. I'm lazy today."

"You deserve to be lazy occasionally," Alice replied just before opening the side door to the house.

Duke handed the permit to Jason. "Do you want to begin your weight training program this morning? We can go into the basement right now. I'll show you the program I have developed for you."

"Yeah. Do I need to change my clothes?"

"You should wear your sweat pants and shirt, and your tennis shoes."

"Okay," replied Jason. "I'll change clothes and meet you in the basement."

By noon, Duke had put Jason through several repetitions of each weight-lifting exercise. Duke had not let Jason put any of the cast iron weights on the lifting bars for fear he might hurt himself. Just as Jason finished his last crunch, Duke said, "Well, my boy. How did you like that workout?"

Jason wiped the sweat from his forehead and replied, "I liked it, except I think it would be better if I could use some of the weights."

"You need to work out at least one more time with the bare lifting bars before you add any weights. If you don't increase the weights slowly, you'll injure yourself. I guarantee you that you'll feel sore as hell tomorrow and the next day. Let's go upstairs and eat lunch. I'm sure Alice has it ready for us by now."

When Jason and Duke entered the kitchen, Alice looked at Jason and said, "My goodness, Jason. You are soaking wet."

"Yeah. Grandpa put me through a good hard workout. I think I've already lost five pounds."

Alice smiled while saying, "Our lunch is waiting for us on the dining room table. I made tuna fish sandwiches and lettuce salads."

"That sounds like a good healthy meal," replied Duke as he headed for the bathroom to wash his hands.

Jason wiped some more sweat from his forehead. "Do I have time for a shower, Grandma?"

"Let's eat, first. You can shower after lunch."

"Grandpa wants me to mow the lawn after lunch."

Alice smiled and replied, "Oh, goodness. I guess you should wait to shower until you finish mowing."

"I'll just change out of this sweat outfit," said Jason as he headed for his bedroom.

Duke and Alice sat down at the dining room table and waited for Jason. Duke said, "I talked with my brother this morning. I told Dave that I would bring Jason over to the house for a visit this afternoon."

Jason sat down at the dining room table as Alice replied, "I suppose you and Dave will drink a few beers."

"That's the whole idea of our weekly visits," replied Duke as he poured some thousand-island salad dressing onto his lettuce salad. We enjoy drinking a few beers while talking about the old days."

"I look forward to meeting Dave," Jason offered. "How old is Dave?"

"He told me that he looks forward to meeting you, too, Jason. Dave is three and a half years older than I am, so he is seventy-two. Actually, he celebrated his birthday about a week ago." Duke took a bite of salad, chewed it a little, swallowed, and said, "We'll go over to his house when you finish mowing. Maybe Dave will tell us some stories about his time in the US Army."

"I hope so," Jason said as he prepared to take a big bite out of his tuna fish sandwich.

"Wasn't Dave a military policeman?" asked Alice.

"Yeah. Dave signed up for a two-year hitch in the army, 1961 and 1962. That's because the draft board was about ready to draft him for duty. He figured he would have a little better choice of jobs if he enlisted." Duke took a bite of his sandwich, chewed, and swallowed. Then, he looked at Jason and asked, "Have you ever used a power mower?"

"No. I don't know anything about power mowers. Dad always hired somebody to do our yard work."

"When we finish lunch, I'll teach you all about power mowers and mowing. Then, you can do all the mowing this summer. I'll do the trimming when the need arises."

"I can do the trimming, too, if you'll show me how," replied Jason as he lifted his glass of freshly made lemonade to his lips.

"Okay," Duke replied. "I'll show you how to trim."

Alice looked at Duke, grinned, and said, "You'll probably become bored if you let Jason take care of the lawn this summer."

"I'll find plenty to do around here," Duke replied while slightly scowling at Alice. "There's always something to do around this place. Maybe, I'll just have to bug you a little more often."

Alice didn't reply, but her grin turned into a huge smile. She swallowed some lemonade before saying, "I suppose that will be okay, Duke. I don't mind when you bug me."

After lunch, Duke and Jason went into the garage where Duke spent fifteen minutes explaining the mechanical aspects and safety procedures for the power lawn mower to Jason. Then, Jason rolled the lawn mower through the small doorway opening of the garage and onto the sidewalk. Duke said, "Roll it out to the front yard before you start the engine."

Jason rolled the mower along the sidewalk toward the front yard. As Duke and Jason approached the chain-link gate, they saw Jo Ann standing on the city sidewalk in front of the house. "Hello, Jo Ann," said Jason as he unlatched the gate.

"Hi, Jason," Jo Ann said as she strolled toward the gate. "I'm on my way to the swimming pool. Can you go swimming with me?"

Jason hung his head a little while replying, "I can't this afternoon. I have to mow the lawn. When I finish mowing, we are going to visit Grandpa's brother."

"Okay," replied Jo Ann with disappointment in her voice. "Will you be home tomorrow?"

Duke interrupted and said, "We'll be here tomorrow afternoon. You're welcome to come back then, if you want to visit Jason."

Jo Ann looked at Duke and asked, "Is it okay if I bring my dad along tomorrow? He wants to meet Jason, and visit with you for a while."

"Tell your dad that he's always welcome here. You can

bring your mother and sister along, too. Alice and I would love to visit with them. I'm going to give Jason some driving lessons in the morning. Can you all come over here at 3:00 p.m. tomorrow? Your dad might enjoy sitting on the porch with me. We could drink some beer."

"I'll ask Mom and Dad if 3:00 p.m. will work for them. I'll phone you to let you know."

"Sounds good," replied Duke as Jo Ann turned and walked toward the city sidewalk.

Jason rolled the lawn mower through the gate opening, and said, "I hope we'll see you tomorrow, Jo Ann."

Jo Ann waved her arm in reply as she began walking toward Byron Park. Duke watched as Jason pulled the starter rope on the lawn mower. The engine started on the third pull, so Duke walked over to the front stoop, sat down, and watched as Jason began mowing the front lawn. Twenty minutes later, they moved the mowing operation to the backyard. Duke sat on the wooden garden bench and watched Jason mow. When Jason finished mowing and shut off the engine, Duke asked, "Are you going to shower before we go over to Dave's house?"

"Yeah, I'd better. I probably stink like an old hog." Jason rolled the mower along the sidewalk and passed in front of Duke. "I'll put the mower away, Grandpa. Then, I'll take a quick shower."

Duke checked the time on his wristwatch. "We'll arrive at Dave's house at 3:00 p.m. if we leave here twenty minutes from now."

"I'll be ready in twenty minutes, Grandpa."

When Duke steered his S-10 pickup onto Dave's driveway, Jason and Duke saw Dave sitting in a lawn chair located just inside the double garage overhead door opening. Duke parked the S-10 and said, "It looks like Dave already has a cold beer waiting for me."

Duke and Jason exited the S-10 and approached Dave. After the introductions and handshakes, Dave handed a cold can of beer to Duke and said, "What would you like to drink, Jason? We have 7-up and Pepsi."

"Pepsi sounds good," replied Jason as he sat down in a lawn chair.

Dave walked toward the doorway leading from the garage into the house. "I'll go inside to get a can of Pepsi for you, Jason."

Duke sat down in a lawn chair, popped open the beer can lid tab, lit up a cigarette, looked at Jason, and said, "When Dave returns, you should ask him if he'll tell us a few stories about his army time."

A few minutes passed before Dave returned and handed a cold can of Pepsi to Jason. Dave sat down and said, "Jason is a lot bigger than you are Duke."

"Yeah. He weighs more than I do, but he isn't nearly as tough. He'll probably be a lot stronger than I am by the end of this summer."

"I doubt that, Grandpa."

"You will be, if you keep working out with weights," replied Duke.

Jason popped open the soda can lid tab, took a huge swallow of Pepsi, glanced toward Dave, and said, "Grandpa said that I should ask you to tell us a few of your army stories this afternoon."

Dave swallowed some beer before replying, "I suppose I could tell you at least one story."

"Tell us the one about when you were on maneuvers in South Carolina," offered Duke.

Smiling, Dave said, "Okay."

A fox squirrel suddenly appeared near the side of the overhead garage door opening. The squirrel stopped three feet in front of Dave, sat on his haunches, and looked at Dave as if begging for something. Jason said, "Wow. That squirrel is really brave."

Dave reached down and picked up a coffee can. "Oh, we feed the squirrels walnuts, so that's why he's begging. Dave reached into the coffee can and took out a few pieces of cracked black walnuts. He threw them toward the squirrel, and when the pieces landed on the concrete driveway, the squirrel began eating a piece. As they watched the squirrel, Dave said, "That male squirrel isn't quite as brave as the female squirrel we feed. She will come up to us and take the walnuts right out of our hands."

Dave's wife, Jolene, walked through the small doorway opening leading into the garage. When she approached the men, Duke introduced Jason to her. Then, Jolene sat down in a lawn chair next to Dave and said, "I see you're feeding one of our squirrels."

"Yeah. He begged me for food, so I gave him some walnuts. I am just getting ready to tell a story about when I was in the army."

"Well, let's hear it," replied Jolene.

Dave took a swallow of beer before saying, "Well, back in the summer of 1962, the 5th Division I was attached to left Fort Collins in Colorado and convoyed all the way out to an army base in South Carolina. After we arrived, we spent a few months playing war games. I remember that it was ungodly hot and humid while we were there. Our pretend enemies were soldiers from the 82nd and 101st Airborne Divisions."

Jason said, "Wow, Dave. You were up against some tough guys. I have read about the training they go through."

Dave smiled and said, "Yeah, the airborne guys are tough, but we had a lot of tough guys in our division, too. Some of the men had been police officers before the draft board drafted them into the army. Our group of men were scattered all through the woods when the airborne guys parachuted into our areas, sometimes during the night. Some of them landed in the trees, so their parachutes caught in the tree limbs, but they cut their parachute strings to free themselves. I remember that one of them had the rank of Colonel. He became very upset about landing in the tree. I also remember that they dropped some jeep vehicles from the planes. On one of them, the parachutes failed to open. My God! When that jeep hit the ground, it made a huge hole in the ground. That jeep was all smashed to hell."

Dave took a huge swallow of beer before continuing. "Our division did okay for a while, but the airborne troops eventually won the battle. Hell! They actually captured some of us and tied us to tree trunks while they hunted down the rest of our soldiers. Of course, we captured some of the airborne soldiers, too. Needless to say, there were a lot of hard feelings created during those few months."

"Did you get a chance to go bar hopping while you were there?" asked Duke.

"We didn't have enough money to go into town, but on the night of the last day of the war games, a group of my buddies and I went to the base PX so we could drink some beer. That wasn't too smart of us, because there were a lot of airborne guys at the PX, many of them had been our enemies during the war games."

Jolene stood up and said, "Well, men. I've heard this story several times, so I'm going inside to start making supper."

Dave stood up and asked, "Do you want another beer, Duke?"

"No thanks. I don't want to get arrested for drunken driving."

"Do you want another Pepsi, Jason?" asked Dave.

"No thanks, Dave. My can is still half full."

"I'll grab a can of beer and be right back," Dave said as he walked toward the entrance door to the house.

As soon as Dave returned, he sat down and popped open the beer can lid tab, took a huge swallow of beer, and said, "Yeah, men. That was quite a night at the PX. We all drank too much beer, and before long, some of the soldiers began harassing each other. About twenty of us soon ended up outside where one of my best friends nicknamed Bunch began fighting with a soldier from the 82nd Airborne. Bunch wasn't an MP like me. He served as an artilleryman. We had met each other during boot camp, and the army eventually assigned both of us to the 5th Division. Bunch grew up on a ranch near Elko, Nevada, and spent his entire youth being a rough tough cowboy. Hell! While we were stationed in Colorado, Bunch spent some of his free weekends riding Brahma bulls in the rodeos, just for entertainment."

"Gee whiz," remarked Jason. "Bunch must be a tough guy. We spent a night in Elko, a while back."

Duke lit a cigarette and said, "So continue with your story, Dave."

Dave swallowed some more beer, and continued, "So anyway, the rest of us all began fighting and we were holding our own, but then, the guy Bunch squared off with found a piece of iron pipe lying next to the building, so he grabbed the pipe and used it to hit Bunch in the face. Just after that, a large group of military policemen from the base arrived and broke up the brawl. I remember Bunch standing there with blood running out of the gash on his cheekbone and part of his lower face. He even had a small gash in his chest. As Bunch stood there slowly weaving from side to side and back and forth, he kept saying, 'I was holding my own until that bastard hit me with the pipe.' The MPs told all of us to leave the area. They took Bunch and a few other men to the hospital for stitches. Bunch returned to our camping area right after a doctor sutured his wounds. He appeared quite sober and somber by then."

"Did you get hurt?" asked Jason as he swatted at a mosquito on his arm.

"Not very much," replied Dave. "I had a few bumps and bruises, but nothing severe. We all had hellish hangovers the next day." Dave looked at Duke and said, "You could tell us one of your navy stories, Duke."

Duke glanced at his wristwatch and stood up before saying, "I'll tell you a story some other time. I want to look at your garden before we leave for home."

Dave rose slowly from his chair and said, "The garden plants haven't grown very much since I planted them a few weeks ago."

As Duke, Dave, and Jason approached Dave's garden, Calvin parked his white Cadillac upon a driveway located in front of a row house in the Bayview area of San Francisco. He saw the dashboard clock displaying 1:30 p.m. *I am right on time,* he thought. I hope Jes'us remembers from our phone conversation yesterday that I told him I would see him today at 1:30 p.m. Calvin exited the car, shut and locked the car door, and stood beside the car for a minute while thinking, *I hope nobody shoots me while I am in this rundown neighborhood.* Calvin slowly and cautiously approached the front door. He knocked, and immediately heard a large dog barking and growling loudly on the other side of the door. A minute later, the front door opened a crack. "Who sent you?" a man with a low-toned, gruff voice asked while the dog continued growling and snarling.

"Jacob sent me. I am Calvin. Are you Jes'us?"

"Ya, man. Wait a minute, while I chain up the dog."

A few minutes later, Jes'us opened the front door and said, "Come in, man."

Calvin followed Jes'us into the small kitchen. "Take a seat, man," Jes'us said as he pointed at one of the chairs by the kitchen table. As Calvin sat down, he saw the sink full of dirty dishes and several empty beer bottles upon the dirty, worn laminated countertop. Jes'us had attached the free end of the dog chain to a hook near the back door. The other end of the chain attached to a huge Rottweiler lying upon the dirty linoleum floor next to a doorway located only five feet from Calvin. Jes'us reached around and removed a .38 caliber pistol from his waistband. He set the pistol upon the table as he sat down in a chair across the table from Calvin. The Rottweiler began growling and snarling while glaring at Calvin. Jes'us hollered, "Shut the hell up, Ace." Ace immediately lowered his head and began whining. "That goddamn dog drives me crazy sometimes," Jes'us said as he stared directly into Calvin's eyes. "So, man. Why did Jacob send you to see me?"

"Jacob told me that you could fix me up with some fake identification cards and driver's licenses."

Jes'us leaned back in his chair and slid his fingers through his shoulder-length, oily black hair. "I can make some of those for you, man, but it'll cost you a lot of cash."

"Jacob said that you could help me with some disguises, too."

"Ya, man. You pay me enough, and I can do anything you want." Jes'us placed his right hand on the pistol and said, "Show me some cash, man. I'll see how much I can do for you."

Calvin removed a folded stack of hundred dollar bills from his right front pants pocket. He held the bills so that Jes'us could easily see them. "There should be enough money here for your services," said Calvin as Ace began growling.

Jes'us slammed the heel of his left fist against the

tabletop and screamed, “Shut the hell up, Ace!”

Calvin had flinched a little when Jes'us screamed, but quickly recovered from being scared shitless. Calvin flipped through the cash and asked, “So are you going to fix me up with some fake driver’s licenses?”

“Ya, man. Let’s go into my office.” Jes'us grabbed his pistol and said, “Follow me, man.”

Calvin followed Jes'us out of the kitchen, through the living room, along a long narrow hallway, and into the office. Calvin could not believe all the electronic equipment located in Jes'us’ office. Computers, scanners, cameras, printers, and video cameras occupied the spotlessly clean room. “Wow, Jes'us. You certainly have a lot of very expensive electronic equipment.”

“Ya, man. That’s why I keep Ace around. He’ll kill anybody who tries to steal anything from me.” Jes'us waved his pistol into the air while saying, “Ya, man. I always have this pistol nearby, and it wouldn’t bother me at all if I had to shoot a thief. Jes'us pointed the pistol toward a chair and said, “Take a seat, man. Tell me what you need.”

Several hours later, Calvin left Jes'us’ house and headed for Elaine’s house. He felt very thankful to still be in one piece and alive. Calvin parked his Cadillac upon Elaine’s driveway at 5:00 p.m. (California time). Just as Calvin exited the Cadillac, Alice heard the kitchen phone ringing. She glanced at the kitchen clock and saw it displaying 7:00 p.m. (Iowa time). “Hello, this is Alice.”

“Hello, Ma’am. My name is Rick. I am the assistant manager at Wanda’s Restaurant. Is Jason available?”

“Yes. Hang on for a minute, Rick. I’ll tell Jason that you’re on the phone.” Alice quickly walked into the dining room and picked up the mobile phone. She took it onto the 3-season porch and handed it to Jason. “It’s Rick from Wanda’s Restaurant.”

Jason answered the mobile phone, so Alice went back into the kitchen and cradled the phone receiver. She returned to the porch and sat down in the wicker chair near Duke. When Jason ended the call and placed the mobile phone upon the glass-topped wicker table, he said, "Hooray! I am now a part-time employee at Wanda's Restaurant. I will work from 5:00 p.m. until 10:00 p.m. tomorrow. I will work the same shift Sunday night, too."

"That's good news," replied Duke. "I'm proud of you."

Jason rubbed the top of his head lightly as he asked, "Will one of you be able to take me to work, and then get me when I finish my shift?"

"I'll do that, Jason," Alice quickly replied.

"Great. Thank you, Grandma."

Alice leaned over, put her hand on Duke's forearm, and said, "I forgot to tell you that the lawyer phoned this afternoon while you and Jason were at Dave's house."

"Oh, yeah. What did he have to say?"

"He said that he had showed all the paperwork we brought from California to a judge. The judge said that he would approve everything and have somebody take care of the Iowa paperwork we'll need. The lawyer said that he'll have all the paperwork ready for us to pick up at his office by the end of next week."

"That's good," replied Duke. "Did he tell you how much that will all cost us?"

"No," Alice said as she grinned. "He probably didn't want to ruin our weekend."

Just then, the phone began ringing. Alice picked up the mobile phone and answered after the third ring, "Hello."

"Hello, Alice. This is Jo Ann. I'm at work, so I'll make this short. I want to let you know that my sister and I, along with our parents will come over to your house at 3:00 p.m. tomorrow."

"That's wonderful, Jo Ann. We look forward to your visit."

"Okay. Good-bye."

At 10:00 p.m. Friday, Mary and Keisha sat down on the edge of Mary's bed. They had finished their showers and dressed in their negligees a short time earlier. Keisha smiled at Mary and said, "Well, we have completed the first five days of the program."

"Yes. The days have certainly passed quickly. I have been thinking about leaving here in a few days, and moving to Iowa. I asked the doctor about it this morning, and he said that my drug problems are minor. He thought I could deal with it on my own from now on."

Keisha placed her right hand upon Mary's right knee. "I don't know, Mary. Do you think you can stay away from drugs if you leave now?"

"I believe so, as long as I stay away from my ex-husband. I do not think that will be a problem, because he has already told me that I would probably never see him again. I miss my son, Jason, so much. He will be my top priority from now on."

Keisha began sliding her right hand lightly along the top of Mary's bare upper right leg, from her knee toward her hip. "I will miss you so much if you leave, Mary. You have been an inspiration for me. I haven't had any desire to take drugs since I have met you, even though we haven't known each other very long."

"You have helped me think much differently about my life, Keisha," Mary said as she placed her right hand on top of Keisha's right hand and gripped it hard in order to stop the motion of Keisha's hand. "You are very important to me, Keisha. I hope we will always remain friends."

Keisha leaned over so that her lips almost touched Mary's lips. As she tried to slide her right hand further up Mary's leg, she whispered, "I want to become more than just friends with you, Mary. Would you please let me show you how much you mean to me, at least just once? Please let me show you tonight." Keisha kissed Mary softly on her lips. A minute passed before their lips separated. "You taste so good, Mary," offered Keisha.

Mary began panting slightly as she relaxed her grip on Keisha's hand. Then, Mary felt Keisha's fingers exploring slowly along her right inner thigh. Mary moaned softly, but then suddenly said, "Please leave me alone, now, Keisha."

Keisha quickly stood up and stormed across the room. She flopped down onto her bed and said, "You don't know what you're missing, Mary. Good night!"

At 10:00 a.m. Saturday, June 11, Duke finished giving Jason driving lessons with the LeSabre at a large vacant parking lot. By noon, Duke and Jason had finished weeding some of Alice's flower gardens. After lunch, Duke and Jason went for bicycle rides, and by the time they returned home at 2:15 p.m., had ridden ten miles. As they entered the 3-season porch, Jason said, "I think I'll take a quick shower and put on some different clothes."

Duke grinned and said, "You must want to look your best for when Jo Ann arrives, huh? You'd better hurry. They should be here by 3:00 p.m."

As Jason went into the bathroom, Duke went into the kitchen where he found Alice preparing a large pitcher of lemonade. Alice kissed Duke on the cheek and said, "I hope Otis and Missy like lemonade."

"Otis will probably prefer beer," Duke replied as he patted Alice's buttocks. "You look very pretty in that floral-print dress. You smell very nice, too, kind of like a bouquet of lilacs."

"Thank you, Duke. I put on a touch of my new perfume. Are you going to freshen up a little before they get here?"

"Yeah, as soon as Jason gets out of the bathroom."

Otis, Missy, Jo Ann, and Monica approached the 3-season porch door at 3:00 p.m. Duke stood up, opened the door, and said, "Come in. I'm so glad to see all of you."

As soon as they entered the porch, Duke introduced himself to Otis and Missy. Alice appeared in the French doorway opening and said, "Hello. I'm Alice." Otis shook Alice's hand and said, "It's nice to meet you." He put his arm around Missy and said, "This is Missy, my lovely wife."

Alice shook hands with Missy and said, "Nice to meet you, Missy. My goodness, you are so petite and pretty."

"Thank you, Alice," replied Missy as she smiled beautifully.

Alice released Missy's hand and said, "Please come into the house and I'll show you around." Alice looked toward Jo Ann and Monica and said, "You're welcome to come with us, girls."

Jo Ann asked, "Where is Jason?"

Alice replied, "He's in his bedroom changing clothes. He should be out pretty soon."

Duke sat down in his wicker chair and said, "Would you like a cold beer, Otis? I'm going to drink at least one this afternoon, possibly more."

"Sure, Duke. I'll drink a beer."

"Do you want to sit here on the porch, or do you want to go into the living room?" asked Duke.

"The porch is fine, Duke," said Otis as he lowered his 6'-2" tall, 200-lb. muscular body into a chair. "It's such a gorgeous day."

"It might be a little quieter out here," Duke said as he grinned. "It'll probably get pretty noisy in the living room when all the women begin talking."

"I'm sure it will," replied Otis as he smiled broadly.

"Well, Otis. I'll go downstairs and get some beer. I'll be right back."

Just as Duke left the porch and walked into the dining room, Jason walked out of his bedroom. "Are you going to join Otis and me on the porch, Jason?" asked Duke.

"Sure, Grandpa, but first I want to go into the living room and introduce myself to Jo Ann's mother."

"Okay. I'll introduce you to Otis when you join us on the porch."

Duke returned to the porch a few minutes later and handed a cold can of beer to Otis. "Thank you, Duke. I have been looking over your backyard. All the roses are beautiful. I especially like all the dark red blooms on the climbers growing up your rose arbor."

As Duke took a seat in his wicker chair, he replied, "Yeah. I planted those climbing roses about three years ago. They have grown quite well, and they're hardier than hell. Those are both Henry Kelsey climbers. I suppose that's the name of the man who developed them, but I'm not sure."

Otis popped open the lid tab and took a swallow of beer. "I don't know much about gardening. I've devoted most of my life to law enforcement."

"How long have you worked for the Waterfield Police Department?" asked Duke as he reached for a cigarette.

"I began working for the department when the Army discharged me in May of 1991. I had just turned twenty-five years of age. I served as an MP in the army, so I already had some experience with police work."

"My brother, Dave, was an MP when he served in the Army, but that was way back in the early 1960s."

"Did Dave continue working in law enforcement?" asked Otis as he pulled a package of small cigars out of his shirt pocket. "Do you mind if I smoke one of these cigars?"

"No, I don't mind at all." Duke stood up and shut the French door. He sat down and said, "Alice gets upset if smoke enters the house." Duke swallowed some beer, and said, "When Dave received his army discharge, he began working at an engineering and land surveying company here in town. When I received my discharge in 1965, I began working for the same company."

"That's cool," said Otis as he lit the cigar. "Did you two get along with each other while working together?"

"Yeah. We did okay. Dave and I didn't have to work together very often. We usually worked on separate projects."

Jason opened the French door, and Jo Ann followed him onto the porch. Jo Ann said, "Dad. This is Jason."

Jason offered his hand for a handshake, so Otis stood up and shook Jason's hand while saying, "I'm Otis. It's nice to meet you, Jason. I've heard a lot about you. As a matter of fact, it seems as if Jo Ann mentions your name a lot."

Jason looked up at Otis and replied, "Nice meeting you, sir."

Otis released Jason's hand and replied, "You can call me Otis."

"Okay, Otis," replied Jason as he sat down in a chair.

Jo Ann brushed back some of her long blonde hair and said, "I'm going inside to visit with the women."

For the next hour, Jason sat silently, almost in a daze, as he listened to Duke and Otis talk about their time in the military and Otis' time as a police officer. As Jason watched Duke and Otis, he thought, *Gee whiz. I feel like a midget when I compare myself to Otis. His black hands are huge. When he holds that beer can, you can barely see it. He must work out with weights a lot, because his muscles are huge, so huge they appear as if they are ready to burst. He seems like a nice man.*

At 4:15 p.m., Duke looked at Jason and said, "You should probably get ready for work, Jason."

Jason snapped out of his daze and said, "I'll be ready to leave here by 4:30 p.m. I want to be at Wanda's Restaurant by 4:45 p.m. Grandma said that she will take me to work."

Otis stood up and stretched a little before saying, "I should probably go inside and gather my family, so we can go home."

"Oh hell, Otis," said Duke as he looked up at Otis. "You don't have to hurry away. You surely can stay long enough to drink another beer."

Otis sat down and said, "I suppose we can stay for a little while longer, if it is okay with you."

"I'd enjoy hearing some more of your police stories," Duke said while smoothing back the grayish brown hair on the right side of his head.

Jason stood up and said, "I'll get a couple cans of beer for you guys."

"Well thank you, Jason," Otis replied while smiling.

"Thank you, my boy," replied Duke.

Chapter 13

The remaining days of June each faded away into the sunset. Then, at 5:00 a.m. Friday, July 1, Duke knocked on Jason's bedroom door and shouted, "Time to wake up, Jason."

"Okay, Grandpa," Jason answered sleepily.

"We need to eat breakfast, so we can begin our weight-lifting workouts at 7:00 a.m. I want to finish working out by 9:00 a.m., so we can accomplish some other things today."

"Okay. I'm getting out of bed. I'll be right out."

Duke went into the kitchen and approached Alice standing in front of the stove baking pancakes and frying bacon. Just as she used a spatula to flip over a pancake, Duke put his hands on her hips and said, "Those pancakes smell delicious, Alice. The bacon smells even better."

Alice turned to face Duke, kissed him on the lips, and said, "Is Jason getting out of bed? I'll have breakfast ready and on the table in about ten minutes."

"Jason is already in the bathroom, so he will be ready to eat by the time you set the table."

Duke poured a cup of coffee and said, "I'll be out on the 3-season porch until breakfast time."

"Okay, Duke."

Five minutes later, Jason walked onto the porch and asked, "What are we going to do after our workouts, Grandpa?"

"Well, my boy. While you were at work last night, I talked with Elmer for a little while. I invited him to accompany us on our bicycle rides today. We will ride along the bike path, all the way to Hinson and back."

"Is Hinson a big town?" Jason asked. "How many miles is it from here?"

"Hinson is a small town located about eight miles south of here, so the round trip will only be about sixteen miles."

Alice opened the French door and announced she had breakfast waiting on the table, so Duke and Jason went into the dining room and joined Alice at the table. Alice said, "Let's bow our heads in prayer."

Jason and Duke immediately bowed their heads and listened to Alice's prayer of thanks, for an entire two minutes. When Alice finished praying, Duke looked at her and grinned. "You shouldn't have to thank the Good Lord again for quite a while, Alice. I didn't think you were ever going to quit praying."

Alice gave Duke a nasty look as she replied, "Oh, shush. If you would thank the Good Lord more often, I wouldn't have to say such long prayers."

Duke and Jason finished working out at 9:00 a.m., just as Duke had planned. With a very red face, Jason stood up from the weight bench, and while rubbing his belly muscles, said, "Wow, Grandpa. I can already do a hundred crunches without stopping."

"Yeah. You're getting in pretty good shape." Duke slid a digital scales away from the wall, "Stand on the scales, Jason. We'll find out how much weight you have lost since your first weight-lifting workout on June 10."

Jason stepped upon the scales and watched as the digital numbers bounced around before finally settling at 190. "Wow, Grandpa. I have already lost ten pounds."

"Yeah. All the hard work you've been doing is paying off for you. I can see that your body is firming up quite a lot, especially your arms and legs. You should be able to play football in school this fall. We'll inquire about getting you signed up for the football team; that is, if you still want to play football."

"Yeah," replied Jason as he stepped off the scales and slid it back against the wall. "I still want to play football."

"Okay. We'll find out when practice begins. I think football practice usually begins a few weeks before school begins in the fall. Well, I suppose we should get our bicycles ready for our rides. Ol' Elmer will be chomping at the bit if we're late. I told him that we would meet him on the sidewalk in front of his house at 10:00 a.m."

As Duke and Jason met Elmer, Larry parked his silver BMW in the rehab center parking lot. He looked at his wristwatch and thought, *I am right on time. It is exactly 8:00 a.m. I hope Mary is ready to leave with me.* When Larry approached the main entrance door of the rehab center, he looked through the entrance door glass and saw Mary standing inside waiting patiently. He saw Keisha standing beside Mary. Larry opened the entrance door, bowed flamboyantly, and said, "Good morning, my dear Mary. Are you ready to leave this place?"

"Yes," replied Mary. "I feel as if I am a completely new person. I am definitely ready to proceed with a new way of living."

"That is wonderful, Mary." Larry grabbed Mary's suitcase while saying, "I will carry your suitcase to the car."

"Okay. I will meet you there in a few minutes." As Larry exited through the exit doorway opening, Mary faced

Keisha and gently grasped her hands. "I will miss you, Keisha. I wish you all the luck in the world."

A tear rolled down Keisha's right cheek as she replied, "I only wish we could have become closer while you were here. I will miss you so much."

Mary hugged Keisha snuggly and said, "Good-bye, Keisha."

"Good-bye, Mary. Good luck."

Mary let go of Keisha and strutted out through the exit doorway opening. She wiped several tears from her cheeks before arriving at Larry's car. Larry opened the car door for Mary, and after she situated herself upon the front seat, Larry gently closed the door. He walked around to the driver's side, and slid in behind the steering wheel. As he turned the ignition key and heard the powerful engine fire up, he asked, "Are you ready to go to the bank with me, so I can pay you for your house and belongings?"

"I am ready, Larry. I will get the deed out of the safety deposit box so you can inspect it before you write the check. I assure you there are no liens or encumbrances attached, but you can check it all out to make sure. Perhaps, Judge Socko will want to inspect the deed."

Larry glanced at his wristwatch and said, "He told me to take care of everything. I trust you, Mary. Do you want to stop at Dave's Restaurant and kill a little time drinking coffee? The bank doesn't open until 9:00 a.m."

"That will be fine, Larry. When we finish at the bank, could you come over to the house with me? I thought you might help me pack some of my personal belongings."

"Absolutely, Mary. I will help you."

Larry and Mary spent thirty minutes at Dave's Restaurant. Then, at 9:00 a.m., Larry parked his BMW in the bank parking lot. He looked at Mary and asked, "Are you going to drive your car to Iowa, or are you going by plane?"

"I will drive my car," Mary replied. "If I get everything packed today, I will leave early tomorrow morning. If I cannot pack all my belongings into the car, I thought that perhaps you would ship the rest of them to me after I am settled in Iowa."

Larry exited the car, walked around to the passenger side, and opened the car door for Mary. "I will gladly ship your belongings to your new address."

At the same time as Larry and Mary entered the bank in Redwood City, Duke, Jason, and Elmer parked their bicycles and sat down on a picnic bench located on the north side of Main Street in the small town of Hinson. Duke looked at his wristwatch and said, "It's already 11:10 a.m. We'll have to ride a little faster on our way back home; otherwise, we'll be late for lunch."

Elmer took a sip of water from his water bottle. His right shoulder jerked several times as he said, "It is quite warm today. It must be about eighty-five degrees. The northerly breeze has increased, so it will be a little harder pedaling on our way home."

"At least it isn't very humid," said Duke as he removed his wide-brimmed straw hat, "not like the last several days. Hell! It was hard to breathe, yesterday."

Jason removed his bicycle helmet and placed it upon the picnic table. He wiped the sweat from the top of his head, and said, "It's definitely hot enough to make me sweat a lot."

Elmer began tugging nervously on the tips of his long gray beard. His right shoulder twitched a few times as he offered, "When we get back home, I will show you guys my new toy."

"So what kind of toy did you get?" asked Duke as he reached into his shirt pocket for a cigarette.

"I purchased a pair of night-vision goggles a few weeks ago," Elmer replied as he used his thumbs and index fingers to form circles around his eyes. "It is amazing how well you can see in the dark with those darn things." Elmer lowered his hands, and with his fingertips, nervously tapped out a drum rhythm upon the picnic table. His right shoulder twitched a few times as he offered, "I should have had a pair of night-vision goggles when I served in Vietnam. Then, I could have seen those slant-eyed gooks a lot better when they snuck around at night trying to kill us. I could have killed a lot more of the bastards."

Duke glanced at Jason and saw the astonished look on his face, so Duke said, "Well, we had better mount our bicycles and head for home." Duke glanced at Elmer and said, "You'll have to show us your goggles tonight, after darkness sets in."

"Okay, Duke. You both come over to my house at about 10:00 p.m., and we'll sit in my sunroom. You can put on the goggles and look out through the windows at your backyard. You'll probably be surprised when you see how many rabbits are in your yard and garden."

Duke stood up and mounted his bicycle as he replied, "That sounds like a good plan, Elmer."

Duke, Jason, and Elmer arrived in front of Elmer's house at noon. At the same moment, 10:00 a.m. (California time), Calvin parked his white Cadillac upon Jes'us' driveway in Bayview. As Calvin exited the car and walked toward Jes'us' front door, he thought, *I hope Jes'us has all my fake identification cards ready. When I was here a few days ago, so that he could take pictures of me with my scruffy, three-week-old beard and newly dyed black hair, he promised that he would have the identification cards ready by today.* With his right hand, Calvin fluffed the right side of his black hair and thought, *I believe I like this black hair better than my natural brown hair. It matches the color of my beard better.* Calvin knocked on the door and immediately heard loud growling and barking. After a few minutes, the door opened a crack and Jes'us peered out through the narrow opening. After Jes'us' squinty, black eyes adjusted to the bright, outdoor natural light, Jes'us said, "Hi, man. Let me chain up Ace. I'll be right back."

A couple minutes elapsed before Jes'us opened the door and allowed Calvin to enter the house. "Okay, man," said Jes'us as he slid his right fingers through his greasy black hair. "Follow me to my office. Did you bring the rest of the money?"

Calvin almost gagged from the putrid smell, but managed to follow Jes'us toward his office. "I have the money with me." *Jes'us must never clean anything other than his office*, thought Calvin. *The smell in this house is rank. It smells like rotting garbage and dog feces all mixed together.*

Jes'us had chained Ace to one of the sofa legs, so when they walked through the living room, they passed within inches of Ace's reach. Ace snarled loudly and suddenly snapped at Jes'us, narrowly missing Jes'us right leg. Jes'us stopped abruptly, jumped back, quickly pulled the .38 caliber pistol from his waistband, and aimed at Ace's head. "It's a good thing you didn't bite me, you son of a bitch," Jes'us screamed. "I will send you to doggie heaven if you keep that shit up." Ace promptly lay down, lowered his head to the floor, and began whining. Jes'us waved the pistol into the air and said, "That goddamned dog drives me crazy most of the time. I don't know what his problem is lately. He has been acting mean as hell for the last few days. The bastard tried to bite me earlier this morning, so I beat the hell out of him."

Calvin thought, *I would not want to own such a vicious dog.*

When they entered Jes'us' office, Jes'us laid the .38 caliber pistol upon the desktop. "Okay, man. Show me the cash, and I'll show you the finished identification cards."

Calvin pulled a wad of cash from inside his right front pocket and offered the cash to Jes'us. "That is the amount you requested. You can count it if you do not trust me."

Jes'us grabbed the money and began counting. When he finished, he opened a desk drawer and threw the cash into the drawer. Then, he removed several different laminated cards from the same desk drawer, and handed the cards to Calvin. "Take a look at those, man. See if you like them. I assure you that if the cops ever run a check on any of those, they will find that everything jives. Ya, man. I spent a lot of time hacking into all the different websites, so I could coordinate everything."

Calvin sat down in a chair and carefully inspected his new social security card, his new Iowa driver's license, and his new California driver's license. Then, he checked out the new proof of auto insurance cards and the auto registrations for Iowa and California. These look great, Jes'us. Are you sure everything will cross check if the cops ever check them?"

"I guarantee that everything will check okay," said Jes'us as he sat down in front of his desk and opened another desk drawer. He removed two new Iowa license plates from inside the drawer and handed them to Calvin. "These plates will match the Iowa registration and proof of insurance."

"I am very curious about how you obtained these new Iowa license plates," said Calvin as he stood up and inspected them.

"Hey, man. I have friends in many places, and those friends have friends in places. You just have to know the right kind of people when you want to get around the laws." Jes'us sat silently for about a minute, as if in a daze. Then, he offered, "If you want to pay me a little extra, I'll give you the name of a very rich Italian businessman who lives in a small town near Waterfield, Iowa. He can help you out with things when you arrive there."

"How could he help me?" asked Calvin as he sat back down in the chair.

"Hey, man. He owns all kinds of rental properties and several automobile rental agencies, so he could provide you a place to live for a while, and let you use some of his vehicles, you know, just in case you want to change cars daily. I think the man is involved in a lot of illegal shit. He is a friend of my friend who lives in Chicago. My friend loaned a lot of money to the man, so that he could start his businesses in Iowa. The Iowa man will do anything for my friend, because he still owes my friend a huge amount of money. My friend in Chicago will do anything for me, because he still owes me many favors."

Calvin thought it over for a few minutes, before asking, "How much extra will it cost me?"

"Give me another thousand, and I'll set it up for you."

Calvin reached into his pants pocket and pulled out a wad of cash. He counted out a thousand dollars and handed it to Jes'us. After Jes'us counted the cash, he reached for the phone receiver and phoned his friend in Chicago. Several minutes later, Jes'us ended the call and said, "He will call me back in about ten minutes."

Calvin and Jes'us carried on a frivolous conversation until the phone rang. Jes'us answered the phone and talked with his Chicago friend for a few minutes before ending the call. Jes'us slid his right fingers through some of his greasy black hair and said, "Okay, man. My friend's friend lives on the western edge of Rainy, Iowa. That's a small town located about ten miles east of Waterfield. His name is Jimmy Shoot, but make sure you call him Mr. Shoot. His address is 100 Studio Street. You tell him that I sent you to see him. He'll help you with whatever you need. It's all arranged. "

Calvin rose from the chair and asked, "How old is Mr. Shoot, anyway?"

"He's about fifty years old. Make sure you show him a lot of respect, because he can be very mean." Jes'us rose from his chair and headed for the hallway as he said, "Hey, man. I need to do some other things today, so we are finished here."

Calvin followed Jes'us through the hallway and when they reached the living room, Calvin asked, "Are you certain these identification cards will all cross check if the cops ever check them?"

Jes'us stopped right in front of Ace, faced Calvin, and yelled angrily, "Goddamn it! I already told you that I guarantee those cards. What more do you want?" Ace suddenly lunged forward with all his might, pulling the chain and sofa along with him. His sharp teeth penetrated the back of Jes'us' left upper leg, and Jes'us immediately screamed from the severe pain. Ace snarled loudly and became more vicious. He began shaking his head from side to side, causing his teeth to rip and penetrate deeper into Jes'us' thigh. Jes'us reached for his .38 caliber pistol, but fell to the floor while Ace continued biting and snarling. Calvin felt very scared when he saw the expanding bloodstains soaking Jes'us' jeans, so he ran all the way to his car. Just after he slid in behind the steering wheel, he heard two gunshots. When he turned the ignition switch and heard the engine start, he thought, *Jes'us must have shot Ace.* Then, Calvin again heard Jes'us' blood-curdling screams, along with Ace's very loud snarling. Calvin quickly backed his white Cadillac out of the driveway and sped away while thinking, *I wonder which one of those two will survive.*

Calvin arrived in Redwood City at noon. He decided to drive past Mary's house on his way to Elaine's house. As he neared Mary's house, he saw Larry and Mary loading some small boxes into Mary's car trunk. Calvin steered his Cadillac onto Mary's driveway and parked behind Mary's Mercedes C300. As Calvin exited the car, Mary asked, "What are you doing here, Calvin? You said that you would not bother me."

"I wanted to see if you were home from the rehab center. I certainly do not plan to bother you."

Larry straightened his necktie as he said, "Hello, Calvin. What have you been doing today?"

"Hello, Larry. I was in the San Francisco area most of the morning. I was en route to Elaine's house when I saw you, so I decided to stop and visit with you and Mary for a few minutes."

Mary closed the trunk lid, looked at Calvin, and said, "Did you grow that beard and dye your hair for Elaine? I think it makes you look older."

"Well, I am certainly glad I do not have to please you any longer. For your information, Elaine loves my beard and black hair."

Mary tugged on her blouse and right bra strap while straightening her bra a little. "You could help us load some more of my luggage into the car while you are here."

"Are you going on a trip?" asked Calvin as he eyed Mary's bright red short-shorts.

"Yes. I am leaving for Iowa tomorrow morning. I will never return to California. I sold the house and furnishings to Larry."

"Really!" Calvin replied while glancing at his wristwatch. "Well, I will leave you two to your packing. I told Elaine that I would be home for dinner at noon. I am already thirty minutes late, so I had better leave now. Elaine will probably give me some of her special dessert after dinner. Good-bye." As Calvin slid in behind the steering wheel, he thought, *I will leave for Iowa Sunday morning. I cannot wait to get even with that bitch and her parents.*

"Good-bye, Calvin," Mary replied as she scowled at him. She watched Calvin back his car out of the driveway. Then, Mary looked at Larry and said, "I hope I never see that bastard again. He really knows how to irritate me."

Larry smiled, but said nothing as he headed toward the house to get another box of Mary's items.

Duke and Jason sat down inside the 3-season porch at 2:55 p.m. Duke glanced at his watch and said, "My ol' brother, Dave, should be showing up before long."

"Do you want me to get two cans of beer out of the basement for you?" asked Jason.

"I was just thinking that maybe ol' Elmer would enjoy coming over to meet Dave and visit with us for a while. I've tried to get him to come over here before, but he always says that he is too busy. I think he might come over if you invite him. He seems to like you quite a lot."

"Do you want me to knock on his door and ask him?" replied Jason as he stood up and grabbed the porch door handle.

"I guess you could go over there and knock on his door. He might open it for you."

Jason opened the porch door and said, "I'll knock on his front door and find out."

Just as Jason opened the chain-link gate and headed for the front sidewalk, Dave parked his pickup next to the curb line in front of Duke's house. Dave saw Jason and said, "Hello, Jason. Is Duke out on the back porch?"

"Hi, Dave. Yeah. Grandpa is out there waiting for you. I'm going next door to ask the neighbor if he wants to come over to visit for a while."

"That's good. I would enjoy meeting the neighbor. Duke has told me a few things about him, but I've never met him."

Dave walked along the sidewalk leading to the 3-

season porch, and when he reached the porch door, Duke said, "Hi, Dave. Are you ready to drink some beer?"

"Damn straight, Duke. I was working in the garden just before I came over here, so I'm thirstier than someone lost in a desert."

As Dave opened the porch door, Duke stood up and said, "Come in and sit down, Dave. I'll go get a couple beers for us."

A few minutes later, Duke returned to the porch and handed a cold can of beer to Dave. Duke sat down in his wicker chair, popped open the can lid tab, and asked, "Do you have many tomatoes on your plants?"

"There are some," Dave replied as he popped open the can lid tab, "but not as many as last year at this time."

"It's kind of a strange summer this year." Duke took a sip of beer before continuing, "We have tomatoes on the plants, but they are all very small for this time of year. Hell! I don't think we'll have many to can this fall."

Jason and Elmer entered the porch a few minutes later. Duke stood up and introduced Elmer to Dave. As Dave shook Elmer's hand, he said, "I'm glad to meet you, Elmer. Duke has told me a few stories about you."

"I hope they were all good ones," replied Elmer dryly.

Dave let go of Elmer's hand, laughed, and remarked, "They were all good, Elmer. Duke said that you were in the army. I was an army man, too."

Elmer managed to grin a little, but Dave could barely see the grin because of Elmer's long gray beard. Duke asked, "Would you drink a beer, Elmer?"

"I guess a beer wouldn't hurt me," Elmer replied softly as he sat down.

Jason quickly headed for the French doorway opening and said, "I'll get a beer for you, Elmer."

Dave looked at Elmer and said, "I'm sure glad you decided to come over here for a visit with us. Duke told me that you are a novelist."

Elmer began tugging nervously on the tips of his beard. "Yes. I have written several novels through the years. I only write part-time now days."

Jason returned to the porch and handed a cold can of beer to Elmer. Just as Jason sat down, Alice exited the garage and strolled along the sidewalk toward the porch. "Well, hello, my dear," Duke said loudly.

"Hello, everybody," Alice replied as she entered the porch. "I'm surprised to see you, Elmer. It's nice of you to come over to our house." Alice looked at Dave and asked, "How are you today, Dave?"

"I'm just fine, Alice. Jolene told me to tell you hello."

"Tell Jolene hello from me. You should bring her over here sometime. Then, I'd have someone to visit with while you guys drink beer."

Alice approached Duke and gave him a kiss on the right cheek. "How are you, my dear?"

Duke reached up and patted Alice's back a little as he replied, "I'm just fine. How was bible study?"

"It was great. A few more women joined our group this afternoon."

Duke took a swallow of beer, and asked, "Did you hear any new gossip from them?"

Alice scowled at Duke as she replied, "We don't gossip. We concentrate on studying the bible."

"Yeah, right," replied Duke.

Alice entered the dining room, and shut the French door behind her. Duke said, "I guess Alice doesn't want to listen to our bullshit."

"Can you blame her?" Dave said as he grinned from ear to ear.

Jason sat down in the chair next to Duke. "So, Grandpa. Will you tell us about the time you drank down your sterling silver dolphins over in Scotland?"

"I suppose so, unless Elmer wants to tell us about when he received his airborne badge."

Elmer's right shoulder quivered and jerked a few times as he tugged at the tips of his beard and dryly replied, "You go ahead and tell your story, Duke. I might tell you my story, someday."

"Yeah, Duke," said Dave. "Go ahead and tell you story. You've never before told me that one."

Duke reached into his shirt pocket and pulled out a cigarette. As he lit it, he said, "Well, we were steaming across the Atlantic Ocean on our way to Scotland at the time I qualified as a submariner. When we arrived a few days later, we tied up to a pier located near a small town, about an hour away from Glasgow. That evening, a couple of my fellow crewmembers and I rode on a train to Glasgow. We soon entered a pub and began drinking rum and cokes. When I had my third drink about half finished, ten of our crewmembers entered the pub. We moved some tables and situated them so that we could all sit together. I saw the senior crewmember remove a set of sterling silver dolphins from inside his jumper pocket. He walked over to the bar and talked with the barmaid for about five minutes, and then returned to sit with us."

Elmer interrupted and asked, "What do those dolphins look like, anyway?"

Duke stood up and said, "Just a minute. I'll go upstairs and get a pair of dolphins, so you can see exactly what they look like."

As Duke opened the French door, Jason stood up and asked, "Do you want me to get some more beer for everybody, Grandpa?"

"You bet, Jason. I'm sure we can each drink at least one more. You'd better get a soda for yourself."

Duke and Jason returned to the porch a few minutes later. Duke handed a set of sterling silver dolphins to

Elmer while saying, "Here they are, Elmer. Pretty neat, huh?"

Elmer inspected the dolphins closely and said, "Yes. These are very nice. I'm sure you are very proud of being a submariner. I know I felt very proud when I qualified as an airborne ranger."

Jason distributed the beer, sat down, and said, "Are you going to finish your story, Grandpa?"

Duke took a huge swallow of beer, and said, "Well, a few minutes after the senior crewmember returned to our table, the barmaid showed up with a very tall glass filled with an ungodly colored liquid. She set the glass upon the tabletop directly in front of me. The senior crewmember dropped the set of dolphins into the greenish, grayish liquid, and said, 'Okay, Duke. It's time to drink down your dolphins. Then, you will officially become a qualified submariner.' I looked at the smiling barmaid and asked her what she had poured into the glass. She replied that she had poured 10 different varieties of hard liquor and 3 different varieties of beer into the glass. The barmaid said that she mixed one shot of Crème' De Menthe into the drink, so that it would taste a little better."

"Good God, Duke," Dave remarked. "That's a lot of booze for one drink."

Duke laughed as he replied, "That's for sure."

Jason asked, "So, Grandpa. Were you able to drink the whole thing?"

"I picked up that glass, smelled the drink for a few seconds, and then drank all 13 shots of booze without stopping. I had one end of that dolphins badge clenched between my front teeth when I set the empty glass on the tabletop. The senior crewmember reached over, took the dolphins, and said, 'Stand up, so I can pin these on your uniform.' I stood up and after he pinned the dolphins badge onto my uniform, he said, 'Congratulations. You are now one of our Silent Service brothers.' All the crewmembers clapped and offered their congratulations."

"Goddamn, Duke," said Elmer while grinning and tugging lightly on the tips of his beard. "How long was it before you began heaving?"

"About thirty minutes," replied Duke while smiling. "Hell! When all that booze hit me, I ran for the bathroom. I kneeled in front of the stool for about ten minutes while heaving out my guts. Then, I lay on the floor in front of the stool while waiting for the next wave of sickness to hit me. I spent at least an hour in that bathroom, part of the time heaving and part of the time lying on the floor in front of the stool. Every once in a while, some of the crewmembers checked on me. I guess they wanted to make sure I hadn't died."

"Do all the submariners have to drink qualification drinks when they qualify?" asked Jason.

"I don't know for sure, but I know that all the men on our boat drank down their dolphins. I don't know how much booze they had to drink, though."

Duke looked at Elmer and asked, "Would you like to tell us about when you received your airborne badge?"

Elmer swallowed the last of the beer from his can before saying, "I will tell you the story some other time. I need to head for home, now. It is already 4:00 p.m. Elmer stood up and shook Dave's hand as he said, "I am glad I met you, Dave. I hope we can all get together again. Perhaps, I can come over for a visit the next time you are here at Duke's house."

"That sounds like a good plan," Dave replied. "You are welcome to come over to my house with Duke and Jason next Friday."

"Thank you. I will see if I can work that into my schedule for next week." As Elmer opened the porch door to leave, he said, "Don't forget, Duke. You and Jason come over to my house at 10:00 p.m. I want you to see my night-vision goggles."

"Okay," replied Duke. "Jason has to work tonight, but he should be home by that time."

Dave stood up and said, "I suppose I'd better head for home, too. I told Jolene that I would be home by 4:30 p.m. Thanks for the beer, as well as the good story."

Duke replied, "You're welcome, Dave. We'll see you next Friday at your house."

As soon as David disappeared around the corner of the house, Jason said, "I need to get ready for work, Grandpa. I have to work from 5:00 p.m. until 9:30 p.m."

"Is Jo Ann working tonight?"

"Yeah. She told me that her dad will pick her up after work, so she said that I could ride home with them."

"That's nice," replied Duke. As Jason exited the porch through the French doorway opening, Duke thought, *Maybe, I'll ask Alice if she's interested in spending a little quality time with me in bed while Jason is at work.*

Later, at 10:30 p.m., Duke and Jason returned home from Elmer's house. Just as they entered the kitchen, Alice answered the kitchen phone, "Hello. Alice speaking."

"Hello, Mother. How are you tonight?"

"I am just fine, Mary. How about you?"

"I am quite okay," replied Mary. "I want to let you know that I will leave here tomorrow morning and begin driving toward Iowa. Is it okay if I stay at your house until I can find a place of my own?"

"That's wonderful, Mary. Sure, you can stay here. I'll get the spare bedroom ready for you. When do you think you will arrive?"

"I should be there sometime late Wednesday, July 6."

"Great. Make sure you drive carefully."

"Yes, Mother. Is Jason still awake? I want to talk with him for a minute."

"Jason and your father just came home from Elmer's house. I'll tell him you want to talk with him." Alice put down the phone receiver and told Jason that Mary wanted to talk with him. Jason walked into the dining room and picked up the mobile phone.

When Jason began talking with Mary, Alice cradled the kitchen phone receiver, and then walked into the living room where she stood in front of Duke sitting on the sofa. "Mary is going to arrive here sometime Wednesday. She is leaving Redwood City tomorrow morning. I'm so excited."

"That's good news," replied Duke. "It'll sure be nice to see her again. Elmer told me a little while ago that he owns a nice two-bedroom house located six blocks from here, over on Third Street. It is completely furnished, and it is vacant right now. He said that he would rent it to Mary for a very reasonable price. Elmer also said that he would buy brand-new mattresses for the beds."

"That's nice of Elmer. We'll tell Mary about it when she gets here. I'm sure she would like to have her own place instead of living with us." Alice sat down beside Duke and snuggled against him. She whispered into his right ear, "You are sure a good lover. I'm still tingling all over from our get together earlier tonight."

Duke smiled as he lightly rubbed Alice's left thigh. "I can see that your face is still pretty flush. You are a great lover, Alice. My heart is still pounding faster than normal. We should get together more often for some of that quality time. I love it, and I love you.

"I love you, too, Duke," Alice replied while smiling brightly.

Chapter 14

Mary parked her Mercedes 300C Sport Sedan in front of Duke and Alice's house at 4:00 p.m. Wednesday, July 6. As she unbuckled her seatbelt and opened the front car door, she thought, *The old neighborhood certainly has not changed very much since I was here the last time. Some of the houses appear in better shape, and some appear more run down.* Just as she began walking toward the chain-link gate, she saw Jason, Duke, and Alice walking out through the side doorway opening of the house. Jason quickly opened the gate and ran toward Mary. "Hi, Mom," he hollered as he ran toward her. When he reached her, they wrapped their arms around each other and hugged tightly.

"I'm so glad to see you, Jason," said Mary as tears welled up in her eyes. She released Jason and stepped away a little. "My goodness, Jason. You appear to be in very good shape these days."

As Duke and Alice approached them, Jason replied, "Yeah, Mom. Grandpa and I have been working out together, and I have already lost ten pounds of my body fat."

Alice hugged Mary briefly and said, "I'm so glad you're here, Mary."

"It is certainly nice to be here," replied Mary.

Duke took his turn hugging Mary and said, "I'm glad to see you, Mary. Jason and I will carry your luggage into the house. I'm sure you're about worn-out from all the driving."

"Yes, it was definitely a long trip, and I am very tired."

With her right hand, Alice reached out and held Mary's left hand, and said, "Let's go inside. We'll drink something cold while catching up on all the news."

As they entered the kitchen, Alice asked, "Do you want some freshly squeezed lemonade? I finished making some about fifteen minutes ago."

"That sounds delicious, Mother, but I need to use the bathroom before I drink anything."

Alice poured two glasses of lemonade and set them on the dining room tabletop. Mary exited the bathroom and paused long enough to peer into the rear bedroom, the bedroom she used while growing up. "It is hard to believe how I ever managed to sleep in such a small bedroom while I grew up," Mary said as she walked into the dining room. "I guess I have become quite spoiled from living in the beautiful house Calvin and I owned in Redwood City."

As Mary sat down at the table, Duke and Jason entered the kitchen, each carrying one of Mary's suitcases. As they walked through the dining room, Duke asked, "Should we set these suitcases inside the rear bedroom, Alice?"

Alice grinned at Duke and replied, "Well, I don't know where else you would set them, Duke."

Duke did not reply as he and Jason placed both suitcases inside the rear bedroom. When they exited the bedroom, Duke stopped beside Mary and asked, "Do you want us to bring all those boxes into the house? There isn't enough room in the bedroom for all that stuff."

"I guess you can leave the boxes in the car for now,

Dad. I plan to rent an apartment, or a house, tomorrow."

"I know where there is a nice two-bedroom house you could rent," Duke said as he rubbed the back of his neck with his right hand and stepped a few steps away from Mary.

"Where is it?" asked Mary.

"It's over on Third Street, just about six blocks from here. Our next-door neighbor, Elmer, owns it. He told me that he will rent it to you for a very reasonable price."

"I guess we could look at the house in the morning. Will you ask Elmer if he will show the house to me at 9:00 a.m. tomorrow?"

"Sure," replied Duke. "I'll go next door and ask him right now."

As Duke walked out of the dining room, Jason put his hand on Mary's right shoulder and said, "Will you give me a ride to work in a little while, Mom?"

"Yes, Jason. What time?"

"We'll have to leave here by 4:45 p.m., as soon as I finish showering and changing clothes."

Mary took a sip of lemonade before replying, "How late do you have to work?"

"I'll finish my shift at 10:00 p.m. Will you come over there to get me?"

"Yes, Jason."

Several hours later, Jason glanced at the wall clock hanging above the kitchen sinks in Wanda's Restaurant. He saw the clock displaying 9:00 p.m. and thought, *I'll really be glad to finish my shift. I am very tired.* At the same time, Calvin steered his white Cadillac off a two-lane highway and onto the parking lot of a gas station located just north of Mahoosa, a small city located about fifty miles south of Waterfield. Calvin parked the Cadillac next to a gas pump, and pumped several gallons of ethanol-blended gasoline into the Cadillac gas tank. When he entered the building to pay for the gas, he saw several refrigerated coolers along one wall. One of the coolers held several different assortments of beer. Calvin opened a cooler door and removed a twelve-pack of his favorite beer. After paying his bill for the beer and gas, he exited the building. Just then, he saw a petite young woman with shoulder-length blonde hair strolling toward him. She wore a very short denim skirt, a skimpy, low-cut white blouse, and a pair of black cowboy boots. Calvin judged her to be in her late twenties, or early thirties. As Calvin continued walking toward his Cadillac, the woman said, "Hey, Mister. Are you heading north toward Waterfield?"

Calvin stopped walking and faced the woman who stood only five feet away from him. As Calvin looked her up and down, he caught a whiff of her lightly scented lavender perfume. "As a matter of fact, I am going to Waterfield. Why do you ask?"

The young woman smiled and rolled her large blue eyes flirtatiously as she used her right hand to flip back part of her long blonde hair over her right shoulder. "My name is Tina. I need a ride to my home in Waterfield."

Calvin walked about fifteen feet to reach the Cadillac. He opened the rear door and placed the twelve-pack upon the floorboard. Tina moved closer to Calvin and said, "I would really appreciate it if you will give me a ride to Waterfield. I have to get home, so that I can go to work early tomorrow morning."

Calvin shut the rear door and asked, "What kind of work?"

"I am the day manager at a restaurant. My shift begins at 5:00 a.m."

Calvin closed the rear car door and opened the front door before saying, "Okay. Get in the car and I will take you to Waterfield. I surely wouldn't want you to miss work."

When Calvin steered the Cadillac from the gas station property onto the main highway, he asked, "Did your car break down, Tina?"

Tina began sobbing softly. "No, I don't own a car. I was attending a party with my boyfriend in Mahoosa, at a house located about two blocks from the gas station."

"How come you left the party?"

"I left because my boyfriend drank some beer and took some kind of pills. He began acting very crazy, and tried to get me to swallow one of the pills. I agreed to have a drink with him, but I refused to take a pill. Then, he insisted that I participate in a foursome with him, his best friend, and his best friend's girlfriend. I bluntly refused, so he became very violent. We argued for a little while, but then he told me to find my own way home, because he was staying with his friends for the night." Tina rubbed her forehead several times while saying, "I'm feeling kind of light-headed. I think my boyfriend mixed some kind of drug into the drink he fixed for me about a half hour before I left the party."

While Tina had been talking about the foursome and the drugs, Calvin began feeling turned on sexually, since he had participated in more than one foursome within the last year. Calvin took a deep breath and caught another whiff of Tina's sexy smelling perfume. He glanced at Tina, smiled, and said, "There is a cold twelve-pack of beer on the back floor. You should drink a beer. That will help dissipate the drugs your boyfriend gave you."

"Really?" replied Tina. "If you think it will make me feel better, I guess I'll drink one."

"Can you reach over the seat and get one of the beers, or do you want me to pull over and park on the shoulder, so that I can get you one?"

Tina unbuckled her seatbelt and scooted around until her knees were upon the front seat. She slid over next to

Calvin and reached over the back of the front seat. Her large breasts had passed within inches of Calvin's face, and he again smelled her fragrant perfume. "Grab me a can of beer, too," Calvin ordered.

Tina managed to open the twelve-pack carton and grab two cans of beer. When she straightened up and handed Calvin a can of beer, her breasts were again very close to Calvin's face. As Tina returned to the sitting position and buckled her seatbelt, Calvin popped open the beer can lid tab, took a huge swallow of beer, and thought, *Tina has really turned me on. She definitely enjoys flirting. I will give her some well-deserved loving, whether she wants it or not.*

Calvin and Tina sat in silence for about ten minutes while continuing to head north at 55 mph along the main highway. Calvin eventually slowed the Cadillac and steered it off the highway onto an east-west gravel road located approximately fifteen miles south of Waterfield, Tina nervously asked, "Why did you turn onto this gravel road?"

Calvin continued driving east along the gravel road. "I saw a realty sign back there at the intersection. There is a house for sale somewhere along this road. I want to see what it looks like. It should not be much farther. I have been planning to purchase a house and acreage for a long time."

"I don't know how well you can see it at night."

"I merely want to see if it is a dump, or a nice place. If I am interested, I can always contact the realtor."

Tina's cell phone rang, so she reached into her long-strapped, small, black leather purse and removed her cell phone. Calvin said, "Do not answer that call, Tina."

"I have to, because it's my boyfriend."

"Don't answer it," ordered Calvin as he forcefully grabbed the phone from Tina's hand.

Tina released her seatbelt and began struggling with Calvin while trying to get the phone out of his hand, but

Calvin suddenly backhanded her very hard across the forehead. Tina immediately blacked out and slumped forward, so Calvin pushed her back into the sitting position against the front seat. A few minutes later, Calvin saw a realty sign located next to a driveway. He steered the Cadillac off the gravel road and slowly entered the farmyard. Tall pine trees lined the perimeter of the acreage. A barn, a few small outbuildings, and a one-story bungalow with an attached oversized double garage occupied spaces on the property. Calvin saw the opened overhead garage door and vacant garage. *This place looks very deserted*, he thought. *Perhaps, it is a foreclosed property*. Calvin parked a little ways away from the garage, and removed a flashlight from inside the glove compartment. He exited the car and slowly approached the house where he looked through one of the living room windows. He shined the flashlight beam through the window and saw only a vacant room with two night-lights glowing dimly. Calvin made his way to another window and looked through it. He saw another vacant room with only one night-light glowing. Calvin quickly returned to the Cadillac, drove it through the garage doorway opening, and parked inside the garage.

Tina began moaning and stirring a little as Calvin shut off the engine. He saw the dashboard clock displaying 10:30 p.m. as he exited the car. Calvin manually closed the overhead wooden garage door. He checked the entrance door to the house, and felt surprised when he found it unlocked. Calvin opened the front car door and pulled Tina from the Cadillac. As he gripped Tina's left upper arm very tightly, he said, "Let's go into the house and have a little fun."

As they walked toward the entrance door, Tina began crying. "I want you to take me home."

"I will take you home when I finish with you. If you

fight me, you will never again see your home."

After entering the house, Calvin opened the basement entry door and turned on the light switch. "We'll go into the basement. That way, if somebody happens to come onto the property, they will not see lights glowing inside the house." When they reached the bottom of the steps, they explored the basement and found a utility room, a workshop containing some tools, and a bedroom containing an ancient double bed with a steel-spindled headboard and a bare, dirty appearing mattress. "My, my," Calvin remarked. "This place still has a bed in it." He shoved Tina toward the bed and said, "Okay, bitch. Take off your clothes. I want to explore your beautiful body."

"Please take me home," begged Tina while standing next to the bed. Her black eyeliner flowed with her tears causing her cheeks to appear streaky. She wiped her tears, smudging the eyeliner even more as she again said, "Please take me home."

Calvin quickly approached Tina and pushed her down onto the mattress. He slapped her across the face before shaking her violently. "Stop crying! I've had enough of your pretend drama".

"Please take me home," Tina sobbed while remaining on her back upon the mattress. "If you take me home right now, I won't tell anybody about you."

"Shut your mouth," Calvin hollered

At the same time as Calvin began violating Tina's body, Alice and Mary sat down on the sofa in Duke and Alice's living room and began discussing Mary's plans for the future. Duke and Jason had already retired to their bedrooms for the night. Alice and Mary talked softly, so that they would not disturb Duke and Jason. They continued discussing different things until midnight, when Alice said, "Well, Mary. I hope everything works out for you, so that you will remain living here in Waterfield. You know your father and I will do whatever we can to help you and Jason."

"Yes, I know you will, Mother." Mary yawned as she stood up. "I am going to bed, Mother."

"Alice stood up and said, "Sleep tight, my dear. I'll see you in the morning."

At 12:30 a.m. Thursday, Calvin stood up and looked down at Tina, who appeared with several bright red welts across her breasts and belly area caused by Calvin whipping her with his belt. Red marks encircled her neck from Calvin choking her during the last minutes of his violations. "Get up and put on your clothes," Calvin ordered as he put on his underwear. He slipped into his slacks, and strung his belt through the belt loops. He again looked at Tina and saw that her eyes were wide open, but perfectly still. Calvin reached down and shook Tina. "Come on, Tina. Wake up and get dressed." When Tina did not respond, Calvin became worried, so he checked to see if she had a pulse. He felt none, so he panicked and shook her some more. *Oh, God*, he thought. *She is dead. I really blew it this time. What am I going to do?*

Calvin finished dressing before sitting on the edge of the bed. He spent the next ten minutes trying to decide if he should leave her there, or if he should hide her body. Calvin finally decided to hide her body. He turned toward Tina and closed her eyelids gently. *I wonder if I can find a shovel inside one of the outbuildings*, he thought. *If I find one, I will dig a hole and bury her. I must have choked her too hard, or too long. Damn! I am really in a lot of trouble.*

Ten minutes later, Calvin entered a small machine shed where he shined the flashlight beam around until he found a garden spade. A few minutes later, with the help of his flashlight and the full moon, he found his way to a large garden plot near the rear of the acreage. *I should be able to dig a large hole in this garden, large enough for a grave*, he thought as he laid the flashlight upon the ground. He rammed the spade into the earth and removed a spadeful of dirt. *This will take a while*, he thought, *but I definitely need to bury her. Nobody will ever know I buried her in this garden plot.* Calvin spent the next two hours frantically digging the hole. When he finished, he dropped the spade onto the ground and wiped some sweat from his forehead. *Boy, it is very warm and humid*, he thought. *My clothes are completely soaked with sweat, and I am tired as hell. I hope I still have enough strength left to carry that bitch out of the basement.* Calvin walked back to the house and entered the basement bedroom. He stood next to the bed looking at Tina. *She is so beautiful*, he thought. *God, I am so sorry, Tina.*

Calvin struggled as he picked up Tina and placed her over his right shoulder. As he began walking toward the steps he thought, *She is much heavier than she appears.* Five minutes later, Calvin gently lowered Tina's body into the hole. He positioned her body to match the shape of the hole. With the bright beam from the flashlight shining into the hole, Calvin could see that there would be about eighteen inches of dirt over and above the body by the time he finished backfilling the hole. Satisfied with the depth, he walked to the house and entered the basement bedroom to retrieve Tina's clothing, purse, and cell phone. When Calvin returned to the gravesite, he threw Tina's clothes, purse, and cell phone into the hole, and began filling the hole with dirt. An hour later, he threw the last spadeful of dirt onto the gravesite. Then, he spent fifteen minutes smoothing out the dirt above the gravesite in order to blend it in with the surrounding area. He picked up the flashlight and shined the light beam onto his wristwatch. *Damn!* he thought. *It is already 4:00 a.m. I am tired as hell, but I need to keep going so I can leave here before daybreak.*

Calvin returned to the basement and checked to make sure he had left nothing incriminating. When he felt satisfied with his cleanup, he looked for a screwdriver. He found a screwdriver lying upon a workbench, so he grabbed the screwdriver and headed for the garage. *I will remove the California license plates and put on the Iowa license plates,* he thought while walking up the stair steps. *I do not know if anyone saw my California license plates at the gas station, but I do not want to take a chance.*

After Calvin changed the license plates, he opened the trunk lid and removed one of his suitcases. He opened it and removed a clean pair of slacks and a short-sleeved white shirt. When he finished changing clothes, he placed the suitcase back into the trunk, closed the trunk lid, opened the overhead garage door, and slid in behind the steering wheel. While backing the Cadillac out of the garage, he thought, *Oh, shit. I forgot to wipe clean Tina's cell phone before I threw it into the hole. My fingerprints are all over that phone. It is too late for me to do anything about it now. I can only hope that nobody will find her body.* After twenty-five minutes of driving, Calvin entered into the southern area of Waterfield. Daylight seemed to be approaching quickly, so Calvin decided to continue driving until he reached the western part of Rainy, Iowa. There he would find a place to park near Mr. Shoot's residence, so that he could sleep for a few hours. As the dashboard clock displayed 5:30 a.m., Calvin parked his Cadillac next to the west curb line of Studio Street, only a half-block north of Mr. Shoot's driveway.

Calvin set his wristwatch alarm for 8:00 a.m. and reclined the front seat as far back as it would go. He leaned back and thought, *I will doze until about 8:00 a.m. Then, I will approach Mr. Shoot's house and find out if he will talk with me. It would be great if I could use one of his cars while I am here. Mary might recognize me if she sees this car parked near her parents' house.*

Jason awoke at 5:45 a.m. Thursday, July 7, but remained in bed while fantasizing about Jo Ann. He exited the bedroom at 6:00 a.m. and went into the bathroom. When Jason finished washing his face and brushing his teeth, he went into the dining room and saw through the windows of the French door that Duke sat silently on the 3-season porch, enjoying a smoke and his coffee. Jason walked into the kitchen and saw Alice tying her apron strings while standing in front of the stove. "Good morning, Grandma."

"Hi, Jason. What would you like for breakfast? I'm trying to think of something different to make."

"I will eat anything you make, Grandma. Are you going with us when we look at the house over on Third Street this morning?"

"I don't know if Mary wants your grandpa and me to look at the house with her. I'll ask her when she awakes." Alice opened the pantry door and stared at all the boxes of food. She fumbled around with some of the boxes, and finally said, "How does oatmeal with some honey on it sound to you?"

"That will be just fine, Grandma." Jason drank a glass of water before saying, "I'm going out on the porch and sit with Grandpa until breakfast is ready."

Just as Jason opened the French door between the dining room and 3-season porch, Mary exited the rear bedroom and went into the bathroom. After Jason entered the porch and closed the French door, Duke smiled at him and said, "Good morning, Jason. Did you sleep well last night?"

"Yeah. How about you?"

"I woke up a few times through the night, but that's not unusual for me."

Jason sat down in the wicker chair near Duke and said, "Grandma is cooking some oatmeal for us."

Duke snuffed out his cigarette and dropped it into the clear glass ashtray. He grinned and said, “That’s good, Jason. The doctors claim that oatmeal helps lower the cholesterol level in a person’s body.”

Five minutes later, Mary opened the French door and stepped onto the 3-season porch. “Good morning. Mother told me that she would like to go with me to look at Elmer’s rental. Do you both want to accompany us?”

“If you want me to come along, I will,” replied Duke.

“I want to see the house,” Jason replied.

“Is Elmer going to meet us at his rental, or are we all supposed to go over there together?” asked Mary as she turned and stepped into the dining room.

“Elmer told me that he will meet us in front of our house at 9:00 a.m. He said that we will walk to his rental property.”

“Great,” replied Mary as she shut the French door.

At 7:30 a.m. in Rainy, Iowa, the part-time police officer, a man in his late fifties named Marvin Lewinski, parked his squad car behind Calvin’s white Cadillac. Officer Lewinski slid out of the squad car and cautiously approached the driver’s door of the Cadillac. He saw Calvin reclined back lying motionlessly in the driver’s seat. Officer Lewinski knocked on the side window several times before Calvin awoke and sat up. Calvin opened the side window and said, “Good morning officer.”

“Hello, sir. Why are you sleeping while parked here?”

“I am here this morning to speak with Mr. Shoot. I arrived a few hours early, so I decided to catnap for a while.”

“I need to see your driver’s license, registration, and proof of insurance.”

“No problem, officer.” Calvin removed his Iowa driver’s license and proof of insurance card from his wallet, and handed both to Officer Lewinski while saying, “The registration is inside my glove compartment. I will get it for you."

Officer Lewinski placed his right hand on his 9-millimeter pistol grip. "Reach into that glove compartment very slowly, and when you remove the registration, move your hand much slower."

"Yes sir, officer." Calvin opened the glove compartment door and slowly removed the registration. He handed it to the officer, and said, "There you go, officer."

"Okay. You sit very still while I go back to my squad car and verify everything."

"Yes sir, officer."

Ten minutes later, Officer Lewinski returned to the Cadillac and handed everything back to Calvin. "Everything checks out okay," said Officer Lewinski, "so I'll be on my way. Have a good day."

"Thank you, officer. Enjoy your day."

When Officer Lewinski disappeared from Calvin's view, Calvin started the Cadillac engine and drove the half-block to Mr. Shoot's driveway approach. Calvin parked a little ways past the driveway approach, and opened the front car door. He slid out from behind the steering wheel, and walked along the edge of Mr. Shoot's concrete driveway. When Calvin approached the garage, the overhead garage door began opening. Calvin stood beside the garage doorway until the overhead door opened fully. Then, Calvin looked toward the front inside of the garage and saw a very large, barrel-chested man exiting the house and entering the garage. "Good morning," Calvin offered cheerfully.

The startled man stopped in his tracks, peered at Calvin, and asked loudly, "Who in the hell are you?"

"Are you Mr. Shoot?"

"Yes, I am Mr. Shoot," answered the stocky built, gray-haired man as he walked toward the overhead garage door opening. Mr. Shoot approached Calvin, and asked, "And who are you?"

"My name is Calvin. Jes'us sent me to see you." Calvin offered his hand for a handshake, but Mr. Shoot declined.

"So what do you need from me," asked Mr. Shoot. "I heard that you might need a place to stay while you are in town."

"Yes, I definitely need a place to stay. I also need a different car to use while I am here."

"That's what my contact in Chicago told me. Climb into your car and follow me. You can stay in a house I own in the countryside. It's located about ten miles south of here. We'll talk more when we arrive there."

Twenty minutes later, after navigating along several different curvy, dusty gravel roads, Calvin followed Mr. Shoot onto a farmyard and parked his Cadillac beside Mr. Shoot's black, 2011 Lincoln Navigator. Mr. Shoot exited the Navigator as Calvin exited the Cadillac. Mr. Shoot pointed toward the house and said, "This is the place, Calvin. It's not very big, only two bedrooms, but the house is completely furnished. I'll let you have it free of charge for the next two weeks. If you need it longer, you'll have to pay me a thousand dollars a month."

Calvin laughed a little and said, "I do not plan on staying here for more than about a week. That is if everything goes okay." As Mr. Shoot handed Calvin a key ring containing several keys, Calvin asked, "Would it be possible for me to rent a car from you?"

Mr. Shoot pointed toward an unattached garage located about a hundred feet from the house, and said, "There is a nice little black Ford Focus parked inside that old garage. You can use the Focus rent-free while you are here. The keys are on the key ring I gave to you. If you so desire, you can park your Cadillac inside the machine shed. Nobody will see it in there, if that's what you are worried about."

"Thank you, Mr. Shoot. I appreciate all this very much."

Mr. Shoot gave Calvin a ten-minute tour of the small house while explaining a few things about what Calvin should do and should not do because of the water well system and septic tank system. As they finished the tour and stood in the kitchen, Mr. Shoot asked, "Do you have any questions?"

Calvin rubbed the back of his neck with his right hand while nervously asking, "Do you know where I can purchase a small quantity of cocaine?"

Mr. Shoot replied, "I'll give you credit, Calvin. You definitely have a lot of balls, asking a complete stranger a question like that one." Mr. Shoot reached into his right front pants pocket and pulled out his cell phone. He flipped open the keyboard, punched some keyboard buttons, and walked into the living room. Calvin heard Mr. Shoot talking with someone, but could not hear the conversation. A few minutes later, Mr. Shoot returned to the kitchen and said, "Okay, Calvin. You will see a car entering this farmyard at 11:00 a.m. The person will park next to the garage, get out of the car, and place a package upon the ground, right next to the overhead garage door. You make sure that you stay in the house until the person leaves the area. The first package is on me. If you want additional packages, you will have to pay me."

"Thank you, Mr. Shoot. I appreciate all your kindness."

"I need to leave for my office," said Mr. Shoot as he walked toward the door.

When they returned outside, Mr. Shoot faced Calvin, stood nearly toe-to-toe with him, and stared directly into Calvin's eyes. Using the tip of his right index finger, Mr. Shoot began poking the center of Calvin's chest. Mr. Shoot continued poking the same spot on Calvin's chest while using a very serious, almost threatening tone of voice, as he gruffly said, "I am doing all this as a favor for my contact in Chicago. I want you to know that if you damage anything on this property, or steal anything from this property, I will have my people hunt you down. When they find you, your life will end abruptly. Is that clear to you?"

Calvin backed away several steps and while rubbing the center of his chest, replied, "Yes sir, Mr. Shoot. That is perfectly clear to me."

Chapter 15

At 9:10 a.m. Thursday, July 7, Elmer, Duke, Jason, Alice, and Mary stood upon the sidewalk leading to the front porch of Elmer's rental house at 4723 Third Street. Elmer removed a key from his right front jean pocket and said, "I'll first give you all a tour of the house. After that, I'll show you the fenced-in backyard and the double garage located near the alley."

"This is a craftsman-style house, isn't it?" Mary asked. "I love the small front porch and those square, tapered columns."

"Yes, it's a craftsman style," Elmer replied. "According to the deed, a well-known local contractor built this house in 1924. The same contractor built many other houses throughout this city. Many of those houses are very huge and fancy. I think you will like the inside of this house, Mary. It has 1,200 square feet of area on the main floor, and has a full basement. The house has all kinds of fancy, solid oak woodwork."

"I adore oak woodwork," Mary replied as they began walking toward the front porch.

Just then, they heard the next-door neighbor to the west of them say, "Good morning, Elmer. Are you getting some new renters?"

Mary looked to the west and smiled brightly when she saw a muscular, handsome man about her age sitting on the front stoop of his house. He had on a pair of denim shorts and a bright white undershirt, much like the shirts Mary had recently heard some young women refer to as wife-beater shirts. Mary thought, *Wow! That man is literally oozing sex!*

Elmer put his hand on Mary's shoulder as he looked toward the neighbor and said, "Well, good morning to you, Tony. I hope this young woman will rent the house, so that you will have a new neighbor."

Tony immediately stood up and strolled toward everybody. He approached Mary closely and looked directly into her beautiful blue eyes. He offered his hand for a handshake while saying, "Hello. My name is Tony."

Mary smiled as she glanced at Tony's brown eyes and perfectly shaped nose. While shaking Tony's hand, she said, "I am Mary." After several repetitions of handshakes, Mary reluctantly released his hand and introduced Tony to Duke, Alice, and Jason.

After the introductions and handshakes, Tony smiled at Mary and said, "I think you will like this neighborhood, Mary. I purchased my house about twenty years ago, and have enjoyed living in this neighborhood ever since." Tony shaded his eyes from the sun with his right hand as he sneaked a few quick glances at Mary's red short-shorts and low-cut white blouse. "It is very humid this morning," Tony said while using his right palm to wipe a few beads of sweat from his forehead. "I'm already perspiring."

Mary suddenly felt very attracted to Tony and while admiring his sweaty, glistening biceps, replied, "I think the exterior of this house is lovely. If I like the inside as much as the exterior, I will certainly rent it."

"Well, I hope you do," replied Tony as he slid his left palm along the top of his crew-cut black hair, causing his left biceps to flex more than normal. "Well, it is nice meeting all of you." Tony lowered his left hand and as he took a few side steps toward his house, said, "I'd better quit bothering you so Elmer can show you the inside of the house."

Mary smiled and said, "I am glad I met you, Tony. And believe me; you certainly did not bother us." Mary could not take her eyes off Tony as he walked toward his front stoop. She felt dazed while thinking, *Wow! Tony has a gorgeous body. He is extremely handsome and very polite.*

Mary came back to reality when Elmer said, "Well. Is everybody ready to go into the house and look around?"

"Yes," Mary replied. "I am ready."

Elmer led them up three steps and onto the front porch where he fumbled around with the door key for about ten seconds before finally turning it the right way to insert it into the brass lock of the solid oak door. Elmer unlocked the door and swung it open, exposing the small vestibule. Elmer walked into the living room as Mary and the others followed behind. Mary saw the recently refinished solid oak floors, and said, "Wow, Elmer! I love these oak floors."

Elmer replied, "All the floors in this house are oak except for the kitchen and bathroom, and they are linoleum covered floors." Elmer pointed toward the edge of the ceiling and said, "What do you think of all the wide oak cove molding? A few years ago, I hired a man to strip and re-varnish all the oak woodwork in this house. Isn't it beautiful?"

Alice quickly offered, "The oak woodwork in this house is absolutely gorgeous, Elmer. I wish the contractor would have installed varnished oak woodwork in our house instead of the white-painted spruce."

From the living room, Elmer led them through the dining room and into the kitchen. When they all gathered in the kitchen, Mary stated, "There is no dishwasher in here, Elmer."

Elmer grinned at Mary and replied dryly, "I thought about ripping out a few cabinets, so that I could install a dishwasher, but that's as far as I went with it. As you can see, there is a lovely double-bowl, stainless steel sink. A few people still manage to hand wash dishes." Elmer scratched his left eyebrow lightly and said, "I purchased this refrigerator and stove about six months ago."

"I suppose I could live without a dishwasher," replied Mary. "Let's go look at the bedrooms and bathroom."

After fifteen minutes of checking out both bedrooms and the bathroom, Elmer led them down the stair steps leading to the basement. As they all stood upon the concrete floor, Elmer offered, "There isn't much in this basement, other than the furnace and water heater. I purchased those last January, so they are still nearly brand-new. I purchased the central air conditioner when I purchased the furnace. This basement is a very dry basement. At one time, I thought about building another bedroom, or a family room down here, but I never accomplished it."

Jason said, "This would be a perfect place for my workout room, Mom. I want to eventually buy a weight bench and some weights."

"It is certainly roomy enough, Jason," replied Mary. "Let's go check out the garage and the backyard."

Fifteen minutes later, they exited the garage and went into the kitchen, where Mary said, "I like this place a lot, Elmer. Can you and I sit down somewhere and discuss the rent options?"

"Sure," replied Elmer. "We can go back to my house and discuss the options, or we can discuss them right here."

Alice quickly offered, "The rest of us can go home,

Mary, if you and Elmer want to discuss the options privately."

"That will work," replied Mary as she walked toward the living room. Duke, Alice, and Jason left through the front doorway opening and headed for home. Elmer went into the living room and sat down at one end of the sofa. Mary sat down at the other end of the sofa and asked, "How much will you charge me monthly to rent this house?"

Elmer's right shoulder jerked several times as he looked at Mary and replied, "The last renter paid me 1,000 dollars a month, but since I have known you and your parents for so many years, I'll only charge you 800 dollars a month. How does that sound to you?"

Mary relaxed and leaned back against the softly padded sofa cushions. She crossed her legs and began sliding the palm of her right hand lightly along the top of her bare left thigh. "That is definitely a fair price, Elmer. How long will it take you to get two new mattresses delivered here?"

Elmer snuck a quick glance at the very bottom of Mary's bright red short-shorts and admired her firm thighs. Then, Elmer smiled and said, "I will phone the store and order the mattresses as soon as I get home. They will deliver them this afternoon."

Mary saw Elmer checking out her legs, so she smiled and rolled her eyes flirtatiously at him. "How can you possibly get them delivered that fast?"

Elmer grinned from ear to ear as he replied, "I do a lot of business with that particular store, so they always try to please me. I own ten other rental houses and two 12-unit apartment buildings in this city."

"Are you kidding me, Elmer?"

"No," replied Elmer as he snickered a little bit. "I should sell all my rental properties, but I don't need the money, at least not yet."

"Would you consider selling this house to me after I rent it for a while? That is, if I like living here."

"How about this scenario? If you decide to buy this house within the next year, I will sell it to you for 100,000 dollars. I will apply all your rent money toward the purchase price."

"Will you write that into the rental contract?" asked Mary as she uncrossed her legs and leaned forward, exposing more cleavage.

"Yes," Elmer replied while sneaking a glance at Mary's cleavage. "We can walk back to my house, and I'll write the contract. All you will have to do is sign it and pay me 800 dollars. You and Jason can move into this house tomorrow."

"That is a deal," said Mary as she offered her hand for a handshake.

Elmer gladly shook her hand as he stared at her cleavage. When their hands parted, Elmer said, "Do you have any other questions while we're here?"

Mary leaned back and said, "I am curious about the neighbors, especially Tony. He seems like a very nice man. Who lives next-door east of here?"

"Arnold and Lucille Smith, a very pleasant couple lives in that house," Elmer said as he pointed toward the east. "They are in their mid-seventies, both retired, and have lived there for about forty years. They always keep an eye on this place for me."

"That is nice of them. What is the scoop on Tony?"

"He is extremely nice," replied Elmer as his right shoulder jerked a few times. "Tony's wife died from ovarian cancer about five years ago. That was a very sad and difficult time for him."

"That is so sad. Did they have children?"

"No," Elmer replied solemnly while using his right

index finger and thumb to tug lightly on the tip of his long gray beard. "She had been trying to get pregnant, but had no luck. She eventually made an appointment with a fertility doctor to find out why she couldn't get pregnant. That is when the doctor discovered her ovarian cancer. Sadly, she passed away about a year later."

"Where does Tony work?" Mary asked as she stood up.

"Tony is a detective with the Waterfield Police Department," said Elmer as he rose from the sofa. "I think he is on his twentieth year at the police department. He made detective grade a couple years ago. Before that, he worked as a patrol officer. I believe he also did some undercover work."

"He evidently does extreme workouts," said Mary while walking toward the front door. "Tony appears to be in top physical condition."

"I imagine he works out. Most cops try to stay in good physical condition. Well, Mary. Are you ready to leave here and go back to my place?"

"I certainly am," replied Mary as she opened the front door.

Elmer and Mary arrived in front of Elmer's house at 11:00 a.m. They saw Duke and Jason rolling their bicycles through the chain-link gate opening. Jason saw Mary and said, "Hi, Mom. Grandpa and I are going downtown for a little while. Are you planning to rent the house?"

"Yes, Jason. We will move into the house tomorrow, so plan accordingly."

Jason mounted his bicycle and coasted to the front sidewalk. "Okay, Mom."

Duke mounted his bicycle, and as he and Jason pedaled their bikes toward the east, Duke shouted, "We'll be back in about an hour, Mary."

As Elmer and Mary entered Elmer's house to draft the rental contract, Calvin looked through the kitchen window of the farmhouse and observed a black Lincoln Continental park near the garage. He saw a man exit the Lincoln and place a small package next to the overhead garage door. Then, the man quickly slid in behind the steering wheel, closed the car door, and drove hastily out of the farmyard. Calvin went outside, picked up the small package, and brought it into the kitchen. He carefully opened it and found two dozen small packages of powdered cocaine. *That should be enough for a while,* he thought. *Now, I need to find a place to hide it.* Calvin searched through the kitchen cabinets until he discovered a brown porcelain teapot. He dropped a dozen packages into the teapot, and placed it inside the highest cabinet. The powder caused temptation for Calvin, so he decided to take the other twelve packages and hide them underneath the trunk floor mat in the Focus.

At 11:30 a.m., Calvin went outside to the machine shed. He struggled while sliding open the huge wooden door that attached to steel rollers hanging from a steel overhead rail. Then, he maneuvered his white Cadillac into the vacant stall of the machine shed and parked. After he closed the huge door, he walked toward the unattached garage. When he arrived, he opened the overhead door and entered the garage. As soon as he finished hiding the cocaine inside the Ford Focus car trunk, he shut the overhead garage door and returned to the house. When he entered the kitchen, he thought, *I should have asked Mr. Shoot if he knew where I could get a woman to entertain me for a while tonight.* Calvin took out his cell phone and punched in the numbers for Mr. Shoot's cell phone. Mr. Shoot answered on the third ring, "Mr. Shoot speaking."

"Hello, Mr. Shoot. This is Calvin. I forgot to ask you earlier if you knew where I could find a woman to entertain me for a few hours tonight."

"I'll have Delbert phone you in about thirty minutes,

so answer your phone when it rings. Good-bye."

Calvin placed his cell phone into his right front pants pocket. He suddenly felt tired and extremely hungry, so he looked inside the pantry to see if there might possibly be something to eat. All he could find was a can of vegetable soup and some soda crackers. As Calvin heated the soup in the microwave, he opened the refrigerator door and found nothing but emptiness. *I should drive into town and buy some groceries,* he thought as he closed the refrigerator door. *No, I will drink water with my soup and crackers. I need to sleep for a while after I eat.* Calvin finished eating the soup along with the very stale soda crackers at 12:45 p.m. As he slid back his chair and stood up, his cell phone rang. He quickly removed the cell phone from his front pants pocket and answered, "Calvin speaking."

"This is Delbert. What can I do for you?"

"I need a little sexual fun tonight. Do you know a woman who might be interested?"

"What kind of woman are you interested in? I know of several."

"I would like to spend some time with a young black woman, a woman who enjoys rough sex. I have never been in bed with a black woman before."

"I know of a woman like that, a woman in her middle twenties, and she will be available at about 11:00 p.m. Do you want me to send her to your temporary home at the farmhouse?"

"What will it cost me?"

"My boss, Mr. Shoot, told me that one of my women could spend the entire night with you, and that it is on the house, but only this one time. After that, you will have to pay normal charges."

"That sounds good to me," replied Calvin. "Can she arrive here by about 11:30 p.m. tonight?"

"I'll give her the order. If you need my services in the future, you can call me. I'll give you my cell phone number." After Delbert told Calvin the phone numbers, he said, "Good-bye, Calvin."

Calvin ended the call and placed his cell phone into his right front pants pocket. He suddenly felt very tired, so he went into the largest bedroom and flopped down onto the full-sized bed for some much-needed sleep. Calvin set his wristwatch alarm for 3:30 p.m. He slept soundly five minutes later.

Duke, Alice, Jason, and Mary finished eating lunch at 1:00 p.m. Thursday, so Duke and Jason went outside to weed the garden and yard. When Mary and Alice finished washing the dishes and silverware, Mary said, "Would you like to go shopping with me, Mother? I want to purchase some towels, sheets, and pillowcases, so that Jason and I can sleep in our new home tomorrow night."

"Sure, Mary. I'll go shopping with you. Do you want to shop at the Crossroads Mall?"

"Do they have any high-end stores out there, or are they all just the big-box chain stores?"

"Well, I'm sure you can find what you want at Sears, J.C. Penny, Younkers, or Dillard's."

"I am thinking more like a Macy's store."

"Sorry, but we don't have anything that fancy around here. You'd have to drive all the way to Des Moines to shop at Macy's. There is a Kohl's store in the Cedar Hills Mall. They have a lot of nice merchandise."

"I suppose we could shop there. I might find something worthwhile to purchase. I want to be home by 4:45 p.m., so I can give Jason a ride to work."

"Well, we'd better get moving," replied Alice. "It's already 1:45 p.m."

Alice and Mary exited the house fifteen minutes later, and found Duke and Jason weeding the garden. Mary said, "Mother and I are going shopping, but we'll be back in time, so I can take you to work, Jason."

"Okay, Mom," replied Jason as he threw a large dandelion plant into a pail.

"Don't spend all your money in one place, Mary," Duke offered as he grinned from ear to ear.

"Do not worry about that, Dad," Mary replied sarcastically as she waved her right hand into the air. "I know how to handle my money."

Duke tipped back his wide-brimmed straw hat, wiped a little sweat from his forehead, and said, "Gee whiz, Mary. I'm only kidding you."

"Oh, I'm sorry, Dad," replied Mary. "I thought you were serious, like you are normally."

"I've been trying to get over being so serious all the time," Duke replied as he reached down to pull another weed.

Alice and Mary walked out of the backyard and toward Mary's Mercedes without saying another word to Duke and Jason. When Duke saw them drive away, he looked at Jason and said, "Your mother always thinks I am serious about everything."

"I used to think that, but I finally figured out that it's just your tone of voice. It is so low, and you speak slowly, just like me. I think you are wonderful, Grandpa. I love you a lot."

Duke smiled broadly as he replied, "I love you, too, Jason. You are a very nice young man, and I am glad you decided to live with us until Mary moved here."

Duke and Jason weeded the yard and garden until 3:00 p.m. Then, Duke began walking toward the porch and said, "It's my beer time, so let's sit on the 3-season porch until it's time for you to get ready for work."

"Okay, Grandpa. That sounds good to me. I'll go to the basement and get a cold can of beer for you."

"You should get a soda for yourself while you're at it."

"I'll just drink a glass of ice water," replied Jason as he held open the porch door for Duke. "I need to lose some more weight."

Duke entered the porch, removed his straw hat, and placed it over the neck of the concrete bust figurine he had made several years earlier. As he sat down in his wicker chair, he smiled while looking at the bust figurine and thinking, *That figurine is sure a good place to hang my hat. Those large busts look so nice jutting out from under the hat brim.*

Jason returned to the porch and handed Duke a cold can of beer. "Thank you, Jason." Duke popped open the can lid tab, and took a huge swallow of beer. "Boy! This doggone beer really hits the spot."

Jason sat down and took a swallow of ice water. "This water tastes pretty good, Grandpa. It doesn't have any calories, either."

"Water is good for you, Jason. It helps flush all the poison out of your body, at least that's what the professionals always tell us." Duke reached into his shirt pocket, pulled out a cigarette, and lit it. After a huge drag, he blew a large smoke ring into the air. Then, Duke looked very seriously at Jason and said, "I want you to know, Jason, that if you ever get into some kind of predicament and you need my help, the secret safe word to use is *Geronimo*; you know, like if you are in trouble and you are talking to me on the phone. If you say the word *Geronimo*, I will know that you are in some kind of trouble and I will come to your aid as soon as possible. I told your mother the same thing when she was a child, but so far, she has never used our secret safe word. I thought she might have forgotten about it, but I asked her last night, and she said that she still remembers the secret safe word. I hope neither of you ever have to use it, but if you do, don't hesitate to use it."

"Gee, Grandpa. Thanks a lot. I'll definitely remember that if I ever get into that kind of circumstance." Jason squirmed around in his wicker chair a little, trying to get comfortable. With the tip of his right index finger, he began lightly rubbing his right temple, and said, "I've been thinking about asking Jo Ann for a date, but I am kind of nervous about it."

"The worst thing she can say is no," Duke replied while grinning. "If you want to ask her, go ahead. I'm betting that she will say yes. What do you have planned if she accepts?"

Jason took a drink of water, swallowed, and said, "I want to take her to a movie at the Crossroads Theaters."

"How are you going to get there?" asked Duke as he reached over and snuffed out his cigarette in the large clear-glass ashtray located upon the glass-topped wicker table.

"We can walk over to Third Street and catch a city bus. I've already checked the bus schedules."

"It sounds as if you have everything planned pretty well." Duke took a swallow of beer before continuing, "When are you going to ask her?"

Just then, they heard the clank of the chain-link gate latch. Fifteen seconds later, they saw Jo Ann appear at the porch door. Jason jumped out of his chair and said, "Hi, Jo Ann." Jason opened the porch door and said, "Come in and have a seat. What a surprise to see you."

As Jo Ann sat down, she said, "Hello, Duke. How are you today?"

"I'm fine, thank you. How are you?"

"I'm okay," replied Jo Ann as she reached up with her right hand and brushed several strands of long blonde hair back over her shoulder.

Jason remained standing near Jo Ann and asked,

"Would you like something to drink, Jo Ann? I will get a can of soda, or ice water for you."

Jo Ann saw Jason's half-glass of ice water upon the wicker tabletop, so she replied, "Ice water will be fine."

Jason headed for the kitchen and said, "I'll be right back."

While Jason went into the kitchen, Duke glanced at Jo Ann several different times. He thought, *Those hot-pink short-shorts and that white, spaghetti-strapped, low-cut blouse sure makes Jo Ann appear sexy. It would be nice to be young again. The girls didn't dress that sexy back in my younger days.* Jason returned to the porch and handed a glass of ice water to Jo Ann. After she took a sip of water, Jason asked, "Do you want to sit on the front stoop with me for a while?"

"Sure," replied Jo Ann as she stood. "Let's go."

As Jason and Jo Ann exited the porch, Duke said, "You two enjoy yourselves. I'll see you later."

Duke glanced at his wristwatch and saw it displaying 4:00 p.m. *Mary and Alice should be back here in about thirty minutes*, he thought. *I may as well drink another beer before they get home.*

At 4:05 p.m., Calvin opened the overhead garage door, and slid in behind the steering wheel of the black Ford Focus. Two minutes later, he drove the Focus out of the farmyard and headed north on a gravel road. After driving a half-mile, he approached an intersection and steered the Focus from the gravel road onto the westbound lane of a county asphalt road. Calvin stepped on the accelerator pedal and when the speedometer displayed 55, he thought, *I should arrive in Waterfield by 4:30 p.m. It should not take me long to find Duke's house, thanks to the GPS in my phone. I will park somewhere near the house, so I can see what is going on there. Mary should have arrived by this time, since she left California the day before I did.*

At 4:40 p.m., Calvin drove east past Duke's house and saw Mary's light gray Mercedes parked on the north side of Klinger Blvd. *This is weird,* he thought. *There is no boulevard on this street. It is just a narrow, two-lane.* Calvin continued driving east for about three blocks until he reached the second intersection. He turned around and drove west along Klinger Blvd. When he reached a point about a half-block east of Duke's house, he parked in between two parked cars along the north side of Klinger Blvd. Calvin shut off the car engine, slouched down in the seat, and thought, *I will sit here for a while and see if Mary leaves the house.* Five minutes later, he observed Mary and Jason leaving the house and walking toward Mary's car. Calvin quickly sat up and started the car engine. When he saw Mary's car leave its parking spot and head west, Calvin maneuvered the Focus from the parking spot and onto the westbound lane. He tried to remain about a block behind Mary and Jason, but followed closer through the intersections containing traffic lights. He certainly did not want to stop for a red light and lose sight of Mary's Mercedes. He managed to stay about a block behind Mary and Jason most the time, and eventually saw Mary steer the Mercedes off University Avenue and onto the parking lot at Wanda's Restaurant.

Calvin quickly steered the Focus off University Avenue and onto a parking lot at a business adjacent to, and on the easterly side of Wanda's Restaurant. He parked the Focus and soon saw Jason exit the Mercedes and enter Wanda's Restaurant. Calvin saw Mary's car leave the parking lot and head easterly on University Avenue. Calvin sped out of the parking lot and onto University Avenue. He followed Mary all the way back to Duke's house. As Mary parked her car in front of the house, Calvin turned the Focus around and parked in the same parking spot on Klinger Boulevard he had parked in earlier. He slouched down in the seat and began watching Duke's house for any kind of activity.

After sitting in the Focus for two hours without seeing a bit of activity at Duke's house, Calvin became very bored, so he decided to find a restaurant and eat supper. When Calvin finished eating, he drove to a grocery store and purchased some basic groceries. Two hours later, Calvin returned to his parking spot on Klinger Boulevard. He checked his watch and saw it displaying 9:20 p.m. Darkness set in quickly and the temperature began dropping slowly, however, the humidity remained very high, high enough to cause Calvin to sweat quite easily. By 9:45 p.m., Calvin tired of the surveillance crap, so he turned the ignition key.

As the Focus engine started, Calvin saw a shadow moving in Duke's front yard. He squinted while his eyes adjusted to the darkness, and then saw Mary walking out of the front yard and toward her Mercedes. Calvin again followed Mary as she drove to Wanda's Restaurant. Calvin pulled into the parking lot adjacent to Wanda's and watched as Mary parked her car. Then, Calvin saw Jason exit the restaurant and enter Mary's car. Fifteen minutes later, Mary parked her car in front of Duke's house. Calvin parked about a half-block east, and watched Mary and Jason exit the car and walk toward Duke's house. When they disappeared from Calvin's view, he thought, *I will sit here for a while and watch the house until all the lights are off for the night.* By 10:45 p.m., there were no visible lights glowing inside Duke's house, so Calvin drove away and headed for his temporary farm home. At one point during the drive, Calvin thought, *I do not know for sure how I will get even with Duke, Alice, and Mary. Perhaps, I will kill them. I do not have anything to lose, since I have already killed Tina.*

Calvin parked the Focus inside the unattached garage at

11:30 p.m., and turned on the overhead yard light. As he closed the overhead garage door, he saw a car entering the farmyard. He remained by the garage and watched as the driver parked the car near the front of the house. As Calvin walked toward the house, he saw the front car door open, and watched as a beautiful, young African American woman exited the car. She saw Calvin walking toward her and said, "Hey there, sexy. Are you Calvin?"

"Yes, I am Calvin. What is your name?"

The woman shut the front car door, opened the left rear car door, and removed a small duffle bag from the rear seat. She shut the door and said, "My name is Jasmine. I'm here to give you some real pleasures. Delbert told me that you like to play rough, so I brought some of my special toys."

Calvin pointed toward the house and said, "Let's go inside and have some fun."

As soon as they entered the kitchen, Calvin turned off the yard light and asked, "Do you want to snort a line of cocaine before we begin?"

Jasmine replied, "I don't mess with drugs, but if you want to do a line, go ahead. Where is the bathroom? I need to freshen up a little before we play."

Calvin pointed toward the hallway and said, "It's right there in the hallway, the door on the right side. We will use the bedroom at the end of the hallway"

Jasmine headed toward the hallway and said, "Okay. I'll put my bag of toys in that bedroom."

Calvin opened the highest cabinet door and carefully removed the brown teapot. He took off the teapot lid and removed a small plastic bag of cocaine. "When you finish in the bathroom," he said loudly, "I will take a quick shower."

"Okay," replied Jasmine as she exited the bedroom and walked toward the bathroom.

Calvin put the teapot back into the top cabinet and shut the cabinet door. He looked inside some of the other cabinets and found a serving tray. He continued searching through cabinets until he found a few plastic soda straws. He took the serving tray, the straws, and the cocaine into the bedroom where he placed the items upon the dresser top. He removed his clothes, all except his white cotton undershorts. Calvin sat down on the edge of the bed and waited for Jasmine to finish in the bathroom. *Man!* he thought. *It must be at least eighty degrees in this house. I wish this house had an air-conditioner. We should not have much trouble sweating.*

Fifteen minutes passed before Jasmine appeared in the bedroom doorway opening. As she stood leaning against the doorway casing, Calvin looked at her and said, "Wow! That is a sexy outfit, Jasmine. I love those chrome spikes embedded into that black leather dog collar you have around your neck. Those knee-high, black leather boots look very sexy on you. I hope you brought a leather whip and some handcuffs. I like kinky sex!"

Calvin watched intently as Jasmine sauntered over to her duffle bag, reached into it, and removed a coiled black leather whip. She smiled as she uncoiled the three feet long braided leather whip, swirled it around a little, and said, "Is this what you had in mind?"

"It is perfect, Jasmine." Calvin's eyes scanned Jasmine's glistening, long muscular legs, her firm abdominal muscles, and her bare breasts for about twenty seconds. "You are very beautiful, Jasmine, and the glistening sweat on your bare body makes all your muscles appear nice and firm. How tall are you anyway? You appear to be as tall as me, and I am 5'-10" tall."

Jasmine threw the whip onto the bed and replied, "I am 5'-10" tall, and weigh about 140 pounds. I work out with weights and kick box a lot to keep in excellent shape.

Then, Jasmine reached into her duffle bag, removed two sets of fur-covered handcuffs, and threw them onto the bed. Jasmine approached the bed and remained standing while straddling Calvin's legs. She snuggled her belly against his chest, looked down into his brown eyes, and placed her hands on his bare shoulders. "You should take a shower, Calvin, so we can play."

Calvin gently pushed Jasmine away and stood up. He hugged her while kissing her on the side of the neck. Calvin released her after ten seconds, and said, "You really smell nice, Jasmine. My insides are already tingling. I will take a shower, right now."

Fifteen minutes later, Calvin, completely nude, exited the bathroom and walked toward the bedroom. Jasmine waited directly inside the bedroom doorway opening for him. When he entered the bedroom, she grabbed him, pushed him toward the bed, and forced him down onto the bed while saying, "I heard that you like rough sex, so I am going to make you happy." She jumped onto the bed and quickly handcuffed Calvin's wrists to the iron-spindled headboard. Calvin tried to resist her aggressiveness, but failed, for Jasmine had much more strength than Calvin did. He could not believe Jasmine's strength and aggressiveness.

Jasmine walked over to the dresser and picked up the serving tray, cocaine, and straw. "Do you still want to sniff some cocaine, Calvin?"

"Yes," Calvin replied as he struggled against the handcuffs.

Jasmine dumped some cocaine onto the tray and formed the powder into a rough line. She crawled onto the bed, took a position on her knees, and straddled Calvin's belly area. She placed the tray on Calvin's chest and carefully inserted one end of a soda straw into his right nostril. "Snort some, now," Jasmine commanded as she pushed her finger against his left nostril.

Calvin took a huge snort as Jasmine slowly moved the straw along the line of cocaine. Then, Jasmine put the straw into his left nostril, "Snort some more, right now," she ordered. "You are going to do everything I tell you, for I am the dominatrix tonight. If you don't obey my commands, you will pay with a lot of pain. I guarantee it."

Calvin took another huge snort while Jasmine moved the straw along the line of cocaine. Five minutes passed before Calvin began acting very crazy. Jasmine said, "Why do you like cocaine, anyway? I have always heard that it dampens sexual drive."

"I guess it does for some people, but it gives me superb sexual drive, along with extra strength."

Jasmine un-straddled Calvin, crawled off the bed, and set the tray and straw upon the dresser top. She looked down at Calvin and saw his glazed eyeballs twitching around a little. "Do you feel high, right now?"

Calvin mumbled rapidly while replying, "I feel like I am flying, as if I am a kite, or maybe a glider. Are you going to give me some sex, now?"

Jasmine reached for the whip and said, "I'm going to give you some rough play before I give you what you really want. I hope you enjoy pain."

"No, I do not enjoy pain," Calvin mumbled rapidly, "but I enjoy giving pain to my sexual partners. It turns me on big time."

Jasmine dangled the whiptail onto Calvin's right nipple for a few seconds, before dangling it onto his left nipple. Then, she raised the black leather whip into the air and snapped the whiptail down onto Calvin's chest. Calvin cried out from the pain. As Jasmine again raised the whip into the air, she asked, "How do you like that pain?"

Before Calvin replied, Jasmine snapped the whip and the whiptail struck Calvin's right nipple. Calvin again cried out from the sharp burning pain, but then smiled. "It feels so good. Whip me some more. It is making me excited."

During the next two hours, Jasmine gave Calvin several different commands, as well as delivering more pain to him. She finally removed the handcuffs at 2:30 a.m. Friday. Calvin felt completely drained, and fell asleep within ten seconds. Jasmine felt very fulfilled and tired, but managed to dress. She packed up her toys before writing a short note to Calvin, reading that she had never had a better lover than Calvin and would enjoy seeing him again. She wrote her personal phone number on the note before placing it upon the dresser top. She drove her car out of the farmyard at 3:00 a.m. and headed for Waterfield.

Chapter 16

Duke awoke at 5:00 a.m. Friday and saw Alice still sleeping soundly, so he reached over and gently rubbed her left upper thigh a few times. He saw a smile appear on her face, but she did not wake. Duke sat on the edge of the bed and dressed quietly. Ten minutes later, Duke opened the French door and walked onto the 3-season porch. Just as he lit his first cigarette of the day, Jason entered the porch. "Good morning, Grandpa."

Duke sat down in his wicker chair and said, "Good morning, Jason. Did you sleep well?"

"Yeah. I slept very well last night. How about you?"

"Well, Jason, some nights I sleep very well, and other nights I toss and turn a lot while staying half-awake all night, all because of my doggone nightmares. Last night was like that, so I didn't get much sleep."

Jason peered through the Jalousie windows at the sky and said, "There is a nice clear sky this morning. It should be another beautiful summer day."

Duke yawned before saying, "Yeah. It sure is humid as hell, though." Duke blew a large smoke ring into the air and watched it eventually dissipate. "Did you get around to asking Jo Ann for a date?"

Jason blushed slightly while replying, "Yeah. I asked

her. We are going to a movie tomorrow afternoon. Neither one of us have to work tomorrow night."

"Well, that's nice. She's sure a pretty girl."

"I think she is very nice, and pretty, too."

Duke looked closely at Jason. "I think you should consider shaving that peach fuzz off your face. Jo Ann might appreciate it."

"I've thought about shaving, but I'm not sure how to do it."

"I'll show you how later today. There's not much to it. You have to apply some shave cream, rub it in, and then shave with a safety razor. Of course, you could use an electric razor, but I never liked those very well. I can't get a close shave with one of those, not as close as when I use a safety razor. I tried shaving with a straight razor once when I was a young whippersnapper."

"How did that work for you?" asked Jason.

Duke snickered before replying, "I almost cut off my left earlobe, because when I looked into the mirror, I moved the razor the wrong way. Then, I took a swipe and sliced into my left earlobe. Blood dripped everywhere. I thought about going to the doctor for some sutures, but I didn't. It finally healed on its own. I never again used that straight razor. I bought a double-edge safety razor, one with a replaceable blade."

"Is that the one you still use?"

"Nope. I use those plastic-framed throwaway razors. They work nicely."

Jason sat down in a wicker chair, and said, "Not to change the subject, but Mrs. Tokin, the owner of Wanda's Restaurant, asked me last night if I would work Sunday afternoon and evening. She wants me to help some of the other employees clean the restaurant. Mrs. Tokin plans to close the restaurant at 1:00 p.m. Sunday, so that we have time to clean the place spotlessly."

"Are you going to help?"

"I told Mrs. Tokin that I would help. She wants us to clean until about 6:00 p.m., and after that, she will take us employees to the Hotel Five Diamonds. Mrs. Tokin will rent rooms for all of us, so we can spend the night there. I guess it's a very fancy place. My boss said that the employees could swim in the huge pool after supper, if they wanted to. Mrs. Tokin's husband will be there, too, so Mr. and Mrs. Tokin will chaperone all of us."

"Doggone, Jason. You sure have a nice boss. Most bosses wouldn't do that for their employees. Did you ask your mother if you can stay overnight at the hotel?"

"She said that I could."

"Are there going to be any female employees there, or only male employees?"

"My boss and her husband took the female employees to the hotel for a night a couple weeks ago, so it will only be the male employees this time." Jason stood up and asked, "Do you want me to get a cup of coffee for you?"

"Sure. That would be great."

When Jason returned to the porch, he carefully handed a cup of coffee to Duke and asked, "Are we going to work out with weights this morning?"

Duke took a sip of coffee, swallowed, and said, "I doubt it, because your mother will probably want us to help her move into the house right away this morning. We might have time to go on a nice long bicycle ride this afternoon. That would give us a good workout. We will probably go over to my brother's house at 3:00 p.m. Elmer might ride over there with us, if you invite him."

"I'll ask him right after we finish eating our noon lunch."

Calvin steered the Focus from Fourth Street onto Klinger Boulevard at 8:30 a.m. Friday. A few minutes later, he drove past Duke and Alice's house where he caught a glimpse of Duke carrying a small garbage bag while walking toward the garage. *The old bastard is still alive,* thought Calvin. *I saw Mary's Mercedes parked in front of Duke's house, so I will turn around and park on Klinger for a while.* Calvin parked the Focus about a half-block east of Duke's house, leaned back in the seat, and began watching for activity. At 8:45 a.m., Calvin observed Jason and Mary loading two suitcases into the Mercedes. Then, he watched them get into the car, and drive westerly along Klinger Boulevard. Calvin followed about a block behind them, and soon saw Mary park the Mercedes in front of a house at 4723 Third Street. Calvin parked the Focus about a half-block east, and watched in his rearview mirror as Jason and Mary exited the car and made several trips back and forth between the car and house while carrying boxes and suitcases.

At 9:30 a.m., Calvin saw Mary and Jason enter the Mercedes. A minute later, they drove past Calvin as he crouched down in the seat, so that they would not see him. He soon followed Mary's Mercedes, and watched as Mary parked it in front of Duke's house. Calvin quickly parked the Focus and watched Mary and Jason exit the car and walk toward the side door of Duke's house. *I will sit here for a while and see if they leave again,* thought Calvin. *They must be moving into that house on Third Street.* The time passed slowly for Calvin as he waited, and when he eventually checked the time on his wristwatch, it showed 11:30 a.m. Calvin felt very hungry, so he thought, *I will wait here until noon. If nothing happens by then, I will eat lunch somewhere.*

Jason finished packing his suitcases at 11:30 a.m. He entered the dining room and approached Mary sitting at the table visiting with Alice and Duke. Jason waited until Duke finished talking with Mary before saying, "Can we haul the rest of our belongings over to the house right now, Mom? I want to go bicycling with Grandpa this afternoon."

Duke cleared his throat, and said, "Let's eat lunch first, Jason. I'll help you load your stuff into the car after we eat. Then, I will help you unload it at the house on Third Street. When we finish, we'll go bicycling."

Alice slid back her chair and stood up. "What does everybody want for lunch? How about if I make some chicken salad sandwiches?"

"That sounds good to me, Alice," replied Duke as he stood up and headed for the 3-season porch.

"I will help you make the sandwiches, Mom," offered Mary. Then, she looked into Jason's blue eyes and said, "Do you think Jo Ann would enjoy coming over to our house on Third Street for a while when you come home from the movie tomorrow afternoon? I want to meet her. Mom and Dad have already told me that she is a very sweet girl."

"I'll ask her, Mom," replied Jason as he stood up and headed for the porch.

Calvin started the Focus engine at noon and pulled out of the parking space on Klinger Boulevard. As he drove past the front of Duke's house, he thought, *I will eat lunch somewhere, and after lunch, I will find a local hardware store, so that I can purchase a few items.* Ten minutes later, Calvin parked the Focus, and entered Roger's Bar and Grill located in a strip mall next to Kane Street. After a five-minute wait, the hostess seated Calvin in a booth near a rear corner of the restaurant. "Wilma will be here to take your order in about five minutes," stated the hostess. "As you can see, we are extremely busy. Would you like to read the newspaper while you wait?"

"Yes. Will you please bring a cup of coffee to me right away?"

"You bet, sweetie. I'll be right back."

A few minutes later, Calvin opened the Friday morning newspaper to page three, and immediately saw an article about a murdered Waterfield woman. The article read that the owner of a farm located about fifteen miles south of Waterfield had arrived at his garden plot Thursday morning to check on some of his tomato plants. He noticed a black leather strap protruding from the ground, so he tugged on the strap, but could not pull it out of the ground. He assumed the strap attached to something, so he grabbed a garden spade and began digging. The man eventually found a small black purse attached to the other end of the strap. He dug a little more, and soon saw a woman's hand. The man panicked and immediately phoned the sheriff's office. By noon, authorities had unearthed the body and called in investigators from the Iowa Bureau of Criminal Investigations. Authorities are not releasing the woman's name until they contact her family members.

Calvin folded the newspaper and laid it upon the tabletop. With his right hand, he picked up the coffee cup, but his hand shook so badly that he immediately set the cup onto the tabletop. *Damn it!* he thought. *I should have checked that gravesite better. I did not see that purse strap sticking out of the ground.* Wilma arrived to take Calvin's order, and when she looked at him, asked, "Do you feel okay, sir? Your face is as white as a sheet."

Calvin managed to smile at Wilma as he replied, "I am okay. I partied too hardy last night."

Wilma laughed a little and said, "I do that occasionally. What can I get you for lunch?"

"I will have a cheeseburger with pickles and ketchup, and an order of hash browns. Can you tell the cook to burn the hash browns? I like them nice and crispy."

Wilma wrote down the order and said, "I'll tell him."

As soon as Wilma walked away from the booth, Calvin

again read the newspaper article. Just as he finished and folded the paper, he saw two police officers sit down at the counter next to the cash register. Calvin thought, *I had better get a shave and haircut this afternoon. The clerk at the gas station might have seen Tina with me in the gas station parking lot.* Wilma returned with Calvin's food fifteen minutes later. Calvin finished eating at 1:00 p.m. and went directly to the cash register to pay his bill. As Calvin waited for the cashier, he overheard the police officers talking about being on the lookout for a white Cadillac bearing California license plates. Calvin immediately turned his back to the officers, paid his bill, and walked out of the restaurant.

Calvin noticed a hardware store located in the middle of the strip mall, so he walked to the store. By 1:30 p.m., Calvin had purchased a roll of duct tape, fifty feet of clothesline rope, two quarts of charcoal lighter fluid, and a butane grill lighter. He had looked at a hunting knife, but decided not to purchase it. As he slid in behind the Focus steering wheel, he thought, *Now, I need to find a barbershop.* As he began driving out of the parking space, he saw a sign for a barbershop at the north end of the strip mall, so he re-parked the car and walked to the shop. Three barbers worked in the shop, and one of them occupied his chair while waiting for a customer. Calvin entered the shop, so the barber stood up, and pointed at his chair. "You can sit in my chair, mister. What can I do for you?"

Calvin sat down in the barber chair and said, "I want a butch and a shave."

The barber placed a cloth over Calvin's chest and shoulders, and as he tucked in part of the cloth edge around Calvin's shirt collar, said, "The heat must be getting to you, huh?"

"Yes. I think it will be much cooler without this beard

and long hair."

Calvin left the barbershop at 2:00 p.m., appearing as a completely different man. Duke and Jason had left for their bicycle rides at 1:50 p.m., and just as Calvin steered the Focus off Fourth Street and onto Klinger Boulevard, he saw Duke and Jason riding their bicycles along the city sidewalk paralleling Fourth Street, heading north toward the downtown area. Calvin saw Duke wearing the wide-brimmed straw hat and thought, *I cannot wait to get even with that old bastard. I am positive he and Alice convinced Mary to call the California cops on me.* A few minutes later, Calvin drove past Duke's house. He did not see Mary's light gray Mercedes, so he continued driving until he reached Third Street. He saw Mary's Mercedes parked in front of the house at 4723 Third Street, so Calvin turned around and parked in between two cars on the north side of Third Street, only three houses east of 4723. *I will sit here for a while and see if anything exciting happens at 4723*, thought Calvin.

A half hour later, Calvin saw Alice and Mary walk off the front porch and into the front yard. He saw Mary pointing toward some flowers in one of the flowerbeds as she talked to Alice. Then, Calvin watched as Alice bent over and began picking some yellow flowers. He saw Alice's exposed pink panties while she remained bent over. Calvin thought, *That old bitch should quit wearing cotton dresses, and instead, wear jeans or slacks.* After Alice picked several flowers, she straightened up and held the flower bouquet close to Mary's nose, so that Mary could smell the flowers. Just then, Calvin observed a man wearing a bright white undershirt, a pair of cut-off jeans, and sandals, exit the next-door house. The man held what appeared to be a bottle of wine with his right hand and a bouquet of red roses with his left hand. Calvin watched with interest as the man approached Mary and offered her the bouquet of roses while saying something to her. A few minutes later, Calvin watched Mary, Alice, and the man enter the house at 4723. *Evidently, that house is where Mary now lives*, Calvin thought. *The man must be her next-door neighbor. He will probably be in bed with that bitch before much longer.* Calvin glanced at his wristwatch and saw it displaying 3:00 p.m. *I may as well sit here and observe things until 5:00 p.m.*, he thought. *Then, I will head for my temporary home. I will phone Jasmine and ask her if she wants to visit me at the farmhouse this evening.*

Calvin picked up his cell phone, flipped open the keyboard, and selected Jasmine's number from the contact list. After pressing the send button, he listened to several rings before hearing the answering service message. Calvin left his phone number and requested that Jasmine call him back. He flipped shut the keyboard and laid the cell phone on the seat beside him. Calvin slouched down in the seat and resumed surveillance on Mary's house. During the next hour, he saw several different people, some with their dogs in the lead, strolling along the city sidewalk as they passed his car. The afternoon sun reached a location in the sky causing the sunshine to shine between the shade tree limbs and through the front car window. Calvin became extremely uncomfortable from the intense heat, so he decided to move to a new location. He started the Focus and moved it to a shady spot, just a little ways east. He could still see the front of Mary's house, so he felt comfortable about not missing anyone entering, or exiting the house. Calvin's phone rang at 3:45 p.m., so he quickly flipped open the keyboard and answered, "Calvin speaking."

Calvin heard Jasmine's sexy voice reply, "Hello, Calvin. You called?"

"Hey there, sexy. How would you like to drive out to the farmhouse tonight and spend some quality time with me?"

"I would love to, but I am booked solid tonight. I could drive out there tomorrow night. Will that work for you?"

"I suppose so, if that is the best you can do, but I prefer seeing you tonight, as well as tomorrow night. Can you cancel your appointments for tonight? I will pay you more than enough to make up for it."

"I will cancel them if you want to pay me double for the cancelled appointments, only the ones for tonight. I will give it to you free tomorrow night, since you are such a good lover."

"I will gladly pay you double. Can you arrive at the farmhouse by 7:00 p.m.? Would you enjoy some wine, or something else to drink tonight? I will purchase something tasty for you."

"Do you like Chinese food?" asked Jasmine.

"Not particularly, but I eat it occasionally."

"I'll stop at my favorite Chinese restaurant and pick up some supper for us. I'll also bring a bottle of my favorite wine."

"That sounds good, Jasmine."

"Okay. I'll see you at 7:00 p.m. Bye, lover."

"Good-bye, Jasmine."

Calvin ended the call just as he saw Duke and Jason walking westerly along the city sidewalk on the south side of Third Street. Calvin quickly turned his face away from them, fearing they might recognize him. He waited a short while before looking towards Mary's house, but looked soon enough to see Duke and Jason enter the house. A few minutes later, Calvin observed Mary's next-door neighbor exiting Mary's house and returning to his own house.

As soon as Duke and Jason entered Mary's living room, Duke saw the bouquet of red roses sprouting from a beautiful cut-glass vase located upon Mary's dining room tabletop. He sat down between Mary and Alice on the sofa, and drawled, "Where did you get the beautiful roses, Mary?"

Mary smiled broadly and replied, "Tony from next door gave them to me for a house warming present. He also brought over a bottle of wine."

"That was generous of him," replied Duke. "He seems like a very nice man."

Mary snuggled against the softly padded sofa back. "I invited Tony to come over here later this evening to help me drink the wine, but he cannot, because he has to work tonight. He will come over tomorrow evening, since he will be off work for the weekend."

"Tony is so polite," Alice offered while blushing, "and darn nice looking, too, if I may say so."

Duke smiled as he looked at Alice and kiddingly said, "Only in your dreams, Alice."

Jason interrupted their thoughts as he said, "I have to get ready for work. Can you give me a ride over to Wanda's, Mom?"

"Yes, Jason. I will also be there at 10:00 p.m. to get you when you finish working."

Alice looked at Duke and asked, "Did you and Jason go over to Dave's house this afternoon?"

"We sure did, and Elmer even tagged along, which surprised me. If Jason wouldn't have invited him, he probably wouldn't have gone with us."

"Did you get a chance to check out Dave and Jolene's garden?"

"Yeah," replied Duke. "We looked at the garden. Their tomatoes are already larger than ours are, but I guess that isn't unusual. Their tomatoes always grow better than ours do. Their garden soil must be more fertile."

"Oh, Duke," Alice replied as she shifted her body slightly upon the sofa. "You always say that, but our tomatoes grow well every summer. We always have plenty of tomatoes to can each fall."

Duke glanced at his watch, stood up, and looked at Alice. "I suppose we should go home, Alice. It'll be supper time before much longer."

"I don't even know what I'm going to make for supper, Duke." Alice rose from the sofa and grasped Duke's right hand with her left hand. "Let's head for home."

Calvin scooted down in the front seat of the Focus as Duke and Alice walked east along the city sidewalk on the south side of Third Street, passing only about sixty feet from his car. When they were far enough away to the east, Calvin relaxed and straightened up. Then, at 4:45 p.m., Calvin saw Jason and Mary enter Mary's Mercedes. He again scooted down in the seat just before the Mercedes passed beside his car. *I imagine Mary is taking Jason to work*, Calvin thought, *so I will wait here and see if she comes back alone.* Five minutes later, Calvin saw an immaculately restored, candy apple red, 1967 Chevy C10 pickup at the intersection a half-block west. The pickup turned onto Third Street and began heading east towards Calvin. When the pickup passed beside Calvin, he saw Mary's next-door neighbor sitting behind the steering wheel. *Mary's neighbor must have had that pickup parked in his garage by the alley*, thought Calvin. *That is definitely one beautiful pickup.* At 5:15 p.m., Calvin saw Mary park her Mercedes in front of her house. He watched as Mary strolled to her front porch and entered the house. He started the Focus engine, and slowly drove out of the parking space. *I may as well go back to the farmhouse*, Calvin thought, *so I can shower before Jasmine arrives. She will probably freak out when she sees me with this butch haircut and no beard.*

Duke and Alice finished eating their fried minute steaks

and hash browns at 5:45 p.m., so Duke grabbed his half-can of beer, slid back his chair, and said, "I'm going out on the porch to finish drinking my beer. Do you want to join me?"

Alice stood up and said, "No thanks, Duke. I want to wash the dishes and clean up the kitchen so we can go for a nice long walk together."

Duke walked through the French door opening leading to the 3-season porch and peered through the Jalousie windows at the sky. He turned and smiled at Alice. "Judging by the sky, it appears as if it will rain later tonight. It might be a good night for me to be in bed with a wild woman and a pint of whiskey."

"My goodness, Duke! You always say that when you think it's going to rain or snow." Alice stood up and began clearing the table. "Now that Jason has moved out, we have the house to ourselves, so I guess I could be your wild woman for the night. How does that sound to you?"

"I look forward to your wildness," replied Duke as he reached into his shirt pocket and pulled out a cigarette. Instead of lighting the cigarette, he returned to the dining room and said, "I'd better go upstairs and turn on the window air conditioner."

"That's a good idea, Duke," replied Alice with a broad smile on her face. "It might get steamy hot up there when we go to bed later."

Duke returned to the porch a few minutes later and lit his cigarette. When Alice finished washing dishes and cleaning the kitchen, she entered the bathroom and freshened up a little. Then, she entered the dining room, looked through the open French doorway at Duke, and said, "I'm ready to go walking, Duke."

Duke rose from the wicker chair and replied, "I'll be ready as soon as I put on my tennis shoes and grab my walking stick."

Five minutes later, Duke held Alice's right hand with his left hand and they began walking easterly along the city sidewalk located on the southerly side of Klinger Boulevard. As they entered the next city block and neared Otis and Missy's house, they saw Otis sitting on the front stoop. Otis saw them at about the same time, so he waved and said, "Hello, Duke. Hello, Alice."

Duke and Alice stopped walking, and each replied, "Hello, Otis."

Otis rose from the front stoop and approached Duke and Alice. He wiped a few beads of sweat from his forehead. "How have you two been? What's with the walking stick, Duke?"

"My brother, Dave, made this walking stick for me. It's plum wood." Duke waved the walking stick into the air in front of him while saying, "I use it every time we go walking, not because I need it, but because I can use it as a weapon if need be, you know, like for mean dogs or criminals."

Alice stepped away from Duke and said, "Quit waving around that stick, Duke, before you clobber one of us." Then, Alice looked at Otis and offered, "We've been fine, Otis. Our daughter, Mary, arrived in town. We have been busy helping her move into her house."

"Oh," replied Otis. "Is she Jason's mother?"

"Yeah," replied Duke. "Jason moved out of our house today, so we are all alone again."

"Where did Mary and Jason move to, now?" asked Otis.

"Mary rented a house located on Third Street, the first house east of Tony Margiotti's house."

"Oh," remarked Otis. "Is that Detective Tony Margiotti?"

"Yes," replied Alice. "He is sure friendly, and extremely polite."

"Yes," said Otis while grinning. "Tony is unusually nice until a criminal irritates him. Then, he can become very mean and nasty. I've seen him take down more than one scumbag criminal."

"I suppose that is because of his Italian temper." Duke offered as he grinned from ear to ear. "It's too bad more cops don't beat the hell out of criminals. Maybe, there wouldn't be so many repeat offenders."

"Well, Tony is sure nice to Mary," stated Alice.

"He is nice, except for when he deals with criminals," replied Otis. "I used to work with Tony when he worked as a patrol officer. I could tell you all kinds of stories about our run-ins with criminals."

"I would sure enjoy hearing some of those stories," remarked Duke.

"I'll tell you a few stories one of these days." Otis again slid the palm of his right hand across his forehead to remove several beads of perspiration. "It is muggier than heck this evening. I'm sweating like crazy."

Alice giggled a little as she rolled her eyes and teasingly said, "You could join us for a walk, Otis."

"No thanks," replied Otis while smiling at Alice. "I am leaving here in about five minutes to drive out to the community college. I'm going to spend some time target practicing at the indoor shooting range."

"That sounds like fun," Duke replied. "Do you have to pay to use the range?"

"No, I don't have to pay. I teach part-time in the police science program, so I can use the range anytime, as long as there are openings. Do you like to shoot pistols, Duke?"

"I haven't shot a pistol since I left the navy, but I really enjoyed shooting those Colt .45 caliber automatic pistols. Gee! What do you teach at the college, anyway?"

"I teach firearms and self-defense. Would you like to go to the range with me? I'm sure Missy would enjoy walking and visiting with Alice."

Duke looked at Alice and asked, "Do you mind if I go with Otis?"

Just then, Missy opened the front door and said, "Hello, Alice. Hello, Duke."

Before Duke and Alice could reply, Otis said, "Hey, Missy. Would you enjoy going for a walk with Alice, so that Duke can go with me to the indoor shooting range?"

"I would love to walk with Alice," replied Missy as she stepped onto the front stoop. "We can visit while walking, and when we finish, we will sit on the back porch and drink some of my delicious homemade ice-tea."

"Great," Otis said as he turned toward the house. "Come on, Duke. We'll have some fun target practicing." As Otis and Duke walked past Missy, Otis said, "We'll be back about 8:30 p.m. See you, then. I love you, Missy."

"I love you, too," replied Missy. "Have fun."

Chapter 17

Duke and Otis entered the indoor firing range at 7:15 p.m. Friday. At the same time, Calvin saw Jasmine driving her car onto the farmyard. He approached the car and opened the car door for Jasmine. With a shocked appearance on her face, Jasmine stared at Calvin as she said, "What in the world happened to your hair and beard? I didn't even recognize you when I first saw you approaching my car."

Calvin slid his left palm across the top of his head and said, "I decided to try a butch haircut, and I was tired of the beard. It made me feel unclean most the time."

Jasmine slid out from behind the steering wheel and stood up straight. She placed her palms on Calvin's head and began lightly rubbing his stubby brown hair. After thirty seconds, she pulled his head toward her until their lips met. Jasmine French kissed Calvin before saying, "I like your butch haircut, but I would like it more if you would have shaved your head. I love bald-headed men. Shaved heads really turn me on for some reason. I guess it's a fetish of mine."

"If a shaved head turns you on so much, I'll shave mine."

"How about letting me shave your head? That will turn me on even more."

"That is fine with me. You can shave my head, but not until after we eat supper."

Jasmine pointed toward the backseat and said, "I brought some Chinese food and a bottle of wine. If you will carry that stuff into the house, I'll carry my duffle bag."

"Is your bag full of surprises for me?" Calvin asked as he opened the rear car door.

"You know it is," replied Jasmine. "I purchased several new toys earlier today, so you will experience some new surprises tonight."

Calvin and Jasmine finished eating supper at 8:00 p.m. Jasmine slid her chair away from the kitchen table, stood up, and said, "I'm going to take a shower and change into something you will love."

"Okay," replied Calvin as he slid back his chair. "I showered a little while before you arrived, so I am all set for some good loving." As Jasmine turned and walked toward the bathroom, Calvin asked, "Do you want to snort a little cocaine when you finish your shower?"

"No," snapped Jasmine as she turned and looked at Calvin. "I told you before that I never mess around with drugs. I don't care if you snort some cocaine, but you should wait until I finish shaving your head. I don't want you acting all hyper and crazy while I have a safety razor in my hand."

Jasmine entered the bathroom and closed the door. When Calvin heard Jasmine turn on the water, he removed the brown teapot from the top cabinet, removed a package of cocaine from inside the teapot, and carefully placed the teapot into the top cabinet. Calvin went into the bedroom, undressed, and crawled onto the bed. He saw Jasmine's duffle bag in the corner of the room, and thought, *I wonder what she has in store for me tonight.*

Twenty minutes later, Jasmine, wearing only a very short white-satin robe, entered the bedroom. "Wow!"

Calvin remarked. "You are so beautiful, Jasmine. I love that satin robe. It really sets off your lovely ebony body."

"Thank you," Jasmine replied as she bent over and reached into her duffle bag. When she straightened up, and turned around, Calvin saw that she held a can of shave cream and a safety razor. "Let's go into the kitchen. You can sit in a chair while I shave your head."

"Are you going to tie me to the chair?" Calvin asked as he slid off the bed and stood up.

"I will if that's what you want."

"Please."

Jasmine set the can of shave cream and razor upon the dresser, bent over, reached into her duffle bag, and removed four pieces of rope, each four feet long. She grabbed the can of shave cream and razor, and walked out of the bedroom. Calvin followed Jasmine through the hallway toward the kitchen while staring at the backs of her firm, glistening legs. As soon as they entered the kitchen, Jasmine moved a chair to a location near the kitchen sink. "Sit down, Calvin," she ordered. Calvin sat in the chair and waited for the next command, but Jasmine remained silent. When she finished tying his wrists to the rear spindles of the chair, she tied one end of rope around his right leg, just above his knee. She wrapped the other end of rope around a lower chair rung and roughly tightened the rope, which forced Calvin's right leg toward the side of the chair. She tied a knot, and then bound his left leg in a similar manner, leaving Calvin in a spread-eagled position. Jasmine stood back and looked at Calvin's nude body for about five seconds. Then, she turned and walked toward the bedroom.

"Where are you going?" asked Calvin.

"I'll be right back."

Jasmine returned a minute later with two more pieces of rope. She bent down and bound Calvin's ankles to the chair legs before saying, "There, Calvin. That should keep you firmly secured." She walked to the sink and turned on the cold-water faucet. After wetting both hands, she quickly turned around and rubbed some water onto Calvin's head. She picked up the can of shave cream and stood behind Calvin while spraying a gob of shave cream onto his head. She placed the can upon the counter, and with both hands, began spreading the cream, being careful not to get any into Calvin's eyes. When she finished, she moved around to Calvin's front side. She stood in front of him for about five seconds before untying her robe belt. As the front of her robe partially opened, exposing parts of her beautiful, firm upper body, she picked up the safety razor.

Calvin's eyes opened wide as he said, "I hope you know what you are doing with that razor."

Jasmine smiled as her large, beautiful brown eyes rolled flirtatiously. "Don't worry, Calvin. I've done this many times. I won't cut you."

Jasmine eventually moved around to the back of the chair, so that she could finish shaving his head. When finished, she used a wet towel to remove the remaining shave cream from Calvin's head. She moved around to the front of the chair and stood at a location four feet in front of Calvin. She grasped the right front opening of her robe with her right hand, and slowly pulled open the side of her robe, exposing the front right side of her body. Calvin's eyes opened wider as Jasmine put her left palm upon her belly and began slowly moving her palm in circular motions. "Do you like watching me do this, Calvin?" she asked with a very sexual tone of voice.

"Yes, very much. You are absolutely gorgeous, Jasmine."

"Do you want to see more of my body?"

"Yes, please show me more."

Jasmine quickly flipped the robe off her shoulders, exposing her shoulders and breasts. Ten seconds later, she flipped the robe back onto her shoulders and tied the robe belt. She looked into Calvin's eyes and said, "I'm really turned on, Calvin."

Jasmine walked over to the refrigerator and opened the door. She reached into the refrigerator and removed an unopened bottle of virgin olive oil. When Calvin saw the oil, he asked, "What are you going to do, now?"

Without replying, Jasmine moved to a location directly behind Calvin, removed the bottle cap, and dribbled some olive oil onto his shaved head.

"Yikes," Calvin cried out as the cold oil puddled on top of his head. "That stuff is ice-cold."

"It won't be cold for long," replied Jasmine as she used both hands to spread the slippery oil over Calvin's shaved head. Five minutes later, Jasmine moved around to the front of Calvin, stood straddle of Calvin's legs, and listened to Calvin's outbursts as she dripped several spots of oil onto his chest. She spread the oil all over his chest and belly area. During the fifteen minutes of Jasmine's expertise, Calvin moaned non-stop. She finally stopped and backed away from him, until she stood four feet away. Jasmine felt as if she could explode by this time, so she suddenly lunged toward Calvin, stood straddle of his legs, and began sliding her hands around upon Calvin's slippery shaved head. As Jasmine leaned over and positioned her luscious breasts against Calvin's face, she whispered, "Kiss my breasts, Calvin."

"Let's go to bed, now," begged Calvin.

Jasmine's entire body quivered for about twenty seconds. Then, she stood up, grabbed a towel off the countertop, and said, "We'd better wipe off some of this oil and take showers before we crawl into bed. I'll untie you, now."

At 9:30 p.m., just as Calvin and Jasmine finished showering together, Duke and Alice left Otis and Missy's house, and began walking toward their own house. While holding hands and walking westerly along the city sidewalk, they saw several intermittent flashes of lightning in the distant, southwestern black sky. "It appears as if we will get some rain before much longer," offered Duke. "The wind has switched around to the east, so we might get severe storms tonight. It seems like every time we have an easterly wind along with rain or snow, we receive nasty storms."

After walking along the city sidewalks for five minutes, they turned and walked along the sidewalk leading to their side door. Duke opened the chain-link gate and let Alice lead the way to the side door. While Alice stood waiting next to Duke, he unlocked the door. As they entered the kitchen and walked toward the dining room, Duke said, "Man! Otis is one hell of a marksman. Every time he fired his pistol, the bullet hit the bull's-eye. Unbelievable marksmanship!"

When they entered the dining room, Alice smiled at Duke and asked, "How did you do with your target? I'm sure you hit the bull's-eye, at least a few times."

Duke sat down at the dining room table and mumbled, "Yeah. A few of my bullets hit the bull's-eye, but most the time, my bullets hit quite a ways away from the bull's-eye. It was a lot of fun, though. Otis is really a nice guy."

Alice walked toward the bathroom and said, "I'm going to take a shower. Will you be ready to go upstairs for a little excitement after we finish taking our showers?"

Alice turned and faced Duke just as he yawned and mumbled, "Gee, I feel very tired right now. I don't believe I will be able to perform very well."

Alice smiled broadly and said, "I told you earlier that I would be your wild woman tonight." Alice winked at Duke and teasingly said, "Perhaps, you can hit my bull's-eye."

Duke perked up a little and replied, "That sounds very inviting, but would you mind if we put it off until tomorrow afternoon? I always feel more energetic during the afternoons."

Alice's smile disappeared as she turned and went into the bathroom. Before closing the bathroom door, she replied with much disappointment in her voice, "I suppose we can delay our fun until tomorrow afternoon."

Alice finished in the bathroom at 9:55 p.m., so Duke took his turn in the shower. At 10:20 p.m., Duke and Alice crawled into bed and snuggled against each other. Alice kissed Duke on the cheek, and said, "Perhaps, you should make an appointment with a doctor and have him give you a physical. It seems as if you are tired a lot."

"Oh, I don't know, Alice. I attribute my tiredness to all my physical activity. Maybe, I should quit working out so often with my weights."

"Well, it wouldn't hurt if you had a physical. You haven't had one for years."

Duke slid over to his side of the bed, and after finding a comfortable position while lying on his back, replied, "I'll think about it, but right now, I want to sleep."

Mary had arrived in the parking lot of Wanda's Restaurant at 10:00 p.m. Jason had ended up working a little late, but exited the restaurant at 10:15 p.m. Mary and Jason arrived in their garage at 10:30 p.m., and as soon as they entered the kitchen, Jason said, "I'm really tired, Mom. I'm going to shower right away, and then go to bed."

"Oh," said Mary with a disappointed tone of voice. "I wish you would sit down with me, so I can tell you a few things."

"May I first take a shower?"

Mary opened the refrigerator door and removed a bottle of white zinfandel wine. "That will be fine, Jason. We will sit on the sofa and have a nice relaxing conversation when you finish showering." As Jason headed toward the bathroom, Mary poured a half-glass of wine. She exited the kitchen, walked through the dining room, and entered the living room where she sat down at one end of the sofa. Mary set her wine glass upon the end table, reached over and picked up a *Better Homes and Garden* from the coffee table. She began leafing through the magazine pages as she waited for Jason.

Jason finished his shower, dried off, and put on a pair of white undershorts, followed by a pair of psychedelic-colored pajama shorts and a black tee shirt. He entered the living room at 11:00 p.m. and sat down on the vacant end of the sofa. Mary looked at him and asked, "Where did you get those pajama shorts? I certainly did not know you enjoyed psychedelic fashions."

"Grandma bought these the first time we went shopping together. She said that I needed to dress more like the other kids dress. She's bought me many new clothes since I've been staying with her and Grandpa."

"Oh," replied Mary with a smile. She reached over and picked up her wine glass, took a sip of wine, and returned the glass to the end table. She slid over next to Jason and put her right hand on his left forearm. She rubbed his forearm while saying, "I am sorry you had to listen to your father and me argue all the time when we lived in California. I realize it must have been terribly hard for you to endure everything you went through. I sincerely apologize to you, Jason."

Jason put his right hand on top of Mary's right hand and replied, "I accept your apology, Mom."

Tears welled up in Mary's eyes, and as a few tears streaked down her cheeks, she said, "I hope you can forgive me. I love you with all my heart, more than I love anyone else in this entire world. From now on, I will do my best to treat you right."

"I forgive you, Mom," said Jason as he shed a few tears. "I'm so happy you quit using illegal drugs. I love you just as much as you love me."

Mary and Jason hugged each other for a solid minute. Then, Mary said, "I have told you everything I wanted to tell you. Do you have anything you want to discuss with me?"

"No, not right now," mumbled Jason while yawning. "I think I'll go to bed. I'm very tired."

"Okay. Sleep tight. I will see you in the morning."

Calvin and Jasmine had consumed almost a fifth of wine by 11:45 p.m. Actually, Jasmine drank only one glass of wine, and Calvin drank the rest. He also had used one package of cocaine. As they lay nude together in bed, Calvin said, "I need some more cocaine."

"Are you sure?" asked Jasmine. "I want to have sex with you at least one more time before I leave."

"You can, but first I want to snort a little more powder." Calvin slid off the bed and stood up. He staggered a little as he headed for the kitchen. "I will be right back. Do not go anywhere."

Twenty minutes later, after snorting more cocaine while sitting on the bed with Jasmine lying near him, Calvin lay down on his back. "I feel like I am flying," he said rapidly with his words running together. "Oh, it feels so good. You should try some cocaine, Jasmine."

Jasmine felt irritated with Calvin and replied, "I don't do drugs. I'm not that stupid."

"Are you calling me stupid?" Calvin asked while speaking rapidly.

"I think the word stupidity applies to everybody who uses illegal drugs. I'm sorry, Calvin, but that's how I feel about it."

Calvin did not reply. He raised his arms into the air

and began flapping them up and down, as if he were flying like a bird. Jasmine leaned against the headboard, and for the next ten minutes, watched Calvin go through several different stages of his drug high. At one point, he began mumbling something about getting even with a woman, but Jasmine could not understand his garbled words. When Calvin finally came down from his drug high, Jasmine lay back down on the bed and snuggled against Calvin. She whispered into his ear, "Are you ready for a little of my loving, now? If not, I'm going home. It's already 12:30 a.m. Saturday."

Calvin rolled onto his side and hugged her. "I am ready for your beautiful ebony body."

Calvin and Jasmine finished making love at about 1:00 a.m. Saturday. After lying still hugging each other for ten minutes, Jasmine pulled away and sat up on the edge of the bed. As she began dressing, she offered, "I need to leave for home. Do you want me to come back here and spend time with you later tonight?"

Calvin sat up in bed and leaned back against the headboard. He scowled angrily at Jasmine and yelled, "No! I never want to see you again."

In shock, Jasmine scowled at Calvin. "Why not?"

"Because you think I am stupid for using illegal drugs. I will find a woman who will enjoy snorting cocaine with me."

Jasmine dressed, and then gathered her toys and put them into the small duffle bag. On her way out of the bedroom, she snapped, "Screw you, Calvin. Don't ever phone me again."

Duke nearly jumped out of bed as he awoke startled to a very loud boom caused by a lightning strike near the house. As he sat up in bed, he felt the wet sheet under him, and thought, *I must have been having another nightmare. I thought that doggone booming sound was a depth charge explosion. My heart is beating a hundred miles an hour. It's a wonder it doesn't jump out of my chest.*

As Duke scooted over to the side of the bed, Alice awoke. She heard the howling wind and saw the room lighting up from lightning flashes. "Are you okay, Duke?"

"Yeah. I must have been having a nightmare. Did you hear that loud boom from the lightning? I wonder if lightning struck one of our trees, or the house."

Alice looked at the clock and said, "I don't know, but I'm going back to sleep. It's only 2:00 a.m. so you should go back to sleep."

"I'm going downstairs for a little while, at least until this storm simmers down a little. The doggone wind must be gusting to about fifty miles per hour. If it gets any worse, I'll wake you so we can seek shelter in the basement."

At 8:00 a.m. Saturday, Duke crawled out of bed and went downstairs. As he walked through the dining room, he heard Alice putting away some dishes in the kitchen. While Duke continued walking toward the bathroom, he loudly said, "Good morning, Peach."

"Good morning," replied Alice cheerfully. "Did you get enough sleep?"

"I think so," replied Duke as he entered the bathroom. A short while later, Duke left the bathroom and went into the kitchen where he hugged Alice briefly. Just as he finished pouring a cup of coffee, the phone rang. Alice answered and heard Jason say, "Hello, Grandma. Is Grandpa there?"

"Just a minute, Jason." Alice handed the phone receiver to Duke and said, "It's Jason." Then, Alice went into the living room.

Duke talked with Jason for a few minutes before cradling the phone receiver. "What did Jason want?"

hollered Alice from the living room.

Duke grinned and said loudly, "He wanted to know if I was going to work out with weights this morning. He had planned to come over here and work out with me. I told him that we would work out the first thing tomorrow morning. I invited him to stay with us tonight. He's going to ask Mary if it's okay."

Duke carefully carried his full coffee cup into the dining room, and sat down at the dining room table. Alice joined him at the table a few minutes later and said, "Do you suppose Jason and Jo Ann will have fun on their date this afternoon?"

"I'm sure they will. It's a good thing it has stopped raining for the day. They might have had a little trouble staying dry while waiting for the city bus this afternoon."

"I would have taken them out to Crossroads if it were still raining. I hope they have a nice time."

"It would be nice to be young again," said Duke as he readied for a sip of coffee.

"I guess so," replied Alice. "What are you going to do today?"

"The only thing I have planned is spending the afternoon in bed with you. You do remember that we have a date, don't you?"

"I most certainly do, and I look forward to it."

Jason and Jo Ann arrived on Mary's front porch at 5:00 p.m. Saturday, just as Tony came out of his house and walked toward Mary's porch. When Tony saw Jo Ann, he said, "Well, hello there, Jo Ann. I haven't seen you for quite some time. Your dad showed me a picture of you a while back."

Jo Ann looked carefully at Tony. After about ten seconds, she felt certain she remembered him, and said, "Hi, Mr. Margiotti. You work with my dad, don't you?"

"Yes. We work at the same place."

Mary opened the front door, smiled, and said, "Are you all going to stand on the porch talking, or are you coming into the house?"

We'll come in," replied Jason, "but first, I want to introduce you to Jo Ann." After the introductions, they all entered the living room.

Mary stood near the oak-trimmed doorway opening between the living room and dining room while everybody else took seats in the living room. "Would anyone like something to drink?" asked Mary. "We have soda and beer in the refrigerator."

Jason grinned from ear to ear and said, "I'll have a beer, Mom."

Mary laughed and replied, "Funny, Jason. I think you are a little too young for beer."

Jason stood up and walked toward the kitchen. "I'll get a couple cans of soda for Jo Ann and myself."

"Am I old enough for a beer, Mary?" asked Tony with a huge smile on his face.

"Yes, I believe you are, Tony," replied Mary while smiling and rolling her large blue eyes flirtatiously. "I will get you a beer."

As Mary turned and walked toward the kitchen, Tony's eyes followed her every move. He thought, *Wow! Mary is very pretty dressed in those dark pink short-shorts and that white tube top.*

Holding a cold can of beer in her right hand while walking back to the living room, Mary's eyes locked on Tony. She thought, *Tony looks so sexy dressed in those khaki shorts and that navy blue and white, horizontally striped golf shirt. I would love to see more of his gorgeous body.* Jason followed Mary into the living room and sat down next to Jo Ann on the sofa. Mary approached the recliner Tony occupied and handed the beer to him before sitting in a chair, the nearest chair to Tony. Mary looked toward Jason and Jo Ann, and asked, "Did you two have fun on your date?"

Jason and Jo Ann each answered, "Yes."

"I am glad you enjoyed yourselves," replied Mary. After about fifteen seconds of silence, Mary said, "We should eat supper, soon. Would you all enjoy some pizza for supper?"

"Yum," replied Jason. "That sounds delicious to me."

"I love pizza," replied Jo Ann as she smiled at Mary.

"Pizza is fine with me, but with one condition," remarked Tony as he winked and smiled at Mary.

"And what is that?" asked Mary while blushing slightly.

"I will pay for the pizzas when they arrive."

"Oh!" said Mary. "Thank you, Tony. That is very kind of you."

Just as the pizza delivery driver knocked on Mary's front door, Calvin picked up a soda straw and began snorting two lines of cocaine. Not long after the cocaine disappeared into his nostrils, he leaned back against the softly padded sofa cushion. Then, he hallucinated while mumbling loudly to himself for about twenty minutes. When the drug high wore off, Calvin stood up and walked into the kitchen where he opened the refrigerator door and removed a cold can of beer. After taking a huge swallow of beer, Calvin thought, *I should get all my stuff together and put it into my small duffel bag, so that I am ready to take care of Mary and her parents tomorrow night.*

A few minutes later, Calvin went outside and opened the Focus trunk lid. He removed a plastic sack containing fifty feet of clothesline rope, duct tape, charcoal lighter fluid, and a butane grill lighter. He carried the sack of items into the kitchen and set it upon the kitchen tabletop. Then, he rummaged through the kitchen cabinet drawers until he found a butcher knife with an integral ten-inch long, razor-sharp blade. He set the butcher knife beside the plastic bag, and then went into the bedroom to get his small duffle bag. He returned to the kitchen and sat down at the kitchen table. After finishing his beer, he removed the rope from the sack and began cutting several four feet lengths of rope. When he finished, he placed the rope and butcher knife into the duffle bag. Then, he emptied the remaining contents of the plastic sack into the duffle bag, and put the duffle bag into the Focus trunk. As soon as he shut the trunk lid, he thought, I am all set to make my strike tomorrow night. I may as well go back inside and snort some more cocaine.

As Calvin opened the house entrance door, he heard a car moving slowly along the gravel road. He paused before entering the house, because he thought the car would turn into the farmyard. The car continued along the gravel road, so Calvin went into the kitchen and removed the brown teapot from inside the top cabinet.

Chapter 18

Mary, Jason, Jo Ann, and Tony finished eating supper at 7:00 p.m. Saturday. Jason slid back his chair and asked, "Do you want me to wash the dishes, Mom?"

Tony quickly offered, "I will help your mother with the dishes, Jason."

Mary smiled at Tony and remarked, "That is generous of you, Tony."

Jason stood up and said, "Well, I guess if Tony is going to help you, Jo Ann and I will walk over to her house. Do you care if I stay overnight at Grandpa and Grandma's house? Grandpa and I plan to work out the first thing in the morning."

"Did you already ask them if you could stay there tonight?" asked Mary as she slid back her chair and stood up.

"Yeah, Grandpa asked me to stay there."

Mary smiled and glanced at Tony. While trying to keep one eye on Tony and the other on Jason, she replied, "Okay, but I want you to arrive at their house by 9:30 p.m. at the latest, and when you do arrive, make sure you phone me to let me know." As Jo Ann stood up, Mary said, "It has been nice meeting you, Jo Ann. I hope you will bring your parents over here sometime and introduce them to me."

"I will," replied Jo Ann with a smile. "It has been nice meeting you, and thanks a lot for inviting me to eat supper with you. I appreciate it." Jo Ann looked at Tony and smiled as she said, "Thank you for buying the pizza, Tony. It has been nice visiting with you."

"I have enjoyed seeing you again, Jo Ann. Tell your mom and dad hello for me."

"Okay, Tony. I'll tell them."

Jason went into his bedroom and packed a few clothes into a small duffel bag. He carried the bag into the dining room and asked, "Are you ready to leave, Jo Ann?"

"Yes, I'm ready."

As soon as Jason and Jo Ann exited the house through the open front doorway, Mary and Tony cleared off the table and took the dishes and silverware into the kitchen. As Mary began filling the sink with water, she remarked, "Jo Ann acts very mature for her age. She is definitely a sweetheart."

Tony leaned against the cabinet next to the sink, crossed his arms, and replied, "Jason and Jo Ann are very polite teenagers."

Mary shut off the faucet as she glanced at Tony's biceps. She placed several dishes into the water and said, "We should open that bottle of wine you brought over yesterday. We can let these dishes soak for a little while."

"Is that bottle of wine in the refrigerator?"

"Yes." Mary opened the refrigerator door and removed the bottle of wine. She set it upon the countertop in front of Tony, and then opened a cabinet drawer and found the corkscrew. She handed the corkscrew to Tony and said, "I'll let you do the honors."

"Gladly," replied Tony as he began screwing the corkscrew into the cork. Mary stood beside Tony while he opened the wine bottle. She noticed a slight fragrance of what she believed to be the remnants of Tony's liquid bath soap. Mary reached into a cabinet and removed two wine glasses. Tony poured the wine as Mary observed his every move. Then, Tony handed a half-glass of wine to Mary as he said, "Shall we sit in the living room?"

"Yes, let's sit on the sofa. We may as well bring that bottle of wine with us. "

When they arrived in the living room, Tony set the bottle of wine upon the coffee table. After Mary sat down on the sofa, Tony sat down closely beside her, which made her feel especially happy. Tony held up his wine glass and said, "Let's toast."

Mary held up her wine glass and as Tony gently clanked his glass against hers, he offered, "Wishing you all the best, Mary."

"The same to you, Tony," replied Mary with a smile.

With that, they each took a sip of wine, after which, Tony said, "So tell me a little about your life, up until this point. I want to hear all about it."

"I will tell you about my life, if you will tell me about yours."

Tony took a sip of wine and leaned back against the sofa cushion before replying, "Okay, but first tell me about your life."

Mary and Tony spent two hours sitting on the couch while drinking wine and discussing their lives. The phone rang at 9:30 p.m., so Mary said, "I imagine that is Jason phoning me." She scooted to the end of the sofa and picked up the phone receiver from the end table. A minute later, she cradled the receiver and slid over to sit beside Tony. "That was Jason. He has arrived at my parents' house."

"That's good," replied Tony as he glanced at his wristwatch. "I didn't realize it was already this late. I should help you with the dishes, because I need to go home before much longer."

Mary put her hand upon Tony's left thigh, and with a disappointed tone of voice, said, "Oh, I hate to see you leave. I would love to visit with you longer."

Tony rose from the sofa and walked toward the kitchen, "I would like to stay longer, but I need to go home so I can pack some of my clothes."

Mary stood up and walked toward the kitchen. "Are you going on a trip?"

"Yes. I'm going fishing with two of my coworkers. They will pick me up at 4:00 a.m. tomorrow. Then, we will make an eight-hour drive to a resort located near Virginia, Minnesota."

Mary began washing the dishes and said, "How long will you be gone?"

"We should arrive home late Friday night."

Tony secretly admired Mary's beautiful, firm body as she washed and rinsed the dishes. When she finished, Tony began drying the dishes. After he wiped each dish, he handed it to Mary, so that she could put it away. Their hands touched several times during the process, and Mary began feeling more attracted to him. Tony began feeling the same way about Mary, and just as Mary turned toward him after placing the last dish into the cabinet, Tony gently placed his hands on her waist, gazed into her gorgeous blue eyes, and asked, "Do you mind if I kiss you?"

Mary did not reply with words, only with actions. She suddenly wrapped her arms around his neck and kissed him passionately. Tony wrapped his arms around her and hugged her snugly, so that he could feel her firm breasts pressing against his chest. One passionate kiss was not enough, so they continued kissing passionately. The kisses soon escalated into French kisses. While swirling the tips of their tongues together, Mary enjoyed feeling Tony's firm muscles while moving her hands around on his arms, shoulders, back, and neck. Tony enjoyed Mary's body pressing against him while listening to her soft moans of pleasure. After a few minutes of French kissing, their lips separated. As Mary snuggled her right cheek against the right side of his neck, he felt short pants of her breath palpitating against his neck. After hugging each other for about a minute, Tony released his hold on Mary. He gently grasped her hands and stepped away a little before saying, "Wow, Mary. That was super great."

In between short pants of breath, with her face flushed crimson red, Mary replied, "Yes, it was exquisite. Are you sure you cannot stay for a while?"

"No, I need to go home." Tony paused for a moment while trying to regain normal breathing rhythms. "As soon as I return from the fishing trip, I'll phone you. We will plan to get together again. Will that be okay?"

Mary smiled brightly as she reached up and fluffed the right side of her blonde hair. "I certainly look forward to hearing from you. I will walk with you to the front door."

Duke and Jason still occupied the wicker chairs on the 3-season porch at 10:00 p.m. Saturday. Duke had been telling Jason a submarine story for thirty minutes, and Jason had enjoyed listening to it very much. Jason stood up and said, "I'm going to bed, Grandpa."

"Gee whiz, Jason. You haven't even told me about your date with Jo Ann. How did that go, anyway?"

Jason sat down, smiled, and replied, "We had a lot of fun."

Duke lit a cigarette before asking, "Did you kiss Jo Ann?"

Jason's face turned bright red as he replied, "She kissed me first."

"Really? She actually kissed you first?"

"Yeah. She wanted to sit in the back row of seats at

the movie theater, so we did. As soon as the movie began, she moved over as close as she could to me and placed her hand on top of my thigh. I didn't know what to do for sure. I didn't know whether I should put my arm around her, or not, but I eventually looked at her and put my arm around her. Then to my surprise, she kissed me directly on my lips. I felt very uncomfortable about it, but I'll have to admit that I enjoyed it."

"It sounds as if she likes you, Jason. Have your parents ever talked to you about the so-called *birds and bees*?"

Jason laughed a little, and quickly replied, "Grandpa! No, they never told me anything about that, but I took a sex education class in school last year. Besides that, I have learned a lot about sex from reading internet articles, speaking of which, are you ever going to buy a computer?"

"I might. Well, in other words, you don't want any of my advice about sex. Is that right?"

"That's right, Grandpa. Don't worry, I know all about the precautions I need to adhere to when it comes to sex."

Just then, they heard the chain-link gate latch clank. Twenty seconds later, they saw Elmer standing by the porch door. He jiggled the door handle a little and asked, "Do you mind if I join you?"

"Hell no, Elmer," replied Duke. "Come in and sit down."

Immediately after Elmer sat down, Jason stood up, and said, "I'm going to bed. I'm tired."

"Okay, Jason," replied Duke. "Sleep tight. I'll see you the first thing in the morning. We'll begin working out about an hour after we finish eating breakfast."

"Okay, Grandpa," said Jason as he walked through the open French doorway into the dining room. "See you later, Elmer."

"Sleep tight, buddy," replied Elmer as his right

shoulder jerked slightly.

"Pleasant dreams, Jason," offered Duke.

"Thanks to you both," said Jason as he left the porch and entered the dining room on his way to the bedroom.

Duke entered the kitchen at 6:00 a.m. Sunday. Alice had already made a pot of coffee. She poured a cup of coffee and handed it to Duke. "Here you go, sweetie pie."

Duke carefully took the cup from her and said, "Thank you, Alice." Duke took a sip of coffee and swallowed before saying, "Gee whiz! Ol' Elmer came over last night after you went to bed. We sat on the porch and visited until 11:30 p.m. I couldn't believe he even came over to visit. He's normally such a hermit."

"Maybe, he's getting lonesome in his old age," replied Alice as she poured a cup of coffee for herself.

"I invited Elmer to eat dinner with us this afternoon. It's supposed to be another beautiful day, so I'll fire up the gas grill and grill some Iowa pork chops. We should invite Mary for dinner."

Just then, the phone rang. Alice answered and heard Mary say, "Good morning, Mother. Are you going to church this morning?"

"Yes, I sure am. I rarely miss Sunday morning church services."

"What time are you going?" inquired Mary.

"I usually attend the 10:00 a.m. service."

"Great! I will attend church with you. We will take my car. I will pick you up at 9:45 a.m."

"I'm so happy you are going to church with me. I'll try to convince your father and Jason to attend church with us. Do you want to eat dinner with us this afternoon? Elmer will be here. Your father is going to grill some nice thick Iowa pork chops."

"Yes. I will eat dinner with you. Good-bye, Mother."

Alice cradled the phone receiver, smiled at Duke, and

asked, "Are you and Jason attending church with Mary and me this morning? Mary will pick me up at 9:45 a.m."

"Wow!" replied Duke as he walked toward the dining room. "I'm surprised she is going to church. Sure, Jason and I will go with you. We'll be done working out in time."

With sleepiness in his eyes, Jason exited the bathroom and entered the dining room. "Are we going to work out pretty soon, Grandpa?"

"Yes, but let's first eat some cereal. We need to be ready for church by 9:45 a.m., because your mother will be here by then."

"I'm glad I brought dress clothes with me yesterday," stated Jason. "I won't have to go home to change. I can shower and change right after our workout."

At 11:00 a.m., Duke leaned over and whispered in Alice's ear, "Do you think Reverend Smith will ever run out of words? We've already been sitting on this doggone hardwood pew for an hour."

Alice bumped Duke's leg with her knee and whispered, "Shush, Duke. He will finish preaching pretty soon."

At 11:30 a.m., Mary stopped her Mercedes in front of Duke and Alice's house. As Duke and Alice exited the car, Mary said, "I will take Jason home so he can get ready for work. I will come back to your house after I take him to work at noon."

"Okay," replied Duke. "Don't work too hard this afternoon, Jason. Have fun at the hotel tonight."

"Don't worry, Grandpa. I'll have fun," replied Jason as Mary began driving toward their house.

Duke and Alice went into their house where Duke continued complaining about the long-winded Reverend Smith. Alice finally grew tired of his complaining, so she said, "I don't think that small amount of time you spent in church this morning has caused you any harm. You should actually spend more time in church, not less."

Duke realized Alice had listened to him long enough, so he opened the stair door and said, "I'm going upstairs to change out of this miserable suit."

At 3:00 p.m., just as Duke, Alice, Mary, and Elmer sat down at the dining room table to eat dinner, Calvin locked the back door of the farmhouse, went into the garage, and slid onto the front seat of the Ford Focus. Thirty minutes later, he drove past Mary's house. He did not see her Mercedes, so he drove past Duke's house. He saw Mary's car parked in front of Duke's house, so Calvin parked his car and began observing the house for any kind of action. The time passed slowly for Calvin while he continued observing the house. Finally, at 9:00 p.m., he saw a man with long gray hair and beard exit through the chain-link gate opening. He watched the man walk along the sidewalk and enter the house next door. *That must be Duke's neighbor*, thought Calvin. *I hope Mary soon comes out of the house.* At 9:15 p.m., just as darkness began setting in, Calvin saw Mary exit the chain-link gate opening and walk to her Mercedes. *I wonder where Jason is tonight*, thought Calvin. *He must be staying at Duke's house.*

Calvin followed Mary into the alley behind her house and saw that she parked her car inside her garage. He drove to the other end of the alley, and a minute later, parked the Focus on Third Street, about a half-block east of Mary's house. *I will wait here until it is dark*, thought Calvin. *Then, I will get my bag of goodies out of the trunk and sneak down to Mary's house. I will have to climb over that 42-inch tall chain-link fence, so that I can get into her backyard. I hope she left the back door unlocked. I do not see any lights on inside the next-door houses, so that is good.*

At 9:50 p.m., Calvin reached over the chain-link fence located along the east side of Mary's property and dropped the small duffle bag onto Mary's backyard. Then, he carefully maneuvered his body over the fence, trying to be as quiet as possible. The fence rattled a few times as he climbed over it, but not enough for anyone inside a house to hear it. He snuck directly to the back door and turned the doorknob. To his surprise, the knob turned freely. *Thank God*, he thought. *Now I won't have to break in.* He placed the duffel bag near the back door and walked to the west side of the house, the side with the bathroom and bedroom windows. He waited near the west side of the house until he saw lights glowing through the frosted-glass bathroom windowpanes. *It is 10:00 p.m., so Mary should be getting ready to take a shower about now*, he thought. *I am going to enter the house.*

Calvin approached the back door and picked up his duffel bag. He slowly twisted the doorknob and swung open the door. He stepped onto the basement stairs landing, removed his shoes, and walked up two stair steps leading to the kitchen where a small under cabinet fluorescent light dimly lit up the area. As quietly as possible, he made his way through the kitchen and into the dimly lit dining room. Just as he entered the dining room, he heard sounds of running water from the bathroom. Calvin listened for a moment before entering the hallway leading to the bathroom and bedrooms. He put his ear against the bathroom door and listened for about ten seconds. He heard nothing but running water, so he assumed Mary had begun showering.

Calvin placed his duffel bag upon the hardwood floor near the bathroom door. As he turned the doorknob, he heard it squeak a little, so he hesitated for a few seconds before turning it fully. He opened the door and saw a white bathtub with a set of frosted glass shower doors attached. As he watched Mary's shadow moving around behind the frosted glass shower doors, he began feeling turned on sexually, and thought, *That bitch definitely has a gorgeous body*. Calvin waited patiently for Mary to finish showering and to open the shower door. When she opened the sliding glass shower door, she saw Calvin and screamed, but her scream ended quickly because Calvin punched her as hard as he possibly could, squarely on her forehead. Mary immediately slumped into unconsciousness and collapsed into the bathtub. When she landed, her right eyebrow slammed against the side of the bathtub.

Calvin's heart raced as he saw blood oozing down the side of the tub. He looked closely and saw a two-inch long, deep gash along the length of her right eyebrow. He positioned Mary so that her back faced him, and then placed his arms under her arms, wrapped his forearms around her chest, and struggled as he lifted her out of the bathtub. He positioned her with her back upon the floor. With a washcloth, Calvin applied pressure to Mary's wound for several minutes. When the bleeding subsided enough, Calvin searched through the cabinets until he found a box of bandages. He pinched together her wound and applied a bandage, hoping that it would stop the bleeding. Calvin grabbed Mary's wrists and pulled her out of the bathroom and into the hallway. After a short rest, he managed to drag Mary through the hallway and into the rear bedroom. He stopped next to the bed, lifted Mary roughly, and dumped her onto the bed. Mary began moaning a little as Calvin proceeded to position her on her back. Calvin rushed into the hallway and picked up the duffle bag. He returned to the bedroom, reached into the bag, and took out several pieces of rope. Mary opened her eyes just as Calvin had finished tying her wrists to the headboard. "Why are you doing this to me, Calvin?" she asked as blood dripped into her right eye, causing her to close her eyes.

"Shut up, Mary," Calvin replied as he grabbed two pieces of rope. When he finished tying her ankles to the footboard, he sat down on the edge of the bed for a few minutes. Then, he reached into his duffel bag and removed both quart cans of charcoal lighter fluid. He set them upon the bed, and then removed the butcher knife from the duffel bag. As he held the butcher knife in front of Mary's face, he said, "Open your eyes, Mary. I want you to see what I am going to use to get even with you."

Mary opened her eyes, the left eye fully, but the right eye only partially. When Mary saw the butcher knife, she said, "Please do not hurt me more than you already have, Calvin."

Calvin lightly pressed the razor-sharp blade edge against her throat and said, "I think this knife is plenty sharp enough to cut your throat." Then, he pressed a little harder, just enough so that Mary cried out in pain as a small amount of blood appeared on her neck. Calvin saw the blood and said, "Yes, this knife will work very well."

"Please do not hurt me," whimpered Mary. "I will do anything you want."

Calvin saw Mary's cell phone on the nightstand, so he picked up the cell phone and placed the butcher knife upon the bed. He looked at Mary and asked, "Where is Jason? Is he staying overnight at your parents' house?"

"No," whimpered Mary. "He is staying overnight at a hotel with his boss and some of his coworkers."

"That is good news," replied Calvin as he began looking through the list of contacts on Mary's cell phone. "I will not have to worry about him showing up tonight." Calvin saw the time displayed on Mary's cell phone. "It is only 10:45 p.m., so I guess we have time to get high together for one last time. Do you want to get high, Mary?"

"No," said Mary as she began sobbing louder, "I do not want any drugs."

Calvin became irritated and said, "That is too bad, Mary. Instead of getting high, I will dial your parents' phone number so you can talk with them. I want you to convince them to come over here right away."

"How do you expect me to convince them?" sobbed Mary.

Calvin thought about it for a few minutes before replying, "Tell them that a bat is flying around inside your house and you need them to come over here to help you catch it. Make it sound as if you are petrified and desperately need their help. You had better convince them to come over here, because if they refuse, I will slash your throat. I want you to quit crying right now, so that your voice sounds normal to them." While Mary calmed herself, trying to quit sobbing, Calvin again searched through the contact entries on Mary's cell phone. After a few minutes, Mary had calmed enough to stop crying, so Calvin selected Duke's home phone number and punched the send button. He used his right hand to hold the cell phone up to the side of Mary's face, so that she could utilize the phone. He used his left hand to hold the razor-sharp knife against her throat, just above her Adam's apple.

Duke and Alice heard the phone ringing just as they sat down on the edge of their bed. "I wonder who in the hell is calling at this time of night," said Duke as he saw the brightly lit display on his bedside clock displaying 11:00 p.m. He stood up and walked over to the combination answering machine and phone charger. He removed the mobile phone and gruffly answered, "Hello. This is Duke."

"Hi, Dad," said Mary with a very excited tone of voice. "Will you and Mom come over here right away to help me?"

"What seems to be the problem? Can't it wait until tomorrow?"

"No, Dad! A huge bat is flying around inside my house. I have been trying to catch it for the last fifteen minutes, but I cannot get him. He moves faster than Geronimo ever did. I will leave the front door unlocked for you."

"We'll be over in about ten minutes." Duke immediately ended the call. He quickly entered Elmer's home phone numbers into the keyboard.

Alice asked, "What's wrong, anyway?"

While waiting for Elmer to answer, Duke said, "Mary wants us to come over to her house. She said that there is a bat flying around inside her house, but I'm certain something else is terribly wrong. I'm calling Elmer. You need to put on some clothes, so that we can leave for Mary's house."

Six phone rings later, Elmer answered, "Hello."

"This is Duke, Elmer. I might need your help pretty soon."

"Sure thing, Duke. What's wrong anyway?"

"Mary just phoned and said that there is a bat flying around inside the house, but she mentioned a secret word we have had together since she was a kid, the word *Geronimo.* I told her to use that word if she ever felt as if she were in danger. She has never used it before now, so I know something is terribly wrong."

"Do you want me to go over there with you?" asked Elmer.

"Alice and I will walk over there as soon as I end this phone call. We should arrive at Mary's place in about ten minutes. It's 11:09 p.m. right now by my clock, so I will call you by 11:30 p.m. at the latest. Will you come over there and see what's going on, if you don't hear from me by then?"

"Sure thing, Duke. I will come prepared for trouble. Good-bye, Duke."

"Be extra cautious if you come over there. Good-bye, Elmer."

As soon as Mary had finished talking with Duke, Calvin left the bedroom and unlocked the front door. He returned to the bedroom and sat down on the edge of the bed.

Calvin pressed the razor-sharp blade edge against Mary's throat and said, "When your parents arrive, I want you to tell them to come into this bedroom. If you scream or warn them, I will immediately cut your throat. Do you understand?"

"Yes," whimpered Mary. "Will you please cover my nude body with a throw, or something?"

Calvin moved the blade from her throat to her right breast. He dragged the blade edge lightly across her right breast, and as Mary cried out in pain, he watched a few trickles of blood appear. Then, he placed the blade against the left side of her neck and pressed hard enough, so that a few more trickles of blood appeared. "That is only a tiny sample of the pain you will experience if you try to warn your parents." Calvin stood up and grabbed a woven throw he saw hanging over the back of a wooden chair. After he placed the woven throw over Mary's nude body, he reached into his duffel bag and removed the duct tape and butane lighter. Calvin sat on the edge of the bed and said, "Now, we will wait for your parents to show up."

"Please do not harm my parents," begged Mary. "They did not have anything to do with the police arresting you. I did not have anything to do with it, either."

"Shut your mouth, bitch!" snapped Calvin loudly. "You cannot tell me what do."

Chapter 19

Calvin and Mary heard the front door open, and then heard Duke say, “We’re here, Mary. Where are you, anyway? How come the lights are so dim?”

“I’m in my bedroom,” replied Mary loudly. “The bat is in here, but I cannot subdue it. Come into my bedroom.”

Duke led the way as he and Alice walked into the dining room, through the oak-trimmed doorway opening, and through the hallway to the rear bedroom. They could not believe what they saw when they entered Mary’s bedroom. Calvin immediately held the razor-sharp knife against Mary’s throat and said, “If either of you scream or run, I will cut her throat.”

Alice began crying as soon as she saw the bloody bandage on Mary’s eyebrow and the blood on her neck. It took Duke several seconds to recognize the baldheaded, clean-shaven man holding the knife. Duke said, “You bastard, Calvin. What are you doing, anyway?”

“Shut up, you old slow-talking bastard.” Calvin used his free hand to point at a wooden chair. “Sit down in that chair, Duke.”

Duke thought, *Should I try to fight him, or should I follow his orders. I’d better follow his orders; otherwise, he will probably kill Mary.*

After Duke reluctantly sat in the chair, Calvin said, "Okay, Alice, I want you to take this roll of duct tape and tape Duke's wrists to the back spindles of the chair, and then tape his ankles to the chair legs. Do it right now."

Ten minutes later, Alice finished taping Duke's wrists and ankles securely to the wooden chair. Calvin said, "Okay, Alice. Now, seal Duke's lips with a piece of tape so I do not hear any more of his slow drawling. When you finish that, sit down on the other wooden chair."

As soon as Alice finished taping Duke's mouth, she sat down as Calvin had commanded. With the butcher knife remaining in his hand, Calvin stood up and approached Alice. He proceeded to tape her securely in the chair, and when he finished, taped her mouth shut. Then, he stuck a large piece of duct tape over Mary's mouth. Calvin stood in the middle of the room and smiled broadly while saying, "Now, you can all watch each other burn to death and enter Hell." Calvin approached the bed, lifted the edge of the woven throw, and picked up a quart of charcoal lighter fluid. He snapped open the lid and squirted fluid onto the sheet, along and next to both sides of Mary's body. Then, he picked up a bed pillow, squirted a large amount of volatile liquid onto the pillow, and placed it upon the floor beside the chair Duke occupied. Calvin emptied the quart can of lighter fluid upon the second bed pillow, and placed it upon the floor near the front of Alice's chair.

As Calvin picked up the butane grill lighter and held it near Mary, threatening to light it, Duke tried to say something while struggling against the restraints, but could only mumble. He heard Alice and Mary's muffled cries and saw tears streaming down their faces. *I hope Elmer soon arrives*, thought Duke.

Calvin laid the unlit lighter beside Mary, and thought, *I do not know if I can actually burn them to death. I guess I will snort a little cocaine and contemplate this situation for a while.* Calvin removed a small plastic bag of powdered cocaine from his front pants pocket, opened the bag, and dipped his right index finger into the white powder. He snorted the powder from his finger into his right nostril. Then, he again dipped his finger into the bag, and snorted some cocaine into his left nostril. He decided to see if Mary had any beer in the refrigerator, so he left the bedroom and made his way into the kitchen.

As soon as Calvin left the bedroom, Duke used his feet and the weight of his body to shuffle his chair six inches back, so that the top of the chair stile touched the middle vertical division of the dark green drape panels hanging from the drapery rod above the west window. He managed to position the back of the chair, so that the top of the chair stile held open the middle division of the drapes a mere crack. *I hope Calvin won't notice the opening in the drapes*, thought Duke. *I pray that Elmer will look through this window before he enters this house.*

Calvin exited the kitchen and headed for a stop in the bathroom before returning to the bedroom. As Calvin entered the bathroom, Elmer, fully dressed in camouflaged clothing and combat boots, as well as sporting a blackened face, beard, and hair, arrived in front of Mary's house. When he saw the dim lighting in the main part of the house, he thought, *Something strange must be happening in the house. It shouldn't be so dimly lit if they are trying to catch a bat.* A minute later, Elmer vaulted over the easterly chain link fence and landed on his feet in Mary's backyard. When he approached the rear of the house, he saw a little bit of light seeping through the dark green drapes covering the south bedroom window. Elmer walked to the west side of the house and approached the west bedroom window. *Good, the drapes are slightly open*, he thought. He squinted while using his right eye to peer through the narrow opening between the drape panels. He saw Mary with her bloody, swollen eyebrow, and saw her wrists tied to the headboard. He also saw Alice tied to a wooden chair. *Duke must be in the chair beside this window*, thought Elmer. *All I can see is part of the chair stile.* Just then, Elmer saw a man with a shaved-head enter the bedroom. *I wonder who in the hell that is*, thought Elmer.

Ten seconds later, Elmer saw the man pick up a butcher knife, and saw that the man appeared to be talking rapidly while pacing back and forth in the bedroom. After a minute of pacing and swinging his arms into the air while ranting and raving, the man approached the bed and picked up the remaining full can of charcoal lighter fluid. He snapped open the cap and squirted a large amount of the volatile fluid onto the bed before squirting more liquid towards Alice and Duke. Then, the man picked up the butane lighter and placed the tip of the unlit lighter within an inch of Mary's left armpit. Elmer suddenly had a flashback from his tours in Vietnam, and viewed the man as a gook. *Oh, shit!* thought Elmer. *That drugged up son of a bitching gook must be planning to burn them to death.* Elmer's flashback faded just as fast as it had appeared, so Elmer viewed the man as he had appeared when Elmer first saw him.

Elmer quickly approached the back door of Mary's house. He opened the door quietly, and made his way into the kitchen where he paused and listened to the man's ranting and raving voice drifting throughout the house. *That bastard has to be high on some kind of drugs*, thought Elmer. *He's talking a hundred miles an hour.* Elmer silently exited the kitchen, entered the dining room, and crept across the room to the oak-trimmed doorway opening leading into the hallway. Elmer remained in the dining room, but stood against the west wall beside the south side of the doorway opening. He heard the man say that he would soon light the volatile fluid, so that the entire house would burn down. Elmer felt the adrenalin pulsating through his veins as he whistled a birdcall, a call he had always used in the dense jungles of Vietnam to let his army buddies know his location. Calvin quit talking, so Elmer whistled another birdcall. Then, Elmer heard the oak hardwood floor in the hallway squeaking a little, as if someone were walking toward him.

Ten seconds later, Elmer saw the man's left hand extend through the doorway opening. He also saw the huge butcher knife extending from the man's left hand. Then, the man took a step toward the dining room, so with both hands, Elmer grabbed the man's right wrist and forearm with the intentions of swinging him around and slamming him onto the floor. As Elmer tried to swing the man's 170-pound body around and onto the floor, the man yelled out from surprise and quickly sliced a gash into the top of Elmer's right forearm. Elmer immediately felt pain, so he released the man's arm. The sharp, searing pain suddenly forced Elmer's brain to enter into a flashback mode, a flashback from Elmer's service in Vietnam. Elmer again viewed the man as a Viet Cong soldier, and hollered, "You son of a bitching gook bastard."

The man quickly raised his left arm, readying to stab Elmer in the chest. Elmer hollered, "So long, you gook bastard," as he used his left hand to deliver a punishing judo chop directly against the man's Adam's apple. The man immediately dropped the butcher knife and used both hands to grasped and hold his painful throat. Elmer immediately kicked the man squarely in the groin. The man screamed as he doubled over and fell upon the floor.

Elmer felt warm blood seeping down his forearm. He looked at his right hand and even though the dining room lighting remained dim, he saw a few drops of blood dripping from his fingertips, which caused him to go into a very mean mode. He looked at the stranger and hollered, "How do you like pain, you goddamn gook bastard?" Then, Elmer began kicking the man in the arms, legs, and ribs, while saying repeatedly, "Take that you son of a bitching gook." After several damaging kicks, Elmer grabbed an oak chair from near the dining room table and located it so that he could position the man's right foot and ankle in between the bottom chair rungs, about six inches above the floor. After Elmer positioned the man's ankle upon the bottom chair rung, Elmer raised his right foot high into the air, and then with all his strength, stomped down onto the man's right lower leg, at a point halfway between the man's knee and ankle. As the heel of Elmer's combat boot slammed against the man's leg, Elmer heard the loud popping sound of the man's tibia breaking.

The man screamed from the severe pain. *That should keep the gook bastard from running*, thought Elmer. For one last measure, Elmer leaned down and punched the stranger between his eyes. Just after the man slumped into unconsciousness, Elmer stood up straight and felt as if he had returned to his normal self. Elmer removed the man's foot and ankle from between the chair rungs, and placed the chair near the dining room table. *The cops don't need to see anything suspicious*, thought Elmer.

The smell of charcoal lighter fluid filled Elmer's nostrils as he entered the hallway. He stopped in the bathroom long enough to grab a towel to wrap around his right forearm, and then entered the rear bedroom. He first checked Mary's wounds to make sure she did not have any life threatening ones. Then, he quickly checked over Duke and Alice before saying, "I'm going to leave you all as you are until the police arrive, so that there are plenty of witnesses." Elmer picked up Mary's cell phone, flipped open the keyboard, and punched the numbers 911. When the operator answered, Elmer said, "Please send the police and fire personal to 4723 Third Street. There is a crazy man here who has a butcher knife. He is threatening to kill us and to burn down the house. There are three injured people here, so we also need the paramedics."

When the 911 operator said that help would arrive soon, and to stay on the line with her until they arrived, Elmer ended the phone call. He sat down on the bed and comforted Mary as well as he could. "It'll be okay, Mary," said Elmer sympathetically as he softly stroked her left arm.

A few minutes later, they heard sirens in the distance, and at 12:30 a.m. Monday, a male police officer arrived on the scene. He cautiously entered the house and hollered, "Waterfield Police."

"Come into the rear bedroom," Elmer hollered. "It's safe. The perpetrator is out cold lying on the dining room floor."

Just as the police officer with his gun drawn entered the rear bedroom, a young female police officer and two paramedics arrived inside the house. As soon as the male police officer saw Elmer's blackened face, long beard and hair, he ordered, "Stand up and put your hands behind your back."

Duke began mumbling as loud as he could while struggling against the restraints. The officer paid no attention to Duke, and quickly snapped the handcuffs around Elmer's wrists. "I'm not the criminal," said Elmer.

The male police officer began frisking Elmer and replied, "The cuffs are for my own protection, until I find out for sure you aren't the criminal."

As the female police officer and the paramedics entered the hallway and peered into the rear bedroom, two fire trucks parked in front of the house. Six firefighters entered the house, and after discussing the situation with the police officers, two firefighters remained in the bedroom with their fire extinguishers at the ready, and the other four firefighters went into the dining room to wait for further orders. After the male police officer snapped several pictures of the scene, the police officers and paramedics quickly cut the rope and tape bindings that held Mary, Alice, and Duke prisoners. The female officer helped Mary put on a cotton robe. As soon as Duke removed the duct tape from his lips, he stood up and hollered, "Where is Calvin, that son of a bitch? I'm going to kill him."

Elmer, still handcuffed, said, "If you are talking about the intruder, he's lying on the dining room floor. He isn't going anywhere." Elmer looked at the male police officer and asked, "Are you going to remove these handcuffs?"

The male police officer grabbed Duke's right arm and said, "Sit down. You don't really want to kill anybody. That man is already darn near dead."

Duke reluctantly sat down, so the police officer released his grip on Duke's arm. Just then, Otis entered the rear bedroom, looked at the male police officer, and said, "Hi Joel. You can remove those handcuffs from Elmer. He is one of the good guys. I know all these people. The baldheaded guy lying on the dining room floor is the bad guy."

As Joel quickly removed the handcuffs from Elmer's wrists, he asked, "What are you doing here, Otis?"

"I heard the call on my police scanner, so I decided to come over here to see what is going on. These people are my friends."

Duke saw one of the paramedics treating Mary's wounds while another paramedic inspected the 3-inch long gash in the top of Elmer's right forearm. Duke looked at Alice and asked, "Are you okay, my dear?"

Alice felt very stiff and sore, but stood up and walked over to Duke. She looked into his eyes as she began rubbing his left shoulder and said, "I'll be fine. Are you okay?"

"Yeah. I'm okay," mumbled Duke while lightly rubbing his reddened sore lips. "We should feel very fortunate that Calvin didn't get a chance to torch the lighter fluid." Then, Duke looked at Elmer and said, "Calvin is the intruder. He is Mary's ex-husband in case you didn't know. Thanks for saving our lives, Elmer. We owe you a lot."

"I didn't know that is Calvin," replied Elmer dryly. "He is a complete stranger to me. You don't owe me anything at all. I'm glad I could help you all."

As soon as the paramedics finished inspecting Mary and Elmer's wounds, they went into the dining room and began treating Calvin. The male police officer ordered everybody to leave the bedroom so the firefighters could rid the bedroom of fire hazards. One of the paramedics asked Mary and Elmer if they wanted a ride to the hospital in the ambulance, or if they wanted to have someone else take them to the emergency room. Mary looked at Duke and asked, "Will you take us to the hospital, Dad?"

"Sure," replied Duke, "but we'll have to use your Mercedes. Out car is at home."

"I'll take Mary and Elmer to the hospital," offered Otis. "My car is parked out front."

Two firefighters carried Mary's mattress out of the bedroom, through the hallway, and into the dining room. "This mattress has to go outside," said one of the firefighters. "It is soaked with lighter fluid. Where do you want us to put it?"

Elmer pointed toward the back door and said, "Just lean it up against the chain link fence in the backyard."

Another firefighter carrying two pillows, sheets, and the woven throw exited the hallway and entered the dining room. "I'll put this stuff outside, right next to the mattress," he stated as he followed the firefighters carrying the mattress.

Otis gently grasped Mary's left upper arm while Elmer grasped her right upper arm. "Let's head for the emergency room at St. Francis Hospital," said Otis.

As Otis, Mary, and Elmer exited through the front doorway opening, Duke said, "Alice and I will come to the hospital as soon as we can."

Otis replied, "I'll stay with Mary and Elmer at the hospital until you get there, Duke."

Calvin moaned loudly from excruciating pain as two paramedics lifted him off the floor and placed him upon a portable gurney. As they rolled the gurney toward the front door, "Duke approached the male police officer and asked, "Is it okay if my wife and I leave, now?"

"Yes, you can leave. The female police officer will give you a ride home. If Mary doesn't return before we finish here, we will lock up the house. The lab officer and a detective will soon arrive. They will probably spend several hours here while gathering evidence. We'll contact you if we need anything else."

The female police officer dropped off Duke and Alice at their house at 2:00 a.m. Monday. When they entered the kitchen, Duke said, "We'd better take showers right away. The doggone lighter fluid soaked into our clothes. That's about all I can smell right now."

"Do you think Mary will be okay?" asked Alice as she walked toward the bathroom.

"I believe she'll be okay. She'll need some stitches in her eyebrow, and she'll probably have a black eye for a while. Let's leave for the hospital as soon as we get ourselves cleaned up."

Duke and Alice arrived in the St. Francis Hospital emergency room lobby at 3:00 a.m. where they saw Otis half-asleep sitting in a chair. When Otis saw Duke and Alice, he stood up and said, "Mary and Elmer are still being treated. Follow me and I'll show you where they're at."

Otis led Duke and Alice through an open doorway and into a hallway. Then, he led them along the hallway until they reached room A-1. "Elmer is in this room." Otis pointed at a door on the other side of the hallway and said, "Mary is in room B-1."

"Thank you, Otis," said Duke. "Are you going to hang around for a while, or are you going home?"

"I'll go home, now that you are here. I'll give you a phone call later today to find out how things are going."

As Otis turned and began walking toward the lobby, Duke said, "Thanks again, Otis. We really appreciate all your help."

Otis waved his right hand into the air and kept walking without replying. Alice knocked on the door to room B-1, and then opened the door. No one occupied the room, but she saw Mary's cotton robe lying on one of the chairs. Just then, a nurse approached Alice and said, "Are you looking for Mary?"

"Yes," replied Alice. "Mary is our daughter."

The nurse said, "Mary is doing fine. Doctor Schultz has already sutured her eyebrow and neck. He gave her a complete examination, too. The doctor ordered a scan for her head, so the aides took her upstairs to the X-ray department. They should be bringing Mary back to this room within the next thirty minutes."

Duke cleared his throat a little and said, "How is the man in room A-1 getting along?"

The nurse smiled and rolled her eyes a little as she said, "Elmer is doing just fine. Doctor Schultz should be putting the final suture in Elmer's arm about now." The nurse walked across the hallway and opened the door to room A-1. She looked at Duke and Alice, and said, "You can go in to see Elmer."

Duke and Alice entered room A-1 just as Doctor Schultz installed the last of 13 sutures to close the gash in the top of Elmer's right forearm. Alice sat down in a chair and stared toward the ceiling, so that she would not see any blood, but Duke remained standing and peered over the doctor's shoulder.

Elmer nodded at Duke and Alice, but said nothing. When Doctor Schultz finished tying a knot in the suture, he turned to face Duke. "Is Elmer going to be okay, Doc?" asked Duke.

Doctor Schultz grinned slightly and asked, "Are you Elmer's relatives?"

"No," replied Duke. "We are his next-door neighbors and good friends."

"Oh. Well, Elmer is a very tough man. He would not let me give him anything to deaden his arm before I sutured the wound. I cannot believe how good of shape he is in for his age. He has a few bruised left knuckles, and of course, the wound in his right forearm. As soon as the nurse bandages his arm, he can go home."

Duke cleared his throat a little and asked, "Are you the doctor who has been treating our daughter in room B-1?"

"Yes, and she is doing fine. If the report for the scan of her head is okay, she will be set to go home. I did not want to release her until I made sure she does not have a severe concussion. She refused the scan at first, but I finally convinced her to have one."

Duke heard two women talking in the hallway. He looked into the hallway and saw a nurse's aide pushing the wheelchair Mary occupied. "Hello, Mary," said Duke. "How are you feeling?"

Alice stood up and entered the hallway as Mary replied, "I am okay, Dad."

Duke and Alice followed the nurse's aide and Mary

into room B-1. Doctor Schultz entered behind them, and said, "I will call the X-ray department and check on the scan report, Mary. If it is okay, I will release you. You will hear from me soon." Doctor Schultz and the nurse's aide exited the room. Alice held Mary's hand while saying, "Do you want me to drive to your house and get some clothes for you, so that you have something to wear home? All you have here is your robe."

"It is warm outside, Mother. The robe will be just fine."

Ten minutes later, Doctor Schultz entered room B-1 and said, "The scan showed that everything is okay, Mary, so you can go home. The aide will take you to the front door, so you may as well remain in the wheelchair."

"Thank you, Doctor Schultz," said Mary as she smiled brightly, even though it hurt a lot.

"You are welcome, Mary. Take care of yourself."

Duke parked the LeSabre in front of Mary's house at 4:30 a.m. As Mary, Alice, Elmer, and Duke exited the car, they saw a police car and a wrecker about a half-block away, near a black Ford Focus. When they all entered the living room, Mary said, "I still smell like lighter fluid, even though the aides gave me a sponge bath. I guess I will take a shower."

Elmer entered the dining room and looked down at the hardwood floor. With a disgusted tone of voice, he said, "I suppose I'll wash the blood off the floors before I go home to get some sleep."

"Alice and I will help you," offered Duke as he heard Elmer mumbling to himself, something about the goddamn gooks.

"You don't need to help," replied Elmer dryly while lightly rubbing his right arm as if trying to ease the pain.

Alice headed toward the kitchen and said, "We are helping you whether you like it or not, Elmer. Where do you keep the cleaning supplies?"

Mary's next-door neighbor, Tony, returned home late Friday night, July 15, after nearly a week of fishing in Minnesota. At 7:00 a.m. the next morning, Tony knocked on Mary's front door. When she opened the door, he saw her black eye and bruised forehead. "Are you okay, Mary?"

"Yes. Please come in. I am so glad to see you."

When they entered the living room, Tony said, "When I phoned my boss at the police station this morning, he told me a little bit about what happened here last Sunday night. I would have returned home right away, if I had heard about it." Tony hugged Mary gently and rubbed her back lightly as he again asked, "Are you sure you're okay?"

"I am fine, Tony. Would you like a cup of coffee?"

"No thanks, Mary," said Tony as he released Mary and walked toward the front door. "I'm leaving for the police station right now. I want to find out what is happening to that scumbag ex-husband of yours. I'll be back later this afternoon to fill you in on the investigation."

"I will be waiting for you. Jason is going to spend the afternoon with his grandparents, so we will have some alone time."

As Tony exited through the open front doorway, he replied, "Great, Mary. I'll see you later."

Mary and Jason finished eating lunch at 1:00 p.m. Saturday. As Jason slid back his chair and stood up, he said, "I'll wash and dry the dishes before I leave for Grandpa's house."

"That is sweet of you, Jason," replied Mary as she stood up. "I will sit in the living room and read for a while. Tony should be arriving here within the hour."

Jason finished putting away the dishes at 1:30 p.m. He freshened up a little in the bathroom before entering the living room. "I'm going over to Grandpa's house, Mom. I'll be back by 4:30 p.m. so I can change clothes before I go to work."

"Okay, Jason. Have fun. I love you."

"I love you, too, Mom."

Tony arrived on Mary's front porch at 2:00 p.m. and knocked on the front door. Mary gladly invited him into the living room where they sat next to each other on the sofa. Tony looked into Mary's eyes and said, "I found out a lot about your ex-husband. We might want to drink a little bit of wine while I tell you a long story about the ongoing investigation."

Mary smiled and patted Tony on his left thigh just before she stood up and said, "I will get a bottle of wine and two glasses."

When Mary returned to the living room and sat down beside Tony, he removed the bottle cork and poured two glasses of wine. "Are you ready for an entertaining, but extremely sad story?"

"I guess so," replied Mary as she readied for a sip of wine.

"Well, it turns out that your ex, Calvin, has quite a criminal history, although it has all happened over the last few months. As you know, the cops first arrested him near the end of May for illegal drugs, but after the judge let Calvin out on bail until his trial, he continued getting into more trouble. The cops have been looking for Calvin since the first part of July. During this investigation, the Waterfield detectives along with the Iowa Bureau of Investigations have learned that on July 1, the Bayview, California, police found a dead man by the name of Jes'us lying on his living room floor. Jes'us owned a Rottweiler, and for some unknown reason the dog attacked and killed Jes'us."

"No kidding?" said Mary as she lifted her wine glass to her lips. "Jes'us must have been very mean to that dog."

"Well, that dog definitely hated Jes'us," replied Tony as he snuggled against Mary and took a sip of wine. "Do you want me to continue with the story, or should we do something else?" asked Tony teasingly.

"I want to hear the entire story."

"Okay. When the police found Jes'us, the investigators began searching his house. They soon discovered that Jes'us had all kinds of equipment in one of the rooms, electronic equipment and computers that he used to make fake identification cards. The police seized all the equipment and had their tech boys in the police department search through everything. On one of the computer hard drives, the police found that Jes'us had made some fake driver's licenses, identification cards, and automobile registrations for Calvin. They also discovered that Jes'us had a contact in Chicago who provided some fake Iowa license plates for Calvin. By the way, the Chicago police arrested that man about three days ago. The California police issued a nationwide arrest warrant for Calvin; I believe they issued that on July 5. The worst news I have learned is that on July 8, a farmer found the body of a Waterfield woman buried in his garden located about fifteen miles south of here. The police lab officers lifted several fingerprints from her cell phone, and the pathologist retrieved some DNA samples from her body. Do you want to guess who left the fingerprints and DNA?"

Mary looked at Tony with a shocked look on her face and said, "Please don't tell me it is Calvin."

"I am sorry, but Calvin is the culprit. The lab officers also found his DNA and fingerprints inside the house. Calvin will never see the exterior of a prison after he stands trial. He will surely receive a mandatory life sentence with no possibility of parole."

Mary drank the rest of the wine from her glass and reached for the bottle. When she finished pouring a half-glass of wine, she said, "I guess the good thing about all this is that he did not get a chance to kill my parents or me, and I will never again have to worry about him. I feel very sad about the dead woman." Mary moved her left hand to-and-fro along the top of Tony's right thigh as she asked, "Do you want some more wine? I should not drink anymore, because I have to take Jason to work at 4:45 p.m."

"You may as well finish drinking the wine you just poured. I will give Jason a ride to work. I've only consumed a half-glass of wine. Do you want to hear more of the story?"

"There is more?" questioned Mary. "Go ahead and tell me."

"Yes, there's still more to the story. When the Chicago police arrested the man Jes'us knew in Chicago, they discovered the Chicago man's connections to a prominent business man by the name of Mr. Jimmy Shoot who lives about ten miles east of here in the town of Rainy. The FBI had been investigating Mr. Shoot for the last several months. Mr. Shoot owns a farmhouse located about ten miles south of Rainy, and that's where Calvin was living.

The FBI agents had been watching that farmhouse occasionally, so they had recorded the license numbers of the black Ford Focus. They had also recorded license numbers of several other cars they observed entering and exiting the farmyard. When the police seized the Ford Focus Calvin had been driving, which is registered to a car rental company owned by Mr. Shoot, they found cocaine inside the car trunk. Of course, Calvin sang like a bird when the police questioned him about Mr. Shoot, so the detectives along with FBI agents went to Mr. Shoot's residence with a search warrant. It didn't take long until the FBI agents arrested Mr. Shoot for several different crimes. Mr. Shoot had been running a huge prostitution and drug smuggling ring for several years. He laundered all the illegal money through his car rental businesses.

That ends the story, except for all the pending trials. I guess it just goes to show, that you should never get involved with illegal drugs, because there is no end to the troubles they cause."

Mary leaned over and softly kissed Tony's right cheek. "I know one thing for sure; I will never again take illegal drugs. I have learned my lesson."

Tony kissed Mary on the lips. Then, he asked, "So, when will the doctor remove your sutures?"

"I will see the doctor Wednesday morning. He is supposed to remove all eight sutures from my eyebrow, and both sutures from my neck. I hope the scars are not too ugly."

"You will always be beautiful in my eyes, Mary, even if you have scars."

Chapter 20

The remainder of July and all of August seemed to fly by quickly, and by September 1, 2011, several interesting events had happened. A few weeks after his encounter with Calvin, Elmer decided to change his appearance and become more sociable, so he went into a barbershop and asked for a crew cut and a shave. For several days afterwards, none of the neighbors recognized Elmer, not until they heard him speak. Elmer began visiting Janice, the neighbor living next-door east of Duke and Alice. Elmer and Janice had become very special friends and had even enjoyed time together while eating in restaurants and attending movies. Some of the neighbors thought Elmer and Janice had become much more than just good friends, but those neighbors had conceived their thoughts from several different rumors floating around the neighborhood.

Near the end of July, Duke had decided to phone his former boss at the engineering and land surveying company. During their phone conversation, his former boss mentioned that he wanted to hire an experienced bookkeeper, but he had not been able to find one fully qualified. As soon as their conversation ended, Duke phoned Mary and told her about the bookkeeping job. She interviewed for the position the next morning, and became an employee at the engineering and land surveying company that afternoon. Mary had also applied to the Iowa State Board of Examiners to take the test for her Iowa accountant's license, so she waited patiently for their response. Tony and Mary had begun spending a lot of time together at their houses, as well as on dates. Tony had occasionally tried to get Mary into bed with him, but she continued playing hard to get, allowing Tony no more than hugging and kissing. During the first week of August, Mary traded in her Mercedes for a brand-new Impala, mostly so she could forget her California lifestyle with Calvin. She had found that she enjoyed the simpler, more down to earth life in Iowa, so in late August, she purchased the house she had rented from Elmer. He acted very happy when she wrote him a check for the full purchase price.

Jason and Jo Ann had both passed the driving skills program and obtained their driver's licenses in late August. Jason and Duke had continued working out with weights. By the time Jason signed up for the high school football team, he had lost another ten pounds. His muscles had become rock hard. After several football practice sessions, the coach assigned Jason as a tackle on the first team. Jason had continued spending much of his spare time with Duke and Alice, and during the last week of August, Duke had taught Jason how to prepare and can tomatoes, dill pickles, sweet pickles, and beets. A few days after Jason had obtained his driver's license, he began hinting that he would like to buy Duke's S-10 pickup, but Duke could not decide if he wanted to part with it.

On Friday evening, September 2, Tony and Mary went out for supper and a movie. Afterwards, Mary invited Tony to have a drink with her at her house. He accepted, and after they each drank a glass of wine while sitting on the sofa, Tony asked, "Where is Jason?"

"He is at work. My mom is going to pick him up after work. Jason is going to spend the night at Mom and Dad's house. Jason wanted to stay there, so that he could work out with my dad the first thing tomorrow morning."

"Jason is definitely a nice young man. He is like a son to me." Tony moved closer to Mary before continuing, "I want to have a housewarming for you and Jason on Labor Day. How does that sound to you?"

"That is nice of you," replied Mary as she snuggled against him. "If the weather is nice, we could have the party in my backyard."

"I've already checked the extended forecast. The meteorologist forecasts perfect weather for Labor Day. It is supposed to be clear, calm, and about seventy-five degrees. I want to invite your parents, Otis and his family, and Elmer and Janice. Do you have anyone else you want to invite?"

Mary thought about it for ten seconds. "No. I cannot think of anybody else. What kind of food and beverages do you plan on serving?"

"Well, you have that brand-new gas grill in your backyard, so I thought I would purchase some extra thick Iowa pork chops. I will also buy some ground round for hamburger patties. I know how to grill chops and hamburgers. While I'm at the grocery store, I'll purchase several different kinds of salads. Potato salad always tastes delicious with pork chops and hamburgers. Macaroni salad and some 3-bean salad would taste good, too. As for the beverages, I will purchase a few cases of beer, a few bottles of wine, and some soda pop."

"Great. I will phone everybody tomorrow morning and invite them to the party. I certainly hope they will accept the invitations. Some of them might already have other plans."

"I hope everybody will attend. As soon as I know for

sure, I will purchase all the food and beverages."

Mary put her left arm around Tony's shoulders and gently kissed him on the lips. When their lips separated, Mary asked with a very sexual tone of voice, "Do you want to pour a couple more glasses of wine while I go into my bedroom and change into something more comfortable?"

Tony could not believe what he had just heard, but quickly replied, "I sure will, Mary." Then, as he grinned from ear to ear, he kiddingly asked, "Do you want me to wait here for you, or do you want me to bring the wine into the bedroom?"

Mary stood up and smiled while rolling her gorgeous blue eyes flirtatiously. She began walking toward the bedroom and remarked, "You decide, Tony."

Tony quickly stood up and followed Mary through the dining room, into the hallway, and into her bedroom. As soon as they entered the bedroom, they locked their arms around each other and kissed passionately. Mary began moaning softly and breathing hard. After a few minutes of French kissing, they helped each other undress, and then fell together upon the bed. Tony and Mary entwined in mad passionate love until 2:00 a.m. Saturday, when they felt as if they had made love in every possible position. They both fell asleep and did not awake until almost 6:00 a.m. Saturday. Tony awoke a few minutes before Mary, and as he sat on the edge of the bed to begin dressing, Mary opened her eyes and said, "Wow, Tony. You are a super-hot lover. Are you already leaving?"

"You are a wonderful lover, Mary. I would like to stay longer, but I have many things to accomplish today."

Mary smiled and replied, "Well, you could stay long enough for breakfast, or else some more of me."

"It is very tempting, but I'll have to take a rain check."

With a disappointed look on her face, Mary said, "Okay, then. I will see you later. Thanks for everything."

As Tony left the bedroom, he said, "I'll probably see you sometime this afternoon. Good-bye, Mary. I'll lock the door as I leave."

"Good-bye, lover," replied Mary as she rolled onto her right side and closed her eyes for additional sleep.

Just before noon on Labor Day, September 5, guests began congregating in Mary's house and backyard. Otis, Missy, Jo Ann and Monica arrived at Mary's house a few minutes before noon. Missy handed a sealed envelope to Mary and said, "That is a housewarming card for you."

"Thank you, Missy. I did not expect a card."

Ten minutes later, Mary saw Elmer and Janice holding hands as they approached her front porch. Mary opened the front door and invited them into the house. Elmer handed an envelope to Mary. "Janice and I brought you a housewarming card, Mary."

"Well, thank you. I will put this with the card Missy and Otis gave me. I will open all the cards later this afternoon."

Duke and Alice arrived at Mary's front door about five minutes later. When Mary peered out through the door window, she saw her parents holding hands. Mary thought, *What is with these old folks? They still act as if they are totally in love with each other. It is certainly very heartwarming.* As Mary opened the front door, Duke bluntly said, "Where's the beer located? I'm thirsty."

Mary smiled and replied, "Open the refrigerator door, Dad. You will find the beer. There is also beer in a cooler out in the backyard. Jason and Tony have spent most the morning getting everything ready for this party."

"When are we eating lunch?" asked Duke as he entered the living room.

"My goodness, Duke!" said Alice. "You shouldn't be so outspoken. Please have a little patience."

Duke smoothed down the right side of his grayish

brown hair while replying, "I'm sorry, Mary. I didn't mean to be so impolite."

"Do not worry about it, Dad. I am used to you." Mary put her right hand on Alice's shoulder and said, "It is okay, Mom. I know Dad gets impatient sometimes. Tony is grilling hamburger patties for lunch. They should be about ready to eat. He will grill Iowa pork chops for supper."

Duke opened the refrigerator door and said, "Tony is sure a good man. I don't know very many men who would organize and do all the work for one of these parties."

Mary smiled and replied, "Tony is a great man. I want to keep him around forever. I certainly hope he feels the same way about me."

"Time will tell, Mary," replied Alice merrily. She handed an envelope to Mary. "That's a small housewarming present for you, Mary."

"Thank you, Mom. I will open it when I open the other cards."

Alice walked out of the kitchen, through the rear doorway opening, and into the backyard.

Everybody at the housewarming enjoyed visiting, eating, and drinking together throughout the afternoon. Then, at 5:00 p.m., Tony fired up the gas grill and began grilling Iowa pork chops. Duke kept hanging around the grill with Tony, so Tony finally asked, "Are you getting hungry, Duke?"

"Yeah," replied Duke as he lit a cigarette. "I guess all the beer I have consumed is making me hungry."

Tony smiled while using extra-long tongs to turn over one of the pork chops. "These pork chops should be done in about a half hour." Tony turned over the other pork chops, and closed the grill lid. He looked at Duke and said, "Man! Old Elmer really did a number on Calvin. I wouldn't want to make Elmer mad. He'd probably kick my butt. "

"Oh yeah?" questioned Duke as he raised his beer can

to his lips for another sip.

"Hell yes. Calvin had a broken nose, three broken ribs, a broken right ankle, a broken right tibia and fibula, and a screwed up Adam's apple. His right knee is also in very bad condition." Tony snickered for about thirty seconds before continuing, "Calvin will never have any kind of sex life again, because his testicles are ruined from Elmer's direct kick. I am quite sure Calvin will limp around his cell for the rest of his life. It rather tickles me in a way, because Elmer only received a gash in his forearm. Old Elmer must have knocked Calvin down, and then kicked the holy hell out of him. I still cannot figure out how Elmer broke both bones in Calvin's leg. None of the other cops can figure it out, either. Actually, it's too bad more criminals don't suffer that kind of pain."

Duke snuffed out his cigarette and said, "I don't know what happened for sure, but I heard Elmer calling Calvin a son of a bitching gook when they were fighting. Elmer probably had a flashback from Vietnam. I heard Calvin scream several different times, as if he were being tortured."

Tony opened the grill lid to check the meat, and said, "Did you know that Elmer holds a 5th degree black belt in some kind of karate?"

"Really? I had no idea."

"The detective who interviewed Elmer for an hour told me about it. He said that Elmer acted quite secretive about everything at first, but after they talked for a while, Elmer provided quite a lot of information about himself. Elmer has taught karate part-time for the last several years at a local karate school. He has a hell of a war record from his time in Vietnam. Elmer also said that he probably should have killed Calvin, so that the taxpayers wouldn't have to support him for the rest of his life."

"It wouldn't have broken my heart if Elmer would have

killed the son of a bitch," replied Duke seriously.

Tony saw Elmer walking toward them, so he said, "Elmer is walking toward us, so we'd better change the subject."

Everybody sat down at the outdoor tables to eat supper at 5:45 p.m. By this time, the flies had found the food, so while eating supper, everybody occasionally swatted at flies. At 6:30 p.m., Tony reached down with his right hand and grasped Mary's left hand. He stood up and gently pulled on Mary's hand, so that she would stand up. "May I have everybody's attention?" stated Tony loudly. When everybody quit talking, Tony reached into the right front pocket of his khaki cargo shorts and removed a small black box. As he kneeled on his right knee in front of Mary, he noticed her smile fading and the appearance of shock setting in. Tony opened the box and removed a diamond engagement ring. As he looked up at Mary and gazed into her beautiful blue eyes, he asked, "Will you marry me, Mary?"

After ten seconds of silence, Mary smiled brightly and replied, "Of course I will, Tony. I love you with all my heart."

Tony slid the diamond engagement ring onto Mary's left ring finger, and then stood up. While Tony and Mary hugged and kissed, everybody applauded and cheered. Mary and Tony continued kissing, so after a few minutes, Duke grinned broadly and hollered, "Congratulations. You two can quit kissing; either that, or take it into the house."

Tony and Mary quit hugging and kissing, so everybody took turns congratulating them. Then, Alice removed three cards from a woven straw basket located upon the tabletop. She held them into the air and asked, "Are you going to open these cards, Mary?"

"Yes, Mother. I will open them right now." Mary and Tony sat down, so Alice handed the cards to Mary. She opened the first envelope, removed and opened a beautiful housewarming card from Elmer and Janice. Inside the card, she found a gift certificate for the installation of a home security system, along with a full year paid subscription for the system. She showed the card to Tony, and looked at Elmer and Janice. "Thank you very much, Elmer and Janice. I will feel much safer after the security system is installed and operating."

Elmer's right shoulder jerked several times while replying, "Yeah. I never again want to come over here and fight someone."

Mary opened another envelope and card. A hundred-dollar gift certificate fell out of the card, a gift certificate for shopping at any of the stores in Crossroads Mall. Mary looked at Otis and Missy, and smiled while saying, "Thank you very much, Otis and Missy. I really appreciate it."

Mary opened the last card and saw her mom and dad's signatures. The card included a hundred-dollar gift certificate for any of the stores in Cedar Hills Mall. "Thank you, Mom and Dad. I love you both very much."

Shortly before 9:00 p.m., Otis and his family left the party. Elmer and Janice left a few minutes later, so Tony and Jason began clearing off the tables. Duke pitched in to help carry the dishes, glasses, silverware, and the leftover food into the kitchen. Alice helped Mary in the kitchen until they finished cleaning up at 10:00 p.m. They went into the living room where Alice approached Duke. She waited until Tony finished talking to Duke before asking, "Are you about ready to go home, Duke?"

With bloodshot eyes, Duke looked up at Alice, grinned, and replied, "Yeah. You might have to hold on to my arm and steady me while we walk home. I've consumed enough beer to float a battleship."

"I will give you a ride home," offered Tony.

Duke stood up and replied, "Thanks for the offer,

Tony, but the walk home will be good for Alice and me. Walking helps get the kinks out of these old bodies, you know."

Tony stood up and offered his hand to Duke for a handshake. Duke shook hands with Tony while saying, "Thanks for everything, Tony. Welcome to our family."

Alice offered to shake hands with Tony, but Tony suddenly hugged Alice and said, "Thanks a lot for everything, Alice. I'm so glad I will be part of your family."

When Tony released Alice, she blushed while replying, "We are very happy to have you in our family, Tony. Thank you for everything."

Jason stood up and hugged Duke briefly. "Good night, Grandpa. I love you." Then, Jason turned and hugged Alice. "Good night, Grandma. I love you."

Duke and Alice each replied, "I love you, too, Jason."

As Alice led Duke through the open front doorway, they each said, "Good night, everybody."

Alice held Duke's hand as soon as they exited Mary's house. When they reached the front city sidewalk, Duke looked up at the full moon and said, "Look at that beautiful full moon, Alice. It is a perfect night."

Alice looked at the moon and replied, "Yes, the moon is so bright and beautiful tonight. Mother Nature is so wonderful to behold."

Ten minutes later, Duke and Alice entered their kitchen. Duke said, "I think I'll take a quick shower before I go to bed."

"Okay, Duke. I'll take a shower as soon as you finish yours. Do you want to have a little fun when we go to bed?"

"I don't know for sure. I'm pretty tired."

"Oh, Duke," said Alice as she sat down at the dining room table. "I'll bet I can get you in the mood for love."

"I'm not betting with you," replied Duke dryly. Then,

Duke grinned and said, "I guess I'll let you try."

Duke and Alice, both nude, crawled into bed at 11:00 p.m. It took only five minutes for Alice to bring Duke to life. Then, they spent an entire hour making passionate love. When finished, they went downstairs to the bathroom and freshened up. Ten minutes later, they crawled back into bed. Duke lay flat on his back upon his side of the bed. Alice scooted over and snuggled against the right side of Duke's nude body. While lightly massaging his right thigh, she said, "It has been a very interesting summer. Another summer in our lives is almost over, Duke. Winter will be here before we know it. I just hate the thought of all that cold weather and snow."

"Yeah. I hate Iowa winters, but if we lived down south, we would have to deal with the hellish hot temperatures during the summer," replied Duke sleepily. "This summer has been very good to us. I'm so happy Mary and Jason lives nearby, and I'm happy Mary accepted Tony's marriage proposal. Tony told me that they plan to get married sometime during the first week of June next summer."

"Really? Mary didn't tell me anything about their wedding plans. Well, I guess I'll have to buy a new dress for the wedding."

"We might not even get invited to the wedding. They might go down to the courthouse and have a judge perform the ceremony, since they've both been married before."

Duke began fading away into sleep as Alice said, "Well, I guess we'll have to wait until we hear more about their wedding plans. I'm sure glad Mary doesn't have to worry about Calvin any longer."

Duke did not reply, so Alice tapped his right thigh a few times. "Are you still awake?" Alice did not hear an answer, so she roughly jiggled Duke's right thigh. "Are you awake, Duke?"

Half asleep, Duke drawled, "I need to sleep, Alice. I love you." After thirty seconds of silence, Alice heard Duke's words fading away as he managed to drawl, "To be continued, Alice."

The End

Author's Note

I sincerely thank you for reading this book, and hope that you enjoyed it. Please feel free to write a book review for this book at the place of purchase. Book reviews help other people decide if they want to read the book, or not. Authors spend many hours writing, proofing, editing, and formatting their books, so reviews are very appreciated and important to authors.

Other published novels by Dallas A. Dixon

Miss Nancy
June 5, 1964
To
September 13, 1964

Miss Nancy and Randy
September 14, 1964
To
July 1, 2007

Contact information

dal629@mchsi.com
http://www.dallasadixon.blogspot.com

www.ingramcontent.com/pod-product-compliance
Lightning Source LLC
Chambersburg PA
CBHW062003170626
46813CB00001B/22
* 9 7 8 0 6 1 5 9 7 7 1 2 6 *